THE INCA CONNECTION

By Spence Wade

RoseDog❖Books

PITTSBURGH, PENNSYLVANIA 15222

ISBN-10: 0-8059-9124-7
ISBN-13: 978-0-8059-924-6
Printed in the United States of America

First Printing

For additional information or to order additional books,
please write:
RoseDog Publishing
701 Smithfield Street
Third Floor
Pittsburgh, Pennsylvania 15222
U.S.A.
1-800-834-1803
Or visit our web site and on-line bookstore at
www.rosedogbookstore.com

For Erin and Kristin

CHAPTER 1A

The day was cloudy-the kind of day when the sky is covered with a blanket reluctantly letting through a modicum of light. The day was foggy-the kind of day when you expect to hear the fog horn in the background bellowing its warning. The day was misty-the kind of day where the mist collects as beads on the windowpane and the droplets slowly inch their way to the bottom. It was the kind of day the San Francisco Bay Area was known for and John's gaze was directed through the window into the gloomy weather. Meeting his gaze were dormitory and classroom buildings under the damp gray skies.

John, Dr. John Kirkwood to be exact, was a professor of Pre-Columbian History at Stanford University. The University, located in Stanford, California, is some 30 miles southeast of San Francisco and considered part of the Bay Area. As John scanned the view out the window he realized he was daydreaming and his class was waiting patiently for him to continue his lecture. He turned from the window and faced the students.

"In the space time flow of the Universe, the random occurrence of apparently unrelated events precipitates history. If we are to analyze historical phenomenon, we must be aware of the multitude of trivial, but in actuality, significant cause and effect relationships on an almost infinite level," John told his Friday morning history class.

After making his statement, he scanned the class and wondered if any students were listening to his words. The faces returning his stare were young, bright-at least most, but probably more interested in the weekend ahead and completely unaware of what life had in store for them. During his sixteen years of teaching at Stanford, John often questioned whether he had made significant impact on any of the hundreds of young men and women who had sat before him.

Rarely is long-term feedback a common occurrence in the teaching profession. Once in awhile, former students would return to tell him how much

1

his class meant to them during their days at Stanford. These special times helped, but now he was yearning for something with more immediate rewards.

Since he was unsure of his effectiveness, he was indecisive about staying on as a faculty member at the University. At forty-four years of age John knew retirement was out of the question. He was single so the demand on him financially was less than if he were a family man, yet John did not have the means to support himself without a well paying position and history was his forte. He toyed with the idea of finding a job in the business community or taking his chances in the political arena. These ideas were thoughts just passing by; contemplated but no real action intended. In his heart his favorite activity was doing historical research, especially on the Incas.

The history of the Inca Indians, an important civilization during the 1400's, was his first love. When John was 13 years of age, his father took him to Peru and the Andes Mountains in South America to investigate this ancient civilization. John was enthralled with the searching for artifacts and digging in the ruins of the long dead culture. He loved the sense of exploration and had made several trips over the past 25 years on his own and with groups to investigate these amazing people. John's infatuation with archeology and history was attributable to his father whom he still missed. His father, having died of a sudden heart attack, and John, only nineteen at the time, were just beginning to look forward to traveling full time together. Sadly John and his father only shared the one trip to Peru, although they did explore several other places together.

As an archeologist, his father traveled extensively all over the world taking John with him during the summer months. On other occasions and while in school, he stayed with his Aunt since his Mother died from a jungle disease she contracted while traveling with his Father. It was still a mystery what kind of infection caused her death and since he was only five years old at the time, his recollections of his mother are few, but at least he had some memories of her to associate with when he sees her picture or her name comes up in thought.

The reason these memories entered his mind now must be due to the nasty weather and dreary day. He told himself to get focused, keep his mind on the task at hand, and finish his lecture.

"If you expect to understand history, its causes and results, then you must realize this or forever be destined to repeat dates and facts without understanding the true meaning of history. The hope of our society is to be able to interpret the relationships of small details to the total effect. We look at past civilizations and are amazed at their level of existence. Some seem to spring out of the blue to become very complicated societies. There is a reason for their development in each case and if we search diligently, even though a multitude of relationships might exist, we may find the key spark or sparks that led to their being," John said as he finished his class for the day.

He reminded his students of the exam next week and dismissed the class. As the students slowly filed out of the classroom, one young girl approached him as he was gathering his papers.

She edged up to him and asked, "Dr. Kirkwood, can you suggest any study groups or readings I could do to improve my grade?"

John eyed the young girl, one of many coeds over the years finding him attractive. Even though he was flattered in a way, he never entertained the temptation of becoming involved with one of his students. Even at forty-four, John knew he was an attention-getter among the ladies. At six foot one inch, average build and with thick dark hair, he felt as young as he did in his twenties. He exercised regularly, jogging being his favorite activity, and diligently watched his diet. He had been involved with several women over the years and on two occasions the relationship did progress to a mutual living arrangement. Both of these lasted less than a year, which didn't say much for his level of commitment, yet he had not given up the hope of finding a soul mate even at his present stage of life.

He replied to her, "Yes. If you will check the bulletin board outside my office door, you will find suggestions and a list of articles to help with your studies." John had handed the same information to his students the first day of class so he imagined she was just using the question as an excuse to talk to him.

She gazed up at John with those blue eyes and fluttered her eye lids as only a young girl can, then said, "Oh thank you Dr. Kirkwood, I just love your class."

"I'm glad. I really need to get going," he said as he moved toward the door anxious to get away from her, "Is there anything else?"

She responded by moving closer to John, brushing against his arm. John repeated he had to leave and exited out the door. With so many cases of sexual harassment in the news, the last thing he needed was to be accused of using his position to take advantage of young girls.

The rain echoed in his ears as it hit his umbrella while he walked to his office in the History Department. He was looking forward to some quiet time away from students and the activity of the University.

Arriving at his building and pouring himself a cup of coffee from the pot in the faculty lounge, he migrated to his office settling into an easy chair. Before attacking the paperwork on his desk, he took a moment to relax. John's office was large compared to most in the Department. It was in an older building, which suited him because he felt older buildings had character and were warmer to the heart. His attachment to things old naturally followed from his love of history.

His tenure of sixteen years had allowed him to obtain a more spacious office than his colleagues. The aroma filling the room came from old books, layers of varnish, cigar and pipe smoke and years of dust collecting in the nooks and crannies. It contained one wall of built-in bookcases rising all the way to the ceiling, a large desk with a chair, a small couch, two easy chairs and a small coffee table. One large window behind the desk let the afternoon sunlight brighten the room on sunny days and the wooden floor made a distinct sound when he walked across its planks reminding him of the creepy sounds from a scary monster movie.

When he was a small boy, his father had an office in their old house similar to his present one. John loved to play in the room because it contained many hiding places, little caves he would disappear into where no one could find him; at least that's what he thought at the time. In a way, these happy memories probably influenced his partiality toward his present office.

John had his feet perched on the top of the coffee table resting quietly sipping out of his cup when a tap at his open door broke the peace.

"Excuse me, Dr. Kirkwood," a female voice said.

Having his back to the door, he looked over his shoulder and discovered the voice came from Cheryl Roberts, a Graduate Assistant in the History Department. Cheryl could sometimes be a pain in the neck because she often stuck her nose where it didn't belong, so if you wanted an item of information to get around the Department, Cheryl would be an ideal candidate to tell since she passed along every rumor coming her way. She was attractive in her own way, extremely intelligent and, in the classes she had taught, received high praise from faculty and students alike. John speculated that if she would change her make-up and dress a little less conservatively, she would make the young men's heads turn every which way.

"Yes, what can I do for you Ms. Roberts," John replied as he turned back around wishing she would go away and leave him to his quiet moment.

"I was passing by and I thought I would let you know a visitor was here for you earlier." She stepped into the room so she could see his face.

Sounding disinterested and expecting to hear the name of one of his students, he asked, "Who was it?"

"I believe his name was Henry Cable and he was only interested in talking to you," Cheryl answered, "He was very old, walked with a cane and said he would return later. The way he looked, he better not make it much later." She expected a smile from Dr. Kirkwood, but received no acknowledgement of her joke.

John was stunned. He solemnly stared off into space as if he had seen a ghost.

"Is anything wrong Dr. Kirkwood?" Cheryl said, disappointed that what she thought was a great quip went unnoticed.

"What-err- no, thanks for the information," he said, still with the dazed look on his face.

Cheryl, a little confused by his response to her message, eyed him a moment then, shaking her head, politely exited the room.

John knew he had reacted strangely to Cheryl's communication. He was just surprised to hear the name. Henry Cable was Dr. Henry Cable, an archeologist renown for his study of the Meso-American Indian Cultures including the Incas. For all he knew, Dr. Cable had passed away, yet here he was looking for John. About twenty years ago, before coming to Stanford, John had met him at one of his lectures and also at a symposium on Latin American Indians. John's day just took an interesting turn due to the mystery of why Dr. Cable was here inquiring about him.

Squirming in his chair and anxious to see Dr. Cable, John got up, left his office and began searching the History Department for him, scanning the different hallways. As he neared the reception area John spied an elderly man with a cane who he assumed was Dr. Cable. Cheryl was correct; he did look very old. He was slowly walking toward the reception desk and was bent over, no doubt reflecting the many years of leaning over a trench at archeological sites. Having snow-white hair and a beard to match, John thought he would make a great Saint Nick. He wore a crumpled suit, an old wrinkled tie, dull shoes, and a hat reminding John of the Indiana Jones character in the movies.

"Dr. Cable, Dr. Cable," John called as he hurried down the hallway to greet him.

Dr. Cable, raising his head, looked John's way and smiled as only a person of his age could, with the lines and creases spreading the grin across his face.

John came up to him offering his hand. "Dr. Cable, I'm John Kirkwood. I am very pleased to meet you."

Continuing to smile, he raised slightly from his stooped position showing a gleam in his bespectacled eyes, and spoke in a raspy yet distinct voice carrying with it a commanding tone. "My young man, the feeling is mutual."

John had not been referred to as young for many years, but understood why he might call him so since Dr. Cable must be close to 90 years old.

Leading him to his office, John took his damp hat and coat, hanging them on the hall tree near the door. After seating him in one of the easy chairs and asking him if he would like anything such as coffee, water, soda or something else and Dr. Cable declining, John sat down on the couch opposite him. He surveyed the elder man again from head to toe forming an opinion of him before they started any conversation or discussion. The distinguished gentleman sitting across from John was impressive even in the latter stages of his life and in old clothes to boot.

"Dr. Cable, I am thrilled to have the chance to meet you again, yet I'm at a loss for the reason you are here to see me."

A faint grin came across his face followed by a bemused look in reaction to John's statement. "My, my aren't we the humble one?" Dr. Cable said as he looked deeply into John's eyes, "You belittle yourself Dr. Kirkwood. I knew your Father and had a great deal of respect for him. I've read your books on the Incas and have always been impressed by your insight and diligent research. Why wouldn't I seek out someone with your reputation?

Knowing he had read John's books and receiving Dr. Cable's praise caused the blood to rush to his head. "You flatter me, but you're the authority on the Inca civilization." He knew Dr. Cable was aware of his notoriety and no one could compare with Dr. Cable's knowledge of the Incas and Aztecs nor was anyone better known throughout the archeological community.

He was in awe of Dr. Cable's demeanor and even though he might be old physically, his mind seemed sharp as a tack and his eyes gave the appearance they were acutely aware of everything coming into their field of view.

Dr. Cable peered over the rim of his glasses making John feel a little uncomfortable. He had a trait some of John's teachers possessed when he was in the public schools; the ability to put the fear of God in you simply by giving you a long staring scowl.

After giving John the once over, he asked, "How do you like your tenure here at Stanford?" Dr. Cable adjusted himself in his chair and before John could answer, added, "I suppose the Hoover Library is a tremendous draw for those in your field."

Dr. Cable was right except it was the Hoover Institution on War, Revolution, and Peace. It was established in 1919 by Herbert Hoover who later became the 31st President of the United States. Scholars studied collections of historical material assembled there to help the world strive for peace. John had spent many hours in its halls conducting research on a multitude of topics.

"Yes, the Hoover Institution is a fantastic facility as are the other resources at Stanford and yes, I have enjoyed these many years at Stanford," John said curious about where the conversation was headed. Dr. Cable was looking over John's office as he sat in the chair just like any archeologist would do at a dig site. He seemed to be as alert as someone half his age.

"I know you are curious as to why I am here so I will get right to the point. First would you please shut the door. What I am about to tell you is best kept between the two of us," Dr. Cable said glancing over his shoulder as if there were spies in the hallway straining to hear his words.

John was intrigued by Dr. Cable's desire for secrecy. He went to the door and closed it, then returned to his seat on the couch wondering what Dr. Cable might be about to divulge to him. His reputation for coming up with new theories was like a magician pulling a rabbit out of a hat. More often than not, these ideas turned out to be correct.

"Would you be interested in learning how the Incas became an advanced culture in what seems like overnight in historical terms?" he asked with a glimmer in his eyes knowing the question would draw John's attention.

John's ears perked up. After all of his research, Dr. Cable was going to drop by and give him the solution to a problem he had been seeking for years. "You know I want the answer," John exclaimed making no effort to hide his enthusiasm.

Many historians consider it a mystery where the Incas of Peru as well as the Aztecs of Mexico came from since no one has found a prior civilization advanced enough to give rise to such cultures. John made it one of his goals to find the answer to this delitescence. He studied the prior Peruvian cultures of the Chavin, Moche, Nazca, and Chimu. In his analysis, none of these cultures had the sophistication to father the Incas. The Chavin was the most advanced of these societies, but they existed around 500 BC which was 2000 years before the Incas' time. Could Dr. Cable have the answer to this puzzle?

"What I am going to tell you will be difficult to believe and you may think these words are the ramblings of a senile old man, but I will ask you not to judge me until I have told you everything." Again, he looked deeply into John's eyes as if searching for some betrayal of his feelings.

Not certain why Dr. Cable would think he wouldn't believe him, John responded, "I will listen with an open mind I assure you, but remember I know something of the Inca civilization." John felt uneasy. Could Dr. Cable really have the answer to the mystery? Now John was becoming skeptical, a trait which made his research into the Incas more trustworthy than some of his colleagues. He never took anything for granted, always testing and re-testing possible solutions or outcomes.

"I know you are knowledgeable about the Incas and it is one of the reasons I'm trusting you with what I have to say." Dr. Cable spoke in a voice John remembered from the lecture he attended long ago. It was forceful and demanding, though lower in volume now, no doubt due to his age.

Dr. Cable took his handkerchief out of his pocket, removed his glasses, and started wiping them off as he began; "I have been involved in many trips and expeditions to Peru over the years. I made my first trip in 1938 when I was 22 years old, a graduate student from Ohio State University, young and eager and very excited about traveling to Peru. I was quite fortunate to earn the opportunity to be a member of a team Dr. Senval Happard was organizing for a trip to Machu Picchu in Peru. Perhaps you are familiar with Dr. Happard."

Having read of Dr. Happard's exploits in archeology in South America, and finding nothing earth shattering in those readings, John replied, "I know a little about his exploits, but I never considered him an authority on the Incas."

"As you wish," putting his glasses back on and a little uneasy with John's characterization of Dr. Happard, "but Dr. Happard was well connected with the government of Peru and the U. S. State Department. These connections allowed him to gain unfettered access to many of the ruins in Peru. He also was a close friend of President Franklin Roosevelt, which he was not shy about letting people know. He did have a knack for searching and analyzing archeological sites so I learned a great deal working with him," He said these words implying he respected the man even if John did not.

"I'm sure you know the place called Machu Picchu, a mountain city discovered in 1911. It was found deserted and no one to this day knows what happened to the Incas who lived inside its walls. The city avoided the invasion by the Spanish Conquistadors who overran the Inca Empire in the 1530's. The Spaniards destroyed the Inca civilization yet never found the city of Machu Picchu, thus it remained intact for hundreds of years," He said, reminding John of some of the history of the Incas.

"Yes, I know. Historians and archeologists have long inquired why the Spaniards never found the city. Perhaps it was because of its location," John interjected.

Machu Picchu lies high in the Andes Mountains at an elevation of 8000 feet. Into the city leads only one narrow and treacherous path. Finding Machu Picchu certainly ranks as one of the most remarkable anthropological discoveries of the twentieth century. Having visited the city twice on his trips to Peru, John was quite aware of its relevance.

"The only thing I will say about its location is the Incas must have guarded the secret of it above all else," commented Dr. Cable as he paused for a moment.

He looked as though he was unsure how to proceed. John admired the man for his accomplishments and felt sad his daring deeds were probably done. He wondered how it would feel to him to know he could no longer go off on expeditions and explore ancient ruins. Hopefully he would not experience such a feeling for a very long time.

Dr. Cable leaned over and brought his hand to his chin as if deep in thought reminding John of Rodin's 'The Thinker'. "What I am about to tell you I have never told to another soul. I don't have much longer in my life and I do not want to carry the information I have to my grave."

John's eyes got bigger. He leaned forward so as not to miss a word. "You have my full and undivided attention. Please continue."

"In 1938 Dr. Happard and I were digging at Machu Picchu and discovered a chamber. The chamber was unlike any room either of us had ever seen. It was a barren chamber containing few artifacts, but-" Dr. Cable paused again, looked at John as though he was trying to gage his interest, then sitting back in his chair, continued. "There was one strange object in the room the Incas should not have had in their possession."

John pressed his hands against the couch as if he was preparing to stand up. He remained seated not exactly clear on Dr. Cable's meaning, so he asked, "Why shouldn't the Incas have it?"

Clearing his throat, Dr. Cable answered, "Because the object was alien to the Inca civilization, and Dr. Kirkwood, not only was it misplaced with the Incas, it was also alien to earth."

8

John was taken aback. He cocked his head. Did he hear him right? Dr. Cable must be losing all his marbles. John had built up his hopes for some exciting new information on the Incas, but his hopes were crushed by Dr. Cable's last remark.

CHAPTER 1B

In the vastness of space, the tiny specks of light called stars twinkle brightly far in the distance and the vacuum between these beacons is filled with absolute cold. Into this bleak arena comes a small man-made space vessel composed of metal, wire, plastic, and silicon. The probe travels at a speed of thousands of miles per hour taking pictures and sending them back to earth millions of miles away. All these thoughts passed through Carol Jacobs's mind as she sat before her console at the Jet Propulsion Laboratory's control room. Having performed her job many times before, she awaited pictures from the latest National Aeronautics and Space Administration's probe nicknamed Talaria.

In Roman mythology, Talaria was the name of the winged sandals worn by some Gods, especially Mercury, but the space vessel christened Talaria had problems needing more assistance than winged footwear could provide. Carol knew the probe originally was to make a circuit of the moons of Jupiter, except things had not proceeded as planned. NASA and JPL had attempted to use the gravity of the planet Mars as a slingshot, giving Talaria a boost in speed so as to arrive at Jupiter's moons earlier. The glitch occurred when Talaria took an incorrect trajectory as it passed Mars. It was given a boost in momentum to be sure, but not toward the moons of Jupiter. Instead it was thrown toward the Asteroid Belt, a group of rocks and planetoids orbiting the sun. Carol was as disappointed with the foul up as everyone else at JPL and NASA.

Carol was an old hand at monitoring space flights when compared to her colleagues in the control room. Approaching the age of forty-two, she had already been involved with many space vessels including Pathfinder, Galileo, and NEAR. In her job at JPL, she took signals from the probes and enhanced and clarified the imagery into the clearest pictures possible. The job had become a lot easier in the past few years with the improvement in computer technology and the development of advanced optics in the on board cameras. Carol took a great deal of pride in her work and was well respected by her fellow team members.

Now after many years with JPL, Carol found herself less enthused with her job than when she first started. The excitement of the pictures coming in from the probes continued to be important, but the months and years in between the probes seemed to drag along. Her feelings did not mean she was no longer interested in space. While growing up in Northern California, she would sit for hours viewing the nighttime stars with a sense of awe. As long as she could remember, being a part of the space program was her life long dream and now, having accomplished the dream, she wanted more. What the "more" was, she did not know exactly.

One desire of Carol's was to be part of the analyzing group at JPL. Each time she had requested a transfer to another division, she had been turned down. She felt the scientists who interpreted the pictures considered her to be a technician, not qualified to render an opinion on pictures from the rest of the solar system. Although she detected a hint of male chauvinism in their attitude, she did not let the issue disrupt her desire to improve her station in life.

She had studied planetary geology at Stanford University and was well versed in space composition, yet her primary engineering degree was in computer science, and the knowledge of computers was the trait landing her the position she now held.

Soon the images would be arriving from Talaria and all other thoughts would fade away as she became busy in her work. The probe had previously taken the pictures of the asteroids as it approached them and now it was aligning its antenna with Earth to begin the process of transmitting the signals across the vast distance of space. It would take almost fifteen minutes from the time it was sent for the signal from Talaria to reach Earth and the Jet Propulsion Laboratory.

The control room at JPL was filled with consoles manned by people monitoring the expedition of Talaria. Receiving all kinds of telemetry, each console was set up like a desk with a computer screen or monitor on top, which gave readings about the flight. On the surface below the screen was a keypad and the surface could also be used to keep notes and papers. In front of all these consoles was a large screen showing the current data being received from Talaria.

"Carol, are you ready to start the process?" The question came from Dale Belfer sitting at the console adjacent to hers. Dale was younger than Carol, not quite thirty, yet already an important player at JPL. His field of expertise was putting color and tint into the pictures making them more life like in the process. He and Carol had worked together on many projects becoming good friends during his initiation period. Dale was stocky, close to six feet tall, and looked like a football player, which he had been in high school.

"Of course I am. I just don't get as excited as I did when I was your age." Carol remembered the elation she felt the first time she participated in a launch. The goose bumps during lift-off had covered her body as the rocket roared into the clouds. The memory was so implanted in her brain, it could have happened yesterday.

"Well, I know I'm anxious to see the finer parts of the asteroid belt for the first time." Dale's starry-eyed look was common place among those working in the space field, especially during the first years on the job.

She reminded Dale of two other probes, Galileo and NEAR, which were sent to the asteroid belt. Talaria was the third probe going to an area of the solar system in between the planets, Mars and Jupiter, where all theory and common sense says another planet should be located. If a planet was positioned there, it does not exist now, only millions of rocks called asteroids orbiting around the sun.

"If I remember correctly, a problem existed getting those probes off the ground or something to that effect?" Dale inquired, keeping his eyes glued to his monitor.

Carol knew Dale had not been at JPL when the Galileo and NEAR probes were launched. Those probes were sent to some of the larger asteroids and NEAR had eventually landed on an asteroid called Eros.

Taking her eyes off the monitor, she turned and looked at Dale. "It seemed at the time no one in the hierarchy felt it was worthwhile going to the asteroid belt except the scientists. Many efforts were made to cancel the programs and cut the funding for both vessels. It was a hotly debated item throughout NASA, Congress, and the space community."

She could never understand why so much pressure was brought to bear to cancel these probes. Sure, efforts had been made to scrub many of JPL's space plans, but not to the extent taken to deter the probes to the Asteroid Belt. It was a mystery to which she still had many questions.

Dale pushed away from his console, swiveled his bulky frame and chair so he faced Carol. "Looks like the scientists won out on Galileo and NEAR and now Talaria is going to the Asteroid Belt by mistake."

"You're right, and heads will probably roll over the goof up," Carol replied as she turned back, closely scanning her monitor and still reflecting on Dale's queries.

The atmosphere at the space agency was not rosy do to the catastrophes of the space shuttle. Sensing added pressure from her supervisors, Carol felt she had to perform to the best of her ability not just for the staff and scientists, but for the press and public as well. Congress was always pushing the agency to perform, because it had the power to cut the purse strings and NASA, like everything else, runs on money. Because of the pressure, many of NASA's decisions might have been political instead of scientific, which disturbed her greatly.

"Is everything set for the pictures?" said a voice coming from behind them belonging to Colonel Gil Pratt who had walked over to Carol and Dale's consoles. He was looking down on them as if he were a teacher waiting for one of his students to make a mistake.

Not turning to acknowledge him, Carol nodded in assent. Gil Pratt was not one of Carol's favorites and she made no bones about letting him know. The Colonel was a representative of the Defense Department in Washington she believed, although he never made it clear which department or branch of the service he represented. He was the typical example of a military man: tall, erect, with a butch hair cut and a chest full of ribbons. Now and then he would drop in for the viewing of pictures sent back by some of NASA's probes.

"We are ready for the picture show." Dale had also turned back to his monitor and spoke to the Colonel with his back to him. "Seen any movies lately at the Pentagon?"

Colonel Pratt did not reply. Every time the Colonel would ask a question at JPL, some of the staff would automatically ask him about the Pentagon pointing out to him how intrusive his questions were and they wanted him to feel the same way.

Carol had been curious for a long time why the Defense Department was interested in pictures from objects in space millions of miles from Earth; besides, the Colonel in Carol's opinion was a snob. He had a "holier than thou attitude" which really pissed Carol off. She became angry when the people at JPL would go out of their way to give him the run of the place and she had not been shy about letting her supervisors know how she felt about his intrusion.

These thoughts faded as Carol's console started receiving the images from Talaria. The first picture was somewhat fuzzy and Carol worked with the computers to improve the clarity. With a few adjustments the picture became sharp and clear. The cameras on Talaria must have worked fine and she knew the scientists at JPL would be happy to see these pictures.

In picture A474-300, she noticed a rock that seemed to be out of place in the cluster of asteroids in the picture. The picture passed as the next one took its place. Carol glanced over at Dale to see if he had noticed anything unusual, but Dale's expression was unchanged, retaining the starry-eyed look she had noticed earlier.

Over a period of hours, the images were sent and received, enhanced, and filed. Carol grew tired as the last pictures were arriving and would be glad to see the end of the transmission since she had been at JPL for twelve straight hours.

As the last image appeared, Carol was ready to call it a day. A few of the staff might stay for the press conference and hash over the day's events, but Carol's desire was a hot bath and warm bed.

She turned to Dale saying, "I'm leaving. I need a bed to crawl into."

Dale looked at her in disbelief. "You're not staying for the news conference."

"No, you go in my place." She gave him a muted grin as she arose from her chair.

Carol walked out of the control room and toward her office. One of the perks of being an oldster, although she never considered forty-one as old, was an office of her own. By being one of the senior staff members, many of the younger people at JPL would seek her out for personal as well as work related advice. She was always professional in her work and at five feet seven inches, was tall compared to other women at JPL. She sometimes felt it put her on a more level playing field with some of the domineering men in her work. Maybe her standing up to management in some cases led others to believe she could help them with their problems.

As she was collecting her things and preparing to leave, the picture with the unusual rock came to mind. Sitting down at her office computer, she hooked into the network using her password and called up the pictures from Talaria.

Opening her notebook in which she recorded the numbers, she found and typed in A474-300, which was JPL code for the number of the picture taken by the probe and its location at the time. The image appeared and she quickly located the object of her interest, a long and slender rock looking like a soda straw.

She enlarged the area of concern and could see the rock did look out of place, but part of the object was blocked from view by another rock. The asteroids had been bumping into each other for millions of years and were covered with cracks, chips, and fractures. Most of them have rounded edges caused by banging into one another, yet the rock in question was devoid of all these characteristics so its surface appeared smooth, but Carol knew an unblemished surface was impossible.

Curiosity definitely had her attention and she wanted to study the picture more so she copied it onto a disc and stuck it in her briefcase. She planned to view it at home on her computer where she would have more time to study it in greater detail.

She knew making copies without permission from the project director was against the rules, but she had taken data home many times before and no one was the wiser. She felt deserving of taking some liberties after having worked here for over eighteen years, and it wasn't like the pictures were top-secret. She exited the JPL building, walked to her Jeep in the parking lot and steered it toward home.

CHAPTER 2A

An eerie silence permeated John's office. It was so quiet, they could hear the sound of chattering people in the hallway slipping through the cracks around the edges of the door. The murmur invaded John's concentration as he sat with his head hanging down attempting to formulate some response to the unbelievable tale. Not wanting to hurt his feelings, John continued to avoid eye contact even though he could sense Dr. Cable's stare.

Gathering his composure, he raised his head and started to speak. Dr. Cable jumped in ahead of him speaking first. "I know you must think what I'm telling you is preposterous and something a crazy man would say, but I ask you to please hear me out before you make a judgement."

Definitely an understatement if he ever heard one, but at least Dr. Cable realized how off the wall his story sounded and didn't expect John to accept everything he said as the truth. Now it was John's turn to stare at Dr. Cable and say, "Yes, well you have to admit, you have gone out in left field with your story. I told you I would hear you out and I will. Go ahead, I'll listen." John thought to himself, this had to be a hell of an explanation.

Leaning his head to the side as if he was growing tired from holding it erect, Dr. Cable, with his rustic voice, went forward with his story. "One trait Dr. Happard had was a knack for uncovering things most people would never notice. The room at Machu Picchu was a case in point. He told us to start digging near a wall and viola, we found an opening leading into a hidden underground chamber."

"What did the chamber look like on the interior?" John asked, trying to picture the room in his mind.

"The floor plan of the room was shaped like a triangle, a tall thin triangle with the small door we discovered located in the middle of the base or short narrow side. The walls were made of stacked stones and as the walls became higher, the stones progressed inward, closer to the center of the room forming an arch-like ceiling. When looking in the opening, we could see a large stone resting at the opposite end where the two long sides narrowed and eventually came together. The chamber contained some artifacts, but as you are aware, the Incas were not very ornate."

"How big was the room?" John inquired showing a keener interest in the description of the room.

Dr. Cable closed his eyes, visualizing from memory the scene from so far in the past. He could almost smell the musty odor emanating from the room when they first exposed the entry. Opening his eyes, which had grown brighter, he continued. "The room was approximately fifteen feet wide at the door and it was about twenty five feet from the door to where the stone was sitting and the two sides of the room came together. The stone resembled an altar similar to what the Incas called inti-huatana or "hitching-post" of the sun. It is where they believed the sun would stop on its passage through the sky; where it could sit and rest for a moment in all its glory."

John knew about the inti-huatana, but was sure Dr. Cable wanted to refresh his memory. He did not mind and actually enjoyed Dr. Cables words. "Where was the unusual object you mentioned?"

"It was resting on top of the stone altar and was in the shape of a cube. If you think of a very large die with plain faces and rounded corners, you have the idea. Each edge was approximately one and one-half feet in length. It had a glassy look and a faint orange glow giving it the color of the sun when you see it through the evening clouds and the light from our flashlights reflected off its surface as if its faces were mirrors or crystals."

In all of John's trips to Peru, not once had anyone alluded to an artifact like the one being described to him. No drawings had been seen or carvings found, which gave reference to anything resembling a cube. If the Incas had it in their possession for a long time, John believed he would have come across some corroboration during his many expeditions to Peru. He told Dr. Cable; "I've never heard of or seen any indications of an object like the one you are describing. What did you do with it?"

Again John was pressing, but Dr. Cable had his own agenda and was not about to change. He said as much, raising his hand and pointing momentarily at John. "I know you have many questions, but let me tell you the whole story then I will answer any questions you might have. Are you agreeable to such a plan?"

He felt like a small boy being lectured to by an adult. "I will wait. You know anyone hearing a story like you are telling is going to have a lot of questions."

"Of course and I will answer them. When we found the chamber and the object, there were three of us present-myself, Dr. Happard, and Don Webster, a college student associated with Dr. Happard and a member of the team. You could assume from the condition of the chamber, it had been undisturbed for many years-possibly hundreds of years. Analyzing the construction of the area, we surmised the doorway I mentioned originally was at ground level. Someone, we assume the Incas, built up the area around the entrance with dirt and rock walls to make it seem like the normal ground level was higher than the doorway. It remained undiscovered for hundreds of years do in part to the great lengths someone took to conceal the chamber," Dr. Cable said calmly and slowly allowing John time to absorb each detail.

Dr. Cable took his handkerchief out and wiped the perspiration off his forehead, causing John to ask, "Do you want me to a crack a window?"

"I'm fine." He again removed his glasses wiping them clean, leaned back in his chair and crossed his legs before continuing with his story. "After entering the chamber, Dr. Happard and I approached the altar having told Don to stay behind and wait near the door. The glow from the cube gave the room a mysterious radiance we soon diluted with our flash-lights. We each progressed slowly shining our lights to each side of the room searching for any artifact or object that might be present. I was nervous and excited to the point of shaking in my shoes. Dr. Happard was all business as he walked a few feet ahead of me, and reached the stone altar first. I was mesmerized by the exhilaration of finding an undisturbed room of the Inca civilization."

Every archeologist's dream was to discover the secrets of an area like the one being described, having been untouched for hundreds of years, and no other modern eyes ever seeing it. John had a similar experience only once in his career, but it was just a small room the size of a closet containing very few artifacts, nothing to compare with what Dr. Cable was describing.

Dr. Cable shifted in his chair and uncrossed his legs searching for a more comfortable position. "As I came close to the altar I could see the cube sitting on a plate made of what looked to be gold. It was obvious the cube was the primary reason for the chamber by its design and its position on the altar. I was near enough to the cube to touch it and of course I could not resist, so I reached out slowly with my hand and gently made contact with my fingertips. It was cool to the touch, and then suddenly a strange surge went through my body. The sensation was like a weak electrical shock or like when you hold a cell phone whose ringer is set on 'vibrate'. Becoming dizzy and disoriented, I pulled my hand away. As soon as the contact was broken all sensations went away; I felt the same as I did before I touched the cube."

Not able to resist, John had to know. "Did you touch it again? What happened?" He was becoming absorbed by the story.

He gave a little smile as he continued, "Yes, not to be deterred, I touched it again and felt the same tingling except the dizziness quickly faded. Now I felt as though someone or something was entering my mind, like there was another person in my brain controlling my thoughts. It was like having a dream while wide-awake with no control of what my mind was visualizing. I could see objects I had never seen in my entire life. Writings appeared in my mind and I heard sounds in a language unfamiliar to me. None of it frightened me, and I was very calm, when all of a sudden the spell was broken as my hand was pulled away by Dr. Happard. He told me never to touch the cube again. He had been in contact with the cube and I'm sure, receiving the same unusual sensations as I had felt."

Listening intently now, John did not think Dr. Cable could invent a story like the whopper he was telling. He must have gotten everything confused. It would be difficult to make up such a detailed story as he was describing. One explanation might be that he had taken a similar story, where he was involved in finding an artifact, and had changed it into a mystic fabrication through his imagination. It was easy to believe a person of Dr. Cable's age could get things mixed up, even though John considered him to be lucid and coherent.

Knowing the end of his tale was close at hand; Dr. Cable leaned forward as if to emphasize the last part. "Dr. Happard removed his shirt and put it over the cube. He told Don and me to leave the chamber and forbid us or anyone to enter. The desire to touch the cube again was burning inside me, but Dr. Happard placed guards at the entrance twenty-four hours a day. No one was allowed in or near the chamber."

"Who were the guards?"

"They were military personnel assigned to our group. The area we were in contained rebels, who had attacked other expeditions," Dr. Cable answered in a creaky voice, weaker than before and his eyes hinted at a touch of pain.

John could understand having military personnel along. He had been on an expedition to Columbia where soldiers, due to problems in the area, accompanied him and his team.

"The activity at Machu Picchu returned to the normal work of excavation and analyzing the layout and structure of the city. I did my job, but I was always thinking about the cube. One night I tried to get into the chamber by slipping past the guards who were half-asleep. I was caught and Dr. Happard threatened to have me sent back to the States if I made another attempt to enter the chamber."

"Six days later we were allowed back in the chamber, but the cube was gone as was the gold plate it rested on. Dr. Happard told Don and me never to speak of the cube again. He also said the object was in the ruins by mistake and not part of the Inca civilization. Of course I knew it was not something created by the Incas and I'm sure Don felt the same. I never discussed the cube with Don and now I am sorry I did not because after returning to the United States he enlisted in the Army and was killed in the war."

"Dr. Happard said if we mentioned it to anyone he would deny its existence and we would be in serious trouble. He said to put the cube out of our minds so I don't know where the cube was taken, but I suspect it is in the United States."

Dr. Cable leaned back in his chair, again taking out his handkerchief and wiping his mouth giving John the impression he was done with his tale. "I think I've covered the entire story. I'll try to answer your questions as truthfully and honestly as possible."

After hearing a tale like the one just conveyed, John was not sure where to begin.

CHAPTER 2B

The low sun created long shadows on the tree-lined street and these dark areas made the lane markings less visible and the ability to spot children in between parked cars more difficult. Carol, in her jeep, drove slower and paid closer attention to her driving than was her normal routine. It was a pleasant drive from JPL to her home and Carol enjoyed the trip. She purchased her jeep two years prior and loved every minute of time she spent in it, especially when she took the top cover off and let the wind blow her hair. Approaching her house and pulling in the driveway, she looked forward to relaxing at home.

Entering her driveway and parking the jeep in the garage, Carol picked up the mail on the kitchen table, (Carla, their maid, collected the mail from the box and placed it there each day), walked into the den and plunked down in an easy chair.

Four years ago, Carol and her husband, Bob, purchased their home, a huge house located in one of the more upscale subdivisions in the Pasadena area. It had three bedrooms and two baths upstairs. The downstairs contained a family-entertainment room, kitchen, dining room, den, formal living area, a small bedroom with bath, and a half-bath in the front hall. All the downstairs living and kitchen area had cathedral ceilings. A door from the den led to an outside patio and located next to the patio was a pool and a small yard. In Carol's opinion, the house was much too big for only two people besides being very expensive, and had told Bob the same before he made the down payment, but he had to buy it.

Carol was resting in the den when she heard the door from the kitchen to the garage open. The door had made a squeaking sound ever since they moved in and at first, she wanted it fixed. Now after four years, it had become a characteristic of the house and alerted those inside someone was entering from the garage.

Bob yelled, "Carol, are you here?"

Yelling back, "Yes, I'm in the den." She could hear him scuffling around in the kitchen.

"I'm getting a beer. Do you want me to get you one?" He asked as he opened the refrigerator door.

"No, I'm fine." Over the last two years, Bob had begun to drink a lot of beer. It definitely showed in his mid section, which had swelled out and since he was stocky anyway, the beer belly did little to improve his appearance. He now reminded Carol more of a used car salesman than a real estate broker.

As Bob entered the den, Carol started to get up and leave, then changed her mind. It was silly of her to avoid contact with him while living in the same house. He sat in one of the two recliners and reached for the mail on the small table between his and Carol's chairs.

"I'm going to the Club to play cards tonight. Are you interested in going?" He asked as he guzzled down some of the beer and thumbed through the mail.

"You know I don't enjoy going to the club, besides you don't want me with you," Carol said avoiding eye contact and surprised he would ask her to go with him.

"What gives you that idea?" He asked, using a tone of voice Carol had grew to despise. It was the accentuation he used that said 'why are you giving me that attitude, I haven't done anything wrong'.

Here we go again Carol thought to herself. Bob and Carol belonged to a Country Club, but she rarely participated in any of its functions. For more than a year Bob had played cards at the Club and he gave Carol the impression it was some of the guys playing poker. It wasn't until four months ago she accidentally found out poker wasn't the only game being played. Rumors had been flying around that on some nights, women not belonging to the Club came in and the game was strip poker. Bob was not the only husband caught as you might say "with their pants down." Carol considered the news, as might be expected, a major turning point in the downward spiral of their deteriorating relationship.

"Let's not get started. You go off to your Club and I'll enjoy my evening here alone. I'll read a book and be quite happy," Carol said. In the last few weeks, her normal evening's entertainment was reading.

Getting up from his chair, he started to reply, thought better and walked out of the room without speaking another word.

Bob and Carol knew their marriage was on the rocks partly because she spent long hours at work and he was engrossed in Real Estate. His business took a lot of time, but he did quite well at selling as his commissions amply illustrated. The house they lived in was proof of his work since he had purchased it with his sales commissions.

Having been married six years, only the first two could be considered happy. After dating for a year and living together for six months, the decision was made to tie the knot. Now it seemed they lived together out of convenience and not having made love for four months, the tension was building between two career-oriented people. She knew they were living on borrowed time and the end was near at hand.

Separation and divorce would seem to be the solution in her mind since there were so many unresolved problems. Their having no children was always an issue with Bob. Carol was the oldest of seven children in her family and after her Mother died, she took on the responsibility of helping to raise her younger siblings. She had no desire to have a baby and raise another family. Carol had made it quite clear to him before they wed she did not want any children, besides she was near the end of her child bearing years. Bob on the other hand had always longed for children and thought Carol would change her mind after they were married.

In many marriages, Carol knew one partner always thought the other would change in some way. No matter how much Bob had tried to convince her to have a baby, she would not give in to his pleas. The love she had for Bob had dissipated and she had little desire to stay with him any longer.

As she sat in the chair, Carol began to think about the picture from Talaria she brought home and, although tired, considered taking a look at it even to the point of getting up and putting the disc in the drive of her computer, but her fatigue won over her desire to view the picture. She grabbed a bite to eat out of the oven. Carla always put something in the oven or on the stove before leaving for the day. Carol showered and crawled into bed for some much-needed sleep. By sleeping in separate bedrooms, she knew Bob would not bother her when he came in, if he came home, since staying out all night was becoming his practice of late.

The next morning Carol entered JPL and proceeded directly to her office. Passing through the hall, she met Rick Watson near her office door. Rick was the program director for the Talaria probe and had been with JPL for many years. He was a short bald man in his late fifties and the oldest person on the Talaria team.

"Great job yesterday, Carol. The pictures from Talaria are some of the best I have seen."

"Thank you, Rick. I can't take all the credit. The new computer programs really make my job a great deal easier," Carol replied with a smile, appreciating his praise. "Has Dale color enhanced any pictures?"

"I'm not sure. I saw him at his console a moment ago, anyway, great job Carol. Keep up the good work," he said as he turned and walked down the hall.

She liked Rick and the way he ran the team even if he was a company man following orders without question. Carol was more cautious in her acceptance of higher-up's statements and did not always assume they were true or correct. The two had worked together many years and Rick was one man who always treated Carol as an equal. Because of his fairness, she had a great deal of respect for him as her boss and as a person.

After stopping by her office, she headed for the control center and upon entering, found Dale working at his console. Due to the large number of people going over the data sent back by Talaria, the control room was noisy so she spoke loudly.

"Good morning Dale."

"Hi to you," He replied, glancing up at her from his seat.

"You're here early." Dale was known as a late riser.

"Yes, I came in ahead of time. I was anxious to get started. There are some fantastic pictures to be processed."

Dale had a great mind and was very talented in adding color to the pictures from the space probes. A large number of the people involved in the early space exploration had retired or passed away and a younger generation had taken over at JPL. Carol had not been disappointed in the new breed of engineers and scientists who were in charge. Sometimes they had a tendency to make rash decisions or decisions she would consider grandiose, but over-all, they performed as well as those of the past. Dale was one of those talented additions.

"Have you finished with any of the pictures yet?" Carol hoped he had completed the one she was interested in viewing.

He stopped his work and turned to face Carol. "I have several done-you can call them up on your screen." Dale reached for the information on his console and gave her the numbers. Carol entered them and viewed the first one, a beautiful picture of two chunks of asteroid material with the stars in the background against the blackness of space. The picture she had in mind was not among the ones Dale had completed adding in the color.

"Dale, could you work on one of the pictures for me? I saw something in it I wanted to review."

"Sure. What is the number?" Dale again halted what he was doing to perform her request.

After checking her notes, Carol answered, "A474-300." She always took notes during her work. It was a habit she developed in college and these notes gave her a reminder of decisions made and actions taken during the hectic time of receiving the pictures from Talaria.

Dale punched in the numbers and appearing on the screen were the words "FILE NOT FOUND". Dale looked at Carol and tried again with the same results.

"Are you sure you have the right numbers, Carol?" Dale asked. "The number won't come up."

Carol was positive she had the right number. Again she scanned her notes made when the pictures were sent, and then she checked the master

23

printout from JPL of pictures taken and their numbers. JPL handed to everyone a computer sheet listing the pictures taken by the probe and at what time. Everything showed the number Carol gave to Dale was the correct one.

"Yes, I am positive A474-300 is the correct number of the picture." Carol moved her hand to her chin showing she was as confused as Dale. After a moment of contemplation, Carol entered the number on her computer to see if she could call it up on her screen.

"I am baffled," Carol said quizzically as the screen showed the same results as Dale's. "Let me check the picture numbers on both sides."

Carol entered A473-300 and A475-300 and these pictures appeared with no problem. She looked at Dale and received back a similar questioning look.

"We better inform the supervisors," Dale said. He knew it was a serious matter when valuable pictures from space are in some way misplaced.

Larry Kelso was the control room supervisor and a fun-loving guy, yet extremely particular when it came to his work. He had joined JPL at the same time Carol came on board, so they learned the ropes together. Larry liked sports and could be one of the guys at the bar drinking beer and watching Monday Night Football. Larry was always on top of things so Carol expected him to know why the picture was not in the system.

Carol got Larry's attention and waved him over to their area. In a few moments, Larry was standing next to Carol and Dale's consoles.

"Okay guys, I mean man and woman, what super extraordinary difficult problem do you have for Ole Larry to solve. I'm always here to serve." Larry spoke with his usual flair and a big smile on his face as she and Dale swiveled around in their chairs to face him.

Larry teased people and made jokes so he sometimes gave the impression to those who didn't know him he was goofy and incompetent. Of average height and a little on the skinny side, it didn't take long, working with Larry, to find out he had knowledge and skill far surpassing most of the people on the team and underlying his kidding was a very intelligent mind.

"We do have a problem Larry, and believe it or not, we-the two of us-cannot solve it," Dale said throwing back some of Larry's play.

"This is serious," Larry said with a little laugh, "If you two can't solve it, then I'm your last hope."

"Enough of your playing around. The reason we need you is one of the pictures Talaria sent back won't come up on the screen," Carol said wanting the two of them to get back to the problem at hand.

"Punch the number in Dale, and let me see," Larry instructed with a more serious tone to his voice.

Dale swung his chair back around to his console and did as he was told with the same results, "FILE NOT FOUND".

"Are you sure it's the right number?" Larry asked assuming they were mistaken.

"Yes, here is my print-out." Carol handed him the sheet.

Larry looked at the paper, then at the number Dale had typed. He was getting a questioning look on his face like Carol and Dale had expressed earlier.

"I assume you have tried it on your computer Carol," Larry asked trusting the ability of the two to try all the checks before bringing him into the scenario.

"Yes," She answered.

A frown came over his face. "I better inform Rick about the problem. I'll look into it right away. Thanks for pointing it out." Larry left to find Rick Watson.

After Larry went searching for Rick, Dale asked Carol, "Have you ever experienced losing a picture at JPL?"

She searched her brain for any tidbit of information from the past related to what they were dealing with now. "No, I can't recall any." Both Dale and Carol were still thinking about the missing picture as they returned to their normal routine.

Time passed and after one hour, Larry returned. As he walked over to their work area, the look on his face told Carol he wasn't pleased with what he discovered concerning the missing picture. "Do you have any answers?" Carol asked in a tone telling him she expected a reply.

"Yes and no," Larry replied without the jokes. He was all business now. "I was told the picture in question is no longer in the system. It has been deleted from the files, and I can not find out why it was erased."

Carol and Dale were dumfounded. They stared at one another and then both looked at Larry with vague expressions.

Larry responded to the looks on their faces. "Yes, I know. It is highly unusual, but the order came from very high up. All I know is your picture, A474-300, is gone, deleted, erased, kaput! I did find out Colonel Pratt had something to do with its removal. I know you are displeased and so am I. I will continue to look into its deletion, but for the time being we are to forget about it."

A look of utter disbelief came over Carol and Dale's faces.

"I have never dealt with anything along these lines since I have been at JPL. As far as I know, it has never happened before. I'm sorry. I don't know what else to tell you." Larry was nearly babbling as he turned and walked away.

Dale sat at his console in solemn acquiescence. "Boy, would I like to see the missing picture. Something must have been of great importance for it to be deleted. Did you see something unusual in the picture?" He asked Carol. Now Dale was very interested in what was in the picture.

Carol thought for a moment. Should she tell Dale about the copy? Letting the idea bounce around in her mind, she decided to keep it to herself for the time being. No need to jump the gun and make a rash decision when she would have ample opportunity to let him know later if necessary.

"I thought something wasn't right with the picture, but I can't remember any particular thing to point out."

Her noticing a difference in one of the pictures had turned into a strange event. Carol went about her work as if nothing unusual had occurred, as did Dale at the console to her left. She continued to hash over in her mind the missing picture from the Talaria probe and what it was in the picture keeping everyone involved reticent.

During lunch in the hall outside the cafeteria, Carol ran into Rick Watson and asked if she could have a moment of his time. Rick and she stepped into a nearby hall leading to an area of rooms not used at the present time. It was a good place to have a private conversation. "Rick," Carol began, "I found out a couple of hours ago one of the pictures from the Talaria probe has been deleted from the file. Can you tell me why?"

Not answering immediately, Rick seemed to be nervous and trying to think of a response to her question. His reaction was not normal because he usually shot from the hip giving a direct reply when questioned.

Puffing up and speaking in a slightly shaky voice, which was also out of character for him, he replied, "Carol, I really can not comment. Just take it to heart the decision to delete came from the highest levels of government. I can't say anymore."

"Did Colonel Pratt have anything to do with it?"

Pointing his index finger up in the air like he was swearing to God, he answered, "I'll only say one thing-Colonel Pratt is connected to the highest levels of government. I hope I've answered your question. I wish I could be more forthcoming."

She had the impression he would like to say more. Anyway, he answered her question. Colonel Pratt definitely played a role in the concealment.

"You know secrecy like we have here bothers me a great deal. It should not be a part of scientific exploration and you are well aware what I'm saying is true," Carol expounded, surprised by how loud she spoke to him. She looked Rick directly in the eyes since she was almost the same height, then turned and walked away.

As she walked down the hall, she was reviewing in her mind the little bit of information received from Rick. From what he said and did not say, there must be something in the picture the Government or the Defense Department did not want the scientists or general public to see. Carol was anxious to get home and view the copy she had made yesterday in her office. She returned to her workstation finding Dale at his console and related to him her conservation with Rick.

"Your talk with Rick sounds like James Bond stuff. All the secrecy is befuddling to me. Is there anyway we could get the picture from the system?

You are aware things don't always get completely deleted sometimes and they can be recovered," Dale said, showing a great deal of curiosity.

Astonished by his eagerness to attempt to break into the computer system, her decision not to tell him about her copy may need some rethinking. "You know we could get in big trouble if we tried hacking into the system, besides people around here know so much about computers it is doubtful a scrap of data remains." Looking at Dale with wide eyes and a grin, she continued," But if I were a betting woman, which I'm not, I'd put my money on you to come up with a way to get it."

Dale was just as competent as Carol when it came to delving into computers. If anyone at JPL could get the picture from the system, next to her, Dale would be the one.

"Thanks for your praise," Dale said smiling, "I know it would not be the smart thing to do, but curiosity is killing me."

Carol then decided to consider letting Dale see the copy. "How would you like to come over to my house after work for dinner?"

Dale's eyes lit up, looked at her with a frown and smiled.

Not meaning it the way it sounded and hoping Dale knew she wasn't making a pass, she said, somewhat embarrassed, "I mean to talk about the picture."

Dale was an attractive man and since Carol's marriage was going down the tubes, it might be interesting except he was too young, besides they work together and she was just being silly even thinking about dating him.

"Seriously, we can have dinner and discuss how to find a way to get a copy of the picture," Carol said trying to work her way out of the dilemma she had put herself in with Dale.

Dale stared at her with a lurid smile.

"Would you quit that! You men!" She said with a girlish grin.

He laughed. "I'm teasing. Yes, your invite sounds like a plan."

Creating an opportunity to feel Dale out about the picture, she hoped to determine if he would blab it all over the place if shown the copy.

Carol called home to tell Bob Dale was coming over for dinner. Bob had made other plans and would not be home but he would tell Carla to be sure to fix something before she left for the day. Carla Sanchez, besides being the maid, took care of almost everything they asked of her.

Carla was another issue between Carol and Bob. Carol could not be a homemaker and still have a career in the space exploration field. Having a job with long hours and a large house to take care of would not work, so it was her idea to employ Carla. They could afford it, so she hired Carla and felt good giving her a job. He had complained, yet he did very little to help keep up the house.

Knowing she could not continue the charade of being a happily married couple and sure Bob was seeing someone else, it was time for her to look for a place of her own. Bob had purchased the house and considered it his so she was quite happy to leave it to him.

It was 5:30 PM Friday as Dale and Carol left JPL. He followed her in his car and they arrived at her house around 6:00 P.M. Carla had left spaghetti sauce on the stove and Carol proceeded to make a salad and spaghetti as well as put some garlic bread in the oven. As she was organizing dinner, Dale sat on a stool at the kitchen bar and opened a bottle of Shiraz and poured them each a glass

Waiting for the water to boil and sipping her wine, she asked Dale, "What is your take on the mystery picture?"

"I'm very curious. What could be in a picture from the asteroid belt giving the government such a problem they would go to the extent of having it removed and who are the highest levels of government?"

"I really don't know Dale. I would love to find out. You would think the picture could not contain anything but some rocks." Carol stared at the large dining room, then said, "Just to throw out an idea. What if the government had been doing some stuff in space, you know, secret things like the CIA, and Talaria by chance took a picture of their project?"

He had never considered such a possibility so it caught him off guard. He raised his head back and gazed upward as if looking to the heavens for an answer to the question. "I doubt the government would be doing anything secretive in the area of the Asteroid Belt. It is too far out to have any useful purpose in my way of thinking."

Dale's curiosity was quite obvious so she decided to tell him about the copy of the picture during dinner. With his help, she prepared the food and after they sat down to eat, she began to relate to him how she came up with a copy.

"I'm going to let you in on a little secret. You have to promise not to tell a soul." Carol watched him carefully to see how he reacted.

Dale nodded in agreement saying nonchalantly, "Sure, what is it?"

Carol re-emphasized. "I'm not sure you understand the seriousness of what I'm about to say. It involves your job so I need your sworn promise. Please think about what I'm asking because it concerns something I did at JPL."

"You know I trust you. I won't tell anyone unless it involves espionage or something like bringing down the government. What do you have to tell me?" Dale's face lit up like a child opening a birthday gift.

"I made a copy of the missing picture before it was deleted; I have it here in the house." Carol again observed his reaction.

Dale was stunned. A piece of spaghetti slid out of his mouth as he stared at Carol. "You know you're not supposed to make copies. You could get into big trouble."

"I know," Carol said sheepishly, afraid she had made a mistake telling him.

Dale wiped his mouth, hung his head down staring at his plate of food, and said nothing. Carol assumed he was thinking about all the problems he could get into just knowing about the copy. Realizing it was a lot for a young technician to handle, she did not press him, but waited to see what other comments he might want to make. It became so quiet, she could hear the creaks and groans made by the house.

Finally, he raised his head with his face returning to the glow it had before and interrupting the silence, he spoke with jubilation in his voice. "Boy, I'm glad you made the copy. Now maybe we can see what all the to-do is about! You will let me look at it, won't you?"

Relief swept over Carol's face.

CHAPTER 3A

In a vintage office at Stanford University, time seemed to stand still. Words echoed back and forth in every corner of the room, eventually settling in John Kirkwood's mind. The most amazing story had just been told here in his office, and if true, would have ramifications for the entire world.

Caught in the moment, and having absorbed every word, John considered the possibility of what he heard being true. As much respect as he had for Dr. Cable, he could not fathom how the story could be real, yet it was a wonderful tale with the hidden chamber, alien artifact, and governmental conspiracy. Now his doubts were superceding his desire to accept the story. Flip-flopping back and forth, he wanted to believe; yet it seemed so far fetched. The whole thing was turning into a conundrum.

Dr. Cable broke the silence. "I have some ideas concerning the events I have related to you and I will be happy to share them since it may help clarify some parts. I know you're having difficulty believing me, but rest assured every thing I have said to you is just as it occurred."

John chuckled under his breath. He needed plenty explained like how could something so amazing occur and no one know about it? The people from Missouri have a saying; 'they must be shown to believe'. The saying described his feeling to a tee. He nodded at Dr. Cable. "Yes, I would be glad to hear your ideas. Maybe in the process you will answer some of the questions I have in hand. Please go ahead."

Leaning back in his chair, wringing his dry wrinkled hands together, he began anew, "First, I have no doubt in my mind the cube was alien. Nothing then or now would convince me in our most advanced technology, we humans had the know-how to create an object of the magnitude the artifact exhibits. I know its existence is the most difficult aspect of my story for you to give credence to, but I'm personally sure my beliefs are correct."

On the matter of the artifact, he was right on target for if the cube was Earthly, then the story takes on a whole new light. John was listening carefully to his analysis.

"I think you would agree with me even with their best minds, the Inca Indians lacked the knowledge or technology to construct such an object and certainly no other civilization of the period was capable of creating it. Prior cultures would lack the ability as well," He said making a clear and concise argument.

"If your portrayal of the object and what it did when you touched it is correct, then yes, I agree. No one would have the ability to construct the kind of device you describe." John conceded the point without agreeing to its existence.

"In my opinion, the cube is a type of information storage device containing all kinds of data. I think you can access the information simply by touching the cube. Dr. Happard was aware of its abilities and saw the potential for such an instrument so through his contacts in the government, I believe he had it removed to the United States. If it contained knowledge we humans did not possess, its value could not be measured in dollars and cents. Heaven only knows what questions it might be able to answer."

Now he was giving opinions and conjectures regarding these events and for John, these would be more difficult to accept as true since the original story was hard enough to believe. His speculation and interpretation might be as correct as anyone's. John offered another scenario. "Dr. Cable, could the chamber you found have been only a few years old, not hundreds as you believe and the whole thing an elaborate hoax being played on the unsuspecting Americans?"

Dr. Cable bristled up. John was getting into an area he had not intended to discuss, but he would answer the question. "You may think Dr. Happard was not qualified as an archeologist, but take my word, he was a talented researcher. After we were allowed back in the chamber, we went over it with a fine tooth comb. Dr. Happard told us, 'I want to know if the chamber is a fake'. We examined every square inch looking for another way into the room. We looked for some item or sign to show it had been used more recently and we found none."

His tenor had changed into a lecture mode as he related the efforts to check for authenticity. "We were sure the way we came in had been covered for a long, long time. The vines had to be growing over the ground for many years and the dirt was compacted around it indicating the area had not been disturbed for a long time. So my answer to you is no, it was not a hoax. If it was a ruse, it began 400 years ago," He said adamantly.

Maybe his impression of Dr. Happard was wrong. It appeared he took the steps John would have used to determine the authenticity.

"From what little information I have obtained, my guess is it was taken to Wright Airfield, now known as Wright-Patterson Air Force Base in

Dayton, Ohio. I believe it stayed there during World War II. You must remember, in 1938 there was no Central Intelligence Agency or National Security Agency. In fact, intelligence gathering and spying was not one of the United States best qualities before World War II. For instance the Peruvian embassy told American intelligence in February of 1941 that the Japanese were planning an attack on Pearl Harbor and we all know what happened in December of the same year. This is only one example of the ineptitude on the part of U. S. intelligence. I think the people in power at the time weren't sure what to do with it so they stored it at Wright Field. Wright Field housed part of Army intelligence during the time period we are discussing."

"Didn't anyone realize its value when it was brought to the United States?"

Dr. Cable twisted in his chair as he raised his hand chest high and pointed his finger in the air. He would have liked to raise it higher, but was unable to. "I'm sure everyone at the top considered it a valuable object. I doubt anyone realized how extremely valuable it was until later. I would imagine the number of people with knowledge of it was kept very small and its existence I'm sure was top secret. The secrecy would seem to go without question since you or I have never seen or heard anything about an object with these characteristics."

Not being familiar with intelligence gathering of the era in question, John asked, "Who would be in charge of such an item in 1938 or 1939?"

"As I mentioned, secrecy and intelligence gathering were poor at the time. My guess is one of two groups would have control of the artifact. One was the State Department, which had an intelligence section and the other would be one of the armed force's intelligence divisions. Having no Air Force at the time, it would be the Office of Naval Intelligence or Army Intelligence."

"If I had to make a choice, I would pick the State Department since Dr. Happard worked through the agency for many years and remember, I told you he had a close relationship with President Roosevelt. The two of them attended Columbia University at the same time and he was at a conference with the President in Buenos Aires, Argentina in December of 1936."

Dr. Cable looked and sounded tired and once or twice appeared to be in pain. John said in a concerned voice. "Would you like to take a break or reconsider the offer of a drink."

"I'm all right. I just slow down as the day goes by." A slight grin appeared on his face.

It was clear Dr. Cable had done some research into what became of the cube. John also sensed he himself becoming enmeshed in his story. He did like exploration and research so he found the story tantalizing, yet in his mind, the possibility of it being true was still miniscule.

He seemed to have gathered his second wind as he asked, "Are you familiar with or have you read about a Project Mogul created in 1945 shortly after World War II."

"No, I don't believe I've ever seen or heard the term used before," John replied.

Dr. Cable leaned forward in his chair as if he was imparting some very sensitive material to John. He lowered his voice. "Project Mogul was classified top-secret and considered very sensitive. It was labeled top priority and designated a secret status like the kind given to one other activity I am aware of-the Manhattan Project, which as you know developed the A-bomb. Project Mogul operated out of Webster Labs located at Wright Field. Few people knew all the activities Project Mogul was involved with since it was so diversified. In control of the personnel and security for Mogul was a Colonel Garland Martin, who worked out of Wright Field, Ohio."

John now knew in his mind Dr. Cable had been investigating and searching for the cube. The kind of information he was referring to isn't just lying around. He noted Wright Field was mentioned for the second time in Dr. Cable's research.

To John, the story could not get any stranger, yet Dr. Cable kept coming up with new tid-bits to shock him again. "So we come back to Wright Field. How did you find out about Project Mogul?"

"It has been de-classified so you can read about it in books, but nothing is ever mentioned about the cube. I think outwardly, even though it was top secret, Mogul was a cover for the investigation of the cube or the cube was hidden within Project Mogul. Part of the Project did launch some balloons over New Mexico and these objects were blamed for the incident at Roswell, New Mexico, which is still a hot topic today. A supposedly alien space ship crash-landed in July of 1947 near Roswell and books have been written about the incident many times over."

It would be ironic to John if Project Mogul did have an alien cube hidden away and at the same time the Roswell Incident occurred through another part of Project Mogul.

"I'm familiar with the Roswell Incident. Documentaries and movies have also been made about the event. I've never heard of Project Mogul in reference to Roswell so if it is de-classified, is the Project still in existence today?"

A serious expression manifested itself on Dr. Cable's face as he gazed at John and replied, "I don't know."

Considering his answer, John eyed Dr. Cable with a bit of skepticism. The whole story seemed preposterous and now John was waffling. He looked into Dr. Cable's eyes and found them staring back at him in all seriousness. Why would a man well known for his life's work in the field of archeology suddenly appear at John's office and tell him such an unusual story?

John arose and walked over to the window behind his desk. The weather seemed to be improving so maybe some sunshine would appear later today. As he stood looking out over the campus, Dr. Cable said, "I think I am done with most of what I have to say. I'll try to answer your questions."

Thinking to himself, so many questions were popping up in his head; it was difficult to keep them all in his consciousness. John turned, walked back to the couch, and stood in front of Dr. Cable eyeing the old man. He said, "Excuse me a moment, I'll be right back."

Leaving his office, he walked to the faculty lounge and purchased two bottles of water from the machine. He returned to his office handing one to Dr. cable and saying, "Your voice seems a little dry."

"Thank you. I could use a little water."

John returned to the couch, sat down, and said, "Why are you telling me, a History Professor at Stanford University, a story about alien cubes?"

After taking a drink, Dr. Cable struggled to replace the cap on the bottle. At ninety, I guess your hands and fingers don't work as well John thought as he started to offer help, but changed his mind. He didn't want to offend him by implying he couldn't do something as simple as putting a cap on a bottle. Dr. Cable eventually replaced the cap.

"Dr. Kirkwood, you are the only authority on the Inca civilization I respect to any great degree. I share it with you in hope, some day, you may uncover more of the story."

"Your assuming I believe what you say is true-a mysterious cube exists somewhere. If your story is correct, what does it all mean? What is it you wish to find?"

"I have had many years to ponder and speculate. I can not prove any of the ideas I have, but I will let you be the judge and jury. I think some very serious questions would be: Where is it? Who is in charge of it? How has it been used? and Is it still being used?"

CHAPTER 3B

The quiet pervaded the house and the night's glow gave a mystical flavor to the rooms with high ceilings. The house was huge by normal standards and although adequately furnished, because of the large rooms, its ambience created an impression of emptiness. Only the voices of Carol and Dale broke the silence. They had chosen the breakfast nook for their dinner preferring it to the large table in the dining room.

The dinner conversation was of a more personal nature when compared to their day to day discussions at work. Carol was shocked to discover Dale was considering a long-term relationship with his current dating partner. Now knowing he had a steady girlfriend, Carol felt bad taking him away from her on a Friday night, but found out later his friend was out of town for the weekend.

Since they had discussed the copy, after dinner he offered to help her clean up, but she was more interested in the pictures so they proceeded to the den for a look. It was easy to see Dale was anxious by the gleam in his eyes and his hurried movements. Still having reservations about telling him, she had gone too far to back out now.

Her computer and other hardware were positioned on a small table in the corner of the den. She sat down at the computer and checked the drive. The disc was right where she left it the previous night so she brought up the program displaying the picture on her monitor.

Looking closely at the screen as the picture appeared, Carol picked out the object she had noticed the previous day at JPL. It was the only part of the picture she considered out of place. Everything else in the photo fit what would be expected in a picture taken in the Asteroid Belt, thus if the government deleted the picture for another reason, it would have to be something Carol couldn't distinguish.

Dale scanned the screen and quickly pointed to the object Carol was eyeing. "Look at this thing. It can't be an asteroid! It almost looks like it could be a man-made object. What do you make of it?" Dale said scratching the side of his head with a questioning look.

The object in the picture capturing their attention was mixed in with other rocks and debris so it was difficult to get a clear look at the item of concern. It was partially blocked from view by another asteroid. Carol gazed at it for a moment before answering. "It looks like a type of structural beam. I might say it could be a part of one of our space probes although I don't think we have sent anything into space having a part like the one shown." Carol spoke with the realization she was not privy to what goes into the making of every space vessel.

Halting the scratching of his head and focusing on the object, Dale spoke with a voice of confidence. "I agree. It looks like a part from my erector set I had when I was a kid. It's long and narrow and it seems to have holes in it or it is reflecting light."

"If we could color enhance it, we might get a better idea of its structure. The reason I inquired into your work at the lab today was to help determine its composition." She was hinting the least little bit hoping Dale would take the bait.

Dale was so engrossed in the picture he gave no response to Carol's comment. Finally he said, "I have the color enhancing program at my condo." He had a guilty smile on his face like a little boy caught in the act of doing something wrong.

Smiling as well, Carol stared at Dale wide-eyed not expecting him to have the program at his home. "I thought I was the only one who took stuff from JPL."

They both laughed, then Dale suggested they take the disc to his place and run the color-enhancing program. Both were curious and neither wanted to wait any longer. Carol thought it was a great idea so she left a note for Bob, knowing he would not care where she was and besides, it was doubtful he would return before she came home.

Carol and Dale both drove to his condo so she could return without Dale having to drive her home. It took twenty minutes to make the trip and on the way, Carol reviewed in her mind the events of the day. The picture or the object in it was extremely important to somebody, but why was the picture so valuable, or maybe she should ask why is the picture so dangerous? The only thing Carol could see in the picture different from the other objects was the odd shaped one she and Dale had just reviewed. A shiver of fear ran through her body as she realized she might be getting in over her head. What if the object was top secret, then she shouldn't have a copy. Slowly the tenseness gripping her eased away as they approached his residence.

Dale lived in a large complex in a yuppie section of Pasadena. When they arrived, Carol was impressed by the size of his condo and commented to him how nice it looked. They had climbed a set of stairs because his place was on the second floor of the building. Dale said he had a life long dream of owning a place like his present home. He asked her if she would like anything, a drink or something, and she declined. Carol was surprised at how neat the condo was kept since at JPL, Dale never gave her the impression of being an orderly person; in fact he gave the opposite sentiment. The apartment was well organized and clean. Oh well, she thought, he can be any way he wishes.

The large living room had a small alcove off to the side and located in it was a desk and computer. He sat at the computer, took Carol's disc and started the enhancing program.

The program was a color-enhancing system developed in part by Dale with technical assistance from Carol. It took all the slight differences in shades of black and white and fine-tuned them into colors and tints. The program did take some leeway in choosing the tints and hues, although the outcome should be close to the actual view if you were out in space looking directly at the object.

"I don't think much will change in the picture. The asteroids are prin- cipally made up of metals which have a dark hue to their color."

"Yes, you are right, yet it could make some difference in the area we are interested in and might change the view," Dale replied.

The computer was loaded and ready so Dale clicked the mouse and the process of coloring began. Slowly the picture faded into different tints and hues with some things changing and others remaining the same. As the area where the object came into view, they both stared at it with mouths agape.

They slowly turned to look at each other checking whether the other was seeing the same thing, then both their pairs of eyes returned to the monitor.

"Do you see what I see?" asked Dale, keeping his eyes pinned to the screen.

Carol nodded slightly not taking her eyes away from the monitor either. She didn't believe the scene being sent to her brain.

"Is your program operating correctly?" She thought there might be some kind of error.

He keyed in a couple of checks, then replied, "Yes, up to its intended performance. Everything checks out."

The picture on the monitor was impossible, yet before Carol's eyes was a long tubular object, if she did not know better, she would say it was made of orange glass. It had a glow to it and stood out in the photo like the proverbial sore thumb. She had been standing, but now searched for a chair as if needing something to support her shaky legs.

So many things were going through her mind. So many questions-it would take her a moment to collect her thoughts.

"I think I may understand why they deleted it from the computers at JPL," Dale said in a quivering voice, "but why would they want to hide it from the scientists. If the object is what I think, it is fantastic news."

"What do you think?" Carol asked, not sure where he was headed.

Dale studied the picture once more. "Unless a malfunction occurred in the camera or an error in the signals from Talaria, it must be something alien. I know of nothing we humans have sent into space having any resemblance to the thing we are viewing."

Carol was struck by the term, humans, used by Dale. Once we start talking of aliens we are all grouped together as one without concern for nationality. Her thoughts then returned to the item at hand. Surely a simple answer exists such as an old space probe gone awry, a Russian secret probe, or one of many other possibilities. Yet a simple solution does not explain the picture, and why all the secrecy. Carol had taken a chair from the kitchen table and was now sitting next to Dale looking at the picture.

"You're leaving out the possibility the object is Russian or something secret the United States is responsible for putting into space. I agree it looks alien," Carol said.

"I suppose your right. Do you want a hard copy?" He inquired.

She responded right away, "No, only the disc." Having the disc was enough of a problem. "I have no clue as to what the object might be. Many possibilities exist so I don't think we should jump to any conclusions and we better not mention the picture to anyone until we understand the consequences of doing so." Carol spoke grimly, believing there was a lot more to the deletion than she first perceived.

"I agree. We could loose our jobs and by it being deleted at JPL, someone wants it kept quiet. If we mentioned something about the picture and it got back to the higher ups, they might conclude we had it in our possession." Dale spoke with the tiniest hint of fear in his voice.

After agreeing to think about the picture over the weekend and discuss any new ideas at work Monday, she left Dale's condo and drove around the city, being in no hurry to get back to her house. Carol had a lot to mull over with her marriage breaking up, the picture at JPL, and her future in the space program, all concerns taking a toll on her well-being. After an hour of driving, she arrived home and seeing no sign of Bob went to bed.

The weekend was a welcome retreat from the activities at JPL. Since Talaria had moved swiftly past the Asteroid Belt, it was taking very few pictures now so Carol could take full advantage of the free time playing tennis at the Country Club. She had become acquainted with another woman who was Carol's equal at the game. It was the only thing she enjoyed doing at the Club. Bob called her anti-social because she wouldn't go into the bar after playing since one of the responsibilities of belonging to the Club was to spend money for drinks or food. Of course he forgot she didn't want to join in the first place and there were other tennis courts in Pasadena.

Viewing the picture off and on over the two days, she still was confused by all the events surrounding its deletion. During the weekend Dale called telling her his thoughts were as unsettled as hers and he had not developed any new revelations or conclusions either. Carol had a problem giving her full attention to the picture because of her difficulties with Bob.

She and Bob argued the entire weekend. Their arguments were about trivial things of no consequence and it was a symptom of their deteriorating relationship.

Once, while in the kitchen preparing food, Bob said to Carol in a sarcastic tone, "If you're so upset with living here with me, why don't you move out?"

"Maybe I will. You're never here anyway. You're always at the "Country Club" (she made the quotation sign using two fingers on each hand) doing I don't know what," Carol yelled back at him.

"You're never going to forget that, are you?"

"You had your opportunity. All I asked was for us to quit the Country Club, but oh no, you said too many business clients are members, so don't give me your old line."

"You never gave it a chance. Some nice people are members, much more friendly than I find at home."

"Carol gave him an evil stare. "Yes, I know some of the women are very friendly. If you like it so much, why don't you move to the club." With her last words, Carol stomped out of the kitchen.

Carol knew she and Bob were over, through, done. Looking for an apartment would be on her "things to do list" for next week. Sometimes two people might like each other, but are not meant to be husband and wife.

Monday morning Carol arrived at JPL in a somber mood. Having now made the decision to sever the ties with Bob, she felt a huge burden had been lifted from her shoulders; one she had been carrying for a long time. Anxious about starting a new life for herself, she checked through security and walked toward her office.

Barbara Sillings, who was Rick's secretary, entered her office. "You are expected in the conference room at 9:00 am for a meeting with Rick."

"What kind of meeting?"

"I don't know. Strangers are walking around the lab this morning. I'm not sure if they have anything to do with the meeting."

Being curious and thinking to herself-could it be in relation to the missing picture? Carol made herself a cup of coffee, did some paperwork at her desk and left for the meeting.

She entered the conference room and noticed more people than usual were in attendance for a typical meeting. Most of the technicians, many of the scientists and engineers on the Talaria team and Colonel Pratt were in the room.

The one person present who was a surprise to her was Ben Hagen, the Director of JPL and someone she rarely saw except when big media events occurred like the pictures from a probe coming into JPL. He sat off to the side of the room with the same aide who always seemed to be around him.

Carol sat down as Rick Watson walked in the room with two men she did not recognize. Everyone turned their attention toward Rick as he started the meeting. "I want to introduce you to Glen Feathers and Greg Johnson. These gentlemen are government agents and will be here at JPL for a period of time."

The two men didn't look like government agents, or at least not how Carol imagined Federal agents looking. They both were overweight and their clothes were wrinkled. Feathers face looked like he had acne and Johnson had let the hair on the side of his head grow long and plastered it over the top in an attempt to hide his bald head. Why do men want to hide their baldness? To her bald men sometimes looked sexy.

Rick looked a little out of sorts as if he had done something wrong and he was fidgeting as he continued. "I have asked everyone to this meeting because we have a problem. A serious breach of security has occurred in our internal system. Last Friday a picture from the Talaria probe was deleted from the system by order of the highest levels of government. I can say nothing else concerning the deletion so don't ask me any questions about it."

Carol just then realized Dale was absent from the meeting. She worried about him, hoping he wasn't sick or in any trouble.

"Now to the matter I asked you here to discuss. In the investigation, the agents have determined a copy of the deleted photo has been made without permission by someone here at JPL." Rick conveyed this information to the group.

Everyone seemed to turn and scan the room staring at one another as if they could ferret out the guilty party by looking them in the eyes. Carol wanted someplace to hide, but instead she looked around the room like everyone else so as not to look conspicuous. She was sure they would eventually tie it to her computer even though she had tried some tricks when accessing the information. It was only a matter of time until someone with a little computer savvy found her out.

As the group eventually turned back to Rick, he nodded at Colonel Pratt who stood to address the group. He was in his usual stiff military form.

"As most of you know, I am Colonel Gil Pratt. I have witnessed the return of pictures from many of JPL's probes over the past several years and I have been impressed by the work you are doing. We really need to know who made the copy and where it is located."

Ben Hagen stood and re-iterated Colonel Pratt's last statement then exited the room with his aide.

Rick interjected, "I will ask all of you to cooperate with agents Feathers and Johnson. They will be asking many of you questions and I know everyone will help so we can get to the bottom of the problem. Are there any questions."

The group raised a myriad of questions about the picture and its removal. Rick was true to his guns when he said he would not say any more about the deletion of the picture. Nothing he said seemed to calm the rising tide of discontent and several people looked as though they were ready to start a riot. Finally things settled down and the meeting was adjourned. As the people began to file out of the conference room, Rick caught Carol's eye and motioned her to stay.

Soon the room was empty except for Rick, the two agents, Colonel Pratt and Carol. She felt the noose beginning to close in around her neck. She told herself to remain calm, act innocent and remember, no information regarding her had been found because if evidence showed she made the copy, this meeting would not have been necessary.

"Carol, we are going to ask you to assist us in any way you can. You have more knowledge about the computers and equipment than anyone else at JPL. We want you to check your station and see if you can come up with anything," Rick said in a calmer and more confident manner after the dispersion of the crowd. He was always better dealing with people in small groups or one on one.

Colonel Pratt added, "We are dealing with a very serious matter and any help or assistance you can provide will be greatly appreciated."

Carol felt some relief. "Right now I know little about the making of a copy. I will check into it and see what I can find out."

Rick responded to her answer. "Thank you for your help. I will be anxious to hear the results of your efforts."

Exiting the room, she was perspiring profusely and hoped no one noticed. Little Miss Hot Shot, you stuck your nose into this one and now it was getting out of hand. Her little stunt of copying the picture is leading her down a treacherous path. Needing to talk to Dale and find out why he missed the meeting, she hurried down the hall toward the control room.

After searching high and low, Dale was no where to be found. Returning to her office, she used the inter-com to ask Barbara to come to her office.

"What can I do for you Mrs. Jacobs?"

"I've been looking for Dale Belfer. He doesn't answer his phone and I can not locate him. Do you have any idea where he might be?"

"Mr. Belfer has been with two strangers in Mr. Watson's office. The three have been in there all morning."

"Do you know what it concerns?"

"I haven't the faintest. If I see Dale I will tell him he's wanted," Barbara said, then left the office.

Carol was worried now. What if they were questioning Dale about the picture? It seemed to be the logical assumption, and if he spilled his guts, then it was all over but the shouting or in the present case, the firing. These people would know she had the picture and they would soon be coming after Carol. As she was contemplating Dale's situation, he entered her office and plopped down in a chair.

"You look awful," Carol said in a sharp tone, surprised by his abrupt entry. His hair hung down in the front as if it had been wet. His shirt had a lower button loose and it was not tucked in completely.

Dale blew out some air as he wiped his forehead with the back of his hand and replied,

"Gee, thanks!"

"Well I mean you look like you've been through the wringer. What happened?"

"I have been through the wringer," He said, repeating Carol's comment, "Government agents are here and they found out I had made a copy of the color enhancing program, thus they concluded I was the culprit who made off with the copy of the picture from Talaria. I've been going through the third degree."

"How did they find out you made the copy?"

"The agents were trying to see who copied the Talaria picture and stumbled on to my copying the coloring program. I goofed up," Dale said, "I should have been more careful. I never imagined someone would check into it, so I took very few precautions to cover my tracks when I made the copy."

"What did you tell them?" Carol asked nervously hoping he did not rat her out.

"Nothing. Oh I confessed to copying the enhancing program, but I denied making a copy of the Talaria picture. Of course I did not make a copy so I was truthful. Carol, what is happening around here? We are talking about a picture taken over 100 million miles from Earth aren't we? I don't understand the cloak and dagger stuff," Dale said shaking his head in disbelief. He was very dispirited.

Carol stared through Dale into space and spoke softly to herself. "Neither do I, Dale, neither do I."

CHAPTER 4A

The morning fog vanished in the air, the rain disappeared into the horizon, and the sun made itself known again to all it touched. In John's office a beam of sunlight penetrated through the window onto the floor between him and Dr. Cable. You could see the dust floating in the air. It was as if the story Dr. Cable had told created such a fury that the dust was just now beginning to settle in the aftermath.

John stared at the suspended particles as he attempted to absorb all the information revealed to him. One item Dr. Cable had not touched on interested John and he inquired of Dr. Cable, "I've followed your story very closely. You never mentioned how the Incas came to have the cube in their possession." As he finished his question, John opened his bottle of water and took a drink.

Dr. Cable winced in pain again and reached in his pocket pulling out a small tin box and removed two pills from the container. Popping them into his mouth, he opened his bottle of water and taking a drink, washed the pills down. He preformed the task of screwing the cap back on the bottle with greater efficiency than he had earlier.

"Are you all right. Is there anything I can do?" John asked worried he might be having a heart attack or something.

"No, no. I'm okay. Just needed to take my medicine."

John wondered if it was pain medication since he seemed to be in pain a moment before he took the pills.

"Now, back to your question. Remember, I am only giving you my conjecture. I did spend many years in Peru trying to discover a clue to assist in solving the problem and I determined, in my best estimate, the cube was acquired by the Incas or their forebears sometime between 1000 AD and 1200 AD. I believe the Incas did in fact gain some knowledge from the cube and the information they obtained spread throughout the Americas. In my opinion, the cube is the reason the Inca, Aztec, and Mayan cultures developed far beyond the other Indian societies of North and South America.

The Incas had control of the cube for approximately two to three hundred years. You know they had a highly organized society and conquered surrounding cultures at an amazing rate."

"I know from your story you think the cube gave them knowledge to advance beyond the other Indian groups in the region."

"Yes I do. The Incas avoided at all costs destroying captured cities because they wanted them intact and did not want to kill the people involved. They let the captured people keep their own leaders, but the conquered people had to accept the Inca language and become a part of the Inca Empire. This was very unusual. It would not be typical today in most cases."

"The Incas built over eighteen thousand miles of roads and paths, some through the Andes Mountains, and the Inca leaders received reports daily from all parts of their empire. Every person was allotted an area to grow more than enough food for his or her family. No one in any part of the empire ever went hungry. These organizational skills had to come from somewhere." Dr. Cable spoke with a touch of pride.

Knowing his tremendous love for the different cultures of the Americas, John knew Dr. Cable was enjoying lecturing him on the Incas so he let him continue.

"Do you have any proof they gained knowledge from the cube?"

Reaching up and slightly loosening his tie, he replied, "Let's look at it in another way. You know Dr. Kirkwood; the Egyptians took thousands of years to develop their society. The ancient Greeks and Romans took hundreds of years to create their cultures, but the Incas did it during one lifetime. Under the leadership of Pachacuti and his son, TupacYupanqui, in a mere 55 years, the Inca lands went from a few mountain communities to an empire stretching over 2,500 miles."

John was becoming frustrated with Dr. Cable's delay in answering his original question. "But where did they get the object. If it is alien like you say, did some spaceship land in the Andes and hand it over to the Incas?"

"You watch too many movies Dr. Kirkwood. It is nothing so grandiose I'm sure. I honestly don't know how they obtained the artifact. Your scenario may be true-I doubt it. A more feasible explanation would be that it was left here by mistake, or it was left in our solar system and wound up on Earth. You remember a few years ago the to-do raised over the meteorite from the planet Mars found on Earth."

"Yes I remember. Some scientists thought there were microbes fossilized in the rock and it would prove life once existed on Mars."

"Very good. The point I'm trying to make is-ah-items move around the solar system due to explosions, objects crashing into one another, and gravity pulling them here and there. You see, we have a tendency to think in terms of our lifetime, 70 or 80 years or in my case, more, where as the solar system changes on a scale measured in millions, even billions of years. The cube might have been left here millions of years ago, long before we humans even existed."

John considered what he said. It would make sense. If the Inca gained information from the object, their civilization would receive a jump-start compared to other cultures. Also the new information would explain why they protected the location of Machu Picchu from the Spaniards, but he was getting ahead of himself. "If it has been here millions of years, wouldn't it decay, dissipate or rot away from exposure to weather and such?"

"Possibly. I have no idea what it is capable of withstanding. Since I or no one else I know has examined its structure. I can only speculate."

"Dr. Cable, what do you want me, a history professor from Stanford University to do about an alien object?"

Dr. Cable was looking at John in a different way as he prepared to answer his last question. The reason he came to see Dr. Kirkwood related directly to his inquiry.

He folded his arms across his chest, cocked his head slightly to the left, and looked at John with a serious stare. "I would hope-that is-I am asking you to continue my investigation and attempt to locate the cube and answer some of these questions we have been posing. I am not able to do what needs to be done. I have reached the limit of my ability to travel around the country and conduct the kind of search necessary to obtain information about the cube. I will supply you with all the funds you need in your efforts."

Dr. Cable had dropped another bombshell on him. He was one surprise after another and the last one ranked right up next to the alien artifact. John leaned back on the couch with his mouth open and quite frankly stunned. Nothing was said by either as John caught his breath. John liked the man who sat before him and he had a way to get on your good side. The request was most unusual, and he realized, to do it right, it would be a full time job. He would not be able to continue teaching at Stanford because in no way could he attempt both and do either justice.

"I can't leave my teaching position. If I did what you ask, I would have to quit my job here at Stanford and I'm not sure I would ever consider making such a choice."

"You could take a sabbatical. In fact I have taken the liberty of conferring with your Department chairman, Dr. Calway, and he has agreed to let you take a leave of absence. I will pay you your present salary plus twenty thousand dollars for at least three years if necessary. My attorney will start an Escrow Account with three years salary so in case something happens to me, you can go on with the search."

"What about my classes. I can't leave until the end of the term if I did decide to do what you ask." John knew sabbaticals were not authorized in the middle of a semester, and for that matter-what was he doing actually talking about leaving Stanford! John Kirkwood, get hold of yourself he said under his breath.

"Dr. Calway has taken care of your classes. He has someone in mind to take over as teacher."

"Who does he have in mind?"

"Cheryl Roberts. A graduate assistant I believe."

He was sure Cheryl would jump at the chance to replace him, as it would be a feather in her cap. "If I did decide to accept your offer, it would be expensive. How can you afford to pay me and also pay all the expenses I would incur? I'm sure it would be a considerable amount."

"I have made a lot of money from the sale of my books and used my expertise on appraising artifacts which brought in a great deal of consulting fees. I never married and have no children, so I have had little to spend my money on over the past years. Money is not a problem."

Dr. Cable's frugality might be apparent from the clothes he wore, but John suspected the apparel was not a legitimate representation of the Dr.'s wealth. His comment indicating money was not a problem surprised John, but it followed because the Dr. had an answer for everything. He must have taken a great amount of time to plan all the details so John asked with an inquisitive frown. "Then why me?"

Leaning toward John and pointing at him with his shaky hand, he responded, "You have an unencumbered life, no spouse, little family ties, and your talent in researching the Inca Culture, which I mentioned to you earlier, all went into my decision to ask you. Your ability at research and exploration is well known."

John stared at Dr. Cable with suspicious eyes. "It sounds like you have planned for everything and are well prepared, researching my life, talking to my superiors, and getting into my mind."

Dr. Cable made no effort to respond to John's comment.

Just when John thought Dr. Cable could not surprise him any more; he had arranged his future life for him. He may give the appearance of a tired worn down old man, but behind those gray eyes was a keen, crafty, calculating mind. "Why do you want to spend your money searching for the object. What I mean is, if I should find it, what would you do with the information?"

"What would you suggest be done?"

"It's your idea," John said, wanting to know Dr. Cable's agenda.

"I wish I had done something in 1938. I was young and inexperienced in the ways of the world. The best experts in the world, not just the United States, should study the artifact. It should be used for the good of mankind-all mankind. I personally want no gain from the cube, only the satisfaction of knowing it is being used for the good of all people."

Truly a noble goal, yet John was not completely satisfied Dr. Cable was telling the whole truth. He sensed other factors might be involved in his desire to find the artifact.

"I'm past my prime. I don't have the energy to continue the investigation. I spent most of my efforts in Peru, but would suggest you work in the United States."

John was intrigued. If the story was true, the possibilities were endless. Maybe accepting the offer was what his life needed to get back in the swing of things, to feel alive again. His purpose had been to teach and explore yet recently his teaching wasn't giving him the good feeling it had in the past. Searching for the object would certainly give him new purpose so his original disbelief was ebbing and the idea of finding an artifact was alluring.

"I would like to have some time to think about your request," John said thinking he must be out of his mind giving Dr. Cable's proposal the least bit of consideration.

"I need to know soon and unlike you, I'm nearing the end of my years, so I don't have time to waste. I'm spending the weekend in town with old friends so I must know your answer by noon Monday. I have other people to ask should you decline."

The time-line Dr. Cable requested jolted him. John was not prepared to make a tumultuous decision in such a short time so he requested more time of Dr. Cable. He again said Monday was the deadline and John would have to live with it or decline now. John decided to live with the time line.

Dr. Cable began to stir in his chair in preparation to standing up. "I want to thank you for your time, Dr. Kirkwood. You have been everything I expected. I'll leave my hotel and room number with you. Contact me anytime over the weekend with your decision or if you have any other questions."

John retrieved his coat for him, handed him his cane and hat, and helped him slowly edge his way toward the door. He hobbled and wavered after having sat for a long period of time and appeared to grimace in pain as he walked.

"Can I take you somewhere, to your hotel, or call a cab for you?"

"No, thank you, I have someone who looks after me and drives me around."

"I need the name of your hotel."

"Of course, I'm so forgetful these days. Here is my card. I've written the information on the back."

His admitting he was forgetful didn't make John feel any better about believing his story.

John opened the door for him. He left the office walking with his cane. John watched as Dr. Cable made his way down the hall and was met by a tall man who took his arm and escorted him out of the building. How sad it is for a man who was at the top of his profession to become weak and frail.

He still had the gift of his mind, and in John's opinion, thinking ability was more important to retain.

The story Dr. Cable told was going around in his head. Could any of his tale have a thread of truth or is it simply the ramblings of a tired old man. It was a dilemma John would have the weekend to mull over and then make a decision.

Eyeing the paperwork on his desk, he decided any chores could wait because after the story he had just listened to, he was in no mood to grade essays. Picking up his briefcase, he left for home. The trip to his house was 15 minutes and after arriving, he could rest, relax and attempt to sort out what he had just heard.

As he neared his house, he pulled into the garage, closed the door, and entered the kitchen. He had purchased the home seven years ago and never regretted it for one moment. His home was an old two story house he had spent weekends remodeling, sometimes using subcontractors to do part of the work.

Twisting the top off a bottle of beer, opening the door and picking up the mail from the box by the door, he continued out onto the front porch and sat down in a lounge chair. Thumbing through the mail, nothing caught his eye because his mind was still on Dr. Cable's story.

If Cable was right and he took a sabbatical, he would have to establish a plan of action. He couldn't go around the country half-cocked. It did seem exciting and he loved research and exploration. He could look into Project Mogul and Wright-Patterson Air Force Base as a start. Did he want to leave his teaching for a time and search for the object? Would it turn out to be a wild goose chase? Would he be better off to forget what Cable had said and continue his present life? He guzzled the beer, laid back in the lounge chair, and let his mind drift.

What to do?

CHAPTER 4B

The halls at the Jet Propulsion Laboratory presented a sullen picture of people passing each other with little acknowledgement. A place where, at times, space accomplishments had the focus of the entire world, now harbored government agents snooping, spying, and nosing in and around the corridors. The questioning by the agents created a morose posture and a great deal of suspicion among the staff. The present attitude was so different from the normal comradery usually pervading the building when a probe's pictures were being received from space.

The day passed far too slow for Carol and every phone call she received and every person who stopped by her office to chat gave her a little shiver of fear. The trepidation of getting caught was a new experience and not one she relished. She now had an idea how people might act when they are afraid of their own shadow.

Dale had not contacted her since mid-morning when he confided to Carol his experiences with the investigators. She felt lonely and was anxious for the day to end, wrap up her work, and remove herself from JPL.

Feeling guilty for causing the upheaval at the Lab, it occurred to her the real culprits were the people who deleted the picture. She had mulled over the idea of confessing to the act and letting the chips fall where they may. One thing deterring her from doing so was the itching in her soul to find out why the picture was removed and who was behind the deletion of the picture.

All her life Carol had worked with computers and loved to use them to solve problems and always followed where ever they led her in her inquires and research. Now she was prevented from pursuing her instincts by mysterious powers who gave no reason or explanation for doing so. It did not set well with her character.

Carol checked into some apartments during the day and her calls resulted in two possibilities; both apartments were more distant from work than her present home. Bob could easily find her a good deal on a place closer to work except she wanted a clean break. Owing him a favor was not the way she wanted to leave and the longer drive wouldn't create any undo hardship.

At the end of the day, she left and drove to the first of the two appointments made over the phone. After walking through the first apartment with the manager, she was quite pleased with its size and location. It was a large one bedroom located on the first floor of an apartment building. Leaving to visit the second one not far away, she found it similar, less expensive, but the surroundings were not as appealing. She called the manager of the first one to tell her she would take the apartment, then stopped by her office to put a deposit down and sign a lease. Since she saw no reason to delay the break with Bob, Carol decided to call a mover tomorrow. The manager gave her the key, a copy of the lease, some rules and a sheet with the phone numbers of the utility companies.

Driving to her house, she entered the kitchen and smelled the dinner Carla had left warming in the oven. Carla was a wonderful person and Carol would miss having her around to take care of things. Maybe someone could come in one day a week at her new place and it would be great if Carla was the one.

A note from Bob said he was showing property and would be home later. One thing Carol and Bob always attempted to do was let the other know where they would be located in case the need arose to contact one another. Carol was sure, in the last several months; Bob was not always in the place his note said he would be.

Entering the den, she sat at the computer and called up the picture. As her computer monitor displayed the picture, she asked herself; what can it be? She searched her brain trying to remember something on one of the space probes resembling the orange piece, but nothing came to mind.

She considered destroying the disc so no tangible evidence would exist pointing her way. Instead, something in the intuitive part of her brain told her to make a second copy and hide it in the house, which she did.

Bob had not come in and probably wouldn't, so Carol ate some of the dinner Carla left and retired to her bedroom to read. Falling asleep with a book in her hand had become her normal evening routine.

The next morning Carol awoke and prepared to go to work. As she passed by Bob's bedroom she noticed the door ajar, so she looked in on him. The room was empty which probably meant he did not come home last night. She left a note on the kitchen counter telling him about the apartment and informing him she would be moving as soon as possible.

Carol wanted to arrive early at JPL to keep ahead of the rumors and scuttlebutt concerning the picture. By knowing what information was flying around, she would have time to plan a defense if necessary or squelch any suspicions leading the search in her direction.

On the drive to work, Carol remembered her days in Northern California, getting six kids up and ready for the day. The two youngest not in school yet, went to a neighbors across the street. She took care of them for four and one half years before going to Stanford. After she left, Robin took over till she left for college. Her father never married again, probably in part do to having the baggage of seven children.

Those times seem so long ago, but they helped mold her into the person she is today. She had to grow up before her time and helping to raise her family had given her a strong affinity for right and wrong, a trait leading her to a precarious position regarding the picture. It wasn't right for someone to arbitrarily delete the picture so she again made a promise to herself to find out why.

Entering JPL and proceeding to her office, she was surprised to find agents Feathers and Johnson going through her papers. Greg Johnson was looking at her books on the shelves against one wall and Glen Feathers was scanning the material on top of her desk as she watched from the doorway.

"Can I help you gentlemen?" Carol asked in as snarly a tone as she could muster.

The agents seemed startled as they both jerked their heads slightly and looked her way. "Ms. Jacobs, I'm Agent Feathers and this is Agent Johnson. We are here to ask you some questions concerning the missing copy of the picture."

Carol did not want to look guilty and kept telling herself to act casual. She decided to put some pressure on these guys. "I know your names. We met in the conference room yesterday morning. When you were introduced no one said what agency you represented."

When Carol became angry, her eyes glazed over just as they were doing now. Seeing these two men in her office snooping around brought out the ire in her personality.

Feathers gave an inquiring look at Johnson as he sat in a chair located in the corner of the office and made no effort to answer Carol's question.

"Ms.... Jacobs, we represent an inter-agency group which investigates matters of national security." Johnson, in an attempt to irritate her, put extra emphasis on the Ms by stringing it out.

"What?" Carol blurted. She noticed Feathers peering at her with raised eyebrows. He had the look of a man offering a little girl candy so she would get into his car, which reinforced Carol's dislike for the man.

"Did something agent Johnson say bother you?" Feathers asked.

"What does a space probe picture have to do with national security?" She asked, astounded at such a remark.

"All you need to know, Ms. Jacobs, is it does involve national security," Johnson said as he moved behind her desk where Agent Feathers had been standing before he sat down. He eyed the material on top of her desk.

"Says who?" She fired back.

"Says Agent Feathers and me," Johnson said forcefully with a cold stare.

The debate was getting away from Carol and her planned cool behavior was losing out to rage and anger. Not backing down she said, "If it is a

national security matter, I need to see some kind of identification please."
She was pushing the envelope with these two characters and their responses
and facial expressions told her she was getting under their skin.

Johnson was slow to respond as if he was going to ignore her request.
Eventually, reaching inside his suit jacket, he produced an identification,
which he held for Carol to see. The ID showed he was employed by and an
agent for the Defense Intelligence Agency.

Carol was confused. What kind of agency was the Defense something or
other? Feathers produced a similar identification.

"I've never heard of such an agency. Where is it located and who does
it represent?"

Johnson walked around the desk and stood facing Carol with little room
between them. He spoke with gritted teeth. "It's in Washington, DC and it
represents the Government of the United States. I think we have answered
enough questions and it is now your turn to answer our questions." His
loud voice caused the words to reverberate in the air.

Carol was at the end of her rope. She could think of nothing else to challenge these two brutes about except to tell Agent Johnson to get out of her face.

Johnson with a sly grin returned to the desk as Feathers began the questioning. "Do you have any information concerning the copying of the picture from the Talaria probe?"

It was decision time for Carol. She could lie and deny any knowledge of
the whole affair or admit to everything and take the condemnation from her
employers and colleagues. With her confession she would never know why the
picture was being kept a secret and all proof of its existence would disappear.

"No, just what I've picked up around the lab." Carol made her decision
to deny copying the picture.

"Have you used the network connection on your computer recently?"
Johnson asked.

"Of course, I use it every day," Carol said smugly. The agents could ask her
questions all day if they liked, but she was not about to get caught in a trap.

"Have you been approached by anyone inquiring about data from this
or any other probe?" asked Johnson.

Waiting a moment before answering, she said, "No, I can't recall any."

Agent Feathers jumped in with a question. "Ms Jacobs, you hesitated
on your last answer. Are you sure?"

"You asked about any other probe. You are talking about a lot of probes
and years of work for me so I had to think back. Also, sometimes reporters
inquire about space probes, but usually they ask others here at JPL, not me."

The interrogation continued with questions about her finances, travel
plans, marriage, and many other topics of both a professional and personal
nature. Before Carol realized, an hour had passed and she was getting tired
both from the questions and the two men she considered goons.

"We are going to have some of our people check out your computer," Johnson said again with a smile on his face implying he already knew she was the culprit.

"We are going to lock your office until our men arrive. You will have to do your work somewhere else."

"Has Mr. Watson given you permission?" Carol said, still standing up to their prying.

"Yes, but we wouldn't need his permission," Johnson said, "We will be in touch." The two agents escorted her out and put a doorknob lock on her office door. The lock was a metal object covering the original doorknob, except when you tried to turn it, the doorknob lock just spun around on the real one.

Carol walked into Ralph's office, which was next to hers. It was empty and as soon as she closed the door, she let the air escape from her lungs. Having never dealt with questioning like she just endured, she felt weak-kneed and mentally drained. Carol could empathize with Dale's experience yesterday when he was put on the hot seat.

The idea a picture from outer space had something to do with national security confused her and she wanted to find the connection. Carol sat at Ralph's computer, which she had used before. Ralph was another technician who was involved with the Talaria probe and other projects. Using the password she remembered from times spent here in the past, she was able to call up the information on a previous space probe called Galileo. It had passed through the Asteroid Belt and taken pictures of several asteroids just like Talaria.

One of the objects photographed was Gaspra, a small asteroid ten miles long, which was passed on October 29, 1991. The pictures of Gaspra came up on the screen. The scaring from many collisions indicated it was two hundred to three hundred million years old and once was a part of a larger object. Two years later, on August 28, 1993, Galileo passed another asteroid called Ida.

Carol sat back and tried to remember what was going on during Galileo's trip. She recalled the presence of Colonel Pratt as a regular during its flight. In fact, it was the first time Carol remembered him at JPL. The only other thing that came to mind was the effort to cancel Galileo. Many higher ups said the probe was too expensive and it was not worth the effort to send a vessel to the Asteroid Belt.

Carol looked at the rest of the pictures sent back by Galileo, and seeing nothing unusual, called up the other probe she was interested in investigating.

It was called NEAR or Near Earth Asteroid Rendezvous, launched on February 17, 1996, and on February 14, 2000 went into orbit around the asteroid, Eros, studying it for one year before eventually landing on one of its cratered faces.

Colonel Pratt was a common visitor during NEAR's flight as well. Originally the NEAR probe was canceled until someone at NASA found a way to make it a part of the "Discovery" program allowing the flight to get off the ground. The Discovery Program was a project involved in purely scientific studies of our solar system.

As Carol searched the records, she checked to see if any of the pictures from Galileo were deleted. None were, so she then checked NEAR for deleted pictures and discovered three pictures were missing from its display. Searching her memory of its flight, nothing came to mind about pictures being deleted or taken away. She had no success trying to call up the deleted pictures-and why didn't she notice the deletion of the pictures at the time they were received.

Next, Carol called up the layout of the pictures. It was a sheet listing the numbers of the pictures taken. Scanning the list she found the three numbers of the missing photographs. The pictures were deleted before they ever got to her console and she wasn't sure how anyone could accomplish a feat so complicated because it would require someone in high authority to override the system.

But if someone could do it on NEAR, why didn't they do it on Talaria? Then the reason came to her; Talaria wasn't supposed to go to the Asteroid Belt so they probably did not have time to set up the over-ride.

As she was contemplating these missing pictures, Ralph entered his office and asked what she was doing. She explained to him how the agents had locked her out of her office.

She left Ralph's office knowing they soon would discover the copy was made on her computer. Carol proceeded to the cafeteria looking for Dale, wanting to discuss her discovery of the NEAR probe's deletions. Finding Dale sitting alone eating lunch, she went over to his table and sat down.

Looking up from his food, he said, "Hi Carol. You not eating today?"

"I'm not hungry. I don't have much time so listen to me carefully. Soon the agents questioning everyone are going to determine the copies were made on my computer. I don't know what action will be taken when they find out so I'm going to ask you to think about doing me a favor."

He put his utensils down and gave her a concerned stare. "You know I'll do whatever I can to help you."

"Dale, think about what I'm asking because it could cost you your job. Remember, we had a similar discussion last Friday night. She wanted Dale to be completely aware of the danger he might be in if he agreed.

He didn't hesitate for an instant. "What is it?"

"When the NEAR probe sent back its pictures, some of them were deleted from the system."

A look of shock came over his face. "You mean like the one from Talaria?"

"Yes, except three were deleted on the NEAR probe! What I want you to do is see if you can come up with copies of those pictures."

Dale did not reply. Carol waited patiently and let him think. Finally Dale's eyes lit up. "It may be possible to dig up the pictures deleted from the network. You would have to get into the main system. I may be able to do it."

"I was hoping you would come up with the main system's data storage, because I had the same idea. If I continue to have security clearance, I will do it myself, because I don't want you to get into any more trouble, but if I'm not able to, I will have to depend on you." Carol knew she was asking a lot from Dale.

Carol and Dale parted and agreed to talk only if absolutely necessary. She did not want to draw any more attention to Dale since the agents were now checking into her activities. Too jittery to sit, she walked over to the control center to listen for any rumors and hearing none walked back toward her office. A great deal of pressure had descended on her and no doubt more was to come. How she would tackle the coming events bounced around in her mind as she passed through the halls.

Reaching her office and finding the door open with no one inside, she immediately knew they had found something because her things had been moved around which indicated someone had searched her office, probably looking for the copy of the picture.

Hearing voices, she turned to see Agents Feathers and Johnson coming through the door accompanied by Colonel Pratt and Rick Watson. The office grew crowded as Colonel Pratt and Rick stood at the door with Carol and the two agents inside.

The noose was tightening again as she attempted to present a calm appearance by not acting surprised at the group of people now hovering in and around her small office.

Colonel Pratt cleared his throat, puffed out his chest thinking it made him manlier and spoke first. "Ms. Jacobs, we have learned the copy of the picture was created on your office computer. We want any and all copies you have made as well as the names of anyone else involved."

Having previously decided how she would answer, she eyed the men staring at her and speaking defiantly, said, "Are you sure it was made on my computer?"

"No doubt at all," Rick said. Carol detected a hint of disappointment in Rick's voice and a look of sadness in his eyes. She had let him down and he was hurt.

"Someone must have used my computer to make the copy. I'm shocked you would think I was involved with any breach of security."

"Is that all you have to say?" asked Colonel Pratt.

"Yes," answered Carol. "How else did you expect someone who is innocent to reply?"

Rick left while Colonel Pratt and the two agents continued to question Carol about the picture. She did not back down and continued to deny any knowledge of the copy. After ten minutes of questioning Rick returned.

Rick nodded to Colonel Pratt.

"Ms. Jacobs, I have no alternative. I am suspending you from JPL until further notice. You have ten minutes to gather any personal items you may want to take with you. Turn in all keys, security cards, and IDs to the agents before you leave. You will not be permitted back in JPL for the time being," Colonel Pratt said, "Do you understand?"

She could see the smirks on the faces of Agents Johnson and Feathers acting like they had pulled a coup over on her. Not giving up, she spoke with a scowl on her face."You are not my boss and I would like to know what gives you the authority to dismiss anyone here?"

Colonel Pratt looked at Rick with a frown. Rick turned to Carol and said, "But I do and what Colonel Pratt told you is the way it will be."

Carol looked at Rick with disdain. "I guess we know who calls the shots around here."

Hoping Rick would back her up at least for a while, her disappointment in him began to show. Since they had worked together for eighteen years, she could not understand why he was being so cruel and not giving her the benefit of doubt. He must be under extreme pressure to act so different from his normal behavior.

"Agents Feathers and Johnson will observe what you take and then escort you off the premises," said Rick with much irritation in his voice.

Still having a look of defiance, Carol began gathering some things on her desk while Rick and Colonel Pratt departed. She began to hash over the last few days in her mind. When Dale copied the enhancing program, it got him a reprimand. Now they think she has copied the picture and it results in a suspension. The picture is definitely considered more important, but why? There is a lot more to the picture than meets the eye.

After handing over her keys, ID tags and security card, the agents led her out of the building. As they proceeded down the hall, they met Dale coming toward them wanting to know what the devil was happening. She made eye contact with him and shook her head indicating to him to say nothing. Dale stopped and moved to the side of the hall to let them pass. His eyes were full of questions that would have to wait for another time to be answered.

CHAPTER 5A

Sleep can escape into the realm of delirium when confronted with a dilemma. The night was not a cordial companion for John. On awakening Saturday morning, he knew his sleep had been restless during the previous night and the decision whether to accept Dr. Cable's offer would not come without serious analysis, intertwined with some pain and agony.

On the one hand he did not want to go off on a wild goose chase wasting a great deal of time he could put to better use. On the other hand, it could be one of the greatest experiences of his life if the story turned out to be true. He would agonize over what to do the entire weekend.

The previous night he called Roger Fry, a college buddy who lived in Chicago. The two of them attended the University of Illinois together, yet had not talked to one another for several years. Memories of the many nights they had spent drinking beer and describing to one another how they would spend all the money they planned to make flowed through his mind. Roger had a degree in biochemistry, which led him to a job with Swab-Dell Pharmaceuticals. He had made a great deal of money where as John earned enough to subsist adequately, thus Roger's spending plans had come to fruition.

After some reminiscing about college and bringing each other up to date on recent activities, John gave Roger a premise to consider: Many of the discoveries, inventions, and devices over the past 50 years were developed do to secret information gathered from German scientists and found in German records at the end of World War II.

"Roger, can you prove or disprove the premise?" He asked, anxious to hear Roger's response.

Roger laughed. "What are you talking about?" He then laughed some more.

"Humor me, Roger. Please try to answer. It is important to me." Too late to back out now, even though it seemed to be turning into a mistake and an embarrassment since Roger thought it was so funny.

Roger's voice became calmer as he replied, "You're not joking are you. Well then, let me think. With so many developments since World War II, some being leaps in technology, it would be hard to prove or disprove the premise," Roger paused before continuing, "unless you had some specific information on particular items of interest or specific examples."

"Give me an example of a leap in technology?" John asked.

"A couple of items off the top of my head developed after World War II would be the transistor, and following right behind it, the silicon chip would be another example of a jump. Saying they were developed with information from the Germans would be very hard to prove unless you had first hand knowledge."

Not giving a reply, John considered the two items he mentioned.

Hearing no response from him, Roger added, "If the premise were true, who obtained the data from the Germans and who controlled it. The people who had the data would make a lot of money so are you going to let me in on what you're talking about?"

"I was just considering something one of my students brought up in class last week," He said, lying to Roger. "I appreciate your opinion. Come see me if you're in my neighborhood."

"The same to you. I'm here in Chicago. You're always welcome."

After talking to Roger, John went to the Internet to check into the history of the transistor and silicon chip. He was surprised to find material showing many historians of the computer age have said no one before 1947 foresaw the creation of the transistor or dreamed about semiconductors based on silicon because Edison's incandescent tube was carbon based. The development appeared to be a genuine leap in technology, but determining if the creation of these devices was influenced by information from an alien artifact seemed impossible, yet it did fit.

The conversation with Roger didn't do much to help John make his decision. Just as Roger said, how would you prove or know inventions were being promoted by advance knowledge unless you had direct information or evidence. You would have to confront the person who invented it. Of course challenging them to prove they did invent it on their own would not be an option.

Saturday passed with little activity for John. His mind, as would be expected, kept returning to the issue of the cube no matter what task engaged him.

He called two other acquaintances during the weekend and presented them the same premise as Roger was given, and the answers he received were similar to those given by Roger. Both people asked him why he was inquiring, but John never mentioned the real reason. Searching for an alien artifact was not something he wanted his friends to know, especially since he was considering taking a leave of absence from his teaching to do that very thing.

He pondered over the decision as the weekend flew by, trying to make up his mind. Sunday night, John needed more information before making a final decision, so he called Dr. Cable to pose some additional questions.

After making a connection on the phone, John asked his first question, "How long have you actively searched for the cube?"

"I wish I could say my efforts to find the cube began the first day I saw it, but I can't. I became more interested in my career, so I paid little heed to the artifact. In 1939, after returning from Peru, Dr. Happard made calls and contacted people who were instrumental in advancing my career in archeology. He helped me in tacit exchange for my silence. I'm not proud of the decision I made so the answer to your question is a few weeks. As you can tell I have not made many inroads."

"Dr. Cable, I'm not the judge of choices you have made in your life. To add a point, I would not want anyone second guessing the decisions I made when I was in my twenties." Again John had an underlying sensation Dr. Cable was not confiding in him completely.

"Why have you waited till now to attempt to find the cube?"

Collecting his thoughts, Dr. Cable replied, "As I continue to age, I begin to see the end of my life. I don't want it to end and in all honesty I dread not being a conscious entity, no longer able to experience life, so I now think in terms of what my life has been, instead of what it is to be. I wish to atone for any wrongs I might have committed and make amends to those I have injured. I take these actions not to insure my soul going to a better place, but for my own personal well being and satisfaction. I have many other areas to deal with in the near future; the cube is just one."

John was right in thinking Dr. Cable's mind was still capable of functioning to a high degree. He turned to another area of concern. "What happened to Dr. Happard?"

"In 1942, I enlisted as most men did. I was sent to the Pacific Theater where I was shot in the leg and returned home a few months later. Because of the injury, I've walked with a limp most of my life and now I walk with a cane. I became involved in my own affairs after the war and never made any effort to locate him again."

"Why didn't you tell your story to the press?"

"Surely you know the answer to your question?" Dr. Cable replied.

Even though he asked, John did know the reply Dr. Cable would have given him regarding the press. If Dr. Cable had told his story to the news media, he would have been labeled a crackpot and no one would have believed him any more. The only people who would have printed his story would have been the tabloids. He would have become a joke in the scientific community and would not be able to enlist the aid of people like John.

"If I accept your offer may I hire other individuals to help with the investigation?"

"Yes, as long as they do not know the reason for your search. You know if the story gets out, you will be considered crazy and no one will trust your sanity."

"Point taken." The door was open now, all he had to do was pick one or the other: either go for the search or stay at Stanford. With his personal history of going on expeditions, John decided to take the step. "Dr. Cable, I accept your proposal with one condition. I go where ever the trail leads me and I don't back off even if you want me to."

"Agreed Dr. Kirkwood with a condition of mine. You keep me informed of your progress at all times. I will also be available to help in any way I can."

Since he was paying for the search, it seemed reasonable to keep him up to date. "One other condition. You call me John from now on."

Dr. Cable laughed. "Ok, I'll call you John if you'll call me Dr. Cable."

Now John laughed. What a wag the old man was turning out to be.

"Let me give you my phone number where I can be reached all the time." He passed the number to John.

John assumed it was a cell phone number.

"My attorney will be in touch. He will have a contract for you to sign, give you information on how you will be paid, and how to get reimbursed for your expenses."

"Does your attorney know my address and phone number?"

"Yes, he does. If you need me to help in anyway, feel free to call. I also want to thank you for taking on a difficult challenge. I hope you are successful," Dr. Cable said as he ended the call.

The decision made, his hat tossed into the ring so to speak, John was off on his newest expedition. Knowing doubts about his choice would start creeping into his mind, he needed to become actively involved in the search. Getting started right away might help alleviate some of these concerns yet he would continue to be skeptical until he found proof of the cube's existence.

Logging on the Internet he started the search for Dr. Happard. Dr. Happard would be around a hundred by now so the chances of him being alive were slim. He still wanted to know what Dr. Happard did before, during, and after the war.

He found in much of the results of his search information about books written by Dr. Happard. There was one interesting notation of his living in Dayton, Ohio and John felt it would be a good place to start especially since Wright Patterson Airforce Base is located near Dayton.

First he looked at an atlas, locating Ohio, and it showed Dayton was forty-five miles north of Cincinnati. He then searched the web for a private detective agency in the Dayton area with several hits coming up on the screen. Scanning the list, he opted for the Kinkle Detective Agency, since according to the ad, it had been in business the longest and might be better at investigating people from the past. He planned to contact them tomorrow.

CHAPTER 5B

The glare from the noonday sun reflected off the windshields of the cars in the parking lot at JPL. The heat radiated from the steel and concrete as Agents Feathers and Johnson led Carol into this festering oven. Proceeding to the car, she could sense the eyes of her colleagues trained on her from the buildings darkened windows. Carol felt very alone at the moment, as though she was put adrift at sea, left to fend for herself. The thought was enough to shake her confidence in the recent decisions she had made resulting in her present predicament.

She put her things in the passenger seat of her Jeep and climbed in behind the steering wheel. Agent's Feathers and Johnson moved back toward the entrance to JPL as Carol started the engine. Before leaving she searched for her sunglasses, finding them on the floor on the passenger seat side. Knowing they were hanging on the dash and noticing a magazine on the floorboard, which had been on the seat, she knew someone had searched her Jeep. Carol checked for anything missing and found nothing gone, but was sure someone had been looking for the copy of the picture. She unlocked the glove compartment and finding nothing gone she took the radio out and inserted it into the console, turned it on and backed out of the parking space.

The jeep eased out of the parking lot and down the street as if it had a mind of its own. The music blared from the radio yet she failed to hear a single note. She felt betrayed by her friends and colleagues because they had no idea she was the guilty one and except for Dale, not a single person took her side or stood up in her defense. So many thoughts were twirling around inside her head; it felt as though her brain was on overload. Getting away from Bob would help her concentrate on problems at JPL so she planned to move into the apartment right away.

Attempting to reorganize her personal life and not letting what happened destroy her future were two concerns at the present. The agents had no proof it was she who made the copy, only circumstantial evidence as they say on the television crime shows.

Safely arriving home and entering the kitchen, she called out for Carla. Receiving no reply, she walked into the dining room calling for Carla again and heard a sound coming from the direction of the front hallway. Peering around the corner of the dining room and looking down the hallway, she saw a chair wedged under the doorknob to the hall closet. At first not understanding what the chair meant, she called out Carla's name again and a muffled sound came from behind the closet door.

She rushed down the hall, pulled the chair away and opened the door. Carla was sitting on the floor, hands and feet tied behind her back, tape over her mouth and a frightened look in her eyes.

"My God, what's going on!" Carol yelled.

She gently pulled the tape from her mouth and Carla started a long scenario of what had happened, much of it in Spanish as Carol looked for something to cut the plastic strap around her wrists and ankles. She found a pair of scissors in the drawer of the hall table and cut Carla free.

As she helped her stand up, Carla continued to tell her story in a mixture of languages and speaking so fast it was difficult to understand what she was saying. Carol interrupted to ask if she was all right and after she answered yes, Carol picked up the phone on the hall table and dialed 911.

The person on the phone told her to leave the house, so they hurried out the front door into the yard near the street. The jest of Carla's story was two men with ski masks entered the house and tied her up, gagged her, and left her in the closet. She knew nothing else until Carol entered freeing her. She had been in the closet about a half-hour.

Carol called Bob on her cell phone and received no answer. She then called his office and talked to the receptionist.

"This is Carol Jacobs. I need to contact Bob," Carol said in a hurried and rushed manner.

"He's out showing property Mrs. Jacobs. Can I take a message?"

She bet he was out showing property. He was more apt to be——no need to worry about his activities now. "Please tell him to return home immediately. Our house has been broken into by someone."

"Have you tried him on his cell phone? He usually has it with him."

"Yes, but there is no answer."

"I will send someone right away to the house he is showing to tell him. Is there anything else I can do for you?"

"No, thank you," Carol said and ended the call.

As she finished the call, police, with lights flashing entered the driveway, exited their vehicles and after conferring with Carol, some officers entered the house to search for the intruders. Soon they returned informing Carol and the other officers the house was empty. It seemed obvious to Carol the perpetrators would be gone with the time factor and the police all over the yard.

While one of the officers began writing down Carla's story, another woman officer approached Carol and said, "Are you Mrs. Jacobs?" She was very polite and very young; too young in Carol's thinking to be a Police Officer, looking to be no more than eighteen years old.

"Yes, I'm Carol Jacobs and I live here."

"Would you please accompany me through the house. We need to know what if anything was taken from the premises."

"What about Carla?"

"She will be fine. The other officers will finish taking her statement," The young Officer said as she pointed toward the front door, indicating for Carol to follow.

After checking with Carla Carol entered the house with the officer.

They walked through the living room first, then the dining room, kitchen, and into the den where Carol stopped. Her computer and everything connected to it were gone except for the monitor. The area around her computer and desk was a mess. Drawers had been emptied and papers scattered over the floor.

Now Carol had an idea what the masked men were seeking, but she did not convey her suspicions to the Police Officer. They continued through the remainder of the house, Carol looking in some drawers where jewelry and other valuables were kept. Nothing else of value was found to be missing. Bob's computer in his bedroom was gone the same as Carol's with his desk in a similar mess. She informed the Police Officer accompanying her the only things missing were the two computers so they returned to the front room where two detectives had brought Carla.

She told Carla she could go home if the police were finished with their questions and Carla accepted the offer from the police to take her home.

The crime investigators stayed at the house for two hours testing for fingerprints, even though Carla had said they wore gloves. Other police canvassed the neighborhood for possible eyewitnesses and during this time Bob called on his cell phone.

"What happened?" He asked.

Carol went through the events with Bob and he was as shocked as she.

Telling her he was on his way, it was only a few minutes before he arrived. Concerned about Carla, Carol assured him Carla was doing as good as could be expected and the police had taken her home.

As they walked through the house, she was surprised Bob was showing interest in Carla because he seldom did in the past. "Why don't you call her later and see how she is doing."

"I will. Are the computers the only things taken?" He asked as they climbed the steps to the second floor.

"Yes, I haven't found anything else missing."

"It seems odd to me they only took the computers when there were other items more valuable in the house."

Carol didn't respond to his last remark. She felt no duty to inform him of the picture or her problems regarding it and while they were talking she said, "I'm going to spend the night with a friend."

"Are you afraid to stay here?"

His expression told her he was upset with her attitude. "In part yes. I just want to get away. I left you a note this morning telling you I had found an apartment and would be moving soon."

He stared at Carol for an instant then asked, "Is anyone staying with you?"

She felt it was a little late for him to be concerned about her, given his indiscretions. "A friend, and no it's not another man." Carol lied because she didn't want Bob to worry since she would be alone.

"That's not what I meant," Bob said in a harsh voice "If it will make you feel better, I'll call you later tonight," Carol said to appease him a little.

"You do what you want." Bob walked away mumbling to himself.

Finally, the police were preparing to leave. One of the officers reminded them to be sure to lock their doors tonight and informed them more patrols would be in their neighborhood.

Carol was sure the thieves were after her copy of the picture. It upset her to know the government was behind breaking and entering since no one else would have a reason to take the computers and leave the many other valuables. She had read in books and seen in movies where the government invaded the privacy of citizens without regards to their rights, but always thought it was make believe. It made her angry and she vowed to get even one way or another. She knew the disc with the picture was in her computer's disc drive and now the government she guessed, or someone knew for sure she was the one who made the copy.

Carol went to gather some clothes and other items she would need along with an air mattress, camping equipment, and sleeping bag to take with her. As she was getting ready to load the Jeep, she went back into the house to the hall closet and picked up a shoebox. Taped to the bottom of the box was the second disc containing the copy of the picture. Living with six siblings placed a premium on being able to hide things so the others wouldn't find them. Her intuition was right to make the second copy.

After loading her Jeep, she drove down the street, then circled around the block to the main avenue. As she was driving she noticed in her rear-view-mirror a light blue van following her every move. Cutting through an alley near by and after entering the street again, she sped up and turned at the next block. She drove for several blocks before pulling onto a side street. At the end of the side street where it met another main thoroughfare was a

Mini Mart. Driving around to the side of the Mini Mart, she parked her Jeep in a position so it could not be seen from the street. Carol went inside, purchased a bottle of water and stood at the window scanning the street in both directions.

The blue van came along the street and edged slowly by the front of the Mini Mart. After it had passed, she waited for a few minutes then left and drove to her bank withdrawing one thousand dollars in cash for expenses she might incur getting into the apartment and just to have some money on hand.

She arrived at the apartment, unloaded the supplies, sat on the carpeted floor and caught her breath. Not knowing whether she was being paranoid, she decided it was better to be safe rather than sorry as the old saying goes. It was a good thing she brought her camping lantern and a small flashlight since there were no utilities. Right now she wanted some time to herself to think about everything that had transpired over the last few days.

The recent events flowed through her mind as she tried to make sense of all the unusual things happening to her. Even though she was not having much success unraveling the reasons behind the chain of events, she knew something in her persona had kept her from handing over the copy from the very beginning. Her desire to know the truth, her strong belief in right and wrong and her inherent tenacity all played a part in placing her in the dubious position she now found herself.

As night approached she would go out to eat, return and call Bob making sure he contacts Carla, then camp out on the living room floor. She needed rest, but after all the activity, she doubted sleep would come easy.

CHAPTER 6A

The morning air gently blowing through the window cooled John's sweating body as he completed his daily exercises on the bedroom floor. Feeling invigorated after making the decision to search for the artifact and knowing it would be a new adventure, he did his regiment with much greater intensity than normal. After a shower, cereal and juice, he called the Kinkle Detective Agency in Dayton, Ohio.

The reply from the man answering the phone was, "Kinkle Detective Agency. Peter Cozid speaking."

The person who answered was either a young man in his early twenties or an older man who had something wrong with his voice. In either case, John was leery from the first moment.

"I'm Dr. John Kirkwood. I'm calling inquiring about hiring your agency to do some research for me." John used his title because sometimes it brought him favored treatment.

"You've called the right place. What kind of research can we do for you, Dr. Kirkwood?"

"I want you to find out all you can about a man who once lived in Dayton, Ohio. He is likely deceased by now."

"What is his name?"

"First, I would like to know your fees?" John wanted more information before he gave him Dr. Happard's name.

"Of course. We charge a retainer of $700 and $150 per hour until we finish or you tell us to stop. $200 of the retainer will pay for the last two hours of work. You will also be billed for all expenses we incur."

John had no experience to determine if the quote was a fair amount. It didn't seem unreasonable besides, it wasn't his money, but he didn't want to throw Dr. Cable's money away. He could always cancel if he found it to be out of line or turned into an exorbitant amount.

"I think I can handle your fee. Can I send you a check or a credit card?"

"A credit card will be fine to start, so we can begin working for you immediately. Now, who is it you want checked out?"

Dr. Senval Happard is the name of the person I would like you to investigate. I know he lived in Dayton, maybe as early as 1920 and might have been connected with Wright Airfield."

After a pause on the line, Peter responded, "It may be more difficult and take longer since we are talking about a period over ninety years ago."

"If you don't feel qualified to do it, I'll find someone else," John said, throwing it back to him.

"No, no, we can handle it. I was only trying to let you know it may take longer to research something so far in the past. Will you please spell his name?"

He gave him the name again and then his credit card number. Peter informed him they would start right away.

Next, at his computer, he clicked on the Internet to look into Project Mogul. No hits were made so John checked into the United States "Freedom of Information Act" which allows citizens to obtain de-classified government material or to request the material be declassified. He wanted to see how difficult it would be to get information using this act. After doing the research, John found out it was not as easy to do as one might think. He had to know which department of the government had the papers and after requesting the specific material it may be years before he would receive it if it was not previously declassified. It seemed the government was not going to give up any material easily. Because of his research, he decided to use another method. He would try to find and contact people involved in the Project and see if they might help lead him to the artifact.

He remembered Dr. Cable making a comment in their discussion having to do with a man who was in charge of personnel or something along those lines for Project Mogul. He would call him later today to ask him the name again.

John left for the University to discuss his decision with Dr. Calway and he also had a class to teach in two hours. Reaching Dr. Calway's office, the secretary at the outer office told him he could go right in.

He found him hunched over his desk scanning some papers. Dr. Calway was close to 65 years old, a large man with a round face and thick glasses. Rumors floating around had the Chairman retiring in the near future. Three people were in line for the job who had more seniority than John so he considered his chances of getting the position slim to none.

Looking up from his papers and peering over the top of his reading glasses, he spoke as he motioned John to sit, "Hi John, how are you?"

John sat in a chair facing his desk. "Fine. I wanted to stop by and see you before I left."

"Of course we will miss you here, but I'm sure Miss Roberts will adequately see your class through the rest of the term. You have been one of our special teachers and I hope you will return after your-," He hesitated, "I'm not sure what you are going to do. Dr. Cable never explained the reason-."

John interrupted him. "Dr. Calway, I know the University policy does not allow sabbaticals to be taken in the middle of the semester. I was curious why you granted me one?" John quickly changed the conversation from the subject of his future activities to the reason he was here.

"You do such a fine job and I felt you deserved more than the unusual consideration."

John was not satisfied with Dr. Calway's answer. From the tone of his voice, he did not seem serious so he posed another question. "And what else?"

Taking his glasses off and putting the left earpiece in the corner of his mouth, he rocked back and forth in his chair. He said with a twinkle in his eye and a slight grin, "I shouldn't tell you so I'm asking you not to repeat what I'm going to say." He didn't give John time to respond. "Dr. Cable offered a very large contribution to the History Department if we gave you the leave."

That old codger John thought to himself, and where did he get all of his money? John had done some appraising of artifacts in the past and he never found it to be as lucrative as Dr. Cable led him to believe. He thanked Dr. Calway and left for his class.

After the lecture, he met with Cheryl Roberts concerning the rest of the semester and her responsibilities. Things were working out and if he completed all his paperwork, he would be free of all commitments by the end of the week.

He walked to the Science Department to meet with Harry Calvert; an instructor in astronomy who he hoped could answer some questions. Harry had been a friend ever since he joined the faculty at Stanford five years ago when he was offered a teaching position. He is in his mid fifties and his hobby is extra-terrestrial life, which is the reason John was seeking his council.

Arriving at Harry's office, he felt sorry for him because the office was extremely small and it made John feel honored to have an office with some space. Harry was sitting with his feet propped up on his desk smoking a pipe. It was fortunate he had a window in his office because smoking in the building is not allowed. Harry was average build with a beard and yellowish teeth from smoking his pipe for many years.

"Hi Harry," John said walking in the open door and leaning against a filing cabinet. "I haven't talked to you for a long time."

Harry responded with a similar greeting. "What brings you over my way? Are you slumming?"

"Very funny. The reason for my visit is a question. I know you do research and venture into the area of extra-terrestrial life. I am interested in knowing what the probability would be that sometime in the past earth was visited by an inter-stellar civilization?"

Removing his pipe and smiling, Harry was amused by John's inquiry. "You've asked quite a question. If you are interested in the reports of alien abductions, crop circles, or UFO sightings, you can read these in the tabloids."

Embarrassed to a degree by Harry's reaction, John responded forcefully, "Absolutely not. Please don't quote me anything from those papers. I'm speaking purely scientifically, what is the chance we have been visited? And please try to make it easy enough for me to understand."

Relenting to John's persistence, he said, "Okay, I'll give you some ideas. To determine the probability you need to know how many planets in the galaxy have life. A scientist by the name of Drake developed what is known as Drake's equation. Using his equation, it comes to 10,000 planets projected to have life in the Milky Way, but let me give you my scenario.

"The universe contains billions of galaxies, but we will stick to our own galaxy, the Milky Way, which is the band of stars you see at night across the sky. The Milky Way has over a billion star systems of which ours is one. We believe at least one third of those stars have planets orbiting them in the same way ours circles the sun."

"How many star systems does that make?"

"Well over three hundred million. The reasonable assumption one could make is some of these systems have planets with life forming capabilities. Out of all these solar systems, maybe one per cent develops some form of life."

"How many are we talking about now?" John jumped in again with a question.

"Three million."

"Three million develop life!" John repeated in a very surprised voice because it seemed like so many.

"Remember we are talking about any form of life. The life could be a flower or a fungus or bacteria so don't get your hopes up so fast. Now we get to the heart of the matter. Of these three million, maybe one tenth of one percent develop intelligent life or sapient entities. The number turns out to be 3000 civilizations," Harry said anticipating John's question.

"Of these three thousand, maybe one percent develop space flight. Now we are down to thirty civilizations. If ten per cent of these thirty develop interstellar space flight, meaning the ability to get from one star system to another, we are left with three civilizations and now the kicker. If you cannot travel faster than the speed of light, or find some way to move from one place to another in a short amount of time, then the answer to your question of whether we have been visited would almost certainly be an emphatic no. If you could travel at the speed of light, it would still take over four years to get to the closest star or sixty thousand years to travel from here to the center of the Milky Way and back."

Impressed by Harry's recitation on the probabilities, John knew he had a command of the topic and appeared to be knowledgeable about his hobby.

"The next thing to consider is whether an alien civilization would want to come to earth. What is special about our solar system to entice someone to come here?

John along with every other child was taught in school about the planets as a part of growing up. Why wouldn't other intelligent life want to come here he thought to himself.

"Another item to deal with is when would they come. My feeling on this aspect is as follows. First, I do not think in terms of my lifetime. Earth has been circling around the sun for four billion years. We modern humans have been here only ten to fifteen thousand years. If I said yes, aliens have visited us, it would be very conceited of me to think it was within the last few years or maybe even within the last ten million years. They may have come five hundred million years ago or farther back or they may not come here for another one billion years. Are you getting the point?"

John nodded his head yes.

"John, basically here is the answer to your question. A small probability exists that our solar system has been visited in the past and a slightly higher probability it will be visited in the future. I'm sure I have not been much help to you."

"Yes, you have helped. One other item-If we have been visited, lets say, one million years ago. What would they have done?"

"One million years ago there were apes and a type of humanoid, which were our ancestors, but they would have been more like animals to an alien visitor. If they had come one hundred million years ago, they would have found the world full of all kinds of dinosaurs, which would have been far more interesting than our ancestors. Even I would like to see the dinosaurs."

"Thanks Harry. You have helped," John said.

"Come on now John, tell me why you're interested in ET's?" asked Harry, a small glint in his eyes as he continued to puff on his pipe.

Knowing ET stood for extra terrestrial, John replied, "Just a personal curiosity of my own. Nothing grandiose. Thanks again. We'll have to get together another time."

Leaving Harry's office mystified by the possibilities, he was starting to entertain the idea that the cube was not extra-terrestrial. Possibly it was created here on earth as a hoax to dupe stupid people like himself and Dr. Cable. John may have made the biggest mistake of his life.

CHAPTER 6B

The Wednesday morning sun entered Carol's apartment through the uncovered windows. She awoke later than her usual time appreciating the well-needed sleep. Lying on the air mattress on the floor and having yesterday's events pass through her mind was like reliving a bad dream. She felt rested though, and the air mattress and sleeping bag had made the night comfortable. Being alone, segregated from everyone, helped her deal with the situation in which she found herself. Because she grew up in a house full of people, periods of solitude were a premium she learned to treasure.

She had no electricity, water, or air-conditioning so getting them hooked up would be a priority for today. After dressing she left the apartment and drove to a food mart down the street where she purchased some coffee and treated herself to a pastry. Setting in her car she called the utility company on her cell to have service turned on in her apartment. The people at the utility said they would have the electricity and the water on this afternoon.

Leaving the food mart and driving down the street to a small park, she got out and walked a trail running along the edge of a small lake located in the center of the park. The fresh air and the open spaces gave her a sense of freedom she failed to find in the stolid buildings of JPL.

After making one trip around the lake, she stopped at a bench perched along the bank under several large trees, sat and soaked in the pleasant spring day. Calling Dale at JPL on her cell phone, the JPL operator put her through to him.

Happy to hear his voice, she said, "Dale, this is Carol."

"Carol, what happened to you. Are you all right? Your name is mud around the lab. The agents have sealed off your office and the word is they are looking for you. You are wanted in regards to possible treason and espionage."

"Treason!" Carol yelled, "They are crazy." After what occurred at her home yesterday, she couldn't imagine anyone having the gall to accuse her of being a spy.

"I know; now calm down," Dale said. "No one here seems to have any idea what's happening. These people are going to come after you Carol so unless you want to be caught, you better watch yourself."

First it was national security, now it's treason and espionage. Carol didn't know what to expect next.

"Dale, you know I would never do anything to hurt my country. I just don't understand."

"I know you wouldn't. I don't understand either, but the government agents are probably looking for you right now and our phone conversation is no doubt being recorded or bugged or whatever they call it. Carol, if you are going to hide, it will be difficult because they can get into your records, credit cards, bank accounts, and telephone conversations."

"Don't worry about me. I'll make do. What about the request I made yesterday?" She hoped Dale remembered their conversation about the other pictures.

"I'm on track. I will determine later today if it is feasible," replied Dale trying not to mention anything in relation to the request in case the line was tapped. He wanted to protect Carol as much as possible.

"I'll be waiting. Good luck."

"You be careful," he said and ended the call.

Leaning her head back on the park bench and looking through the leaves toward the blue sky, she thought to herself; a few days ago she made a copy of a picture from a space probe and now she was being accused of treason. She promised herself again to find the answer to what was in the picture and let the world know the results.

Carol enjoyed the quiet time sitting in the shade of the trees before walking back to her Jeep, and returning to her apartment. As she was getting out of the Jeep in front of the door to her building, she noticed near the end of the parking lot, a light blue van similar to the one following her yesterday from her house. Carol asked herself, 'am I becoming paranoid?'

Upon entering her apartment, she sat on the air mattress, then laid back on it, putting her brain to work. She knew the government had many ways to find her so she needed a method to escape because she didn't need the worry of looking over her shoulder all the time. She noticed, as she was lying on her back, a reflection in the air vent in the ceiling. She had looked at the vent this morning before getting up and didn't remember a reflection or anything shiny in the vent.

She walked around the apartment checking the other vents. Using her flashlight to aim a beam of light at the vent in the bedroom, she saw a reflection in it as well. As she looked closer, she was sure it was a small electronic device or maybe a microphone. She went to the bathroom, checking the vent out, again seeing a reflection. Now she was pissed. If they were going to spy on her they didn't have to put one in the bathroom. She checked to see if anything was missing from the apartment. Fortunately, nothing was gone and she had kept the disc with her in her purse. If they had found it, she would have no proof the picture ever existed.

In her mind she formulated a plan to find the answer to what was shown in the picture. The effort would require her to leave the area, but first to get away from these perverted bastards.

She walked out the patio door of her apartment and entered the green area called the commons, which contained trees and shrubs. Reaching the street on the other side, she walked one block to a drugstore. At the store, she used the pay phone to call her sister who lives in San Bernardino.

Thankfully, her sister Robin was at home.

"Robin, listen carefully. I need some help and I need it soon," Carol said trying to talk calmly.

"Sure, big sis, what have you got yourself into now?" Robin called her by the name all her siblings used. Carol was the mother figure to most of her siblings.

"I'm serious. I'm going to give you a list of things to do and directions to my apartment."

"What happened to your big fancy house?"

"Nothing, are you going to listen to me or not?" Carol was becoming frustrated at Robin's delays.

"Yes, yes, go ahead. I'll help in anyway I can. You know I will."

She gave her a list of things to do. Robin should be at her apartment in about two hours.

As she was leaving the drug store after buying some cleaning supplies, she noticed cell phones with built in minutes behind the counter. Purchasing one, she then retraced her steps back to the apartment complex. Upon entering the apartment, she began straightening around where she slept and washing the kitchen cabinets.

Two hours later, a white Camry pulled up next to her Jeep, a woman got out and went to the door of Carol's apartment. Knowing the woman was her sister, she opened the door and ushered her into the apartment.

Robin was the oldest next to Carol and a spitting image. Only seventeen months between their ages, they were often mistaken as twins when they were younger.

They talked about decorating the apartment and Robin made suggestions on what could be done as Carol guided her to the walk-in closet in her bedroom and pulled the door almost shut. She hoped to convince the people spying on her Robin was a home decorator there to give her advice. While in the closet the two women took off their clothes and exchanged them, each donning the others apparel. Robin wore a wig, which Carol now adjusted on her head with help from Robin. Robin gave her the bag she was carrying which contained IDs, credit cards, and then she put some of her own personal items in the bag. Carol wrote some things down for Robin on a pad as they were talking about redoing the closet. Robin wrote down a question asking where Carol was going.

Carol wouldn't tell her and wrote down not to worry; she would contact her in a few days. Exchanging car keys, giving Robin a hug, and whispering thanks, they exited the closet. Carol left the apartment, got in the Camry, and drove out of the parking area.Checking in her rear view mirror to see if the blue van followed and seeing no movement she crossed her fingers hoping the masquerade proved fruitful.

She drove to her bank and withdrew $5000 from her money market account. Then leaving the Pasadena area, she steered the Camry North along the coast of California. Robin would wait an hour before she took Carol's Jeep home.

For many reasons, Carol was feeling much better knowing the people following her had been left behind. Driving along the Pacific Ocean wishing she were in her Jeep with the top removed, she rolled down the windows of the Camry, but it wasn't the same. She always felt free in her Jeep with the air rushing around her and the warmth of the sun caressing her body. She drove for several hours, sightseeing along the way, until she came to Monterey where she stopped at a shopping mall and purchased clothes, some personal things, and a duffelbag to carry all of these items. She spent over two hours shopping, eating in the food court, and watching other people going about their daily lives. She wondered if her life would ever be as simple again.

While at the mall, she used the pay phone to call for the number of the Science Department at Stanford University. After locating the number she called and asked the lady who answered if she could talk to Dr. James Hillvale. He was not available so the lady asked if she wanted to leave a message and a phone number. Carol declined and said she would try again later. She tried an hour later and he was still not in his office so she asked for his home phone number and after some persuasion, the lady provided the number. Dr. Hillvale was a professor in the Geology Department and her favorite teacher while at Stanford. She hoped he could provide some counseling and guidance.

It being late in the day, she left the shopping mall, and found the Happy Valley Motel, a small family owned business away from the main thoroughfare. The rooms were clean and neat even though the Motel was built many years in the past. After paying cash for a room, she went through all her purchases trying them on to make sure they fit and organizing them for travel. Taking a long needed shower, she let the warm water flow over her body helping to wash the tenseness out of her muscles.

Carol had let her hair grow long, another issue between she and Bob. He preferred her hair long and she had acquiesced, spending a great deal of time each day taking care of it. Tomorrow morning she was going to find a salon and have it cut short, very short, extremely short. She was not going to spend the time drying and brushing every day as she had been doing for the last six years. It would be her statement to Bob and the world she was through trying to satisfy him and was beginning a new life to please herself.

After her shower she stood before the mirror toweling off looking at her body. She had a long sleek body and her breasts were small, yet none of the men she had been with ever complained. She couldn't understand why a woman would put implants in her body to make her boobs look like they were ready to burst, and why men would like them that way. Oh well, she was quite happy with her body. Knowing many women her age would die to have her physique, she ran her hand over her soft breasts then slowly down to her navel and over the slight swell of her tummy. Her hand continued, then stopped-enough she thought; she hadn't had sex in over four months and this was making it worse.

Putting on a pair of sweats purchased at the mall and snuggling into the bed, she called a friend of hers in Los Angles who she ran around with when they were both single.Martha Bryant was a divorced mother of two teenagers who taught at a private school in Beverly Hills. When she received the call from Carol she was surprised and happy to hear her voice. They had not talked for almost a year.

After the amenities were over, Carol got to the point.

"Martha, the reason I'm calling is to ask you a favor. I want you to call some one for me and give him a message."

"Oh, are you having an affair?" Martha asked, sounding intrigued and immediately jumping to conclusions.

"No, would you listen."

"Is he single?" Martha chimed in, still enunciating with excitement in her voice.

"Look, he is single, near thirty, good looking and all yours if you'll simply do me a favor first, all right?"

"Yes, what do you want me to tell him?" She relented.

"Tell him to go to a pay phone and call me on my cell phone. I'll give you the number."

Martha hadn't changed a bit. She was always on the prowl for a man. Carol gave her the number and ended the call.

Next Carol tried calling Dr. James Hillvale's home on the room phone. A woman answered who she assumed to be his wife, Dana. Carol explained to Dana that she was a former student of Dr. Hillvale and had done some graduate work with him. Carol had met Dana before, but realized she probably would not remember. Dr. Hillvale was at a neighbor's house at the moment so Carol asked if she could leave a message for him to call her when he gets back. Dana agreed to give him the message.

Shortly after speaking to Dr. Hillvale's wife, Dale called on her cell phone. "Carol, are you alright?"

Knowing he was worried about her by the tone of his voice, she answered, "Yes, Dale, just listen to me and remember what Martha told you. Someone had bugged my apartment and I think they put cameras in the ceiling vents. Your phone is probably bugged too and I'm not sure we are on safe phones now, so be careful what you say. How is the research going?"

"You will not believe what is going on at JPL. They found where you had checked into the other probes which made my research more difficult."

"If it is too dangerous, forget it. Were you followed to the pay phone?"

"I'm sure I wasn't. I went out like I was jogging. No one could follow me here unless they were running too. I did get what you wanted. I had to go to the basement and hook in with my laptop. You won't believe these."

"Great Dale. Send it to the Professor I'm always talking about. Don't say his name."

"Will do. You know this cloak and dagger stuff can be thrilling. Some people said my life is dull. Heh, what do they know. I feel like I'm living on the edge."

"Easy Dale. Remember the seriousness of what we are doing. I don't know when I'll talk to you again, but thanks for everything, and remember, be careful," Carol said as she ended the call.

Carol was enthused about the pictures from the NEAR probe Dale had found. Cloak and dagger! Dale was really getting into the sneaking around and copying the pictures. He has to remember what we are doing is not a game. She would hate it if Dale lost his job or something worse because of her indiscretions.

The room phone rang and Dr. Hillvale was on the line.

He was thrilled Carol had called. "Carol, it is wonderful to hear from you. I've often thought of you, doing all the exciting things with the space program."

"Yes, it has been quite an experience." She was so happy to hear his voice and felt safer just knowing she was in contact with him.

They talked for awhile, and then he agreed to meet her at his office tomorrow afternoon.

"I'll see you at your office around three o'clock," Carol said and then hung up.

The day was nearing its end, and a difficult day it had been for Carol. Feeling safe she snuggled into her bed and sleep, when it eventually came, was deep.

CHAPTER 7A

The scent of spring filled the air as the blossoms on the trees made themselves known to the senses of sight and smell. Students were lying on blankets under these flowered trees savoring the sunshine after a long winter hibernation. As with most people, spring invigorated John and his step had an extra spring in it as he walked across campus.

When he returned to his office, he made a call to Dr Cable to inquire about the man who worked for Project Mogul. Dr. Cable answered his call.

"Dr. Cable, this is John Kirkwood. I'm calling to ask for some information."

"Hello John, I hope everything is progressing in a favorable way."

Dr. Cable's rustic voice brought back some of the enthusiasm he had when he decided to undertake the search for the mysterious artifact even though the tone was not as sharp. "I am wrapping up my responsibilities at the University. The reason I called is when you were talking about Project Mogul; you mentioned a person in charge or involved with the program. Could you give me the name again?"

"I can, except I'm not sure what name I gave you. It probably was one of these two people. Either Garland Martin or Frank Wisner."

"Garland Martin was the one. Who is Frank Wisner?" John did not remember him mentioning his name.

He was a person involved with intelligence throughout the 1940's and 1950's. He was tied in with many covert operations."

"Thank you Dr. Cable. I am following several different paths. I have hired a private investigator to look into Dr. Happard's activities in Dayton, Ohio. Also your attorney contacted me and we took care of the paperwork."

"Who is the private investigator?"

"The Kinkle Detective Agency in Dayton," John answered.

"I'll send you a credit card to use. It has a limit of $50,000. I'll increase the amount if necessary. Please use it for all your expenses and give it to the

Kinkle Agency for their expenses. You should be receiving it very soon. Keep me informed."

Because Dr. Cable sounded weak, John wished he had asked him if he was feeling all right. Knowing he was 90 years old put a different flavor into interpreting whether he was sick or not.

John tackled paperwork on his desk the rest of the afternoon attempting to bring everything up to date before he returned home.

Later in the day, walking into his house, he checked his messages and one was from Peter Cozid. He dialed the number of Peter's office and received a recording. In the message was another number to call, which John assumed would be a cell phone. He punched in the number and Peter answered. Peter informed him information would soon be in hand and he would call back later today. John asked him to call back on his cell phone.

Leaving for dinner, he met Judy who had been an off and on companion over the past year. At one time he enjoyed her company, but lately all she wanted to talk about was the two of them having a committed relationship. He was not so inclined and expected to have his last meal with her tonight.

During dinner John received a call on his cell phone from Peter. He excused himself to the entryway of the restaurant where he answered the call.

Peter said, "I have found some information on your Dr. Happard. He did live in the Dayton, Ohio area during the 40's and early 50's. He was married and had a child. Both he and his wife are deceased and his only child, a daughter, Joyce Carter, is retired and lives with her husband in the Sarasota, Florida area. I could not find what work Dr. Happard was doing in Dayton, but if you want I will continue searching his history. I did call his daughter and she would not answer any questions concerning her father."

"Give me her phone number and address. I'll try calling her later and keep looking into where he worked. Also, I want you to find out any information on a Colonel Garland Martin. He worked at the Wright-Patterson Air Force Base in the late 40's. Also a Frank Wisner who I believe was in the Army during the same period."

"You don't have anyone easy to find do you. I was lucky with Dr. Happard. I found a friend of his daughters still living in Dayton. I will get back to you if anything turns up," Peter said as he terminated the call.

John was pleased with the quick response to his request to find Dr. Happard. Peter Cozid may be a good choice to help him in his search. He returned to Judy at the table and apologized, telling her it was a very important call. He did not mention to Judy his taking a sabbatical leave and after dinner, as they were leaving, she asked if he wanted to go to her place for a drink. John said no and told Judy he enjoyed her company, and he only wanted to remain her friend and did not want a relationship. Judy was upset, stomped out of the restaurant toward her car and drove off, squealing her car's tires in the process.

Feeling like a heel and knowing the idea of remaining friends was probably out of the question, he drove back to his house. Tomorrow he would call Joyce Carter in Florida and finish the last of his paperwork at the University. He crawled into bed letting the dreams have their way.

The next morning after exercises and a shower, John placed a call to Joyce Carter, the name Peter had given him over the phone. A woman answered responding with the same name.

"Mrs. Carter, I'm John Kirkwood, a professor of History at Stanford University in California and I'm doing research into people who studied the Inca civilization. One of those I am investigating is your Father, Dr. Senval Happard."

"Mr. Kirkwood, I really have little to say about my Father. Are you friends with the man from Ohio?"

John hesitated before answering. Which way to get what he wanted? He chose honesty. "If you're talking about Peter Cozid, then yes I am. He does work for me and I apologize if he offended you in anyway. Mrs. Carter, I really do need information on your father if I am to finish my research. I can guarantee Mr. Cozid will not contact you again." John was trying to appease her in every way possible.

"I don't like to talk about my Father," She repeated.

"Let me explain if I may please. I did research in Peru just like your Father, which is why I have a special interest in him. You can answer only the questions you wish."

"I'm really busy. I don't have the time."

"What if I came to talk to you in person. Would it be all right?" John said realizing he was about to strike out. He did not receive an immediate response, which meant she might be wavering.

"Well, I might consider talking to you in person. I'm still not sure I would say much about my father."

Yes! He had his foot in the door. "I will call you when I have made arrangements. Would those conditions be acceptable to you?"

"I guess." She spoke faintly with little or no emotion.

"Thank you very much. You don't know how much it means to me," He said, ending the call.

Getting off the phone, John was exasperated. He almost lost her and now he had to go to Florida to get information about her father. It was a long way to go to see someone who didn't want to talk to him, thus the possibility of making a long trip and getting nothing in return loomed big in the back of his mind. Leaving for the University, he would attempt to tie up all the loose ends so he could fly out by the weekend.

When he arrived at the University, he made arrangements to complete his duties on Thursday and by letting Cheryl start his class on Friday, he could reserve a ticket for a flight out early Friday morning.

He had to make another stop at the University to see Dr. Ron Williams, also a professor in the History Department. John and he were professional colleagues; beyond which they had little contact. John was interested in his knowledge of the intelligence community, because he completed his thesis on the spy game and also wrote a book on the subject.

Dr. Williams was to be in his office at 3:30 P.M. for the meeting so when John arrived and found his office vacant and locked, it did not surprise him. Dr. Williams was perpetually tardy for his classes and appointments. His ego was so big, he felt people should wait for him and not the other way around.

John left the building, breathing in the fresh sea air blowing in from the west, and walked around the department until he had made a full circle. He felt connected to the University life and knew it would be difficult for him to break away after so many years. A nostalgic feeling spread through his body as he thought of all the friends he had made while teaching here at Stanford.

Returning to Dr. Williams's office, he found the door open and he entered greeting Ron. Dr. Ron Williams was in his late forties, tall and slender, and recently divorced.

"What can I do for you," he said in his usual 'why are you bothering me' tone. His attitude was one of the reasons John had as little contact as possible with Ron.

"I'm interested in the intelligence community during the late 1930's and 1940's. What in general can you tell me about the spy game during these years?"

He looked at John with a quizzical frown saying, "What is the reason for your interest?"

"Humor me, Ron. I can't tell you, really," John answered in a stern manner thinking it was none of his business.

Dr. Williams spoke in a very authoritative voice. "Let's see. Late 1930's. Intelligence gathering during the period was fragmented among various agencies and organizations. Little exchange of information occurred among these groups, which is somewhat of a problem in the spy agencies today. The two military intelligence arms at the time were the Navy and Army, the Navy being the better. Another was through the State Department, called the Office of Chief Special Agent, which looked for subversive activity.

During World War II, 1941 to be specific, President Roosevelt founded the Office of Coordinator of Information headed by William T. Donovan. Donovan had attended Columbia University with Roosevelt and later became the head of the Office of Strategic Services or OSS in 1942. During the war the military created the Joint Intelligence Agency and in 1946 Truman created the Central Intelligence Group, which became the Central Intelligence Agency or CIA in 1947.

"I think I have covered everything in general. Does the information help you?" Ron said in a condescending tone.

"One other question. In 1938 or 1939, if the Government obtained a defector from Germany or Italy, who would take charge of the individual, or more specifically who would Roosevelt let interrogate the defector?"

"You pose an unusual question. Sumner Welles was Under Secretary of State and ran the State Department during the time period your asking about, because Cordell Hull, the Secretary of State, was sick. Welles roomed in boarding school with a brother to Eleanor Roosevelt and was in her wedding to FDR, so he had frequent contact and access to the President.

I give you these facts because Welles would have a lot of influence with Roosevelt in this kind of situation, therefore I would predict the intelligence section of the State Department would be the one. They would have control, unless President Roosevelt over-ruled them."

"Where would the defector be taken?" John asked, trying to pin Ron down to more specifics. Dr. Williams seemed taken aback by his last question. John assumed he did not have an answer and Ron always acted like he knew everything.

"I don't know the answer. I could look into it if you like."

"I would appreciate all your help. Also could you find out what Welles did after the war. I'm going on a sabbatical so I'll give you my cell phone number. You can contact me if you find any information."

"Yes, I suppose I can agree to your terms. Someday you will tell me what your inquiry is about, won't you, Dr. Kirkwood and what kind of sabbatical."

Even though Ron was a royal pain in the ass, John agreed to tell him about his inquiry knowing he never intended to give him any information and he ignored the question concerning his leave. He left Ron's office and walked toward the parking lot and his vehicle.

John had taken notes during the meeting as he did in all of his investigations, knowing he might need it at a later date. He placed the notes in his briefcase as he drove home to prepare for the trip to Florida.

CHAPTER 7B

The curtains denied the morning sunlight access to the interior of the motel room as Carol slept quietly under the blankets. Having blinds so dark they block the daylight must be a requirement for motels. Many people leave the bathroom light on with the door cracked to prevent hurting themselves if they should happen to get up during the night.

Having stubbed her toe before, Carol left her bath light on yet she did not venture out of bed during the night. She awoke, showered, dressed, used a small amount of make-up as was her practice, and packed her stuff in the duffel bag. Trying to make her life simple had always been one of her characteristics and a trait she continued to cherish. When something could be done in two steps instead of three, she felt a real sense of accomplishment. Carol didn't mind being teased about it by people who knew her, since she was happy to be a simple kind of woman.

Checking out at the office and paying for her phone calls, she thanked the couple who ran the Happy Valley Motel. Being far from fancy, it had provided her a clean, quiet, and safe night for which she was very grateful.

The couple at the motel had directed her to a local restaurant, which prepared breakfast and near to it was a hair salon they recommended. It opened at 9:00 A.M. Driving to the restaurant, she had a craving for pancakes and coffee. The restaurant, set in between a hardware store and a video store, had delicious pancakes and along with juice and coffee, helped to rejuvenate her and she felt ready to tackle whatever was thrown her way.

After paying her check, she walked to the hair salon a short distance down the street. She entered the small shop containing three chairs facing mirrors along the wall to her right. A young woman greeted Carol as she walked through the door. The woman was talkative, wore giant earrings, used too much eye shadow, and had a head of hair that put Carol's hair to shame. It reminded Carol of a movie whose name she couldn't quite pull out of the air.

The woman's name was Vonda and after hearing what Carol wanted done to her hair, Vonda said she would look like a boy with it cut so short. Carol teased her by agreeing and telling her she wanted to look like a man. Finally, the hair was cut close enough to suit her even though Vonda resisted cutting more off at each stage. She paid her with a smile on her face knowing she would never see Vonda again.

Carol left Monterey driving toward Stanford planning to arrive by noon, visit some of her old haunts, and then meet with Dr. Hillvale. Respecting his opinion, she hoped he would have some insights regarding the picture and her situation.

Another lovely spring day followed Carol as she drove the Camry along the road north toward Stanford. Day dreaming about the picture, concerned about showing it to Dr. Hillvale and what to do after the meeting inundated her mind. Concentrating so much on her thoughts, she was jolted back to reality by a shock shooting through her neck and down her back when she noticed in the rear view mirror a light blue van. At first her muscles weakened from the sight, then tightened up as her body tensed with fear.

In the entire world, how did they find her? Her mind searched for any mistake she could have made bringing them to her location. The only thing popping into her mind was last night's telephone calls. They must have known her cell phone number by tapping in on Dale's phone line and from knowing her number they would know the area where she received the call. Of course-how stupid of her. When Martha called Dale, she gave him the number over Dale's line. By this time they would have surmised she was in a white Camry. Damn, she should have been more careful and then again, maybe it's just coincidence a blue van appears on the same highway.

The freedom she had been feeling dissipated from her body. Out smarting the people following her had given her a false sense of security and she had taken it easy, rested on her laurels, and now was back to square one. Whatever possessed her to think she could evade agents experienced in finding people escaped her now. She was mad at herself even though she was not schooled in these techniques.

The distance between Carol and the van remained the same, which led her to believe they were following her as opposed to stopping and arresting her on the spot. She deduced they were not the police or FBI because they would have taken her into custody right away if she was wanted for treason. Surely they knew she could see them so what was their game? What were they after?

She needed another plan to escape again. Whether to continue to Stanford University or attempt to lose them at another location was blurring her mind at the moment.

Obtaining another vehicle would be necessary if she wanted to continue traveling by car. She made a decision and developed a plan to elude her stalkers. Whether it would work or not, she did not know, but she would continue on to Stanford. At the University the advantage would be in her favor since she knew the campus, assuming none of the people in the van attended the college. The van continued to keep the same distance behind her and stopped across the road when she stopped for gas. Back on the road, it continued to follow so she knew definitely it was following her.

Entering the campus, she immediately drove to a section of residence halls grouped together with the blue van still trailing behind. She pulled into a drive, which ran up to the dorm and back to the street in a semi-circle. At the front near the door, little room for parking was available so a van would find it difficult to maneuver.

She parked the Camry close to the front of the dorm, exited with her bag, left the keys on top of the tire, and entered the residence hall. Looking over her shoulder, the van was at the corner of the drive and two men were exiting from it. Quickly making her way through the lobby to the stairs, she walked down one flight to the basement. Having worked part time on the maintenance staff her freshman year, she knew the group of residence halls was connected underground. Carol hastily moved toward the hall farthest from the one she entered checking behind her all the way. She zigzagged through the maze of rooms and passageways filled with pipes and conduits until she reached another flight of stairs.

After climbing the stairs to the lobby of a different residence hall, she exited, making her way across campus to geology corner and the office of Dr. Hillvale. Arriving early at his office for their meeting, she found the door locked and no one responding after she knocked. She walked down the hall to a restroom and changed clothes-no sense making it easy for them to spot her on campus. Being on the run may look exciting in the movies, but to Carol, it was a scary situation-one she preferred not to be in at the present.

Returning to the hall, she passed a room with a man and a woman sitting at a table having a cup of coffee.

Entering either a lounge or work area, she addressed the two people. "Hi, I'm a friend of Dr. Hillvale. Would either of you know where he would be at the moment?"

The woman, who Carol guessed to be a worker, had a ring of keys attached to her belt and wore blue jeans and a gray shirt. She was under five feet tall and a little overweight. She responded to Carol's question. "Yes, I know him, but I haven't seen him lately."

Looking around the small room, she asked, "Would it be all right for me to leave my duffel bag in the corner till he comes back?"

"Why don't you leave it in his office?" the woman asked. She looked to be in her thirties and had dyed her hair bright red which gave her a cheap look.

84

"I can't because it is locked," Carol replied.

The woman got up from the table, took one more sip from her coffee cup and looked at Carol saying, "Follow me."

Leading Carol to his office door, the woman grabbed the large set of keys and fumbled with them until she had the one suiting her needs. Opening Dr. Hillvale's office, she let Carol put her bag inside, then locked the door and turned to Carol saying, "How's that?"

It turned out she was a custodian and had keys to all the rooms in the building. Carol thanked her and walked away.

Checking the time, she had two hours till the appointment with Dr. Hillvale. She wanted to avoid being seen, yet detested sitting here just to kill time. Knowing a sandwich shop was near, she decided to walk to it avoiding the street and staying between the campus buildings. Checking the inside of the shop after arriving, she looked for anyone suspicious. It was set up like a coffee shop with a few tables and chairs scattered here and there and a couch or two.

Seeing no one in the shop she considered a government agent, at least in her mind what one would look like, she ordered a sandwich wrap, bottle of water, and retired to a corner of the shop. A daily paper was lying on the table, so she picked it up to read and to use it as a screen to hide behind.

Leafing through the paper for news of the space probe, she found only a short story referring to the pictures sent back to earth. Carol could find no mention of her stealing the picture or being accused of treason. Using the phone book yellow pages next to the pay phone, she looked up the name of a wrecker service. Calling and telling them to pick up the white Camry, she informed them the keys were on top of the left front tire. Carol gave them Robin's credit card number to pay for the towing and storage. After biding her time for over an hour, she left to see if Dr. Hillvale had returned.

He was in his office examining her duffel bag as she came through the door. Looking up, his face turned from a frown to a wide grin. They hugged. Dr. Hillvale seemed much older than she expected, but it had been ten years since they had been in physical contact. A man of average height and a little thin, his hair had turned grayer, yet he wore the same style of clothes as ten years ago-a pair of gray slacks and a light blue shirt. She also remembered the loosened tie at the neck was his style.

He was one of the nicest men she had ever known. Devoted to his field of geology and the teaching profession, he showed Carol the caring she failed to get from others in the education arena. During her last year at Stanford, she was his teaching assistant in the geology department.

Carol and Dr. Hillvale sat down in his office and she explained how the duffel bag got in his locked room. Past experiences were a topic as they brought each other up to date on their careers, though Carol did not mention her current problems.

After talking for a half-hour, she brought up the reason she was here at Stanford. "I have several questions concerning the recent NASA probe, Talaria, and the pictures sent back from the asteroid belt."

"I'm well aware of the mission. I have been watching and viewing the pictures released to the public."

"I know you keep up on all the probes NASA sends into space and your knowledge on the topic is one of the reasons I came to you. Besides Galileo and NEAR and now Talaria, are you familiar with any other space probes sent to the Asteroid Belt?"

He stared at her with questioning eyes. "Why are you asking me when you are the one involved in the space program. Surely you know more than I do?" He was confused by the question because it referred to the field in which she was employed. Dr. Hillvale would have understood if it was turned around the other way; he asking her the question.

"I know. I want to show you a picture and I'm going to ask you not to share with anyone for the time being. Would you agree to look at it?" Carol hoped she was making the right decision. He was the one person in her life she was sure she could trust and one who would give her sound advice.

"I will keep it to myself if you wish."

"May I use your computer," she said as she pulled the disc from her purse. Dr. Hillvale let her sit in his chair and he pulled another one next to her. She entered the disc in the drive and ran the program to call up the picture.

As they both watched, it slowly appeared on the screen. "I have on the disc one of the pictures from the asteroid belt taken by the Talaria probe. I want you to look at it closely," she said as she got up to give him a better view.

After putting on his glasses, Dr. Hillvale moved in near the monitor, put his index finger on the screen dragging it across the picture eyeing the area directly above his moving digit. He came to the object in question and stopped. Gazed at it for a moment, then said, "Is this a flaw in the picture?"

Carol delayed answering immediately, letting the object fuse into his mind's eye. "No, it is the true picture sent back from the asteroid belt."

"What is it? It's not an asteroid!" He pointed to the mystery rock, obviously confused by the picture.

"What you are seeing is why I'm showing it to you. I don't know what it is. Now watch as I change the picture." The enhanced picture slowly appeared on the screen.

"Carol, I'm mystified. This area should contain only asteroids unless the object is from something NASA or the Russians sent there without mine or anyone's knowledge."

Knowing she had his undivided attention, she would attempt to solicit his ideas and opinions. "I feel the same way. I know of no probes with parts like the one in the picture. Can you speculate on what we are seeing?"

Dr. Hillvale sat examining the picture for an inordinate amount of time. In taking his classes years ago, she remembered he would put a rock or mineral before the students in his class and have them stare at it for an extended period to imprint the object on their brain.

"What do the scientists at JPL think it could be?" he asked still questioning why she was asking him. It was still unclear to him why Carol would bring a picture here instead of conversing with all the scientists at JPL.

"I'll tell you a little later," she replied. She wanted his opinion before they discussed her predicament.

"I can think of one possibility. Let me give you a scenario. You are aware that meteorites hit the earth constantly, most being very small. Meteorites are believed to be asteroids from the asteroid belt. What you may not know is military satellites built for detecting nuclear explosions and missile launches in other countries like Russia regularly detect explosions of small asteroids hitting the upper atmosphere causing as much as a one-kiloton explosion. Surprisingly that is half the size of the atomic bomb dropped on Hiroshima, Japan in World War II. The satellites have recorded these and determined the explosions happen about once a month."

Shocked by the information, she said, "Why didn't I know this?" Having a degree in Planetary Geology, she should be aware of such data. Since she didn't work in the area and hadn't studied geology for over twenty years, she must have let it escape her or the ability to detect them came after her studies, which was more likely.

"These explosions are high up and so fast, rarely anyone on the ground ever sees one, yet they are an everyday occurrence in our solar system. Just look at the cratered surface of any solid body such as the moon. We on earth have a false sense of security since weather and erosion erase the scars of impact."

"I know we are hit with objects constantly. I wasn't aware the explosions they created were as big as you describe. We see the flying stars at night, yet you're talking about something much bigger."

"Yes, a great deal bigger. A group did statistical research and found the earth has a one to five megaton explosion at ground level every few hundred years. The last one was in the Tunguska area of Russia in June 1908. That's around five hundred times bigger than the Hiroshima A-bomb. A twenty megaton blast occurs every 50,000 years like the Meteor Crater in Arizona and an impact we suspect caused the dinosaurs extinction thankfully only occurs every 100 million years."

"Even though your scenario is amazing and interesting, what does it have to do with the picture?" Carol was becoming frustrated and not understanding where he was going with his story.

"You haven't made the connection have you? Since most asteroids are in the asteroid belt and they regularly impact earth, they can be devastating. Isn't it possible some agency in the United States or Russia has sent other probes or vessels to investigate the asteroids with, maybe, the idea of controlling their movements in an effort to avoid future catastrophes. We do not want to become extinct like the dinosaurs. We have only been here a couple of million years where as the dinosaurs ruled the Earth for 170 million years."

"The government would want to keep the investigation secret so as not to alarm the public. The picture could be a part of a failed attempt to survey the asteroids," Dr. Hillvale said. The chance the United States was working in space to prevent such a catastrophe as he had been describing was fascinating to him and he would love to find out more information.

Carol wasn't buying the part about the secret mission or missions to the asteroid belt. She saw no way they could hide those space launches. "Is your idea the only thing you believe could be the reason for the object in the picture?"

He was still thinking about the asteroids and how a country would keep a project so large a secret. "What-uh-there are many more possibilities. One might speculate the object is from another civilization. You know-aliens," he said gingerly, "Why haven't I seen the picture in the news releases?"

She trusted him so confessed to the deed by saying, "I'm not suppose to have the picture. The government or someone confiscated it from JPL." I made a copy before it was deleted from the system."

Dr. Hillvale looked worried. He was troubled and concerned about Carol.

"Can you get in hot water for having the picture in your possession?"

"I'm already in hot water as you say!"

Putting his hand to his chin and looking at her with a kind, warm face, he said, "How can I help?"

A peaceful continence came over her body and eased her mind as Dr. Hillvale spoke his last words.

CHAPTER 8A

The hum created by hundreds of voices echoed throughout the San Francisco Air Terminal as people scurried here and there to make their flight connections. The airport is huge with three terminals for domestic flights and one for international flights. Into this din came John Kirkwood looking for the ticket counter of American Trans Air. His flight leaves at 6:30 A.M. with a three-hour layover in Chicago. It arrives in Tampa at 6:23 P.M.

John obtained his ticket and turned toward the security area. Airline travel had changed since 911 displeasing him immensely. In airports today, security had become a maze of walkways, aisles, scanners, and checkers. What was once an enjoyable venture had turned in to an ordeal. Never the less, he was prepared for the malaise.

Packing enough clothes for a week, he decided to take advantage of some Florida sunshine while he was visiting Mrs. Carter. His sense of excitement was, in part, due to the freedom he now felt not having a time schedule to follow. He was free to stay as long as he desired and for someone who had taught for the last sixteen years with a weekly schedule of classes and summers crammed with expeditions, it was a fantastic feeling.

He passed through the metal detector removing his shoes, being singled out to have extra checks made of his person, no doubt because he was alone with a one way ticket.

The trip was uneventful as he arrived in Chicago at noon and placed a call to Mrs. Carter during his layover at O'Hare Airport. On the phone, she was still hesitant about talking about her father and again John was positive he would have gotten little from her over the phone. Their discussion resulted in a decision to meet tomorrow morning at 10:00 A.M. at her house, which was on Casey Key, a long narrow strip of land peppered with beach-front homes located south of Sarasota. She gave him directions to get to Casey Key over the phone, then ended the call.

To pass the time, John made a few more calls to friends, found a restaurant for lunch, and read the paper. He reviewed what few notes he had on Dr. Happard before boarding his flight to Tampa.

In Tampa, renting the car was easier than expected and he was on the road by 7:30 P.M. headed south to Sarasota. At 9:00 P.M. he found a room at a Comfort Inn, went out to eat, then to his room and bed.

Early Saturday morning John awoke and drove to the beach, jogged for awhile, then return to his room to shower, shave, and dress before leaving for his meeting with Mrs. Carter.

Casey Key was in Osprey, Florida a short drive south of Sarasota. Reaching Osprey, John turned west toward the ocean, passing over the water inlet onto Casey Key. The street running through the key was narrow, tree lined, and homes were located on both sides. As he headed south, those on his right had ocean beach backyards. The homes were nice, but older and smaller than he expected, nothing like the large monstrosities being built today.

John found the Carter home to be on the beach side of the road and one of the more modest homes. He pulled into the drive, walked to the front of the house and knocked on the door. An attractive woman looking to be in her early to mid sixties answered the door. She was a tall, thin woman with blond hair and blue eyes and could have been a model in her more youthful days. John introduced himself; she replied she was Joyce Carter and invited him into her home.

Entering the house, he met her husband, Bill, who was sitting in a lounge chair watching a sport show. Remaining in his seat, he said hello. He turned back to the television show as Joyce offered John coffee or juice, which he politely declined.

She guided him to a screened in porch or sunroom in the rear of the home with a beautiful view of the Gulf of Mexico. Each sat in a chair around a small table and after some small talk about the house and location, John led the conversation toward the topic he was here to discuss.

"Mrs. Carter, I'm a researcher doing similar things your father did in his younger days. I've been to Peru many times on archeological trips just like your father and those excursions have led me to do research on people with his background. I don't want to cause you any discomfort yet I do want any information you feel like providing me."

The time between his question and her answer seemed like an eternity to John. He remained quiet and calm and waited for her response.

"Mr. Kirkwood, I have not spoken of my father for over 25 years, so when your friend, I think his name was Cozid, called the other day I was stunned to here someone mention my Father's name. I will tell you one thing; my father and I were never close because he was seldom there for me during the time I was growing up. I have very little respect for him since he didn't treat my mother any better than he treated me and the reason I haven't discussed him in the past is because of the way he treated us. Why are you so interested in him particularly? Many other people worked in the ruins in Peru," she asked, looking at him with those grayish blue eyes.

John had no intention of telling her the real reason or divulging anything related to the artifact. "I am interested in all of the archeologists who worked in Peru, including your father. My research also indicated there was no record of Dr. Happard doing any research after World War II. Can you shed any light on why he wouldn't continue his work?"

"I wasn't born until 1940 so I don't know much about him during the War. I do know we lived in Dayton, Ohio at the time. We moved to Albuquerque, New Mexico when I was twelve. I returned to Ohio to attend college where I met my husband, Bill. We lived in the Cleveland, Ohio area until a few years ago when we retired and came to Florida. I never knew what my father did, nor really cared."

"Do you remember anything about his activities, anything at all?" He hoped to squeeze out as many facts as possible while she was in a forthcoming mood.

"I do remember a few things, most making no sense," she said with less enthusiasm than her last answer.

No doubt her mind was recalling details she had long forgotten. "I don't care how silly the items may seem. I'm still interested." It appeared she was debating in her own mind whether to dredge up old memories.

"For example I remember sometime in the 1950's my father was so excited a vaccine for polio had been found. I never understood what he meant, but I remember he said something like 'the president would be proud of me'. His attitude surprised me because I always had the impression he hated Eisenhower."

John could tell she spoke without understanding her Father's statement, and he was just as confused as Joyce when he responded, "Everyone knows Dr. Jonas Salk developed the vaccine."

"I know. As I said, it makes no sense."

"Did he say anything else making no sense?" John was not pleased with the conversation. He was obtaining little help.

"He talked about some other developments as if he were personally involved," Joyce said, "I was a teenager interested in my own world, so I never thought much about it. I don't recall what they dealt with, only that they seemed silly."

Deciding to try another line of questioning, John asked, "Whom did he work for in New Mexico?"

"I never was sure. I assumed it had something to do with the military. He never mentioned to me what his job involved. Sometimes army people would come to our house to get him. That's why I say it had to do with the military."

"Do you know of anyone he worked with at his job?"

Joyce didn't respond to his question. She turned cold in her demeanor; thus it seemed he had touched on something she did not want to discuss. She sat and stared out at the ocean. John felt he needed to do something before he lost her completely-maybe a change in atmosphere.

"Would you like to show me the beach?"

She raised her head and a small smile appeared. "Why, yes-of course," she said and arose from the table. "I'll be right with you." She left the sunroom to tell her husband she was going for a walk on the beach.

Mrs. Carter returned to the sunroom. "I'm sorry. My husband does not want to walk on the beach. He has been ill and does not feel like company."

"Mrs. Carter, no apology is necessary."

They stepped off the porch into the sand and walked out to the beach, where a steady breeze was blowing in from the ocean. They walked along the shore, after deciding to stroll north along the beach so the sun would be at their backs. John took his shoes off and walking closest to the water's edge, let the waves lap at his bare feet and the sand scrunch between his toes. The wind blew the spray from the waves against his face and arms counteracting some of the heat from the mid-day sun.

"How long have you lived here?" John asked, hoping to revive the conversation.

"Bill and I purchased our house twelve years ago as a retirement home. We moved here permanently eight years ago. Due to Bill's health he took early retirement."

"You have a nice home, a beautiful beach for a backyard and I imagine the weather is nice year round."

"The weather is very good especially for two people from Cleveland. We had nasty winters back in Ohio," she replied with another little smile. John took her smile as another chance to pry into her past.

"Who did you say your father worked with?" John repeated the earlier question hoping he would get a response from Joyce.

Again, she gave no reply and John didn't exert any more pressure. He stayed by her side without speaking until they reached an area where several large rocks were embedded in the sand. The stones were rounded from the years of pounding surf and sand and some were as large as a small sofa.

She suggested they sit for a moment so they each picked a rock on which to rest. A small sailboat was visible in the distance gliding quietly across the water. For John, the moment was peaceful; the only sounds were the waves washing against the sandy beach and the wind blowing in from the sea.

After several minutes of quietly watching the sea, Joyce spoke without him asking a question. "There was a woman either working with or working for my father. I'm not positive which one, or maybe my father worked for her."

"Do you know her name?"

Hesitating, she stared at the waves as they tumbled onto the beach, and finally turned to look at John. "Her name was Karen Doddson."

Joyce definitely has some issues concerning the woman named Karen Doddson. John was not sure whether to continue questioning her on the subject, yet he knew here and now may be his only chance to interview Mrs. Carter. "Do you know where she lives?"

Again a pause was needed to work up the will to answer. "She lives in Albuquerque, New Mexico the last I knew, but you understand I'm talking about many, many years in the past."

"You seem irresolute talking about her," he said trying to be careful, knowing he was on delicate ground.

"She was not one of my favorite people. I felt she kept my father from me because the time he spent with her should have been mine."

John was at a loss for words. He did not want to make a painful subject worse for Joyce, so he decided not to mention Karen Doddson again.

"How long did your father live?" he asked.

"He passed away in 1959. He was 60. He was 41 when I was born. My mother died in 1971," she said showing on her face more concern for her mother than her father.

He sensed she might not wish to discuss her family any further and as they walked back toward her house, John was sure more hurt and anger were buried deep inside Joyce. It was obvious she needed to attempt to conquer the ghosts in her past, but he was not one qualified to help her deal with her problems. To travel down that road, she would need to seek professional help.

Facing the sun on their way back, John squinted his eyes as he asked one more question, "Have you ever heard of a Project Mogul or remember anyone using such a term?"

Joyce was thinking to herself and she started to say something then held her right hand in the air as if she intended to scratch the back of her neck, saying, "I have heard the term, but I don't know what it means. I heard Karen Doddson mention the word mogul."

"Do you remember when she used the word?"

"It must have been when we first moved to Albuquerque."

John and Joyce returned to her house and he offered to take the two of them to lunch. It was the least he could do since he felt he had stirred up bad memories for Joyce. Both Joyce and Bill declined so he thanked her, wished them well and left.

John was disappointed he found no more information about Dr. Senval Happard. He would have to find Karen Doddson.

As he walked to his car, he surveyed the neighborhood. What would it be like to retire to an area along the ocean with the beach outside your back door? None of the neighbors seemed to be out and about. It was very quiet and peaceful with everyone just sunning himself on the beach—and the solitude would no doubt drive him crazy!

Driving back to the motel, he hashed over the conversation he just had and reviewed the topics discussed. He agreed with her assessment of some of the things her father had said-they didn't make sense unless somehow knowledge from the cube was used to effect certain events such as the polio vaccine. A scenario he considered extremely far-fetched and he dismissed it as unlikely. He would return to the motel and write down the things he had learned from Joyce Carter and see if he could come to any conclusions.

CHAPTER 8B

In the past, when the child was caught with their hand in the cookie jar, the game was over and only the punishment was left for debate. Carol may have had her hand in the jar, but she had not been caught and no penalty had been prescribed. She believed her punishment had already been assessed, by being on the run with the fear of getting caught her constant companion.

At the present time, Dr. Hillvale's offer of help was a godsend-her having no car and no place to stay. She informed him of her situation and he offered to let her spend a few days with Dana and him to which Carol readily agreed.

Carol spent the next hour telling him her story, trusting him with all the details including knowledge of the pictures Dale would soon be sending his way. Dr. Hillvale was surprised at Carol's tenacity, and regretted it had led to her present dilemma. He suggested they leave for his home and get her away from the people following her.

Dr. Hillvale gave Carol a jacket and hat of his to wear. After donning them, she could pass for a man more so than a woman with her hair cut so short, but her duffel bag would be a problem since the men saw her get out of the car with it draped over her shoulder. She and Dr. Hillvale decided to take a chance hoping it would not be as noticeable on a college campus where many students carried backpacks and large bags.

She slung the duffel bag over her shoulder as he picked up his briefcase and together they walked out of his office. Carol kept her head down and peered over the top of her sunglasses searching for any conspicuous people.

As they walked along the sidewalk in front of the building heading in the direction of the parking lot, Carol suddenly stopped. She grabbed Dr. Hillvale by the arm and said, "The man standing by the tree next to the parking lot is one of the men who was in the van at the residence hall."

He pulled her behind a hedge running along side the walk. "Give me the duffel bag and jacket. My car is the light green Honda Civic near the left rear of the parking lot. I want you to take my briefcase and proceed around the building on our left and enter the lot from the rear. I'm sure they won't have enough people to cover every block, so you should have no problem getting there unseen."

"What about you?" Carol was not sure what Dr. Hillvale was planning.

"Don't worry about me. Here are the keys and my briefcase. Get in the backseat and wait for me. Got it?"

She did as he instructed and left him behind the hedge. He waited for a minute, then slung the dufflelbag over his shoulder so it would be difficult for someone to see his face. The jacket's length was to his knees and would hide his body shape.

He then purposefully walked toward the person Carol had pointed out to him in the parking lot. As he approached the man, he could feel his eyes on him. He kept the duffel bag on his shoulder blocking the man's view of his head and face. After he passed, he could hear the man's footsteps following behind him. He slowed his pace, and as he let him get closer, he put his pipe in his mouth. The man behind him said something. Dr. Hillvale stopped and slowly turned around, lit his pipe, and said to the man, "May I help you?"

Dr. Hillvale enjoyed to his great satisfaction the surprised look on the man's face. The man looked at him, apologized, and said he thought he was someone else, then turned and walked away.

Dr. Hillvale, grinning from ear to ear, continued through the parking lot to his car, got in and told Carol who was in the back seat, to duck down. Pulling out of the lot, they left the University, and hopefully the people looking for Carol. Later, he pulled to the side of the road letting Carol get in the front seat and he related to her what happened in the parking lot.

"Things must have changed, for the man in the lot approached me. I suspect they may be planning to take you into custody."

"I'm sorry for getting you into my mess. Please just drop me off somewhere."

"Are you kidding! I enjoyed tricking the man more than anything I've done in a long time. You're not getting out of my helping you that easy." They both laughed; knowing in their hearts it was not a laughing matter.

"You will be safe at our house and you can stay as long as needed. No one will know you are there."

"I don't know how to thank you enough," Carol responded.

As they drove to his house, she considered his proposal concerning the United States Space vessels being sent to the asteroids as far-fetched. Yet to say it is an alien object is going farther out on a limb; probably going out to the very end if she is honest with herself. She needed to check on United States space launches over the past 20 years, yet knew it would be difficult since many of the military launches were secret.

Speaking very bluntly to Carol, he said, "I have an idea why they may want to take you into custody. Since they suspect you might still have a copy of the picture and you drove to a University, the conclusion would be that you are here to try to find out what is in the picture. Of course, it is why you are here so they may want to arrest you now to prevent you from showing it to anyone else."

"You could be right. If I wasn't in trouble before, I definitely am now. Do you know of anyone else who might be as knowledgeable about space as you who could give me more information about the object in the picture or have another opinion?" She asked knowing her time in Stanford might be limited and information about the picture would not fall into her lap.

Dr. Hillvale continued to steer his car through the streets. He heard Carol's question and was going over in his mind who he might recommend to her. After thinking of several people, he said, "A person you might talk to here at Stanford is in the Science Department. He is interested in the space program, space travel and extra-terrestrial life."

Replying back very quickly, she asked, "Is he some crazy UFO, aliens are coming sort of person."

Dr. Hillvale chuckled, then said, "No, no, he is a very sensible person. He has been here at Stanford for a few years teaching Astronomy."

"What is the expert's name?" She said in a disgruntled tone.

"Harry Calvert."

Carol considered his suggestion while she gazed at the trees lining the street and the leaves budding out on their spidery limbs pass them by.

Dr. Hillvale lived in an older area of the city containing two story homes once housing families involved in the shipping business. During the 1800's San Francisco was a major player in the transportation of people and supplies from the East Coast to the West Coast, an honor revived during the 1960's when Japan, China, and Hong Kong began the influx of products to the United States.

Tall trees surrounded the Hillvale's large two story Victorian house with an extremely narrow drive, which ran along the right side of the house leading to a small unattached garage in the rear.

Pulling into the drive, Carol wasn't sure the car could pass through without hitting the house or the hedge on the other side. Zipping past the objects without a scratch, Dr. Hillvale drove to the back of the house without a second thought and parked in front of the garage. Sitting in the car, she asked, "Dr. Hillvale, are you going to tell your wife?"

He studied Carol, then talking in his old familiar lecture tone, said, "I keep very little from my wife and since your staying with us, my wife deserves to know your situation. We have an open relationship sharing our lives with one another and not keeping any secrets."

Carol admired Dr. Hillvale's caring tone when speaking of his wife. She hoped any future partner of hers would exhibit the same regard.

Entering the house, Dr. Hillvale introduced her to his wife, Dana. She was a short woman, medium build, with short brown hair interspersed with gray, and brown eyes.

"I'm so happy to meet you," Dana said.

"The feeling is mutual. I did meet you twenty years ago when I was a student at Stanford, but I'm sure you don't remember."

Dana led her to a bedroom on the second floor where she deposited her dufflebag.

Because Dr. Hillvale and his wife were so warm and friendly, Carol felt safe again and she was starting to relax after being uptight since the van followed her to the University. The next couple of days would be a great chance for her to continue developing a stratagem and she knew Dr. Hillvale would be an excellent advisor in the process.

In the dining room, they sat down to a wonderful dinner prepared by Dana. With the dark woodwork and flooring, the house had an eerie flavor negated by the Hillvale's smiles and inner beauty.

During dinner, he told a short version of Carol's story to his wife and Dana asked some very pertinent questions giving Carol a view of two very intelligent people conversing. Appearing so perfect for each other, Carol wished her marriage had been as compatible and before becoming involved in a relationship again, she also would make it a point to know the man first.

After dinner, Dr. Hillvale said, "Why don't you call Harry Calvert and see if he would have a discussion with you."

Carol agreed to his suggestion as he searched the faculty directory for the number of Harry's house. Using the Hillvale phone, she dialed the number and Harry Calvert answered.

"Hello, I'm Carol Jacobs-a friend of Dr. James Hillvale who suggested I call you."

"Yes, what can I do for you?"

"I would like to have your opinion or ideas on a couple of questions if you are agreeable?"

"I'll try to help you if I can. What are the questions?"

"I'm sure you'll think I'm crazy for asking, but here goes-what is the chance our solar system has been visited by people from other parts of the galaxy?"

The reply she received was laughter, making her feel foolish and sorry she had asked the question. Could Dr. Hillvale be playing a trick on her?

"I apologize for the humor, Ms Jacobs. You see-you are the second person in the last two days to ask me the exact same question. I find the chances of two people asking so close together too co-incidental."

"Listening to your laughter, I was beginning to think you thought I was crazy. Well, I now know there is another person in the world as silly as me. Who is the other person like me?"

He returned a question of his own. "Have I missed something in the news or newspaper recently, which would lead people to ask such a question. The person who called me the other day would not tell me why he wanted to know."

"I really can't tell you either, especially not over the phone," Carol said sorry to disappoint him.

"Well then, I might not give you an answer if you can't tell me why."

"I'm sorry. I can't. Would you be willing to meet me in person? I might be able to give you more information if we were face to face." Even though she felt safe at the Hillvale's home, she was still wary of telling anyone about her situation over the phone.

"We could meet I suppose. Could you come to my office at the University Monday?"

"I'm sorry, I can't. Is there another place we might meet besides the University?" Carol did not want to chance running into the men from the van.

"Would you be willing to come to my home? If you are, we could meet tomorrow."

"I'm sure I can if you will give me a time and directions."

Harry set a time of nine in the morning and gave her his address and directions to his home.

After hanging up, she related the conversation to Dr. Hillvale and he also thought it unusual someone else had recently inquired about the same topic. He asked Carol, "Did he tell you the name of the other person?"

"No. I asked, but he didn't answer. I'm uncertain whether to show him the picture or not."

"The other person he was talking about might have a copy of the picture. I would suggest you play it by ear."

The more people Carol let see the picture, the greater the chance of her getting into more trouble yet she couldn't get closer to the answers without help. The knowledge another person was asking similar questions about aliens led Carol to speculate: could Dr. Hillvale be right and someone else does have the picture and is going around searching for answers? If someone else knew about the picture, then she wasn't alone and maybe her efforts wouldn't turn out to be a lost cause.

CHAPTER 9A

The oppressive Florida heat pounded the concrete patio next to the motel pool and the sun's glare reflected off the water blinding anyone gazing directly into its fiery radiance. John sat in a lounge chair allowing the sun's rays to wrap around his body as he wrote down his recollections of the conversation with Joyce Carter.

The name, Karen Doddson and the move to New Mexico were the only valuable leads arising from the discussion unless you count polio vaccine as a lead! The next step would be to locate Miss Doddson or a relative if she is deceased.

After finishing his notes, he picked up his cell phone and punched in Peter Cozid's cell number in Dayton, Ohio. Peter answered.

"Peter-John Kirkwood. Have you any more information for me?"

"I do. It is in regards to Frank Wisner, the other name you gave me. It is extensive."

"Give me the short version. Send a copy of your total report to my address in California."

"I will. I want you to know I found the information in reference books at the library. Now for the highlights: Frank Wisner worked as a lawyer on Wall Street in the late 30's. In 1941 he joined the Office of Naval Intelligence which later became the new organization of the Office of Strategic Services or OSS during World War II. After the war he returned to Wall Street."

"He had no other connection with the government." John stated thinking Frank Wisner was a dead end.

"No, In 1947 he returned to work for the State Department, then later for the Central Intelligence Agency better known as the CIA, until 1960. His talent was in two parts. First he was put in charge of many covert operations during the early part of the cold war. Secondly, he was very good at diverting funds from one place to another, thereby hiding his covert operations from scrutiny."

"Is he still alive?"

"No. He committed suicide in the mid sixties."

Disappointed it was not a fruitful direction, John asked, "Anything else?"

"A boss of his got into hot water when a congressional sub-committee on intelligence was investigating CIA expenditures in 1949."

"Do you have more information about his boss?"

"Yes," Peter replied, "You know, it would help if I knew why you were looking into these people. I could eliminate stuff not pertinent to your investigation."

"Yes, yes, we've already had this conversation. I'm not revealing my intentions yet, so would you please continue." As long as he kept providing good information, John saw no reason to let him know what the search was intended to discover and Peter my not be as energetic if he knew John was looking for something as far fetched as an alien object.

Peter continued, "I'm not sure if Frank Wisner knew anything about the diversion of funds. His boss certainly did. Someone was spending money on a covert operation and the money was disappearing and no one could account for it or determine how it was used. Much of the testimony the sub-committee heard was behind closed doors. It will be difficult to obtain much data from its records."

"Who was Wisner's boss?"

"David Hanson. His official title was Special Projects Manager or Supervisor."

"What projects did he control?"

"Various projects connected to the CIA and Defense Department. One was in New Mexico," Peter answered.

"Find out more about David Hanson. Forget Wisner and concentrate on Hanson," John said.

"The other name you gave me; Garland Martin. A colonel- He did work at Wright Air Field in the late thirties, but I have found no record or information on what kind of job he performed."

"Keep checking on him. By the way, how many people work for your agency?"

A long pause ensued. Peter said nothing. John could hear him breathing on the other end. "Peter, are you there?"

"My agency has been going through some problems in the past, but things have been picking up. Currently, I am the sole employee, owner, and private investigator working for the Kinkle Detective Agency. I hope my position as sole proprietor does not make you feel less confident in the services we provide."

"You seem to be doing fine thus far. I will make a decision next week about your agency." John smiled. Peter still used the pronoun, we, even after telling John he was the only employee. The call ended with John thinking about Karen Doddson.

John was considering asking Peter to take care of checking out Karen Doddson in New Mexico thinking others in the agency would continue looking into the other names. Since Peter was the only employee, obviously John's idea would not work. He would have to give some consideration in the next few days about keeping the Kinkle Detective Agency or hire an agency in New Mexico.

Later in the day, as John drove to the beach, he received a call from Ron Williams.

"John-Ron Williams. I have some information regarding the questions you asked a couple of days ago."

"Very good. I'm in my car. Let me pull over. It will be just a moment."

John looked for an area along the beach for a parking spot. Saturday must be a popular day at the beach for the people of Sarasota. Parking was at a premium. He finally decided to pull onto a side street and stop along the curb. He knew Ron would be upset because of the length of time it was taking.

"Okay Ron, sorry for the delay. I had trouble finding a place to park. What do you have for me?"

"First, your question about where a defector would be taken. It looks like Wright Air Field in Ohio would be the prime candidate. At the end of World War II, many captured German scientists were taken to Wright. Does the information help with your inquiry?"

"Yes, very much. I have another source who mentioned Wright Air Field."

"Another source. What are you now-a reporter-having sources?" Ron asked a little confused by John's use of the word.

"No. I'm doing research in the intelligence area. I have asked others similar questions I posed to you." Caught off guard by Ron's question, he hoped the answer satisfied his curiosity.

"Sounds fishy to me, by the way, where are you?" Ron's voice was laced with skepticism.

"I'm in Florida."

"What are you doing in Florida?" Ron exclaimed in a surprised tone.

Ron was getting nosey. John needed to end the conversation.

"Ron, do you have any other information for me?"

"You wanted to know what Sumner Welles did after the War. He never made it to the end of the war in government. He and the Secretary of State, Cordell Hull, seldom got along. Hull was jealous of Welles's connection to Roosevelt. In 1940 Roosevelt sent Welles to Rome, Berlin, Paris, and London to meet with those countries leaders. Hull was upset to no end. He implied Welles was incompetent do to personal reasons. Roosevelt accepted

Welles resignation in August of 1943. Welles retired and wrote books until he died in 1961."

"What were the personal reasons Hull used to get rid of Welles?"

"He said he was a homosexual. No proof I know was ever presented to Roosevelt, but in those times the mere fact of suggesting it was often enough to ruin a career."

"Not too different than today-thank you for your help. I appreciate all your efforts. I'll talk to you when I get back," John said knowing he had no intention of looking up Ron when he returned.

"Are you going to tell me what's going on?"

"I'll talk to you sometime. I can not reveal anything at the present time. Thanks again." John ended the call and knew he must be more careful in what he says to people about his efforts. The remark about sources was unnecessary. Ron did mention Wright Field and it was becoming an area John would have to look into, even to the point of going to Dayton, Ohio.

He phoned Dr. Cable and received no answer; he left a message.

He drove to the beach, found a parking spot, and sat in his car watching the people frolicking in the ocean waves. The gap between people playing in the sand and an alien culture leaving an artifact on Earth daunted the imagination. The significance of one compared to the other was exponentially related, yet the people on the beach represented human kind. They were the apexes of our development after millions of years of evolution. They could not be pushed aside as insignificant. John recalled his lecture from the previous week when he told his students: 'The hope of our society is to be able to interpret the relationships of small details to the total effect'. Would he be able to understand the effect on history of all the events he was trying to unravel?

CHAPTER 9B

In her sleep the dreams came one after another. It was one of those nights where she woke up every hour or two, each time having experienced a completely new dream. Fortunately none of her dreams had anything to do with her present predicament, but it was not a restful sleep. Carol knew more rest was impossible because she had to be at Harry Calvert's house in less than two hours.

She showered, dressed and went downstairs to find Dana in the kitchen.

"Good morning, Dana."

Sitting at the kitchen counter, Dana looked up from the newspaper she was reading and said, "Why good morning Carol. Would you like some breakfast? I will be glad to make some for you."

"No thank you, but I will have a cup of coffee?"

Dana poured a cup and handed it to Carol.

"Is Dr. Hillvale here?"

"No, he drove over to the University. According to him, he won't be gone long. His idea of what is long often varies a great deal. Did you sleep well?"

"I was restless, but not because of the surroundings." Carol did not want Dana to think she was unhappy with the room or the bed.

"I understand. You can use my car to get to your appointment. Are you sure you know the way?"

"Yes. I haven't been here for a few years, but I spent a lot of time in the area while attending the University." She was relieved the conversation did not delve into anything concerning the picture.

Carol thanked her for the use of the car, finished her coffee, and hoped she could get the car out of their drive without hitting the side of the house or the hedge. Walking out the back of the house, and toward the garage, she saw a Dodge Neon sitting inside which brought Carol a smile and relief. Driving out the lane next to the house would not be a problem with a small car, she hoped.

Exiting out the driveway turned out to be a breeze, but if she lived here, the hedge would have to go. She drove out of the inter-city to a suburb containing split-level style homes probably built in the 1970's or 80's. Harry Calvert's house was not distinctive, blending in with the others on the street. She parked along the curb near the front of the house.

A man stood in the doorway to the house smoking a pipe. He presented himself to be in his fifties, average build with salt and pepper hair and a similar colored short beard neatly covering his face. Walking out the door and moving down the driveway, he greeted Carol with a smile. If she had to picture a college instructor, Harry Calvert would fit the role perfectly. He could be the poster boy for College Professor's Monthly!

After greeting one another, he escorted her into the house, and then on to the rear of the home. He gave her the option of either sitting at the kitchen table or going out on the deck. Carol chose the deck and welcomed Harry's offer of coffee or a drink. She opted for bottled water while he poured himself coffee. They exited the house to the deck, which was adorned with flowers planted in a box running the entire length of the deck. It gave the deck area brightness and charm making Carol feel very content. The lawn chairs they sat in were situated around a small table with a top made of glass. The table had a potted flower sitting upon it with some papers scattered around that Harry hastily gathered into a pile and shoved to one side.

Carol inquired about the flowers adorning the deck and was told he spent a lot of time tending them because they were a special part of his wife's life. She died of complications from diabetes one year after they came to Stanford.

"I'm sorry for your loss."

Harry acknowledged her statement of sympathy and then began the conversation saying, "So you are the one interested in determining if aliens have visited our little planet earth." Harry spoke with a hint of sarcasm.

"Yes I am. I suppose you might also say I am one of the crazies you read about in the papers; 'Seeing flying saucers at night and little green men'," She replied.

Harry continued puffing on his pipe eyeing Carol with curiosity. "Are you here because you've seen objects in the sky you can't explain?"

"No, not exactly. According to Dr. Hillvale, you have spent a great deal of time researching the area of alien civilization. I'm interested in what you have found in your studies about extra terrestrials. Is it possible our solar system has been visited by, as you call them, aliens." She spoke with a determination in her voice she previously had not shown.

"One thing is clear, you are serious. Many people who find I have an interest in extra-terrestrials ask me these types of questions to tease me."

"I assure you, I am not here as a joke. I have no desire to criticize your interest, only to learn from your efforts and research."

The idea of pulling a joke on Harry had never crossed Carol's mind. She understood how he would feel if people made fun of his hobby and knew the joking would probably make his research more difficult. It would be hard to obtain information if everyone smirked at your questions and did not take you serious.

"Tell me, Mrs. Jacobs, who are you, besides knowing my colleague from Stanford, Dr. Hillvale?"

Carol had not expected to be questioned about her personal life. She couldn't really deny him the right to ask, since he had invited her into his house at her request.

"I grew up in Northern California, attended Stanford University, obtaining a dual degree in Computer Science and Planetary Geology. The Jet Propulsion Laboratory in Pasadena, California has employed me for the last 18 years. I am presently separated from my husband, have no children, but a large number of siblings, nieces and nephews."

"You work at JPL and you are interested in extra-terrestrial life. You may know more about aliens than a fifty year old college professor," He said with a questioning look.

"I am sure you are more informed than I could ever hope to be in my entire life. I was involved with many of the space probes, but they had little to do with alien life forms."

Harry covered the same material he discussed with John Kirkwood a few days prior to his present conversation. The discussion followed a similar pattern as well and when he had finished, he asked Carol again why she was interested in aliens.

Carol turned over in her mind whether to inform Harry of the picture. She was unsure how much knowledge to pass along. "Yesterday, you told me I was the second person who recently asked you about extra-terrestrial life. Was the other person interested in the same things as I am?"

"I see-answer a question with a question. I can't really say because he never told me exactly why he wanted to know about the subject and he never told me to keep his name a secret. I'll think about telling you so now, what about my question, 'Why the interest?'" He was forcing the issue again.

The possibility of someone else having a copy of the picture entered Carol's mind again. If so, whoever it is might be searching for answers to the same questions.

"Do you have a good computer in your house?" She asked deciding to let him view the picture.

"I think it is. My son talked me into purchasing it over the winter. Do you want to see it?"

"If you don't mind, I'd like to show you a picture, but you have to promise not to tell anyone about it," Carol said closely watching his reaction to her request.

With a frown on his face, Harry eyed Carol in a questioning way not sure how to answer. "I'm not crazy about secrets. I prefer everything to be out in the open. I'm not sure I want knowledge I can't discuss."

Liking his answer because it showed he valued openness and honesty, she replied, "The reason I ask you not to tell is I'm not supposed to have the picture, yet I feel it should be viewed by everyone."

"If you think everyone should see it, why do you want me to keep it a secret?" He responded in a skeptical voice.

"Because I'm already in trouble for having it in my possession and if found, the picture will be confiscated, and no one will ever see it again. Is that reason enough for you not to say anything?"

His eyes widened with her last remark. He took his pipe out of his mouth and laid it on the table. "A contraband picture which must deal with aliens in some way-and you could be arrested. I won't say anything-show me the picture," He said, quickly changing his mind.

Carol was sure he would answer in the affirmative. Anyone interested in extra-terrestrial life presented with an opportunity to see something having to do with the subject could not resist.

They went to his study, a bedroom converted into a work area strewn with books, papers and periodicals. The computer was located on a table at one end of the room where the headboard of a bed was still attached to the wall. She took the disc from her purse, loaded it in the computer, and brought the picture up on the screen.

Harry sat in front of the screen, scanning the monitor in a deliberate manner. He sat for a moment then said, "Where was the picture taken?"

"The Asteroid Belt between Jupiter and Mars."

Harry continued eyeing the picture. She waited giving Harry plenty of time to study the picture.

"The picture was taken by the Talaria probe, was it not?" He spoke in a confident way, sure of the answer to own question.

"Yes. How did you know?" Surprised by his knowledge, she gained some respect for his ability.

"Remember my field is astronomy. I view the pictures sent back by all the probes. NASA sends me all these pictures, yet the one you have I never received."

Carol backed up a step fearing Harry was an agent for NASA ready to turn her in for possessing the picture. Her knees began to wobble. Had she made a big mistake showing it to Harry?

"Has anyone given you an explanation for the object in the picture?"

"Yes and no. No one at NASA or JPL has analyzed the picture to the best of my knowledge. The reason it was not forwarded to you and the reason I'm not supposed to have it in my possession is it was deleted from the JPL system," She said feeling a little better. "Some people think it may be a part of a Russian or United States space probe, others believe it is a piece of alien material. What is your opinion of the picture?"

"Unless a secret mission into space has been sent, I would say the picture should not be kept a secret. I would lean to the side of a secret probe. If you published the picture claiming it was alien material, it would be another case of hocus-pocus-faked, fabricated. You've told me why you want to keep it a secret, but I don't know why NASA wants to hide it," Harry explained to her. "Every picture I have viewed purportedly representing aliens has turned out to be some Earth based object. I'm sure your picture will turn out the same. Besides, no one believes you if you say it's alien."

Carol was glad Harry felt the same as she did regarding showing the picture to the scientific community. If enough people saw it, maybe it would be accepted as a factual picture and then it could be determined scientifically what it represents. She wasn't ready to go broadcast it to the world just yet. If it is alien, Harry was right, too. No one would believe her and she would be branded a fool. The object in the picture had to be a part of an earthly venture.

CHAPTER 10A

Palm trees, sand, and rolling waves created a picturesque view from the beach chair John was occupying. He was taking advantage of the weekend in Florida by spending the rest of Saturday and Sunday at the seashore. Participating in a game of beach volleyball with a much younger crowd wore him down though he was still proud to say he held his own and the team he played on won most of their games. The last two days had been a pleasant break from the University routine of the past months.

While at the beach, Peter called to tell John he had found Colonel Garland Martin. He was in a nursing home in Miamisburg, Ohio, a town south of Dayton. According to Peter, he was in poor health so John decided to go see him right away. The plan was to fly to Cincinnati, rent a car and drive the forty-five miles north to Dayton. He discovered the Cincinnati, Ohio airport was in Kentucky, which seemed unusual.

John finished writing a summary of all the information he had accumulated thus far and made a list of items he wanted to check on in Dayton then walked through the sand on the beach to the water's edge. As he stood watching the waves roll in, the Sunday evening sun was sliding below the horizon. It emitted a dull orange glow reminding him of Dr. Cable's description of the mysterious cube. If it existed, what an event to tell the world: there are other sapient beings in the Universe and we were not alone. The various religions covering the earth would probably not find the knowledge comforting. He walked back to his beach chair, gathered his material, and drove back to his motel.

Monday morning, rain greeted John as he loaded his rental car for the drive to the airport. It came in torrents creating a difficult driving situation so he pulled to the side of the road to wait and in a short time the spring shower passed and he was back on his way.

The trip to Cincinnati, renting the car and the drive to Dayton took a large part of the day. John arrived in Dayton at five o'clock in the evening.

The address Peter had given him for the Kinkle Detective Agency was on Main at Lincoln just south of downtown Dayton.

John pulled up to the building Peter had described to him over the phone. It was an old, two-story red brick building. Pulling onto Lincoln Street, he found a place to park and walked to the front door of the building. He was not impressed by what he saw. It reminded John of the eerie buildings shown in the movies when the main characters' car breaks down and the group of people riding in the vehicle walk to a castle with dead vines covering the facade. The windows and the trim of Peter's office building needed painting and some bricks had worked loose and needed replaced. The entire outside of the building was in general disrepair. He opened the door and entered the building.

What was in need of fixing up on the outside was contradicted by the condition of the interior. The very clean entryway led into a reception area where a desk, chair, and a couch with tables were located. The room was neat and orderly with oil paintings on the walls and the floor covered with a slate appearing to be a recent addition. John was amazed at the difference between the deterioration on the outside and the elegance of the inside.

No one was at the desk and John had not expected to find a lot of people since Peter was the only one working in his business. The desk was wooden with a phone, pad and pen, pencil holder, and bud vase arranged neatly upon its shiny top. Having called Peter on the phone earlier, he knew he was in his office.

John called out Peter's name and a reply came from behind the desk where a door led into another room. The voice was Peter's and he yelled for John to come on back. He passed through the door into an office even more impressive than the reception area. It contained two couches in front of a fireplace and the carpeted floor met wood paneling at the wall that ran up to the height of a chair rail.

Peter sat behind an attractive oak desk in a large leather chair. In front of the desk were two smaller, no less impressive leather chairs. He motioned John to have a seat as he was taking a phone call. John walked around the room, examining the entire office, then sat in one of the chairs facing Peter.

Peter finished his conversation, stood and walked around the desk to greet John. Peter Cozid, dressed in blue jeans with a coat and tie, was much younger than John expected. He looked to be in his twenties with blond hair and a baby face. Being almost as tall as John, his body was very muscular indicating he did a lot of workouts. Peter shook his hand and sat in the chair next to John saying, "I'm glad we have a chance to meet face to face. You look younger than your voice indicated."

"I could say the same thing to you except your voice sounded young to me," John returned, "I must ask you about your office building. The inside is so impressive compared to the outside. Why the difference?"

"Most clients ask the same question. I've even lost some business because of the outside condition. Prospective clients drive over, see the building, and don't even take the time to come inside. The building was my grandfather's and he ran an agency here many years ago until he passed away. My father worked for him part time, but was not enthused about being a private detective so after my grandfather died, he and my mother closed the agency. I know I'm going around your question. Patience, I will give you the answer.

My father decided to fix the building up to sell. On weekends he did all the interior work and he was leaving the outside to finish last. He became ill and did not complete any of the outside work. My parents finally acquiesced after a great deal of debate and let me have the building after I convinced them I wanted to be a private investigator. I spent most of my money furnishing the office so I didn't have any left to do the outside. An apartment is located on the second floor, which is where I live. Have I answered your question?"

"Quite extensively," John replied not really wanting such a detailed history, but finding it interesting never the less.

John noticed an open door leading to another room. "Is the adjacent room part of your office also?"

Peter arose from his desk motioning for John to stand and follow him. "In here is where I do a lot of my work. I have computers hooked to the Internet, photo equipment, copying machine, a layout table, reference books, and police scanner among other things. Much information can be gleaned through electronics as opposed to shoe leather. I don't mean to say I spend all my time in a little room. I put in many hours on the go, but information can be obtained much quicker if I can locate it using these items."

His knowledge and the organization of his office impressed John. He asked him if he had more clients and the reply from Peter was yes.

"Actually business has improved in the past two months. I'm presently interviewing for a receptionist and a part time private detective to assist me in serving my clients," Peter said proudly with a tempered grin trying not to be too boastful.

"I see you are very dedicated to your business. You seem to enjoy being an investigator."

"I spent a great deal of time here with my grandfather. He let me help in small ways and from the beginning, I always knew what I wanted to do in life."

The more John knew about Peter, the more confidence he had in him and the more he liked the young man. The interest and dedication Peter showed to his work and his clients impressed him.

Returning to the office and sitting down, John said, "I need the address of the nursing home where Garland Martin is living?"

Peter reached for a folder on his desk. "I have a map of the Dayton area, the location of the home and an address with directions. The location of your hotel is marked on the map. Also brochures on Wright Patterson Air Force Base and the Museum are included in the file. Can I do anything else to help?"

John told him no, arose shaking his hand, thanked Peter and walked out to his car. He drove to the Holiday Inn, checked in, and after putting his stuff in his room, decided to go to the bar for a drink before dinner. Feeling tired, he would turn in after eating dinner and prepare some questions for tomorrow.

The next morning, John was out and on his way to the Oak-Brier Home. It was a twenty-minute drive from his hotel. He arrived at the home at nine am and talked to one of the attendants to find out where Colonel Martin's room was located.

The attendant directed John to the reception office. John followed his directions and met an elderly man sitting behind a desk in a small room functioning as the reception area. John walked through the open door and told him whom he wanted to see.

The man asked him to sign the register, write in the time of day, and be sure to sign out when he left. The man also wanted to know why he was here to see Colonel Martin.

John saw no reason to tell anyone why he was visiting Colonel Martin, so he asked the man why he needed to know. He told John it was part of the rules to protect the people in the home. If he would get the manager, John would tell him or her why he was here. Of course John had no intention of telling anyone.

The man's attitude changed and he said it was not necessary and John could go ahead to Marty's room. John considered the exchange between the two strange. Was the guy just nosey or did the home really have a policy requiring the reason for his visit. He let it fade from his mind and proceeded to Colonel Martin's room.

The home had many residents in wheel chairs, sitting in the hall without any intended purpose and there was the distinct odor of body fluids and waste along with a disinfectant smell. John was saddened by the fate of the people he viewed at the home and he hoped the end of his life would not be spent in such a place. Many of the residents were bright-eyed at seeing a new face and said hello to John as he passed by. He returned their greeting with a smile and a 'hi' of his own.

The door to Colonel Martin's room was open so John knocked on the door at the same time he scanned the interior of the room. A man was sitting in a rocking chair with his back to John gazing out a large picture window. He knocked harder and saw no movement from the man to acknowledge John's presence.

"You'll have to knock a lot louder if you want to get his attention," someone said behind John.

John turned to find another elderly man standing beside him. He was wearing a pair of thick glasses and bent over a walker. John sized up the gentleman prior to responding to his comment. "I'm looking for Colonel Garland Martin."

"Why you lookin' for him?" He asked in a raspy voice with a slow southern drawl.

"I'm a friend of a friend of his," John replied stretching the truth. A new trait he had started using the last few days.

"Who's the friend?"

"Senval Happard."

He replied immediately without having to think about the name John dropped on him. "Dr. Happy!" the man said. "I haven't heard his name in many, many years. So you know Dr. Happard-my-my." Obviously he was talking to Colonel Martin since he seemed to know Dr. Happard. John was curious why he called him Dr. Happy.

"I presume you are Colonel Martin?"

"At your ser'ves. My friends, they call me Marty. Who might'n you be, Mister?"

Of average height, Colonel Martin was completely bald and thin as a rail. John was sure the skinny body was do to his poor health.

"I'm John Kirkwood," He replied to the Colonel

"Come in, sit down," he said, "That's my roommate, Charlie. He k'un hardly hear anything a'tall. Sit in the chair. I'll sit on my bed."

John entered and sat in the chair next to the bed. Colonel Martin followed him, moving slowly with the walker and sat on the edge of the bed. John told him he could lie down if he wanted. Charlie continued to rock in his chair showing no sign he was aware of John and the Colonel. The space the two men lived in was more like a hospital room, except a little smaller with two beds, two dressers and two chairs. A door to a bathroom was located in the corner of the room near the door.

"Would it be alright if I asked you some questions?"

"Sure, go ahead, fire away!"

"Where are you from originally?"

"I grew up in Pikevu'lle, Kentucky." Colonel Martin spoke the words with some pride. John never heard of Pikeville, Kentucky and wondered why the Colonel was so proud of coming from the place.

"How long have you been in the home?"

"I've been here seven years. I came to the home when I was 79 'cause my knees gave way. That's the reason I have to use the walker. I could have gone through the Veterans Administration, but I wanted to stay here."

"I was told you were ill. You look fine for someone in his eighties."

"On the outside maybe, but cancer is eating me away on the inside. I don't have much longer to live."

"I'm sorry. I hope my being here isn't discomforting to you." John wondered if all the people in the home were waiting to die.

"Naw, I'm glad to have someone to talk to," Marty said with a smile on his face, "Charlie and me-we don't get much company."

"Colonel Martin, would it be okay if some of my questions pertained to your work with Dr. Happard at Wright Air Field? I'm doing some research into his life."

"No, I won't answer anything more if you keep callin' me by that name. Call me Marty. Everyone else does." He leaned back on the pillow pressed against the headboard.

"Alright. I agree. When did you first meet Dr. Happard or Dr. Happy as you called him…Marty?"

Marty collected his thoughts. John knew he was trying to remember his life during the period. "It must have been shortly a'fore the end of the War. No, wait a minute. It was after the war. Yow, I met him after the war. I saw him 'round Wright Field during the war, but I didn't meet him till afterward."

"How long were you stationed at Wright Field?"

"Let me think. I was there from 1941 till 1961. I was involved with security for the airfield the whole time. A'fore I retired, I was head of security for the entire old section of Wright Field," He said proudly.

John was surprised he rose to such a level, but his dialect may be giving him a false impression of his ability. He definitely had a good memory. "Do you know what Dr. Happard did at Wright? Can you tell me anything about his work?"

Marty turned to look out the window. John wasn't sure if he was thinking or did not hear the question.

Finally, Marty turned back to John saying, "I never talked about my work at the time, it being so secret and all, but now it doesn't matter, being so long ago. I never did know what they did in that there building, A-19 it was called. It was off limits to almost everyone at Wright including me, except fer Dr. Happy and a few others. After the war, I was assigned to a section called Project Mogul. My official title was Personnel Director, but my real duty was to provide security and funding for Dr. Happy. That's how I come to meet him. It was after I became a part of the new Air Force and Dr. Happy helped me make Captain cause of my help."

"If you were involved with security, why were you providing funding?" John was confused by the dual responsibilities.

"It was a secret project. There were a lot of secret projects at Wright and most of the buildings were off limits except'n you had a pass. I'd get a lot more money fer security and personnel than I needed, so Dr. Happy would take what was left over fer, I guess, whatever they were doing in that building."

"Who approved the money for your security?"

"The Special Projects Supervisor, David Hanson," Marty said, "He approved of all the money I used."

"Do you know who was over him, up the chain of command?"

"I'm not sure-he wasn't military. It may have been the State Department or one of the intelligence groups. There were a lot of them people at Wright. I remember one time a bunch of big shots from the State Department were visiting and I was assigned by Hanson to escort some guy with a funny first name like Spring or Summer."

"You mean Sumner Welles?" John interjected.

"Yea, that's him. He wanted to see A-19 and I thought I was going to see it too since I was assigned to him, but even he didn't have clearance, so what ever was in there was pretty special."

John was grateful Colonel Martin had his mental faculties about him. It allowed John to better accept what he said as true. Some of the information he had been collecting was starting to connect.

"Marty, tell me what you did-tell me how you were involved with Dr. Happard."

"After I came to Wright Field, I was assigned to security. I had recently made Sergeant so I was proud to be at Wright. I knew Dr. Happard worked in A-19, but had no idea what they were doing in there or any other building for that matter. Security was very tight all 'oer the air field."

"During the War, Wright Field went from about 3000 people working there to o'er 50,000. In 1941, there were 40 or so buildings. By 1944, there were o'er 300 plus buildings. We got a boat load of money to do security, which wasn't too easy with that many people coming and going."

"They also built two large hangers right in front of building A-19. There was construction continuously at Wright during this period."

Obviously, Marty was very proud of the job he had done and seemed to be conscientious in his work. His down-home country talk made him likeable and loveable. Both traits and his relationship to Happard and Hanson would have helped him in attaining the rank of Colonel.

"Marty, was it a common practice to over budget one area to fund another?"

He grabbed his side and winced in pain. Seeing John start to get up, he said, "I'm okay. They come and go. I'll take some pain pills if they continue."

John felt helpless knowing he could do nothing to alleviate the pain. "I can leave if you want?"

"No, stay and the answer to your question is yes, I guess. I asked Hanson about it once and he told me that a guy named Carter working for President Rouse'velt used the White House Scholarship Fund to help Britain buy guns a'fore we even got in the war, so I fig'red if the big boys were doing it, then it wasn't a big deal."

Marty appeared to be very relaxed. John wondered how much pain medication he was taking. "What kind of people were allowed into A-19? Were they military or civilian?"

"The regular people, scientists and engineers."

John was confused. "Why do you call them regular people?"

"Wright Air Field was involved almost entirely in research and development. Most non-military people were eggheads and there were a lot of them. We called them the regular people."

"How long did you provide security for Dr. Happard?"

"'Till he left. In the middle of the night they loaded seven trucks with I assume everything in building A-19. I say that 'cause I was able to enter A-19 after they moved and noth'in was left in the building, not even a scrap of paper. I never saw him again and never knew where he wound up. That was in 1951 or 52."

Marty was very forthcoming. John was beginning to get a better understanding of the situation at Wright. "Was your main boss Hanson or Dr. Happard?"

"Dr. Happy was in charge and that was unusual. Always a'fore, my boss was always someone in the military. There was someone who had control over just about everyone. He was in charge of what was called Internal Security for Project Mogul. His name was Robert White. He could enter A-19."

"By the way, why do you call him Dr. Happy?"

"'cause he always had such a serious look on his face," Marty said with a smile. "He always gave the impression that he was out to save the world's problems and some of the other people at the base called him by that name. He didn't seem to mind."

John stood, shook Marty's hand, thanked him for all the information, wished him the best, and walked over to Charlie. He told Charlie he hoped they didn't disturb him and Charlie still gave no sign he heard John's remark as he continued to stare out the window at the birds in the yard.

CHAPTER 10B

The psyche can be elevated in various ways such as having someone agree and accept your interpretation of an event. Carol was excited to have Harry reinforce her ideas about how the picture should be used, but was disappointed he had no more insights into the item depicted in the picture.

The weekend passed quietly which was a big change for Carol considering her recent experiences. Feeling safe from the people pursuing her was one big plus the Hillvales had provided with their warm hospitality. Making contact with her sister, Robin, Carol let her know she was fine and safe. She told Robin her car was in storage, but she would not be able to return it in the near future. In response, Robin didn't seem to care since she was enjoying driving the Jeep.

Making one more call on the pay phones in the area, she contacted Bob to inform him she would be away for awhile. He was not as congenial as Robin had been and Bob informed her he had retained an attorney to start the divorce procedure. She detected a great deal of bitterness in his voice and expected to have some hard times herself before the divorce was final.

Monday morning, as Dr. Hillvale was leaving for the University, he asked Carol, "Can I do anything for you while I'm at the office?"

Carol thought for a moment, then said, "If you could ask security if anyone has been inquiring about me or snooping around the campus, nosing into things, I would appreciate it."

He agreed to check it out as he left the house.

After Dr. Hillvale left, Carol and Dana had a cup of coffee together at the island bar in the kitchen. The two sat on stools at the counter and discussed Carol's marriage breakup and her problems associated with the coming divorce. Carol and Dana had made a connection over the weekend, even with Dana eighteen years her senior; they related to many topics and to each other. Dana was such a kind and caring person, no wonder she and Dr. Hillvale seemed so happy together.

After talking for a long time and about to go shopping, they heard someone enter the back door. Both turned to see Dr. Hillvale coming into the kitchen. Surprised by his early return, Dana asked if there was a problem.

"Follow me to the front room," He said without stopping or giving any kind of explanation.

Carol and Dana followed him to a room at the front of the house where their computer was located and there he showed them a package from Dale Belfer.

"Dale sent the pictures!" Carol exclaimed. "Let's have a look at them!"

Carol sat at the computer and put the disc in and ran the pictures up on the screen. While the computer was working, Dr. Hillvale told Carol he didn't have a chance to talk to Security at the University. She acknowledged his comment and turned back to the monitor.

Silence can echo through a room in the same way the sound of a dropped pan bounces off the walls of a kitchen. The expression "a picture is worth a thousand words" never rang so true than it did in the present situation. No exchange of words passed between the three as they stared at the monitor, the only sound was the tick-tock of the grandfather clock in the entry hall. Each stood almost paralyzed as the pictures flashed before their eyes.

Eventually, Dr. Hillvale was the first to speak, "These pictures pretty much tell us where we need to be looking. They obviously are not-."

Before he finished his explanation, Dana poked her husband nodding for him to look outside. She had heard a noise and was looking out the front window. A van had parked in front of their house and people were getting out and walking toward the front door of the Hillvale's home. Dr. Hillvale recognized one of the men as the man in the campus parking lot last Friday.

He said to Carol, "You have to get out of here. Follow me." He reached over and ejected the disc from the computer, handed it to Carol, grabbed her by the arm and got her up and going toward the back of the house.

Stumbling as she grabbed her bag, Carol put the disc in it and followed him to the back door having no idea why she had to leave. He abruptly stopped at the rear door because people were entering the back yard from the alley behind the garage.

"What's wrong?" Carol asked as she came up behind him where she could see the people entering from the alley. "Oh, I see…" Her voice trailed off as she watched them.

"You have to get away from here. We can't go out this way. There are people out front also." He turned and pushed Carol towards the hall. He opened a door to a stairway leading down to the basement.

"Come on. I have another idea." He scurried down the steps with Carol close behind. They could hear loud knocking at the front door as they descended the steps.

"If you'll go through this door and take the steps up the outside of the house, there is a gate through a fence into the neighbors yard and you might have a chance of avoiding getting caught. Because of the shrubbery, you can't be seen from the front or back of the house. Now hurry. You don't have much time." He urged her out the door.

She gave him a hug and kissed him on the cheek, then ran out the door, up the steps and through a gate into the neighbor's yard. This yard had a high wooden fence between it and the Hillvales blocking the view of the people in the rear of their house.

Running to the back of the yard where another gate was positioned leading into the alley, she peered down the lane. Another van was parked in the ally directly behind the Hillvale's garage. Now what to do?

Having no other option and no fence on the other side of the yard, she continued on to the next yard. Reaching the third one, she came to a fence too high to climb and no gate. The only way out was toward the front of the house or back the way she came, so she walked to the front and looked down the street toward the Hillvale's house. Her eyes were met with another shock.

Agents Feathers and Johnson were standing near the front of the Hillvale's home. She gritted her teeth, vowing they would not catch her. Since the street was lined with large trees and the yard in front of the house she was hiding behind had one of these trees, she decided to use it. She darted the fifteen feet across the lawn to the large tree in front of the house and stood behind its trunk. She used the tree as a shield to block the view of her from the people standing in front of the Hillvale's house.

Carol proceeded to work her way from one tree to the next through the front yards along the street putting distance between her and the Hillvale's home. Eventually, turning the corner of the block and taking out in a full run, she continued to the next street turning again, zigzagging her way through the residential area.

She reached a main street, found a food mart with a pay phone and called for a cab. It showed up in less than five minutes. She gave the Driver the address of a house near Harry Calverts. All during the drive, she worried about the Hillvales-what had she brought on them and how would they be treated by the agents?

The cab stopped two houses down the street from Harry's and after paying the taxi driver, she walked to Harry's and rang the doorbell, but received no reply. After several minutes of ringing and even knocking, she assumed he was gone. Walking to the back of the house and sitting in one of deck chairs they used last Saturday, she stewed over her predicament and where to go. She had hoped to solicit Harry's aid in escaping.

Finding pen and paper in her bag, she wrote a note for Harry in which she told him what had happened at the Hillvale's house and she would be in contact soon. Asking him to check on the Hillvales when he could, she also told him about the new pictures sent by Dale.

Attaching the note to the rear door on the deck, she walked to the house next door and knocked. No one answered. She continued down the street one house after another until someone answered his door. Asking to use a phone to call a taxi, the lady who answered the door brought her a cordless phone and phone book. Carol looked up the number of a cab company and called, with the cab arriving quickly. She thanked the lady and rode off in the taxi.

Remembering from her college days a lake resort with cabins for rent located East of San Francisco, she asked the cab driver to take her to the resort office. He told her it would be expensive. She said she could pay, still having a large amount of cash in her bag. On the way the driver stopped at a drug store where she purchased some personal items, and a timed wireless phone since in the rush to leave, she had left hers at the Hillvales.

The cab driver took her to the resort office and after she rented a place on the lake, drove her to the cabin and helped her with her stuff. Carol paid him, giving him a nice tip before he left her alone. The small cabin was one room with a bath, a small kitchen, and it was nestled in a cove near the shore of the lake. She lay down on the bed. Her muscles ached, and her body felt drained, more from being tense and the strain of her plight than from exertion. The bed caressed her skin as she let her body drift as if she were floating on water. The afternoon sun peeked through the drawn curtains as she listened to the songbirds outside her cabin announce their presence through chirps and whistles.

CHAPTER 11A

The lines in the pavement flashed by the rental car as John drove Interstate75 back to Dayton. Driving slowly due to his consciousness being consumed by what he had just learned, other cars and trucks flew by becoming a blur in his peripheral vision. Colonel Martin's story led credibility to Dr. Cable's belief the cube was taken to Wright Patterson. Since Colonel Martin never saw what was in A-19, John could not assume the cube was in the building. He knew during the 1940's something connected with Dr. Happard, an archeologist, was mysteriously kept secret in a building at Wright Airfield which was probably unusual for an Air Force Base.

The lobby of his hotel contained several chairs surrounding a piano and two settees with some end tables and lamps thrown in for good measure. Returning from the nursing home, John chose one of the chairs to sit in and wrote a synopsis of his conversation with Colonel Martin. After completing the notes, he used his cell phone to place a call to Dr. Cable and was rewarded with the distinctive sound of his voice.

"John, how are things going?"

Using his notes, John reviewed the conversation he had with Joyce Carter. Dr. Cable listened intently as John completed his report.

"Have you any knowledge of a Karen Doddson?" John inquired of him.

"No. The name means nothing. When did the Happards move to Albuquerque?"

Checking his notes, John determined Joyce was born in 1940 and was twelve when she moved. "It was around 1952," He answered.

Hearing no comment, John conveyed the information he received from Colonel Martin.

"When did they move out of building A-19?"

John was curious why he was interested in these dates. He would try to remember to ask him later. "I was told it was either 1951 or 1952. Colonel Martin could not remember exactly."

"How long are you staying in Dayton?"

"I'm not sure. I want to go to Wright-Patterson Air Force Base before I leave. Did you have something you wanted me to do?"

"No, I was curious," He replied.

"Where are you?" John had a sense Dr. Cable was not in California.

"I'm in Minnesota."

The tone of Dr. Cable's words sounded different from the last time they talked. John did not pursue it and told him he would keep in touch.

After the call, John sat in the lobby for a long time watching the guests enter and exit through the front door of the Hotel, but his mind was not seeing the people. His instincts were telling him Dr. Cable was not the same. Something definitely was peculiar in the inflection of Dr. Cable's voice, and why was he in Minnesota? He made mental notes of these thoughts for the next time they talked.

Returning to his room, he dialed Peter Cozid.

"Peter, I've met with Colonel Martin and he was some help. Thanks for finding him."

"That's my job."

"There are some things I would like to talk over with you. Could we meet this evening to discuss our progress?"

"I have a better suggestion. How about talking over dinner? I know an excellent Italian place." Peter said enthusiastically.

"Yes, very good. I'll treat. What time?""

"I'll be at your hotel at 7:30."

"I will be in the bar; see you then," John said as he ended the call.

After eating lunch in the hotel restaurant, John drove to Wright-Patterson Air Force Base. The entrance looked like a pay station on a toll road with several gates to go through. Driving into one of the slots, the man in the booth was dressed in a camouflage uniform, which everyone now knows, do to the Middle East Wars, to be combat gear. The soldier did not look a day over eighteen as he asked John for his ID. John pulled out his California Driver License and handed it to the guard. The guard looked at John with a little smirk on his face and asked John if he was playing a joke.

John told him it was his only ID with his picture and quickly found out you don't get in without an Air Force I.D. and pass. He was told to follow the two guards standing behind the entrance gate.

The guards directed John through the gate and around a side road, which led back to the highway outside the gate. As he drove out the gate, he saw in his rear view mirror one of the guards writing down his license plate number. He discovered you don't just drive onto a military base.

He entered the highway and driving down the road, he saw a sign displaying the words "Air Force Museum". Maybe he would have better luck at the museum.

He did have a better outcome. No guards were stationed at the gates so he drove through the opening and into the parking lot in front of a large building. Behind the building were three larger buildings, which he presumed were airplane hangers. No one said a word to John as he entered the building. He saw a booth occupied by two elderly women and walked over in front of the counter and asked how much it cost to enter the museum.

The ladies looked at each other and smiled. One lady stood and told him everything is free except the Imax Theater and he could wander as he pleased throughout the hangers. The buildings were full of airplanes from the Wright Brothers to the Stealth Bomber. If he wished, he could take a bus over to Wright Field where they have some of the former President's planes.

John asked if he could drive over to Wright Field and enter the museum. The two ladies smiled at each other again. They told him no, you can only get in if your on the bus.

John wandered around for a short time until the next bus left. The bus ride to Wright Field took only a couple of minutes.

At the gate to Wright, again the security people were dressed in full battle gear toting guns. The guards checked the bus driver's papers without the first hint of a smile. The bus driver must have passed through these gates several times already today, yet they treated him like a stranger.

The bus stopped in front of two large hangers built during World War II. The hangers contained former President's planes and experimental planes such as the X-1 and X-2. John went through them quickly looking for a way out the rear of the hangers. No rear doors were there unless he wanted to go through the emergency exit and set off no telling how many alarms. None of the windows allowed him to look at the area in the rear of the hangers.

Two men were manning the front door in a small booth next to where the tourists entered the hangers. John slipped out the door when the men were occupied talking to another tourist. He walked swiftly along the front of the hanger, hoping to get to the corner before he was spotted.

He made it without being seen and quickly went around the hanger. Peeking around the back of the hanger, he saw an old building with a parking area containing several vehicles in between him and the building. He started to walk toward it when from around the corner of the building a soldier appeared carrying a gun. He walked in front of the door and stood at attention. Above the door was a sign with "A-19" on it and below the sign was another stating "No Admittance. Restricted." John started back-peddling returning to the corner of the hanger. At least part of Colonel Martin's story was true, but why was it guarded now. He was almost back to the corner of the hanger when a Jeep came from behind building A-19 and was on him in a flash.

The Jeep contained two soldiers who yelled at him to halt. John stopped, turned and saw what to him were kids again. The soldiers were out of the jeep with guns at the ready asking him for identification. John again gave them his California Drivers License, which these two did not think was at all funny.

He was escorted across the expanse in front of the museum hangers to one of the buildings located about three hundred yards away. Taking him inside to an office, they instructed him to sit and wait. One of the soldiers left leaving the other to watch over John.

In what seemed to be an eternity, which was actually only twenty minutes, a large man in a blue uniform entered. He had gray hair and a rigid face, reminding John of an airline pilot on one of his recent flights. He stood over six feet with broad shoulders and a very traditional style haircut.

"So you are John Kirkwood. Am I correct?" He asked as he stood over John.

"Yes, I am. Is there a problem?" John replied innocently.

The man looked at John with a rather mean tenor and said, "Yes, Mr. Kirkwood, you were apprehended in a security area. We consider your entering the area a serious problem."

John started to reply then thought it would be better to avoid any confrontation.

"What were you doing behind the hanger?"

Having already planned what he would say if asked, John replied, "I was sick and wanted some room. I guess I just wandered around the hanger getting some fresh air."

"We take very serious people's wandering around as you say in restricted areas, especially since 911."

"I had no idea it was a restricted area. Only an old building was back behind the hangers."

"The building you refer to has been restricted for as long as I have been here and that is over fifteen years."

John did not reply. He found it odd the old building would be under scrutiny to the extent illustrated by his capture.

After sparing some with the man whose name was Major Hampton. He decided to let it rest. Major Hampton was in charge of security for Wright Field and when he found out John taught History at Stanford, he backed off of his interrogation.

Major Hampton called in the soldiers and they ushered him out of the room and into the jeep. They quickly took him back to the museum, John riding in the passenger seat and one of the soldiers behind him as the other drove.

124

Reflecting on what had just occurred, he found it unusual the old building behind the hangers was being guarded today. It must be used for something else important since the cube was supposed to have been sent to another location out West.

Upon returning to the hotel, he dressed for dinner. Not knowing what type of restaurant Peter would pick, he elected to wear a coat in case it was upscale. He strolled down to the bar taking in the layout of the hotel and lobby, then sitting at a table in the bar, he asked the bartender for a gin and tonic.

Not having checked his messages at home since leaving Friday, he used his cell phone to call home. When his answering machine came on, he punched his code in and it played back the messages. Several were from people at the University, one from Judy, and one from Harry Calvert.

In Harry's message, he asked John to call as soon as possible. John decided tomorrow would be soon enough to return the call.

When he noticed Peter entering the bar, he put his cell phone away and motioned him over to the table. "What are you drinking?"

Peter said, "I'll have a gin martini." John relayed the order to the bartender.

John reviewed with Peter his experiences at the Air Force Base with Peter smiling and laughing in some places. His drink came as he told John he might want to stick to teaching history and not go prying around an Air Force Base.

As they sat sipping their drinks, Peter said, "See the man sitting by himself in the back corner of the bar."

John gazed over his shoulder, saw the man then turned back around.

"Have you seen him in the past few days?" Peter asked.

He thought awhile and looked again. "I don't think so. Why?"

"When I see a person like the man at the table in the rear of the bar, I get suspicious. Since the man and woman at the bar and the two of us are the only ones here, and he was here when I came in, I thought he might be watching you." Peter spoke without once looking in the man's direction.

"You noticed all those signs. Are you always checking out an area?" John was a little in awe.

"My Grandfather and I used to play a game where he would ask me the occupation of strangers in a bar or along a street, then he would approach them and find out. It becomes a habit in my line of business. For example, the lady sitting at the bar sells Mary Kaye Cosmetics and the man talking to her sells pharmaceutical supplies."

John was skeptical of Peter's knowledge, but made no comment.

"Let's find out if he is interested in you. My car is outside. Listen-I'll tell you what I want you to do." Peter gave directions to John, thanked him for the drink and left the bar.

John took some time finishing his drink, paid the bill and walked to the bar and asked the man and woman who they worked for and they both replied as Peter had said. Shaking his head, he went to the front of the hotel and hailed a cab, got in, and the taxi sped off down the street.

In a couple of minutes, he received a call on his cell phone from Peter. All he said was plan B. Plan A was an all clear and John was to take the cab to the restaurant.

John told the cab driver to take him to the Marriott Hotel. When they arrived, he paid the cab driver, walked through the front door into the lobby and exited a side door into the parking area where Peter was waiting. John got in and they drove away down an alley in back of the hotel eluding his pursuers.

"He was following me?" John asked as an expression of concern came across his face.

"They!" Peter replied.

"What do you mean, they?"

"Another man was outside the hotel in a car. When you left, the man in the bar followed you out of the hotel, got in the car with the other man and they drove out after your cab."

John didn't say anything. He was trying to understand the ramifications of what Peter was telling him. Having never been followed before, at least not that he knew, he had no idea why someone would be doing it now. Peter steered the car to the restaurant and by having a table in a secluded part, they could talk without worrying about someone listening, which of course was Peter's idea.

"No one usually cares what I say, especially the students in my Friday history class."

Peter laughed at John's comment saying, "Well, someone thinks what you're saying now and where you are going is extremely important."

Peter had John go over his entire itinerary from the time he flew out of San Francisco until the present. As he conveyed the story to Peter, they had ordered and begun to eat their food. He mentioned his conversation with Colonel Martin and told him the Colonel called Dr. Happard, Happy or Dr. Happy, thinking it might help in his investigation. John also told him David Hanson's name came up in his discussion with the Colonel. He was his boss at Wright part of the time."

John's story and their dinner ended at the same time with John ordering some coffee and Drambuie and Peter opting for only coffee.

"Nothing in your story causes me to think you have done something to step on anyone's toes-," John let out a sigh of relief, but it was premature, "except," Peter continued, "the man at the nursing home who wanted to know why you wanted to see Colonel Martin and the incident at Wright."

"What about those two?"

"Most people in nursing homes are thrilled to death-maybe that's not the way to say it-they are happy to see visitors, any visitors, because they usually get so few. Just to see a different face, whether the person came to see them or not is important to each resident. Yet the man at the reception desk was more interested in why you came to see the Colonel. He could have been told to call someone if any strangers ask to see the Colonel. I'll check into it tomorrow. As far as getting picked up at Wright, they probably have people wander off over there quite often, but we cannot discount the event as a slim possibility for the reason you were followed."

"What am I to do now, if someone is following me?"

"You saw how we eluded them tonight. You can think of ways to evade them if you put your mind to it, Professor!" Peter replied with a sheepish grin.

"Who could it be-who would want to follow me and why? Who would care if I talked to Colonel Martin." John was at a loss to understand his problem. Surely his looking for the artifact would not result in this kind of attention. He might have to re-evaluate the importance and power of the people in control of the cube.

Peter sat looking at him, trying to calculate what John was after or trying to accomplish. In most of his cases Peter would know what the issue was and the details of his clients problems.

"Well, since I don't know what your problem is about or what you are looking into, I can't answer your question," Peter replied sharply, letting John know he was not happy to be left in the dark.

John was not going to tell Peter any more than necessary. Sometime he may find the conditions right to let him in on all the details; not yet.

"Peter, would you be willing to travel?"

"Yes. Remember though, it costs you more money."

"I want you to continue looking for David Hanson and I also want you to find Karen Doddson. She did live in Albuquerque, New Mexico in the 1950's. Go there and see what you can find. Also Colonel Martin remembered another man connected to his work at Wright. His name was Robert White and he was in charge of internal security at the same time Hanson was serving."

"Do you realize these people are probably dead. Even if I find them, there is nothing they can tell you, yet I will leave as soon as I can get a flight. I want to check out the nursing home and I've also hired a receptionist. She is to start in the morning so I'll have to be there to show her the ropes."

John was glad to hear Peter was expanding his office with additional help. "Fine-I'm not sure how much longer I'll stay in Dayton."

"One thing John, if the people following you happen to be government agents, they have many ways to tail you. You may find it tough shaking them and maybe you don't care if they follow you. One thing to consider would be to just let them and not worry about it. I can't advise you because I don't know what you are doing." He again spoke the last with a sharp tone to his voice.

"I'll think about your suggestions."

"I'll get out to New Mexico within a couple of days. I need for you to take a cab back to your hotel. I don't want them to know I'm working for you if I can help it, who ever "them" are, so the less I'm seen with you the better. I know they did see us together in the bar tonight."

"Before you leave, tell me how you knew the occupations of the people in the bar."

"By simply watching what goes on around you. For example, women who sell Mary Kay are often dressed in pink."

"Yes, but the lady in the bar wasn't dressed in pink."

"I saw her in the lobby with someone dressed in pink who I took to be a Mary Kay representative. I deduced she was a new employee going through training."

"She did say she just started working with them. What about the man?"

"I was in the parking lot when he got out of his car and in the back seat were boxes of pharmaceuticals."

"When did you do this?"

"I was here this afternoon on another case."

"My, you do develop a knack. Your grandfather must have been proud of you."

"Before he died, I was getting almost half correct. He told me I was getting better than him."

After Peter left, John paid the bill, and asked for a cab. One came shortly and John was on his way back to the Hotel. He entered the lobby, searching for anyone who looked suspicious. Seeing no one, he went to his room thinking the whole deal was a farce and it may have been coincidence the man left the bar right after him.

When we are away from our home, in a strange place, and sleeping in a different bed, sleep can be an ordeal. The mot juste of having cobwebs in our brain is very apropos. John awoke Wednesday morning in a daze and glancing at the bedside clock gave him a start. He had overslept and would miss his class. Sleeping so hard he thought he was back at his house in Stanford and had classes at the University to teach. Soon the reality of his location came into his cloudy mind and he felt foolish losing his sense of time and place.

John went through the routine of showering, dressing, and eating breakfast in the hotel café. Afterwards, he stopped in the lobby and used his phone card at a pay phone to call Harry. The people following him might try to listen to his phone call so the card came in handy. Forgetting about the time difference between Ohio and California, John woke Harry when he called and he was droggy at first before coming to his sensible self.

"I see you received my message. Thanks for returning my call at what ever the hour." Harry spoke with less enthusiasm than the last time he and John talked.

"Sorry. I forgot the time difference," John said apologizing for the inconvenience. "What did you want to talk to me about?"

"Where are you," Harry asked knowing he must be far away with a time variance.

"I'm in Dayton, Ohio."

"I'm not going to ask why," Harry said as he collected himself to tell John about Carol. "When you were in my office last week asking questions about aliens, had you seen an object or the picture of something that led you to ask the question of me?"

John was hesitant about answering since the first thing entering his mind was somehow Harry had found out about the cube.

Answering carefully, he said, "I'm not sure what you mean?"

"All I want to know is did you find something out recently causing you to ask me about aliens?" Harry pressed him.

"First, before I answer, why are we having this conversation?"

"Since I asked you to call me, I suppose it is only fair for me to explain myself. A few days after you inquired about aliens, I received another visitor with basically the same question. I found the coincidence quite unusual except there was one difference between the two of you. She showed me why she was asking and you did not."

A shiver of excitement ran through John's body. The possibility of another person having some kind of proof the cube existed would be great news and help his search. The individual might have seen the cube in real life.

"What did-you said she-what did she show you?" John fumbled the words out of his mouth, excited by the possibilities.

"No, it's your turn John. Why did you ask me?"

As much as he liked Harry, the temptation to inform him of the alien artifact was not strong enough to overcome his promise to Dr. Cable. "I'm really not able to say at the present time. Information I have come to know led me to ask you about aliens. I'm not sure I can give you any more information because what I know was given to me in strict confidence," John said hoping his explanation would satisfy Harry.

A long pause on the phone followed as Harry was obviously thinking about what John had said. "Well, I may be overstepping my bounds, but a woman had a picture of an unusual object in the solar system. I thought maybe you had seen the same picture causing you to ask me about extra terrestrial life."

Was Harry being serious? He wanted to know some more. "Are you giving me another Unidentified Flying Object hoax? What was in the picture?"

"No. In my opinion the picture is real. It's hard to describe the photo. You would be better off looking at it on your own and establishing its authenticity for yourself."

"Do you have it, the picture?"

"No, the lady who was here has it."

"Who is the woman you're talking about, anyway, and how can I get in touch with her?"

"Her name is Carol Jacobs. She works for the Jet Propulsion Laboratory in Pasadena."

"Do you have a phone number where I can reach her? I definitely would like to talk to her if you think what she has is genuine and not a fake UFO."

"You may have a problem contacting Miss Jacobs. She has disappeared-vanished and no one seems to have any idea where she is at the moment. Monday she left a note on my back door saying she had more pictures of the object and she would be in touch, but I haven't heard from her since."

JPL, pictures, disappeared-the story sounded full of intrigue. "Harry, I'm going to try to get a plane to California today. I'll stop by and talk to you tomorrow if it won't be an inconvenience for you."

"Yes, sure, we'll work out a time after you return. Call me when you get back in town. By the way, what are you doing in Dayton, Ohio? Did aliens land there?" Harry said with a slight chuckle.

"Didn't you hear about the sightings. It was in all the newspapers and on all the news programs," John said with a smile of his own.

After the conversation with Harry, John was anxious to get back home and find Carol Jacobs. If the woman had a picture of the cube, it would be fantastic, yet why did Harry say 'in the solar system' instead of someplace 'here on earth' or something similar? His search for the illusive cube was creating more questions than answers.

He called the airline, getting a ticket for a flight leaving Cincinnati at 4:40 PM today with one stop in Dallas. John went to his room to pack his things. He checked out of the Hotel, got his rental car and drove to Peter's office. On the way he remembered he could be under surveillance. He had forgotten to check if the man in the bar last night was around when he left the Hotel. The excitement of the picture had clouded his mind and he had dropped his guard.

Pulling to the side of the street and stopping, he sat trying to decide what to do. If he drives to Peter's, he would give him away if he were being followed. He decided to by-pass Peters and drive on to Cincinnati. He would call Peter after he returned to California.

John entered the Interstate Highway heading south for Cincinnati where he planned to stop at the library and check into JPL before going to the airport. His mind returned to the picture and the mysterious vanishing lady who has it in her possession.

CHAPTER 11B

The water of the lake cooled the afternoon air as it settled among the shoreline trees and caressed the limbs over-hanging the water. The surface of the lake gave the appearance of a sheet of glass, smooth as silk and uninterrupted by not the least little ripple. Early in the day, Carol walked a hiking path curving around the lake, estimated to be between six and eight miles in length. The trail led up into the hills overlooking the lake, which made it a vigorous hike and she loved the beauty of the open air in Mother Nature's garden. Growing up in Northern California, she had spent many hours on walks in the woods to get away from the noise and hubbub of her family life.

Carol spent the afternoon at a shopping area a short walk from the rental cabin office. She purchased some clothes and other items she needed. It seemed she had started a pattern over the last few days; leave one place with nothing and then have to buy a new set of basics at the next. Fortunately the money she withdrew from her money market account several days ago had become a lifesaver in recent circumstances.

She also gave a lot of thought on how to proceed and again, she considered returning to JPL and accepting the consequences of her actions.

Worrying about Dr. Hillvale and Dana, she was aching to call them, but resisted the temptation. Already feeling bad about the trouble she had brought into their lives, she didn't want to cause them anymore pain. Harry was partly in the dark and keeping all the information from him would have been the more prudent path rather than leaving the note on his door.

Three years before she was married, she had worked on a project with an engineer who was employed by Boeing Space Systems. He had been involved in the design and construction of space probes and rockets for years and the knowledge he had in his field might help her in understanding the picture. Believing he lived in Seattle, Washington, she decided to find him and get his take on the pictures.

Tuesday afternoon she called a rental car company and made arrangements for them to come to the cabin rental office and pick her up. Later in the evening she called directory assistance for a Harold Anker in Seattle. Fortunately they had a listing and phone number for him so she called the number and happily, it turned out to be the same Harold Anker from Boeing who she had worked with in the past.

"Yes, I'm Harold Anker. Who is calling?" He answered to her query.

"I'm Carol Jacobs. We worked together several years ago at JPL." She hoped he remembered.

"Of course. Yes, I remember. How are you?"

"Fine. I hope I'm not intruding?"

"No, of course not. I'm happy to hear from you." He said in a friendly way.

"I'm going to be in the Seattle area in a couple of days and I would like to know if it would be possible for us to meet?"

"I have a better idea. My wife and I have not been out for some time. Why don't we meet for dinner and that way you'll get to meet her too."

"I would enjoy dinner and meeting your wife." Carol was a little disappointed. She would prefer to discuss the picture only with Harold.

"Why don't you give me a call when you arrive and we can confirm the time. When will you be here?"

"I should arrive Friday afternoon so in the evening on Friday would work for me. I also want to solicit your opinion on a picture I have."

"Sure-I'll talk to you Friday," He answered as he ended the call.

Harold and she had worked together on a project and when it was done, they had gone out to dinner a couple of times before he moved to Seattle. He was a nice guy, but just a little spooky in a way she couldn't put into words. Her feelings caused her not to want to become involved with him. He was somewhat of a neat freak, and always wanted everything in order.

Next she called Harry Calvert. After he answered she said, "Harry, Carol here. I want to apologize for any trouble I may have caused you."

Harry replied, "Nothing you have done has created any problem for me. I am much more concerned about your welfare. Are you in a safe place?"

"I am for now. How are Dr. and Mrs. Hillvale?"

"The Hillvales are fine, but they are very worried about you. After the people searched their home and found nothing except your clothes, they left them alone. Dr. Hillvale called the police, but there was nothing they could do since the people invading their home were government agents. Carol, who are these people?

"I'm not sure who they represent," Carol answered.

"The Hillvales told me of the new pictures you have found and I'm anxious to see them."

Carol was so relieved the Hillvales were unharmed and not arrested, but she still considered it dangerous to contact them. "I'm going away for a few days. When I return I'll bring them by to show you."

"I look forward to seeing them. One other thing. You remember I told you someone else had asked about aliens a couple of days prior to your asking. (she responded yes) I have talked to him and he is very interested in talking to you," Harry said in a questioning tone.

"I'm not sure I want to bring anymore people into my ordeal. Everyone I've talked to has had problems. Did you tell him about the pictures?"

"Yes I did. He acted very enthused, but he wouldn't tell me why he was looking into aliens. Did your pictures have anything to do with Dayton, Ohio?"

"No. Why Dayton?"

"The guy who wants to talk to you is in Dayton. He wouldn't say why he was there, but I'm sure it was connected to his search in some way since he lives in California."

The way Harry was relating the story confused Carol. Why would someone be looking for aliens in Dayton, Ohio? "Who is the man you're talking about?"

"Dr. John Kirkwood. He is a professor of History at Stanford."

"Why would he be interested in extra-terrestrial life. Is it a hobby?"

"I'm sure it's not. That's what is so unusual about the whole thing. His hobby is the Incas of Peru. I have no idea why a professor of Pre-Colombian History at Stanford University would suddenly become interested in aliens. Why don't you talk to him?"

"I'll think about it when I return. Thank you for everything Harry. I'll contact you when I get back," She said as she ended the call.

She had packed her meager supplies and the rental car people were at the office the next morning as she had requested.

After the trip to the rental Car Company and paying with cash to hopefully avoid discovery, she was on her way to Seattle. While driving through Northern California where she grew up, she promised herself she would return in the near future to renew old acquaintances and visit past haunts.

She spent the night in Oregon and continued her trip to Seattle. Sight seeing along the way, the next night she stayed south of Seattle, then drove into the city the next day. Checking into a downtown hotel, she had called and made plans to meet Harold and his wife at a restaurant near where she was staying.

Carol took a cab to the restaurant and since she arrived first, decided to be seated at their table. Harold and his wife entered a few minutes after Carol and as they reached the table, Harold greeted her and introduced his wife, Beverly.

She was very attractive with long dark hair. Carol guessed her age to be in the mid-thirties. "Nice to meet you," Carol said.

Beverly eyed Carol's short hair, but made no comment. "It is nice to meet you also. Harold told me you two dated several years ago."

Carol wouldn't call going to dinner twice dating, but she let it drop. "Yes, it was a long time ago. Let me assure you I'm not here trying to steal your husband away. I'm sure you will understand in a little while." Carol spoke with as warm a smile as she could muster.

They sat down at the table, ordered drinks and discussed what had happened to each of their lives in the intervening years.

"You two make a lovely couple." Carol added this to their conversation only for the reason of sucking up to Harold. No reason not to soften him up since she wanted his help.

"Beverly and I have been married for three years, and are quite happy with our life," Harold said and then asked, "What are you doing in Seattle?"

"Actually, I came to see you. Don't you feel honored?"

Harold acted embarrassed before answering. "How can I help you?"

"I have some pictures in my purse. I would like you to look at them and give me your opinion on what you see. They are on computer discs."

"How about after dinner, we return to our home and we can look at them on my computer," Harold said. "Would that be okay?"

"Very much so. We have a plan," Carol said.

The dinner passed pleasantly, Carol informing them of her recent marriage problems and current leave of absence. She did not tell them the trouble she was in by having the copies in her possession. Harold and Beverly shared recent experiences of their marriage and professional life. As the dinner ended, Carol realized she had been missing time with friends and determining what was important to her would be one part of her new beginning.

Driving to their home in the suburbs, they arrived at a large house reminding Carol of the home she and Bob had shared. The three of them went into a room full of papers, diagrams, computers, and other paraphernalia, which Harold explained, was his study where he did a lot of his work. Everything in the room was neat and orderly as Carol expected from her previous experience working with him.

"Is it okay if I look at your pictures too?" asked Beverly.

"Of course," Carol said knowing she didn't have much of a choice.

The first disc was put in the computer and as they waited for the pictures, Carol gave them some background. "The pictures were taken in the Asteroid Belt between Mars and Jupiter by the Talaria probe."

Harold viewed the picture, then inserted the disc Dale had sent from NEAR, and these pictures increased his interest as illustrated by his moving his head closer to the monitor and using his finger to touch some of the objects being displayed. He said nothing as he jotted down some notes on a pad of paper.

134

Finally, he told Carol, "You have some very unusual pictures. If they were taken as you said, in the Asteroid Belt, you have made a major scientific discovery in my opinion."

"Explain to me why you think so, if you would please?" Carol asked. Beverly, looking over his shoulder, also noted her curiosity.

"Okay, here is the picture from Talaria. It shows a long slender orange item and by itself could be anything."

He then brought up one of the pictures from NEAR. It showed a long black object close to an asteroid. "Look at the first picture from NEAR. Again by itself, it could be anything. Here is the next picture from NEAR. The small orange object in it is different, but in no way can we determine its origin. Now the last picture and here is where things begin to connect."

The fourth picture they were now looking at was some kind of structure. It looked like an Eskimo igloo slashed in half. Part of it was reddish-orange and part was black. The edges were jagged where it appeared to have lost some of its parts. It seemed to be put together with a combination of black and orange boxes; some long and slender, others short and fat. Because of the breakage, the items were all in a jumble.

"I believe all four pictures are of the same thing. It appears to be a container or housing for something. It is definitely some kind of structure or should I say 'was' some kind of structure. What it contained or what it was used for is anyone's guess. The material is new to me. It could be a kind of crystalline substance. I know of nothing we have sent into space resembling this kind of material. The damage seems to indicate it was torn apart by some means. The picture does not look like an explosion broke it, but more likely a case of two objects crashing together and breaking apart. Something may have smashed into it and ripped it into pieces," He said as he finished his analysis.

"Are you sure the object we are viewing is not a Russian craft or something secret from the United States?" Carol asked.

Harold scanned the picture on the monitor again. "I know of no technology we or the Russians have to match what is shown in these pictures. Of course I can't positively say the United States or Russia did not put the object into space. I'm not aware of anything looking like the structure ever rocketed into space, at least by the United States. Are these pictures available to the general public?"

Carol knew she would eventually have to deal with the topic. She did not want Harold or Beverly to get involved so she decided to lie.

"The pictures are top secret. JPL is trying to determine their identity and if they are an indication of anything harmful." She told the fib, not very convincingly.

"I would love to make copies and study them if you will allow me to do so. What do you say?"

Carol was afraid to let Harold have copies because she would have no control over how he used them. "I'll tell you what I'll do. I see you have the equipment here in your den. Make me two hard copies of each picture and when I get clearance, I'll mail you one of each."

"First, let's have some coffee while I make the pictures," Harold said.

Carol and Beverly agreed and they went to the kitchen where Beverly made coffee while Harold started making the hard copies of the pictures. Soon, he joined them at an island bar located in the center of the kitchen.

Carol asked, "Harold. Are there any other people I could talk to or show the pictures who might shed more light on the object?"

Harold thought for awhile. "I can think of one person who might help. He has a great deal of knowledge and a keen interest in the composite elements of a material. He would be someone who could help determine the make-up of the material composing the object in the photo."

"What's his name and where can I find him?" Carol said, grateful for the suggestion. If someone could determine the chemical composition, then she would have a better idea if it was man-made.

"The last I knew, he was working at the solar observatory in Sunspot, New Mexico."

"I know a little about the place. I'm not exactly sure where it is located in relation to the State," Carol said.

"It's near Alamogordo, in the mountains east of white sands."

"Do you have any idea what kind of work he is doing at the observatory?"

"I believe he is using the solar telescope to study the composition of the sun," Harold answered.

"Give me his name and I'll give him a call in the next few days. Can I use your name as a reference?"

"Evan Daily is his name. I don't know a whole lot about him. We met when he was doing some consulting work for Boeing and of course, you may say I sent you if you wish."

Harold went to the study to get the disc and the copies for Carol. He had made two copies of each of the four pictures and handed them to her. She insisted on taking a cab back to the hotel even though Harold offered to give her a ride. Hearing the horn of the cab outside their house, Carol thanked them for everything and left the house, sliding into the taxi.

The lights of the city reflected off the taxi's window like the stars scattered across the night sky. Somewhere out in the darkness a strange orange and black object was floating in space and Carol was on her way to discovering its identity.

CHAPTER 12A

The plane chased the yellow rays across the horizon as it soared west into the sunset. After a short layover in Dallas, it had taken off again gaining hours passing over the time zones below. John finished reviewing his notes looking for some connection to the Jet Propulsion Laboratory. No correlation seemed apparent from the data he had collected the past few days.

From what he knew and had looked into at the library in Cincinnati, JPL was an outgrowth of a group of students at California Institute of Technology in 1936. It organized for the purpose of rocket research and was associated with the Army until 1958 when it became part of NASA. Since JPL was connected to the Army in the forties and fifties, John saw a possibility of involvement with the cube, yet it was only his conjecture for the present.

JPL has built and sent space probes to various parts of the solar system. The scientists at JPL monitor and examine the pictures and data sent back from these probes. Harry said she had pictures. Could they show something about the cube? Could there be more than one? John considered it a priority to find and talk to Carol Jacobs.

Landing in San Francisco, John looked for directions to the garage where his Sport Utility Vehicle was located. Finding the right level and section, he was relieved the search took so little time because once in the past he had combed the garage for almost an hour looking for his vehicle. Since that escapade, he had become more conscientious about where he parks his truck.

After checking the exterior for damage, he got in, started it up and exited the garage heading toward Stanford and his house. A pleasant feeling flowed through his body from knowing he was returning to familiar surroundings, as it typically did for anyone coming home.

During his trip back, he had tried to determine if he was being followed. At no point did he see anyone watching him, or see the man in the bar so he concluded it was all a coincidence. John rolled down his window to feel the cool evening breeze flow through his SUV as he drove home.

The next morning was a clear spring day and John looked forward to spending some time outside. The itinerary for the day involved a trip to the University, a call to Harry, and checking in with Dr. Cable and Peter. He planned to see if Harry was in his office at the school before he called him on the phone.

He first put his jogging clothes on and left the condo for a jaunt to the park several blocks away. He had made the trip many times since moving to his present home. The route took him through a housing area, then by some condos, and finally into the park.

After covering two blocks he noticed a blue van behind him creeping down the street which was probably a repairman looking for a particular house and not some fiendish spy following him. He had to quit being so paranoid and seeing danger in every strange occurrence entering his life.

Upon reaching the park he had several choices to continue his run. He chose the path leading through the center of the park where the various paths and trails all fanned out from the central fountain. Several other people were jogging, skate boarding, roller-blading, roller-skating, and just having a good time enjoying the beautiful morning in the park.

As he ran past the fountain, he caught a glimpse of another man jogging behind him. The man looked vaguely familiar and he tried to remember where he had seen the other runner? He shrugged it off until later when he saw the same man again and this time the man was almost exactly the same distance behind him as he was earlier. Normally, the coincidence would not surprise John, but he had stopped once since he saw him at the fountain. Planning to confront the stranger, John turned and started running toward the man. As he approached the other jogger, he was shocked to meet the same man Peter had pointed out in the bar in Dayton.

John stopped and hailed the man. "Don't I know you."

The man did not stop, continued past him, turned, looked at John, and shook his head.

John turned and followed saying, "I'm sure I saw you in a bar in Dayton, Ohio."

John increased his speed coming up along side of him and as he did the man increased his pace also until finally the man slowed down. John could tell the other runner was becoming fatigued. As John's pace matched his again, he said to the man, "I know I saw you in Dayton a couple of days ago. Are you following me?"

The man turned and said, "I was not in Dayton. You have me mixed up with someone else. Now would you leave me alone."

"Tell me why you are following me and I will."

John's ire was beginning to show itself. He considered pursuing it further, but decided not to press his luck and he had no idea if the jogger would try to harm him if he continued to hassle him. Dropping back to a short distance behind the other runner, John stayed close enough to keep him in sight. As they neared a city street, the man veered across a grassy area to a blue van, which John thought, might be the one he noticed before. The van stopped along the curb, the man hopped in and the van sped off down the street.

Stopping and wiping the perspiration from his forehead, John now knew for sure someone was following him. Taking a moment to assess the situation, he was positive no one followed him on his trip from the Hotel in Dayton to his home so they must be tracking him in some other way. He considered the possibility of a bug planted among his clothes or bags. Things were becoming more complicated.

John approached his house as he finished his run and saw Patricia outside planting some flowers in a pot. Patricia, a divorcee with two small children, lived in the house adjacent to his own. Stopping near her, John said, "Hi Patricia, looks like you're into spring planting."

She looked up from her work, not hearing him approach. "Hi John, I haven't seen you around the last few days."

"I've been on a trip, taking some time off. By the way, did you notice anything unusual going on around my house?"

"With my two young children, I hardly know what's going on in my own home. Wait a second. I did see a water company truck parked in front of your home yesterday morning. It was parked there for at least an hour I would say. I don't know if that's what you mean by unusual."

"Thanks for your help, Patricia. I appreciate the information. How are you getting along?" Patricia was young and attractive, but with two small children, had difficulty finding single men.

"Still looking for a good man like you."

"If I see any, I'll send them your way." Patricia had always shown an interest in John even when her husband and she were together.

He entered his house, showered, dressed and left for the University.

When he arrived he stopped by Bill Chaff's office. Bill was the director of security at Stanford University. John had become acquainted with him during an exhibit of some Meso American artifacts two years ago on Stanford's campus. He was a big burly guy with a very kind heart.

"I need some information about surveillance devices and how to determine if you are being spied on," John said.

"One of your old girlfriends on your tail," He replied with a sneering laugh, "or maybe an irate husband." Bill then laughed louder.

John gave a little smile to acknowledge his joke and waited for Bill to calm down. "No, I'm serious. Can you help me?"

Collecting himself, Bill answered, "There is a store on Market Street specializing in paraphernalia involved in surveillance. I can't remember the name. It's near the old mill."

Thanking him, he walked to Harry Calvert's office, which was empty, so he left a note on the office door telling Harry he would stop by later in the day.

John next stopped at his office, which was Cheryl's for the time being. The door was closed so he knocked and heard her voice call out for him to enter.

"Hi Professor Roberts," John said teasingly, seeing Cheryl behind the desk with her glasses on looking at student papers. "How are things going with the classes?"

Cheryl gave him a big smile and said, "I'm doing fine. I understand you have been quite the traveler."

How she knew of his travels was a mystery he decided not to get into. "I've been here and there," He responded to her remark. "I'm glad you're not having any problems and I feel my classes are in good hands. I stopped by to see if I had any calls or messages?"

"Yes, Harry Calvert had called earlier in the week and another man who wouldn't leave a message or his name called yesterday."

Having no way of determining his identity, John thanked her and walked to the faculty lounge. He visited with some of the staff, drank a cup of coffee, and took some ribbing about his leave of absence then walked back to Harry's office, finding him at his desk.

"I see you're hard at work," John said as he walked in the open door to Harry's office.

He looked up from the work on his desk with a sheepish grin. "I could say the same about you since you seem to bounce around all over the place."

"I did learn some things on my trip. Nothing earth shattering though. I wanted to ask about the woman you mentioned on the phone the other day."

Harry pushed the work on his desk away and sat up in his chair. "Yes, Carol Jacobs. I told her I had talked to you. She said she was going out of town for a few days and would contact you when she returned."

Disappointed, John was looking forward to meeting her and possibly seeing the picture she had shown Harry.

"Is she still searching for an answer to the picture you mentioned?"

"As I far as I know she is looking for answers. I don't have a clue whether the trip she is on has anything to do with her quest or not."

"Do you have any suggestions on how I might contact her before she returns?"

"She has a cell phone, but I can't give you the number without her permission. The next time I talk to her I'll ask. She seems to be secretive about her where-a-bouts."

"Thanks Harry for letting me know someone else was interested in aliens. I'll talk to you in a couple of days."

"Are you going to let me in on your secret?" Harry asked feeling left out in the dark by John.

"Not yet; maybe soon," John replied as he walked out the door. Harry was a good friend, but he still wanted to honor Dr. Cable's request for secrecy, at least for the time being.

John left the University after reviewing his notes from his conversation with Bill and headed toward the electronics store he had referred him too. After talking to the owner of the store and examining several devices, he purchased two types of electronic detectors costing almost one thousand dollars. The man said they should trace most bugs used today and while he was at the store, he asked the man to show him how to use it by debugging his SUV.

The owner of the store said, "Sure, since you purchased the equipment here, I'll show you, but it only works if you have a bug on your vehicle. The chances of anyone having a device are very slim. People come here thinking they are under surveillance and when the detectors don't find anything, they think something is wrong with the equipment I sold them."

"Humor me, then." John replied.

He took out the UE-64 detector for hidden transmitters, turned it on and immediately got a hit. He localized it in the front dash area and eventually found it under the dash. He glared at the bugging device then gave John a strange look as he held the bug in his hand.

"You have a very sophisticated microphone and locator. Who ever placed it here is no $10 dollar an hour private dick."

John gave him a questioning stare. "What do you mean?"

"What I'm saying is a bug like the one in your truck is top of the line and very expensive; someone wants you followed real bad."

"Who is after you?" The Owner asked.

John did not answer his question; instead asked him if any other bugs were in his truck. He took the other detector and scanned the vehicle and it came up negative so John thanked him, got in his SUV and drove away.

He went over possibilities of who could be following him as he drove back to his house. It would have to be someone in government. No, it could be a corporation-big business because whoever it is has money. Someone or some group may be protecting the alien artifact from nosy people like John and in some way they found out he was searching for the cube.

As soon as he arrived home, he took the detectors, and using them, scoured over his clothes, furniture, and rooms. What he found shocked him. John came up with six bugs and three small objects that could be some kind of camera. He knew his situation was serious and considered calling the police, yet their help would be limited and cursory at best.

John left his house and drove to a busy intersection near by. Waiting for the light, he moved into the far right lane, then when the left turning arrow became green he crossed in front of the traffic making a left turn. He ignored the honking and drove quickly down a crossing street, turned into an alley, then pulled into a large garage where cars were being repaired. He knew the owner so was not worried about being questioned. He left his vehicle, went to a pay phone across the street, and called Peter's cell phone.

Peter answered, "What's up John?"

"Listen and listen good. I am being followed. I have just found seven bugs and three cameras in my house and SUV. Someone is very serious about knowing where I am," John exclaimed in a very concerned and worried way.

"I told you I was sure someone was following you. The guy at the home where Colonel Martin lives finally coughed up a phone number after some persuasion. He was to call the number if anyone came looking for the Colonel. I'm checking the number now. I hope you are on a safe phone, otherwise they will know I'm working for you."

John now knew how they discovered he was seeking information on the artifact. "I'm on a secure phone so don't worry. I'm not completely incompetent in the spy game."

"How did you find the bugs?" Peter asked.

"I bought two detectors at an electronics store and using them I found the things."

"Stop at a drug store and see if they sell cell phones that you buy over the counter, then call me and leave me your cell number."

"I will buy one right away. What have you got for me?"

"David Hanson is deceased as we thought he might be and Robert White is alive we believe, but we don't know his location yet. The surprising thing about Hanson is he committed suicide the same as Wisner?"

"You're right. That is odd. Peter, where are you now?"

"I have a flight to Albuquerque tonight. We are going to have a problem contacting each other so write this down. Duke 32-35@Scanmail.com. Duke is the last name of my new receptionist."

"What's the 32-35-no, never mind!"

"You're no fun. Anyway, the password is SECRET. I'll send you messages through the Internet. Don't use your computer at home or office. Got it?"

John replied he had it and ended the call.

Next he punched in Dr. Cable's number. Receiving no answer, he walked back across the street and thanked the owner of the garage for letting him park for a few minutes, then drove back to his house.

Picking up the bugs and cameras, he drove to a store in a strip mall and purchased a cell phone and another phone card. On his way out of the store, he tossed all the bugs into the back of a pick-up truck parked near his SUV. That should give them a fun trip he thought. He had a lot to think about and also plan his next steps.

CHAPTER 12B

The knowledge of another life form existing out in the chasms of space could be a mind-altering event. The comprehension of the idea we are not alone creates a different outlook on who we are as an intelligent entity. Carol awoke from her dreams Saturday morning with these thoughts clogging her mind. Even for her, with the knowledge she had, it was hard to fathom the existence of other sapient beings in the Universe. The results of her search would determine whether the picture proved aliens had visited our solar system or it would show somebody here on Earth had been fooling around in space and trying to keep it a secret.

Having completed her morning exercise, she showered, dressed and took the elevator to the Restaurant near the hotel lobby. Picking up a newspaper on the way to breakfast and sitting at a table waiting to place her order, she opened the folded paper to an article concerning the Talaria probe.

The article criticized JPL and NASA and their failure to direct Talaria to its intended target. Inside the article was a quote from Rick Watson pointing out the need to garner as much information from a probe no matter where in the solar system it was located. The statement made what little hair Carol had on the back of her neck stand up because if Rick really meant what he said, the picture causing her problems would be common news and she wouldn't be in hiding.

The man in New Mexico could be a big help if he could determine the composition of the material in the picture. She considered the possibility of going to Sunspot and besides, it might be a safe harbor for her since she doubted anyone would look for her in the mountains of New Mexico. How to get there was the question?

Calling information, she got the number of the Sacramento Peak Observatory and made the call.

"Sacramento Peak Observatory. Benita speaking. May I help you?" The voice said on the other end.

"I would like to speak to an Evan Daily please."

"I don't see a Daily listed. Do you know what building he works in?" She asked.

She expected it to be easier. "No. He is trying to analyze the composition of the sun," Carol replied surprised the observatory would be such big a place.

"I'll put you through to the Dunn Solar Telescope," She said.

The phone rang again and a man answered.

"I wish to speak to Evan Daily, please," She said.

"He's not here on weekends. Call back Monday-." Then the connection was broken.

Damn, Carol said to herself. At least she knows he is at the observatory. Now how to get to New Mexico?

Flying would be the quickest and easiest way to get to Sunspot. You have to show ID's to get on planes now which means they could track her if she used her own.

Robin's passport was going to be a lifesaver. She looked a lot like Robin and any differences could be attributed to Carol's short hair. At least she could try, which was better than driving hundreds of miles in a car.

Finishing breakfast she asked the Hotel's front desk if they could check on flight times to New Mexico. They suggested she call the airlines from her room. Not having a map can be a problem if you wish to get from A to B and B doesn't have an airport. She needed an Internet connection.

She called the front desk, and asked about getting on the Internet. One block from the hotel was an Internet café where she could log on.

Walking to the café and using the Internet, she determined the closest airport was El Paso, Texas. Viewing the schedules, she could leave at 2:40 PM and arrive at 10:50 PM on Frontier or leave at 8:00 pm and arrive at 2:32 am on American West. She should be able to get to the airport, drop off her rental, and buy a ticket long before the 2:40 flight if seats were available. Using Robin's credit card, she booked the 2:40 pm flight.

Stopping at a luggage store on the way back to the hotel, she purchased a carry on bag with wheels, knowing it would be much easier to pack around than her duffel. The cash she had withdrawn before she left Pasadena had been a smart move because she didn't want Robin to have a heart attack when she received her next credit card statement in the mail.

Returning to the hotel, packing her stuff in the new piece of luggage, she checked out of her room and asked for directions to the airport at the desk before leaving in the rental car.

Turning in the car did not take long. It was 12:30 PM. Having over two hours before the Frontier flight departed, she went to the ticket counter where the lady looked at Robin Stewart's passport, then at Carol.

"You look different than your picture," She remarked.

144

Expecting the question, Carol remained calm and she replied to the ticket agent, "I had my hair cut very short as you can see so my picture looks different."

The lady looked at the picture again, then at Carol and said, "Yes, I understand. My husband told me he thought he was going to bed with another woman when I had mine cut short. I must say, I did not have it cut as short as yours." The lady handed her a boarding pass, smiled and Carol left.

Glad to have the ticket out of the way, she walked down a ramp and in doing so saw a man resembling Dr. Hillvale. She felt terrible not calling them so she found a pay phone and dialed their number.

Dr. Hillvale answered and finding out who was calling, gave a sigh of relief.

"Dana and I are so happy to hear from you. We have been concerned about your well being."

"I know. I'm sorry I haven't called sooner. Harry told me you were okay. I'm sure they have your phone tapped so be careful what you say. I can only talk for a short time." Carol knew they could trace her call.

"I understand. The agents treated us fine, but they did search our house. They had a warrant from some Judge but I'm not sure how they obtained one. I have a receipt for all your clothes and personal items they took with them. I think they found us through the package from Dale Belfer."

The statement shot through Carol like a dagger. It would mean they knew Dale sent the package and was the one who had made the copies of the pictures. Becoming so disheartened, she began to feel sick to her stomach thinking they may have Dale in custody.

"I have very little to tell you except I'm safe and still investigating. If I learn any more news, I'll call."

"Fine-take care of yourself and be very, very careful," Dr. Hillvale said.

"I will, and thanks again for all your help," She said as she hung up the receiver.

In less than two hours Carol was aboard the plane and going to Sunspot, New Mexico to talk to a man she wasn't positive would be at the observatory. She felt like someone grasping for straws, not sure of any steps she was taking.

Arriving at the El Paso Airport, she took a cab to a Howard Johnson's and spent the night. In the morning, she would rent a car and leave for Sunspot.

CHAPTER 13

Universities are like a city within a city. They have their own theaters, libraries, sports facilities, recreational activities, cultural centers, and police force. A person could be a part of a University and have very little to do with the community surrounding the campus.

John spent most of the day Friday at the University and then returned during the evening to attend a play at the auditorium. He had always appreciated the activities at Stanford and the play reminded him of the life he was giving up to go on the search for the artifact.

Saturday, he took his morning jog to the park and was constantly scanning the area for the man who followed him Thursday. Seeing nothing suspicious gave him hope they would leave him alone. Knowing his thoughts were probably just wishful thinking, he needed to let Dr. Cable know someone was watching him.

He stopped at the Hagerty Motel along the way home, found a pay phone in the lobby, and using his phone card dialed Dr. Cable's number, and received a response. "It's about time you called me. I thought something must have happened to you," Dr. Cable said in a scolding tone.

"I tried to call you before today. No one answered at the time." Dr. Cable's voice was still weak, but clearer than the last time they spoke.

"How is your effort progressing?"

"I have been busy spending a couple of days in Dayton, Ohio, then returning to Stanford. I have one problem to discuss with you. I think I'm being followed and I'm damn sure my house has been under surveillance."

Silence met John's remark, then he heard Dr. Cable clear his throat before speaking. "Being followed presents new problems. I didn't think they would go as far as what you suggest is happening. Listen to me, John, if you wish to back out of our agreement, I will understand. I can talk to the University about your returning."

Surprised by his offer to let him quit after all of John's effort, there was no way he would give up. "I told you when I took on this challenge, I would follow it wherever it leads. I'm not about to back out now, and who are 'they'?"

"Are you calling from a pay phone?" He asked avoiding giving a response to John's last question.

"Yes. How did you know?"

"My caller ID tells me. You need to be sure when you call me you're on a safe phone. Be careful. Where are you going to be?"

"I think New Mexico," John replied still curious who "they" would be.

"Okay, keep me up to date."

"I will, now who are they-Dr. Cable-Dr. Cable?" John's query was met with complete silence.

Did Dr. Cable know who was following him? His comments did not appear to be on the up and up. The next time they talked, he would delve more into Dr. Cable's knowledge of who was watching him. He also did not get around to asking about his weak voice because Dr. Cable always made their phone conversations short. Leaving the Motel, he continued his jog toward his house.

Dressing in jeans and a T-shirt and using the surveillance detectors, he checked his SUV for bugs. He drove to the same intersection he had used before to evade anyone following him. Staying in the right lane till the light turned to green, then crossing two lanes to turn left. Instead of pulling into the garage, he continued down the street. On the way to Harry Calvert's house, he stopped at a deli for lunch. Finishing lunch and arriving at Harry's, he knocked and as the door opened, he said, "I hope I'm not intruding, Harry."

"Of course not, come in. I have been working in the garden in the backyard and was taking a break. Do you want anything to drink?" Harry asked. "I was getting some ice tea for myself."

He could see Harry's dirty hands as he entered the house. John decided to get right to the point, "No, thanks. I'm not thirsty; I just ate. Could I ask a favor of you? I need to get on the Internet and my computer isn't working?" John told a lie without flinching. The knack of fibbing was becoming second nature. Real spies were no doubt able to trick the lie detector machine.

"Sure, it's in the den. Follow me. You came over here just to use my computer?"

"No, but it does seem like it," John replied smiling.

Harry led John to the computer and showed John how to get to the Internet, then went to the kitchen for ice tea.

John sat before the computer, logged on, then called up the e-mail address Peter had given him. A message was waiting and read: FRIDAY,

FOUND KD, ALAMOGORDA, N.M., COME SOON, APACHE
LODGE, PC

Peter was something else. He couldn't have been in Albuquerque for
more than a couple of days and he had already found Karen Doddson. John
sent one back saying simply: TRY TO BE THERE SUNDAY EVENING,
LEAVE ME A NOTE IF GONE. JK.

Next, John looked at the flights available for tomorrow from San
Francisco to Alamogordo. None were possible for Alamogordo. He could
fly to El Paso leaving at 8:00 am and arriving in El Paso at 1:20 PM. on
America West. He booked the flight by using the credit card from Dr. Cable.

John logged off as Harry returned with his tea; they went out to his
deck in the rear of the house where Harry and Carol had their conversation
days ago. A cool spring breeze blew across the deck making the afternoon
quite pleasant.

"How's the SETI search going?" Harry asked, taking a drink of tea,
then lighting up his pipe.

John knew Harry was using an acronym describing various scientific
research efforts known as the Search for Extra Terrestrial Intelligence. "I
know what SETI means and I actually have taken a couple of days off from
my search. I have had some problems."

"What are your problems- or have you come up with more stuff you
can't tell me?" Harry spoke with disdain, upset for being left out.

John thought about Harry's question. "I see no reason to keep it a
secret. I have been followed, my place has been under surveillance, and I am
at a loss to explain who or why except it could have something to do with
my investigation."

Harry eyed John with an unusual stare. It appeared to be one of confu-
sion and bewilderment as John stared back with puzzlement of his own.
Harry was in a daze looking right through John as if he wasn't there.
Harry's reaction would be normal if one of your friends told you such a
story, yet his look was different in a way John didn't understand. "Harry, are
you all right? You look like you're in a dream. I know having someone follow me is unusual, but you seem to be over-reacting."

"John, I better tell you something. Remember the lady, Carol Jacobs,
whom we discussed the other day?"

"Yes, I remember," John said wondering how she came into the picture.

"She is also being pursued."

Now it was John's turn to stare with eyes wide open. The coincidences
were piling up in regards to the mysterious woman.

"Are you sure?" John asked.

"Yes, positive. Except now they are also trying to apprehend her and I
presume take her into custody, which is more serious than having someone
follow you."

The surprises kept coming. Could the people after her be the same ones stalking him? "Does she know who it is?" John wondered if they would try to arrest him!

"Supposedly, they are people from the Defense Intelligence Agency," Harry answered, speaking with his pipe hanging out of the side of his mouth. Sometimes it was difficult to understand Harry's words when he talked while chewing on it.

"I've never heard of an agency called-what did you say?"

"Defense Intelligence Agency," He repeated, "and neither had she. They showed their credentials to her and also to Dr. Hillvale."

"What does Dr. Hillvale have to do with her. He's in the science department isn't he?" Now another instructor's name was being brought into the conversation.

Harry described to John the incident at the Hillvale's house when the agents came looking for Carol and her conversation with him when she visited. He tried to remember all the details that he was privy to. John listened intently as Harry presented his rendition and when he finished the two men sat for a moment in quiet solitude. John absorbing all he had been told and Harry relaxing from the narrative. Having been talking for over an hour, the late afternoon breeze felt cool on John's skin. So many questions needed answered in regard to the woman Harry and John were discussing.

"I need to get in contact with Ms Jacobs. You can understand things have changed since we both are being pursued."

"When she told me she was going away for a few days, she didn't tell me where." Harry knocked the ashes out his pipe into the flowerpot on the table in front of him.

"How do you contact her?"

"I don't. She calls me, either from a pay phone or on her cell phone."

"Do you know her number?"

"Yes. I told you I promised not to reveal it to anyone," Harry said guardedly.

"You have to give it to me or at least call her and tell her I want to talk to her." John was nearly begging Harry for the number.

"I will if you will tell me why you're looking into extra-terrestrials," Harry said, trying to squeeze information out of John.

Now it was John's turn to be in a dilemma. The promise to Dr. Cable not to tell anyone was creating a hardship yet maybe he could get around it again.

"I will tell you one thing. I am searching for an object which might be supernatural," John said, hoping a little bit of information would appease Harry.

Harry perked up with John's comment. The stories just kept getting better and better. "Now, John, something not of this world. You've got to tell me more. Don't leave me hanging here," Harry pleaded more anxious than ever to know more.

John did not want to say too much to Harry and give away the whole story, yet he desperately wanted to contact the woman. He could see the agony on Harry's face as he waited for John to reply.

"Harry, what I just told you is more than I should have conveyed. I can't tell you any more without putting myself in jeopardy."

"John, John, you have me on pins and needles. Please," Harry begged.

"I'll make another agreement with you. After I talk to the lady, I'll elaborate on my answer to your question. Would you accept those terms?" John said trying to satisfy Harry for the time being.

Harry hung his head down knowing he would relent to John's terms. "All right. I guess. I'll try to get Carol on the phone now," Harry said finishing his glass of ice tea. He went in the house and retrieved his cordless phone, returning to the deck and dialing the number of Carol's cell phone. No answer came so Harry said he would try later.

"I'm going home so I'll give you my cell phone number and you can call me if you make contact. I'm leaving tomorrow for New Mexico and will be out of town for several days. I still want to talk to her."

The traffic was murderous on Saturday night and feeling hungry, John changed his direction, deciding to go to a restaurant to eat instead of home. Only dressed in jeans and a T-shirt, he picked a steakhouse with tables outside on a patio. After dinner, he ordered coffee and Drambuie. John was bewildered by the events of the past week. He had planned on a slow methodical investigation and search for the artifact. Instead, his investigation had been erratic and all over the place, taking on new twists at every juncture. The pre-conceptions of the expedition he had envisioned were becoming misconceptions, yet he was not about to quit. Finishing his drink, he paid his check and left the restaurant.

When John arrived back at his house, something was amiss. Not being able to immediately grasp the difference, he walked through the rooms and checked the closets when it dawned on him. Someone had searched his belongings. Checking his clothes in the closet, they were very close to the way he usually kept them, but not exactly and other items were moved slightly or turned a different way. Trying to recall if things were different the last time he was home, he didn't remember anything out of place, yet someone may have went through his things when they planted the bugs.

The surveillance and the searching of homes required warrants. These people John was sure had none, so how could they be the same group after Carol. Harry said the ones following the Jacobs woman worked for the government. John didn't think they would spy on Americans without authorization of some kind, so he planned to put these questions to the lady if he had the opportunity. He decided not to wait so he called Peter and asked him.

Picking up the phone, he stepped out on to the patio and moved over between the wall and shrubbery, not wanting to take any chances on some-one over-hearing his conversation.

"Peter, this is John. I have a question. Can the Government search your house without a warrant?"

"John-John-where have you been. The Patriot Act allows the Government to use what they nicknamed 'sneak and peek'.

"What does 'sneak and peek' mean?"

"They can break into your house and take property or other items and they don't have to tell you right away. So you may think your house was robbed when in reality the Government broke in and took the items. They may not tell you for months that they have your property."

"Your joking aren't you?"

"Sorry John, no I'm not. It's the way to combat terrorism."

"It's a way to loose your constitutional rights in my opinion."

"Well call your congressman. It passed. Anything else I can do for you?"

"No, thanks Peter." The call was then ended.

Things had changed since nine-eleven. John had no idea how much and after having his home violated, the new power of the Government scared him.

After going to bed and sleeping for two hours, his cell phone rang. Sitting up in bed and turning the lights on, he attempted to get his wits about him.

He answered, receiving a reply from Harry.

"John, are you awake?" Harry asked.

John stepped out on the patio. "I am now. I'm hoping you made con-tact with Carol Jacobs."

"Yes. I want to ask you something. You said you were leaving for a few days. Where did you say you were going?"

"New Mexico, my plane leaves in the morning. Now what about the woman?"

"Where in New Mexico?"

"Why do you have to know?" Why would Harry call to ask about his destination?

"I just need to know."

Having no idea why this was so important, he reluctantly gave him an answer. "Alamogordo."

John waited and hearing no reply, eventually asked, "Harry, are you still there?"

"Sorry. I was looking at my atlas trying to locate Alamogordo."

"Come on Harry. Who cares where it is! Tell me if you made contact." John's frustration grew by leaps and bounds with Harry's delays.

"You're not going to believe what I'm about to tell you so get a grip on yourself. Carol Jacobs, the woman I've been talking about will be 40 miles from Alamogordo tomorrow."

Now it was John's turn to delay a reply. He was shocked. Every time the woman's name was mentioned, he was astonished to learn of another aspect they had in common. It was uncanny and scary at the same time. He asked Peter, "You're pulling my leg, aren't you?"

"I just talked to her and she is in El Paso, Texas. Now are you going to tell me what's in New Mexico because she wouldn't?" Harry's frustration was also building to a crescendo.

"Give me her number. I want to call her." Hearing no reply, John said, "Come on Harry."

"Oh, all right. I'll tell you, but I'm to be the first to know what you two find and I want you to keep in contact with me while your gone," Harry said full of questions and about to burst.

"I will Harry, now the number please."

"I'll give it to you because she said it would be okay."

John was sorry he had to deny Harry the whole story. The number was passed to John and he immediately punched it in his phone. No one answered right away, and then he heard a feminine "hello".

"Hello, I'm John Kirkwood, a friend of Harry Calverts. I have been trying to get in touch with you for a couple of days."

"Yes, I know-Harry told me. Why do you want to talk to me?" She said with little enthusiasm.

The sound of her voice did not lend itself to him having a willing partner at the other end. "It is my understanding you and I may be on a search for the same thing."

"Harry told me a little bit about you and your efforts. I seriously doubt we are looking for the same answers or talking about the same thing."

Not wanting the effort to dissipate away, he asked, "Would you be agreeable to meet tomorrow? I will be in Alamogordo tomorrow afternoon. It may be beneficial for both of us."

"Why are you coming to Alamogordo?"

"I could ask you the same question."

"Okay. Even though there is the smallest chance our goals are related, it would not hurt for us to meet. Harry said you were being followed so are you going to be able to get here without being tailed?"

"I have some plans to foil anyone spying on me. By the way, who are these people and how do they get by without warrants?"

"I don't know. You're asking the wrong person."

The reply seemed abrupt to him. "Anyway, I'm going to be staying at the Apache Lodge in Alamogordo. Could you meet me in the lobby around 5:00 PM tomorrow evening."

"I'll be there. How will I know you?" She asked.

Trying to think of a good description, he finally said, " I'm six foot one, one hundred eighty pounds, dark hair, and will have a San Francisco Giants hat on. How will I know you?"

"I will be the woman with brown hair cut so short I may look like a man."

Thinking this was a strange way to describe oneself, he said, "Fine, I'll see you tomorrow."

Looks like a man. What kind of woman is this Carol Jacobs? It sounds like she might be a touch on the weird side.

Of all the places she could be or John could be, they wind up in not only the same State, but also the same area of the State. Amazing! He went back to bed staring at the ceiling attempting to think of reasons why she would be in New Mexico. None coming to mind, he turned over, still curious about the mysterious woman.

CHAPTER 14

New Mexico is described in the State brochures as the Land of Enchantment, yet the area around Alamogordo is mostly brown desert. To the West is the area known as White Sands, a desert of white gypsum particles glowing in the noon time sun. The City lay in the Tularosa Valley in between the San Andres Mountains to the West and the Sacramento Mountains to the East.

Two people in two different places were viewing the scene from dissimilar perspectives. In her rental car, Carol Jacobs was scanning the horizon from ground level while John Kirkwood was surveying the area from twenty thousand feet in the air. Neither knew the others eyes were, at the same time, observing the same scenery, only that they had a rendezvous in approximately five hours.

Driving into Alamogordo, Carol found the Apache Lodge, which from the outside appeared to be a nice Inn. With a name like Apache, it would have to be a place with southwestern flavor. She had decided to stay at the Inn so after checking in and putting her bag in her room, she left the lodge and drove East on Highway 82 toward Cloudcroft, a small tourist town eighteen miles away. The information at the New Mexico Welcome Center had shown the town to be full of small shops containing items with a western flair. She planned to spend a couple of hours browsing before returning to Alamogordo.

All during Carol's activities, John was descending into El Paso, renting a car, and driving to Alamogordo. He planned to meet Peter at four o'clock at the Apache Lodge prior to his appointment with Carol Jacobs. After his phone conversation with her, John was not expecting much of an outcome. Harry had given him very little information about her background, and from his conversation with the lady on the phone, he was not impressed.

The trip from the airport took a couple of hours putting him in Alamogordo at 3:30 PM. Arriving at the Apache Lodge, he checked in and looked around the hotel. The Lodge was a three-story building with the office-lobby area in the middle. Behind the lobby was a restaurant and bar with doors leading from the bar outside to a patio and pool. If you pictured a hotel in the Southwest, Apache Lodge would fit the mold to a tee. Totem poles, arrows, tomahawks, pictures of horses, Indians and cliff dwellings, and other items hanging on the walls or standing in corners were dispersed throughout the Inn.

Putting his stuff in his room and using his cell phone to call the front desk, John asked for Peter Cozid. The desk connected him to Peter's room. No one answered so he left the room to look around the Lodge.

After walking around the pool, through the patio and into the lobby, he asked at the desk if there were any messages for him. Having none, he entered the bar and spotted Peter sitting on a stool having a drink. Working his way through the tables toward the bar area, he started to approach Peter, thought better, and walked to the opposite end of the bar.

He said to the Bartender, "Could I have a beer and would it be all right if I take it out to the patio area beside the pool?"

"I'll have to put it in a plastic cup. What kind of beer would you like?" the bartender asked in English with a Mexican accent.

"I'll have a Miller Lite," He glanced at Peter making eye contact in the process.

Peter acknowledged with a nod to John. "Put mine in a plastic cup too. I think I'll go out by the pool and see if any good looking women are sunning themselves," Peter said as the bartender was pouring John's beer into a cup.

Paying for his beer, John moved through a set of glass doors to the pool area. After walking outside the bar and next to the pool, he sat at a table with an umbrella providing shade. The patio was located between the bar and the pool. Peter followed setting at a table next to John's.

Music was playing in the background and three young children were frolicking in the opposite end of the pool. Two women were lying on lounge chairs watching the children. A teenage boy and girl were laughing and kissing in the corner of the pool nearest John.

"I'm glad you didn't come running up to me in the bar. You're beginning to learn. You may make a Secret Agent yet." Peter reveled in John's efforts as he kept his eyes focused forward toward the pool.

"Since my search turned into something out of a spy novel, I have been more cautious." He also did not look at Peter while they were talking. The music would block the sound from anyone listening so they both assumed their conversation would be private.

"So you found Karen Doddson, and very quick. How do you do it?" John asked amazed Peter located her after only a couple of days.

"I'm good. I know where to look and I'm lucky. I play with dates, addresses, names, and ideas on the Internet and on my computer," Peter said with a hint of self-praise in his voice.

"How did you find her?" John asked as he glanced out of the corner of his eye at Peter.

"She doesn't go by Karen Doddson and the best I can tell hasn't for 50 years."

"You must have been lucky. What can you tell me about-what's her name now?"

"Happy Valsen," Peter said with a smile on his face. "Think about the name."

The name had already struck John the instant Peter spoke it. It reminded him of something. What was it he asked himself? The Happy part, yes of course. Colonel Martin had referred to Dr. Happard as Happy and the Valsen-Senval. John had told Peter about the Happy nickname when they talked in Dayton and it had come in handy.

"I get the connection. Obviously you did too." John took another quick glance at a young man with an unusual ability to find people and solve problems. His grandfather did an excellent job teaching him to be an investigator and it appeared he had honed his skills to a high degree.

"How about those apples?" Peter was definitely patting himself on the back.

"All right, fill me in? And yes, I am impressed." John gave him his due.

"Karen Doddson or Happy Valsen has been living here for the last twenty years. From what I have found, she is a recluse. The people around consider her touched-using an Indian expression. In other words, crazy. I'm not sure why you want to talk to her, but here she is!"

"Where? Here in Alamogordo?"

"You noticed the hills to the East of town. Some homes are perched on the side of these hills and she lives in one at 4300 Thunder Road."

"I'll go see her tomorrow. I'm meeting someone here this evening at 5:00 o'clock. A Carol Jacobs."

"Oh, having a little tryst while you're here?" Peter teased enjoying getting a jab in at the forty-four year old bachelor.

Sometimes, the way Peter talked, you would never believe he had talent of any kind. "No, I've never met the woman. She says she looks like a boy, so I'm not expecting much. I want you to keep an eye on her while she is in the area. The reason for her visit to the Alamogordo area is a mystery I'm interested in solving. Also check into her background and see what info you can find out about her life. My room is 219. What's yours?"

"I'm in 108. Avoid coming to my room in all cases. I still don't want anyone to know I have anything to do with you and unless they made a connection between us in the bar in Dayton, I should be clean. You were no doubt followed here so I'll keep an eye out for you also. Are you going to let me in on what you're doing?"

John knew Peter deserved to be told since he had done so much of the legwork, yet John was still hesitant. "Soon, hopefully very soon. I think I'm getting close especially if Karen Doddson pans out."

"Let me leave first-you stay and have another beer."

"Before you go, did you check on the phone number from the man at Colonel Martin's Nursing Home."

"Yes, I did. The number was no longer in service. Someone works very fast. Sorry it was no help." Peter got up and walked across the pool area into the Lodge.

The dry air and the cold beer soothed John's psychic as he looked froward to obtaining new information today and tomorrow. A feeling of euphoria flowed through his body as he lay back in his chair, enjoying the moment.

Checking his watch, it was one half-hour till he was to meet Carol Jacobs so he finished his second beer and went to his room where he changed into jeans, T-shirt, and tennis shoes. Searching for his Giants ball cap in preparation for the meeting, he again wondered what kind of woman was he about to meet.

Two hours of visiting the shops in Cloudcroft was enough shopping to do her for awhile. It turned out to be a cute little town located up in the mountains to the East of Alamogordo. It had one long main street lined with small shops and eating establishments.

After Purchasing an Indian Blanket, a white summer dress, and a beaded necklace, she drove down the mountain toward Alamogordo. Nearing the bottom of the mountain, off in the distance she could see the shine from the white sands. The glow produced was in such stark contrast to the brown desert that the white sand seemed like something alien. Carol thought there might be something to the phrase "Land of Enchantment" used to describe New Mexico.

Contemplating the meeting coming up with John Kirkwood, she almost wished she had declined. He no doubt was some four-eyed pipe smoking fat professor off on some wild goose chase and having no leads to follow, ran into Harry who told him about her picture. She would meet him, talk for a little bit, and that would be the end of the story.

Driving into the parking lot in front of the Apache Lodge, she was right on time. Entering the lobby, she saw no one, so she walked over to one of the chairs in the lobby area and sat down. Looking across the lobby into a stairway, a man was hopping down the stairs two to three at a time. Carol stared at him thinking he was very good looking. When he reached the bottom, she decerned a baseball cap on top of his head. Surely, he couldn't be the professor from Stanford. Not being able to read what was on his cap, she tried to remember the San Francisco Giants colors. Could it be orange and black-she wasn't sure, but the man was walking her way. As he neared, she could see the letters 'SF' on the cap. He was definitely not the kind of person she expected.

Running late, John bounded down the stairs to the lobby. Scanning the room, he saw only one person sitting there. From the bottom of the stairs he could not tell if it was a man or a woman so he moved closer and then realized the person was a woman with extremely short brown hair. As he approached she stood and gave what looked like a halfhearted smile. Why had she cut her hair so close, but even with the short hair she was very attractive, not what he expected.

Having noticed the wedding band, he said, "Mrs. Jacobs, I'm John Kirkwood. I apologize for being late." John gave her the once over as he moved closer.

Carol extended her hand, upset with herself because she still had her wedding ring on. She meant to take it off-just never got around to it. Damn, why hadn't she taken care of that small chore?

"Hello, and please call me Carol," She said as she shook his hand and took in a better picture of the man-John Kirkwood.

"Fine, and I'm John."

"Agreed."

"A bar is located down the hall. Would you like to have a drink while we talk?" John asked as he measured her presence. She was tall for a woman and that combined with the short hair gave her the appearance of a man. Her loose fitting clothes allowed her to keep her figure hidden from view.

"Sure. Why not," She replied.

John directed her down the hall and they moved toward the bar. As they did he said, "You said your hair was short and you weren't kidding. I imagine it's very easy to take care of when it's cut that close." He was trying not to make too much of an issue of her hair and doing a very poor job of it. It was the one major characteristic anyone would notice when looking at her for the first time.

"Yes," She replied with a quizzical look. Why is he making such an issue of her hair? He acts like he has never seen a woman with short hair-well maybe he hasn't seen one cut as close as hers!

They entered the bar and picked out a table in the rear of the room away from other people. Many more patrons were in the bar compared to earlier when John and Peter were here drinking. A waitress came over and took their order. Carol opted for a glass of Merlot and John asked for beer.

"Now, where to begin," John said.

"Since you asked for the meeting, the ball is in your court," She responded noticing a little bit of hesitation in his voice. Could he be nervous? She must be mistaken since the man was a college professor at one of the most prestigious institutions in the United States. Having meetings with strangers would not be something new to him.

"Mrs. Ja-Carol, from my friend, Harry, I learned you were asking similar questions concerning extra-terrestrials as I have been asking. He told me you had pictures of an object taken somewhere in the solar system. I'd like to see the pictures." John was very blunt in his request.

Carol stared at him with penetrating eyes. "I don't even know you. Why would I show you the picture? How do I know your not a Government Agent, and besides, what's your story?"

He told himself to back up and slow down before he lost all hope of viewing the picture. The woman had a lot of spunk, which was not apparent from their previous conversation. John decided a change of approach was sorely needed if he wanted to keep open the chance of seeing the pictures.

"Let's start over." He said with a frown on his face. "First I'll tell you about myself, then you can relate some of your history. Will you agree to share your experiences and maybe we can get off to a better start?"

"I can agree to share," She replied, not happy with his demeanor. She interpreted his request as almost a demand and she had enough demands put on her over the last few days.

"Good, I'll begin. I am a professor of Pre-Columbian History at Stanford. I grew up in the Chicago area and attended the University of Illinois. I do a lot of research into the Indians of Latin and South America especially the Incas of Peru.

Both my parents are deceased. I am an only child and have never been married. I live in the Stanford area and am currently on Sabbatical Leave," John said speaking rather quickly. He felt nervous, but did not know why.

Never been married she thought-how odd. A man of his good looks and intelligence would obviously be a good catch for all the manhunters. A flaw must exist in his character, which keeps him from tying the knot, or maybe he has a dark side hidden under his manly exterior. "Have you traveled to Peru?" She asked.

"Many times. All were on archeological trips to investigate the Inca culture. Now how about you?"

"I grew up in Northern California and was the oldest of seven children. My mother died when I was thirteen so I became the mother to my siblings. I attended Stanford, getting a degree in Computer Science and Geology, and have worked for JPL for the last eighteen years. My work involves the pictures sent back from the space probes. Currently I am separated from my husband and I am in the process of getting a divorce. We have no children. I am presently on leave from JPL."

He suspected her family did not have much money with seven children. She must have been able to attend Stanford on scholarships, which meant she had an extremely intelligent mind behind those blue eyes. "What kind of leave?" He asked.

"I'll tell you later maybe." She did not want him to know how much trouble she might have to deal with in the near future.

Things were going a little better in John's way of thinking and his confidence was returning. The waitress returned with their drinks. John picked up his glass holding it in the air, and he said, "Shall we toast to something."

Carol responded by picking up her glass of wine and saying, "How about to the aliens." They both smiled as they clinked their glasses and sipped their drinks.

Now he would try to get back to the purpose of the meeting. "Harry is a friend of mine and he is always looking into the possibility of extra-terrestrials. When I recently sought out his advice concerning aliens visiting our planet, and then later you asked of him similar questions, we both considered it a strange coincidence. The reason I'm here is I told Harry I would like to meet you and look at your pictures." John now hoped to get a better response.

If this guy thinks he can just waltz in here, tell me what he wants and get it, he is very mistaken. "Before I do anything. I would like to know a few things about your inquiry, since you seem to know so much about mine."

"I suspected you would ask, but I can't tell anyone what I'm looking into. You see-," John was interrupted by Carol.

"Then we have nothing to talk about," She said as she got up and walked toward the door of the bar.

Caught off guard, John sat for a moment, then jumped up and followed her. "Mrs. Jacobs, wait." She slowed down looking over her shoulder at him. "Maybe if I can explain why I can't tell, you might understand." He stared into her eyes giving her a puppy dog look.

Carol just stared at him holding back a grin. She enjoyed seeing him squirm.

Receiving no verbal response from her, John spoke to her nervously. "I am here alone so maybe if you like-I mean would you be interested in having dinner this evening?" Damn, he thought, why was he so nervous?

Realizing she was attracted to the man and not wanting to give her feelings away, she delayed responding. After making him wait, she answered, "Okay, I'll meet you here in the bar in two hours," making the decision where and when they would meet.

"Good! I'll see you in two hours," John said and returned to pay for the drinks.

Carol Jacobs appeared to be a hard case and it may take some time to talk her into letting him see the pictures. He had no intention of going down without a fight.

Carol walked toward her room, number 312, thinking John Kirkwood must be used to getting what he wants. We will just see about that she mumbled to herself.

CHAPTER 15

When objects collide in space, one or both are shattered into pieces and the parts are scattered everywhere or the two objects simply knock each other off course. When two immovable objects collide, the results are not as easy to describe. The latter may be the case when John meets Carol for dinner tonight.

He had jeans and a T-shirt on and now he was changing into slacks and a shirt. In the back of his mind, he wanted to look good. Her immutability and resoluteness was refreshing when compared to his recent female contacts. They had been conciliatory and acquiescent in their relationship to him, which caused him to quickly lose interest. Carol Jacobs had a way about her; he just didn't know yet if it was good or bad.

In another room at the Lodge, Carol had unpacked and walked down to the pool before returning to get ready for dinner. John Kirkwood may think he can pull the wool over her eyes, but he better think twice before he goes too far. She decided to wear the white dress and beaded necklace she purchased at Cloudcroft earlier in the day.

As John was preparing to leave, his cell phone rang and Peter was on the line.

"You were right. The lady does look like a man, otherwise she's not bad," Peter teased.

"Would you give me a break. I don't need your commentary and I don't need you spying on me," John replied to Peter's joking around.

"I told you I'd watch your back and you told me to keep an eye on her so I did. What's the matter? The lady getting under your skin?"

"It's not my skin I'm worried about. Have you found anything?"

"I see no evidence you or the lady are being followed. I will continue to keep my eyes open and my mind alert. Also the Lady is suspended from her job. I don't know why, but I'll keep searching for the reason."

"Good, we're having dinner tonight. Where is a nice place to eat?"

"I see your moving right along. I've only been here a couple of days, but I would recommend the Santa Fe Trail. It's a western type place with good steaks and I understand the other food is good too."

"Thanks, I guess?" John said. Peter gave him directions to the restaurant, then hung up.

So she was suspended he repeated to himself. He was anxious to find out why and from what little he knew about her, he doubted it would be nick and pick stuff.

Leaving his room, he entered the bar expecting to find Carol waiting. Not seeing her in the bar, he discovered it was his turn to bide his time. He started to order a drink then thought better since they would more than likely get one at the restaurant.

Remaining in her room, she was determined to be later than John in getting to the bar. She called the bar asking the bartender if a man fitting John's description was in the room. Receiving a positive response from the bartender, she walked to the bar to meet him. On the way she thought she might be playing too many games with him, or acting like a high school girl, then told herself, no, he deserves it!

Sitting at a table with a view of the door, John spied Carol entering the room. He couldn't miss her with the short brown hair, but it wasn't the hair that had his attention. The white dress accented her slim body and the light coming into the darkened bar from the hallway behind her gave an angelic appearance to her movement. The dress was tight at the waist flowing to just below the knees: what he presumed would be called a sundress. Shaking his head, he told himself to keep his mind on the business at hand, then stood and greeted Carol.

"The short hair may give the impression of a man, but the dress leaves no doubt what you are," John said realizing it didn't come out the way he intended.

"Thank you I guess," Carol said hoping he doesn't think I'm wearing the dress because of him even though she was. She noticed he had changed into dressier clothes as well.

"Where are we going to eat?" She asked feeling uncomfortable standing in the middle of the bar room.

"The Santa Fe Trail was recommended. Would it be alright with you?"

"Sounds like a hoot'n-toot'n place," She quipped with a quizzical look on her face.

Thinking she was disappointed in the choice, He said, "If the restaurant doesn't sound appealing, we can look for another."

"No, it will be okay." With this remark, she turned and walked out of the bar with John close behind.

John drove his rental car to the restaurant which was a large building shaped like a barn with seating in the front and a loft above overlooking a huge dance floor with a small stage at one end. The interior was made up of wooden beams, wooden floors, and constoga wagon wheels hanging on most of the walls. Peter had omitted a great deal when he told John about the restaurant.

Having their choice of eating downstairs or upstairs, they both chose the loft. After being seated next to the railing overlooking the floor below and ordering drinks, they buried their heads in the menu.

"We must be in cattle country. I see steak is the main item." John repeated what Peter had said earlier.

"It appears to be. As they say, when in Rome," Carol said with a grin.

John and Carol ordered steaks and sipped their drinks; both having chose a margarita.

"It must be exciting-being involved in the space program, getting to plan and analyze the missions. Are you involved from the ground up or just when pictures are sent back?"

"I'm not fortunate enough to do much of the planning or analyzing. I am involved from the beginning, but more in the technical end. I deal with the equipment taking the pictures and transmitting them back to earth."

John got the hint of a little bitterness in her statement from the tone of her voice. He sensed she probably felt more qualified than some of the people in her area.

"So what do you do when you're not teaching Pre-Colombian History?"

"The archeological expeditions, especially to Peru, take up most of my summers. I jog on a regular basis. My schedule has been hectic lately, so I haven't been able to do many of the things I like."

"Yes, mine too. In the expedition you referred to, have you made any big discoveries?" She was truly curious about his escapades. Searching in ancient ruins sounded exciting to her.

"I'm sad to say no. I have made some, but I wouldn't consider them big. I did write a book on the Incas, which was well received. How about your extra time? What do you do in your spare time?"

"I enjoy tennis. I read a lot. I swim some since Bob and I have a pool or had a pool." Not wanting to mention her marriage, she found it difficult to keep it out of the discussion.

John was surprised how easy the conversation was going. Trying to be aloof, he was now finding her to be a very intelligent dinner companion and his petty games were unnecessary. He had not felt so comfortable with someone in a long time. Her responses interested him and he genuinely valued her opinions. The conversation continued covering many topics. The steaks came and they ate their meal as they talked.

The evening was not going as she thought it would. She expected him to be a little snotty and pushy. She was in fact enjoying the evening and feeling at ease with the Dr. John Kirkwood she just met.

"Why are you getting a divorce, or is the question too personal?" John inquired wishing he hadn't asked after the words came out of his mouth. The more interested he became the more personal the questions would normally become.

Jolted by his question, she at first started to fire back at him for his nosey question, then changed her mind. "I usually don't discuss my personal life, but I'll make an exception in this case. Bob and I were never made for each other. I thought we were when we first got married. For one thing, our lives are too busy to spend much time together and neither of us wanted to give up our career. It just didn't work out."

Enamored by her openness, he pushed some more. "Those are excuses, not reasons. What is the real reason?"

Why is he pressing me on this-she thought to herself? She should tell him to mind his own business and why is he so interested in my marriage. "What do you mean?" She asked.

"Why did you get married? In any relationship, a basic reason for staying together is always underlying the union if you will admit it."

She should tell him to take his-no-why did she get married? She thought for a moment about her feelings for Bob before responding.

"I was 35 and I guess I thought I should. My brothers and sisters, who are all married now, used to tease me about being an old maid. I never realized—-." She was now in her own thoughts being honest to herself. She likes Bob. Now she wasn't sure if she ever did love him the way a woman should love her husband. Maybe he just came along at the right time or the wrong time depending how you look at it."

Coming back to reality and a little embarrassed, she said, "I'm sorry. I was off in my own world. What about you? Never married?" She would put the question back in his corner and let him talk about his personal life.

"I never really fell completely in love with anyone. I would think I was in love, then when it got down to the nitty-gritty and I spent some time with her, I discovered she was not the person I wanted to be with the rest of my life." He was being open and honest with Carol.

"How many "shes" have there been?" She said with a cutesy grin.

"We won't get into that, but the way you look, I would imagine not any more than the " hes" you had before you were married," John said admiring her inherent beauty once again.

Carol saw a look of admiration in John's face as he spoke the last words. She became a little red-faced with his last comment and decided to make no reply.

"So are you going to tell me how you got on the trail of the aliens?" She asked starting to become uncomfortable with the direction the conversation was taking, not planning for it to become so personal so quickly with someone she just met.

164

"I can explain why I can't tell you," John said, but was tempted to let her in on the entire story.

"Tell me something!"

Okay, here goes he thought to himself. "I received information from a man who made me promise never to tell anyone what he had told me. It is that simple. I understand how you feel since I'm asking you to reveal your information to me and denying you mine."

As he finished, music began to play and a man and woman came out onto the stage below. Using a microphone, the woman asked everyone to come out on the dance floor and learn a new line dance. Sunday night must be a special time to get out and party here in Alamogordo.

John and Carol finished their meal as the instructions for the line dance began. They watched as 25 to 30 people lined up to learn the new dance. The man on stage spoke into the microphone and called for more people to try their hand at a new dance.

John looked at Carol with a questioning grin and a twitch of the head. She knew what he was asking without speaking.

"Why not." She said as she slid her chair away from the table.

Making their way down the stairs to the floor, they fell in line with the other people. The man talked them through the dance steps the woman on stage demonstrated the correct moves.

John and Carol tried to follow along, Carol doing a much better job than him. The leaders walked them through the dance once more, then put it to music and they did the line dance to the song coming from the large speakers on the stage.

When they finished, John and Carol were laughing having bumped into each other several times when one of them made the wrong move. They came up to each other at the end where a hug would have been appropriate and looking at one another backed away-the moment becoming awkward just as the conversation had earlier.

Going through one more line dance, they had just as much fun as they did on the first dance. They were smiling, laughing, and enjoying themselves. Returning to the table, they paid their check and left for the car.

On the way back to the Lodge, Carol said, "That was fun, I can't remember the last time I was out dancing."

"Neither can I. I should go out dancing more often."

The rest of the trip to their hotel was quiet, both evaluating the evening with respect to what they had anticipated and how it actually turned out. The evening had not been what either expected.

John finally broke the silence. "I'm going to see a woman tomorrow who may help me in my search. Would you be interested in going along? You might learn a little about why I'm investigating aliens."

"Yes, I would, but before you visit her, you have to go with me to see someone."

"Does it have to do with the picture?"

"Yes," She replied as they drove down the street. She found herself staring at him in the faint light from the street. Why did this man come into her life now? It was so sudden after her decision to end her marriage. How would she have reacted if she were still living with Bob? Most aptly, she would have denied her feelings.

As they neared the Lodge, feeling her eyes on him, John wondered what she was thinking.

Pulling into the parking lot at the Lodge, they got out of the car and walked toward the door to the lobby. He suggested they meet at eight in the morning here in the lobby and she agreed.

"Thanks for a nice evening," Carol said, a little disappointed it was ending. She had not enjoyed a night like this for-well she didn't know how long.

"You're welcome and thank you too. I also had a good time," John said.

The moment was again becoming awkward. Finally Carol said good night and left for her room. John watched her walk away thinking to himself how unusual a woman had just come into his life. Until he was sure her efforts would not conflict with his, he needed to keep the relationship on a professional level. She was in any case, an interesting woman who definitely had his attention.

CHAPTER 16

The turquoise accents in the lobby of the Apache Lodge along with the totem pole left no doubt you were in Indian Country. To the northeast of Alamogordo was the large Mescalero Apache Indian Reservation. The landscape was full of contrasts, with brown and tan desert in one area, white sands in another, and green pine forests in the hills and mountains.

Returning from his morning jog carrying coffee and an egg sandwich, John entered the lobby and headed for his room. He had rolled out of bed earlier feeling better than he had in a long time, in part do to the memories of last night, which gave him good sensations.

Juggling the coffee, sandwich, and keys, he finally succeeded in opening the door to his room and found the message light flashing. Putting his breakfast down, he picked up the receiver and punched the message button. It was from Peter and all it said was 'call PC'.

Walking over to the table by the window, he picked up his cell phone and dialed Peter's cell number. He answered after a long series of rings.

"Peter, I'm returning your call. What did you want?"

"How was your night. Get much sleep," Peter teased.

"Get to the point, I'm running late." John said becoming frustrated with Peter's ribbing.

"Your Carol Jacobs was put on leave pending an investigation. It sounds like the lady is in trouble. Rumor has it she has an arrest warrant out for her regarding stolen property or something. She may not be the person she represents herself to be."

John didn't answer right away. He was listening to every word. The thought of Carol being a fugitive on the run didn't exactly fit, unless he was a terrible judge of character. Harry had told him the people following Carol were trying to apprehend her. There appears to be more to the lady than meets the eye. John's thoughts slowly came back to his phone call. "Do you have anything else?"

"I have not forgotten Robert White-will get back to you regarding him. What's your plan for today? You and the Lady going on a picnic?"

Peter was starting to get on John's nerves. He would have a talk with him soon. "We're meeting at eight in the lobby. We are going to see someone she's here to meet, and then I'll take her with me to Karen Doddson's."

"Be careful," Peter said as he hung up.

Waking with a nice feeling, Carol stretched her legs and arms much like a dog would do lying by the fireplace getting up from his nap. She felt last night was one of the better times she had spent recently even if a few of her muscles were stiff from the line dancing. Carol knew it was normal, when completing an activity different from our routine, for some muscles to ache.

After doing her exercises, showering, and dressing in jeans and a denim shirt, she went down to the Restaurant in the Lodge for some coffee and breakfast. Carol had some fruit and toast from the buffet and with a half-hour remaining before the time to meet John; she walked down the street in front of the Lodge. A small shop containing items aimed at tourists was open and browsing around, she bought a baseball cap with the word "Apache" written across the front.

Returning to the Lodge, she found John waiting, dressed similar to the way she first saw him here in the Lobby yesterday except the T-shirt was different. The shirt was white with a small Stanford University logo on the left chest and he had his giant's ball cap in his hand.

He noticed the ball cap covering her short hair, smiled and said, "You look like you're ready for a ball game."

"I played on a softball team at JPL for a few years, so I know a little about the game," She said returning his smile and making a swing with her arms like she was at bat hitting a ball.

Watching her in the pantomime, he said, "Strike one!"

"Giving John some big eyes, she said, "It was a home run. Didn't you see it sail over the fence?"

They both laughed at the banter between them.

"Where are we going?" John asked, taken by the softness of her facial features and her bright smile. He knew his attraction for her was increasing.

"Sunspot, New Mexico," She replied, still grinning.

"What may I ask is in Sunspot New Mexico?"

"The sun. Actually a Solar Observatory. It's up in the mountains northeast of here. It will take about an hour to get there."

"I thought you were meeting some one."

"I am. He just doesn't know I coming."

"Well then, let's go meet the person who doesn't know we're coming."

Carol wanted to drive, so they left the lodge in her rental car.

Driving the same route she had driven yesterday to Cloudcroft, Carol pointed out some of the sites along the way such as the White Sands glowing in the distance. Passing Cloudcroft, they proceeded to Sunspot. The only thing in Sunspot was the various observatory buildings and visitor center. You could not really call it a town. It was the place where they built the telescopes.

"Are you going to tell me why you're contacting someone here?" John wanted to get some preliminary information so he could be thinking about possible questions.

Carol made no reply to his question. She gave him a look out of the corner of her eye telling him he should know better than to ask after he refused to give her any information yesterday.

They reached Sunspot and checked at the visitor center, asking for Evan Daily. The attendant there sent them to the solar telescope, which was a short walk away. Approaching the building, John and Carol entered asking a man at the gate, "We're looking for Evan Daily."

"Visitors are not allowed into the section of the building where Mr. Daily is located. I'll call him," He said.

After making the call, the man said, "Mr. Daily will be down in a minute."

John asked again why she wanted to see Evan Daily and she responded the same as before, declining to give him any information.

A man who looked to be in his mid-thirties came slogging toward Carol and John. The man moved as though he was pulling a plow. He had long red hair tied in a pony tail, blue jeans with holes in the knees, a long red messy beard down to his chest, and a T-shirt with "Solar Power" written on the front. He was of average height and a touch overweight.

"Are you the people looking for Evan Daily," He asked with an accent having a New England ring to it. He stared at Carol, probably not sure at first if she was a he with her short hair and baseball cap.

Carol expected an older man, more like Harry Calvert than like the one standing in front of them. Hesitating, she finally answered, "Yes, are you Mr. Daily, the person who studies the composition of objects in the solar system."

"I am and whom am I talking to?" He acted as though he was involved with more important things and did not want to be bothered.

"You don't know me. A friend, Harold Anker, who works for Boeing Space Systems, sent me to you. I'm Carol Jacobs and this is John Kirkwood. They shook hands then Evan, mumbling at first, said "Harold Anker— Harold Anker, I'm not sure I know –wait, yes-from Seattle. I did some consulting work there several years ago. Why did he send you to me?"

"If you have the time, can we go someplace private?" Carol did not want to talk in public about the picture.

"We have a conference room inside we could use. First, what is it you wish to discuss?"

Harold had said Evan had a degree in Chemistry and a graduate degree in Geology. These were ample credentials to give an opinion concerning the picture. Carol waited, formulating exactly what to say to entice him. "I have a picture of an object in the solar system on which I would like to have your opinion."

"You can go to the library and find out what is in your picture. You don't need me to help," He said in a condescending tone.

She returned with, "I have and what is in the picture is not in any library in the World."

Now he began to look interested. He pulled on his beard, then said, "Follow me." He led them through a door marked "Employees Only" into a hallway, then through a large room into a small office with barely enough space for the three of them.

Evan spoke first saying, "Have a seat. Now, let's have a look-see at your mystery picture."

Sitting in front of the desk with Evan behind it in a chair and John standing to the side of Carol, she reached into her bag and pulled out the pictures. She handed him the picture from the Talaria probe and Evan reached for his glasses hanging around his neck, adjusted them on his nose, and eyed the picture.

"The large object looks like it might be a plantoid or an asteroid. What is the item in the background? Does the picture have a defect."

With Evan's comment, John moved over next to him and peered over his shoulder wanting to see what he was describing.

"The picture has no defects," She said. "It has been checked out."

"Then I'm assuming you're interested in the orange thing." Evan reached in his desk and pulled out a magnifying glass, which he placed over the picture.

"The object looks to be man made. You want to know what substances make up its composition. Is that right?"

Carol did not answer. She sat quietly letting Evan and John look at the picture, which they both did with a concentrated interest.

"Where did you get the picture?" He put down the magnifying glass, his attitude quite different now. She had captured his full attention.

"I'll tell you later. Do you have an idea what the composition of the material making up the object would be?"

Evan was pulling on his beard again, studying the picture. "Is the object part of a space probe?"

"What do you think?" Carol asked not wanting to influence him in any way.

John was about to burst and itching to get into the conversation. He had many questions, but on the way to Sunspot he had promised Carol not to say anything during the meeting with Evan. Now he had to stifle his interest in the photo and was sorry he had made the pact with her.

"Don't hold me to it. I'd say it could be made of some type of glass, silicon based maybe. Another possibility would be carbon based and in this form it would have to be made of diamonds. It would have to be the biggest diamonds ever known! It seems to have some kind of heat or light source the way it seems to glow. Maybe it contains small amounts of the element radium or uranium, but no, that would be impossible. If I had a different angle, I might have a better idea," Evan said.

Carol reached in her purse and pulled out the picture from NEAR of the large igloo type structure.

"Whoa, what do we have here?" Evan said as he held the picture in front of him almost taking his breath away. John was also in a daze staring at the picture over Evan's shoulder.

"Carol, is it-are you going to tell me where you got these pictures?" Evan asked.

"In good time. Here's two more." She handed him the other two pictures from NEAR and chuckled to herself knowing she had the men in the palm of her hand.

Evan used his magnifying glass again to examine the pictures. After muddling over the picture for almost five minutes, he pushed his chair back away from the desk, pulled on his beard some more, looked at Carol and said, "Is this some kind of joke? Did Harold Anker put you up to showing these to me?"

John backed away slightly, his movement limited by the tiny office and glared at Carol thinking her pictures must be fabricated.

Slightly offended by Evan's words and John's reaction, Carol said forcefully, "I'm not joking. The pictures were taken in the solar system! Now are you going to give me your opinion?"

"You are aware pure carbon in crystalline form is a diamond and diamonds have impurities giving them different colors, yellow being the most abundant and red being the rarest," Evan said.

"I've never heard of a red diamond. Have you Carol?" John jumped in for the first time, deciding to get into the conversation.

"I believe I knew that at one time. I do know diamonds are one of the hardest substances."

Evan replied, "Yes, they are. The hardness of a substance is measured on a ten-point scale and diamonds are a ten. Now an atom of another element may take the place of a carbon atom in the crystal lattice structure of a diamond, but usually no more than one such atom for every 10,000 carbon atoms. These impurities are what give them the different colors."

"What are you trying to say?" Carol asked not sure where he was going with his line of thought.

"In my opinion, if I had to make an analysis, I would say the orange part of the structure is composed of diamond crystals with a lattice of other elements besides carbon mixed together. The orange glow could be an isotope providing energy. For what purpose I would have no idea. As far as the black

171

objects, I am at a loss as to what composes them or what type of material makes up the substance," Evan said.

"Where would you get so many diamonds, and especially diamonds as big as in the picture?" John asked.

Evan looked at John, then at Carol. Smiled and said, "You can't, that's why the pictures have to be a joke. You also can't have the kind of elements mixed together to form a diamond with energy locked in and for what purpose would they be used. To have these you would have to live in never-never land."

Evan started laughing as he finished. "Harold has put a good one over on you," and laughed some more as he looked at Carol and John. He laughed hilariously until he saw that Carol and John never cracked a smile; in fact they looked more serious.

Finally, he stopped his laughing and spoke. "This is a joke isn't it. It can't be real, can it?" Evan turned back to the pictures again giving them another once-over.

"What shape do the diamond crystals form in?" John asked.

"What shape," Evan repeated as he adjusted his glasses, "In nature diamonds take on the shape of an octahedron or tetrahedron. The perfect shape for a diamond if formed in a controlled environment would be in the form of a cube. Very rarely does that happen."

John stared at Evan then turned to look at the object in the picture. He said nothing, yet Carol could tell something had clicked with Evan's answer to his question. John leaned over and looked at the pictures more seriously than he had before.

Carol got up from her seat, reached over onto the desk, and picked up the pictures. "I want to thank you for your time." She then turned to John and said, "Let's go."

"Wait-are you going to tell me where you got the pictures?" Evan had the look of a child who had their toy taken away.

Carol stopped, turned and said, "The pictures were taken in the Asteroid Belt between Mars and Jupiter.

She eyed John; they thanked him again and left.

"What's wrong?" John asked Carol as they walked out of the building.

"I don't want to talk about it. Let's just get out of here." Carol responded notably upset.

172

CHAPTER 17

The distance between Sunspot, New Mexico and the Asteroid Belt might be millions of miles, but the difference between the understanding of the object in the picture and what they knew it was composed of could make that distance seem insignificant. The suggestion given by Evan Daily implying part of the object in the pictures was made of diamonds, not diamonds the size of gemstones or jewelry but crystals the size of basketballs and baseball bats was mind boggling. On the ride back to Alamogordo, John hashed over in his mind the possibility the cube and the structure in space were connected, and if they were, how did the cube wind up on earth? He had hundreds of questions to be answered before he would understand a possible connection.

Looking at Carol as she drove down the mountain, John sensed her mind was also in deep reflection. Evan Daily had thrown out a lot of opinions all leading to the potentiality the object was a hoax. When the solution to a problem is more difficult to explain than the problem itself, then conceptualizing defies rationale.

Wishing the answer had been a United States or Russian project, now Carol was left with only one solution. Some other civilization besides Earth had placed the object in the Asteroid Belt, which is the most difficult answer to explain. Now she could see herself being called a space-nic spouting slogans like "The Aliens are coming", and "ET's have landed in ships made of diamonds". If she made it public, it would be the joke of the day around the water cooler. The trip to Sunspot had not helped her feel any better about the predicament she was in up to her neck.

John broke the silence. "I understand your feelings. I've been dealing with the same ones for the last two weeks. I'm going to tell you something to help ease your mind." He decided to let her in on some of his knowledge.

"The only thing you could say to help me would be a story where you've seen an alien, except of course no one would believe you." Carol spoke dejectedly. "The announcer on TV would say that a space ship has landed on Earth and it is made of, would you believe, diamonds. So if you don't mind, just keep your opinions to yourself."

Taking his cap off and running his hand through his thick dark hair, he said, "No, I haven't seen an alien, but I believe a piece of what is in your picture is located here on Earth."

"What!" Carol exclaimed. Jolted by his statement, she lost control of the car and ran off the side of the road. Dust and gravel spewed up into the air as John put his hands on the dash to steady himself. She steered the car, two wheels on the pavement and two wheels in the gravel along the side of the road, until it slowed enough to drive completely off the road and stop.

She stared at John with disbelief. "You're not saying that just to make me feel better, because if you are buster, you can get your ass out of the car right here and now." Carol had fire and anger in her eyes.

John definitely hit a nerve with his last remark. She was probably as much upset with her driving as she was with him. "Why are you mad at me? I didn't say the object in the picture was made of diamonds. The tone of John's voice was also laced with anger.

"Yes-well you just said 'parts of it are here on Earth'," She fired back with a little less fury in her voice and a lot less rage in her eyes.

"What do you think caused me to start looking. I'd never seen the pictures you showed Evan until today, so there had to be some other reason I was searching." John was upset with her attitude.

"I just didn't expect the answer to be something alien. I always knew it would have to be some man made thing and now it's this thing made of giant diamonds and no one is going to believe me," Carol said in a disgruntled way.

John looked at Carol. "No one is going to believe us." She had bent her head down with her forehead on the steering wheel. Carol turned her head sideways so she was looking at him. With a saddened look she repeated, "Believe us." Then she half-heartedly smiled and John gladly nodded his head and grinned at Carol.

"You want to tell me where this piece is supposed to be."

"I don't know. It's what I'm trying to find out."

"So you haven't even seen it, have you?"

"No." The answer rang throughout the interior of the car.

Getting back on the road and proceeding to Alamogordo, neither spoke again until they reached the city. Carol had a craving for a deli sandwich. Stopping at Subway, they sat in the restaurant eating their sandwich wraps. John said, "You certainly had a lot of spunk to take the pictures from JPL without permission. Did you realize you would be in your present situation at the time you took it?"

"How did you know I took them without permission?" Holding her sandwich in front of her mouth, she looked over the top of it directly into his eyes.

John almost slipped up, telling information he had received from Peter. He quickly tried a diversion. "Your not being followed because of the way you look—I mean you look fine—I mean people would follow you because your—oh the hell with it."

She enjoyed watching him dig himself in deeper, then she laughed.

"You know what I mean. Now where did you get the spunk Miss Jacobs?"

"When you raise six kids, you must have spunk as you call it." She could see him thinking about her with six kids and knew the next question.

Remembering she had told him there were no children in her marriage, he asked, "Where did the six kids come from?"

"Remember I told you I had six brothers and sisters and my mother died when I was thirteen years old, so being the oldest, I helped raise the others. Are you satisfied with the answer?"

He was getting a better understanding of the woman whom he had just met. She seemed to have overcome a lot of diversity in her life to reach her present position. Leaving Subway and proceeding out Thunder Hill Road from Alamogordo, they drove up the slope east of the city. The landscape was barren with scrub brush and cacti growing between the rocks. The road was narrow in places and curved up the hill toward the houses built sparsely along the bluff. One of those houses was supposed to contain Karen Doddson.

"Who is the woman you are to meet today?"

"Her name is Happy Valsen," John informed her knowing it was an odd name. He could think of only one other woman called Happy. She was Vice President Nelson Rockefeller's second wife, Margaretta, who was called Happy, though he did not know why.

She was having second thoughts about John's ability to conduct an investigation. Nothing he had said or done gave her much confidence in him and not being open and frank with her could be a smoke screen for his ineptitude. "What is the woman's connection to the aliens?"

"I'm not sure there is any connection. We will just have to see." John did not want to tell Carol anything about her especially if the trip turned into a dead end.

Their car climbed up the hill with a drop-off to their right. Peering out his window at the valley below, John hoped Carol stayed away from the edge. As the road began to level out, it turned left away from the drop-off. The house they were searching for was around the next turn on the right. It had a small yard running back toward the road, and enclosing the yard was a chain link fence at least twelve feet high.

The fenced in area was similar to the backyard of people with children where they enclose it so the toddlers can run and play without getting out. With a fence as high as the one before their eyes, convicts would have a hard time getting away. On the far side of the fence was a drive running up a slight grade from the road to the house. It was a one story home perched on a cliff over-looking the valley below.

"I bet the house has a great view. What does the lady do?"

"She is in her eighties so I assume she is retired. Her intelligence must be high because she has a degree in chemistry and biology from Columbia University where she graduated magna cum laude in 1945. Around here, they call her 'Crazy Happy'."

"I have to ask. Has she seen any flying saucers or UFO's, or maybe she was abducted. Why are we here?" Again she put the question to him, this time in a disgruntled fashion.

John gave her a smirky look, frowned and quipped, "Oh, ye of little faith. Don't ye believe in me?"

Carol decided she was leaving as soon as they returned to the Lodge. John Kirkwood was probably crazier than the Crazy Happy lady they were here to see. She should have gone by her instincts and never agreed to meet him, but no, she let her libido lead her into visiting a lunatic in the middle of the New Mexico desert with a Professor of questionable ability.

Passing the fenced in area, they reached the driveway, which had a bar across it with a sign saying, "No Trespassing". Carol stopped the car in front of the bar and John got out to open it. The bar was pad-locked so he walked back to the car and informed Carol.

Turning off the engine, Carol got out of the car and they proceeded to walk up the driveway located next to the fence. Halfway to the house, Carol, walking closest to the fence heard a growling. As she turned to look through the fence an animal of extreme proportions lunged against the fence, mouth open, teeth and fangs bared, and saliva dripping from the sides of its mouth.

She let out a scream as she fell toward John. Never in her life had she been so frightened. As John pulled her away from the fence, he being shaken as well, another large animal just as ferocious as the first, lunged into the fence causing it to sway back and forth. At first John feared the fence would give way and come crashing down on top of the two of them with the animals close behind. After viewing the fence with closer scrutiny, he was sure it would hold and remain intact.

John thought these were the biggest dogs he had ever seen as they continued to growl and yelp running back and forth along the fence showing their fangs, jumping up against the fence growling and snapping at them with their ferocious bared teeth.

Now being nearer to the house than to the car, both John and Carol were in limbo. "Let's get out of here," Carol yelled trying to pull John back toward the car.

John, on the other hand, stood his ground knowing now why the fence was so high and not fearing the animals in quite the same way as before.

"It's all right. They can't get at us." He attempted to calm Carol down. He held her in his arms and liked the feeling of protecting her from harm.

She pulled away from him. "I don't care. Let's get out of here," She said in a loud trembling voice still holding on to his arm trying to move him toward the car.

Just as quickly as the animals had appeared, they were now gone. They stood scanning the yard for the large animals.

Carol was relieved and feeling a little calmer now that the animals were out of sight.

"Carol, please, I need to talk to the woman who lives here. It's safe now and we're only a short distance from the house."

She decided not to have any part of visiting the lady. "Well you talk to her, I'll stay in the car," then as she turned and started to trot back to the car looking over her shoulder, she yelled, "I want no more part of this crazy Lady or her crazy dogs."

"Come on Carol," John pleaded as she moved away from him. "Oh be that way." He turned and continued up the drive.

As he came to the house, the fence on his right connected to the end of the house. This set up might allow the dogs access to the inside of the house. He stood in front of the door and looked West and was greeted by a beautiful view overlooking of the City of Alamogordo and the White Sands glimmering far off in the distance.

He took in the scene, then looked back behind him down the drive to the car with Carol sitting inside. He shook his head and approached the wooden door with two small panels of glass near the top. Finding no doorbell, he knocked a few times. Receiving no response, he knocked again and was rewarded with a female voice inside saying, "Go away. Leave me alone."

John countered with, "Miss Valsen, I need to talk to you. Please. Won't you let me in to see you."

"Go away. I don't want to talk to anyone. I have a gun," was the reply coming from inside.

"Miss Valsen, or should I say Miss Doddson," John said loudly to be sure he was heard. No immediate reply came after his reference to Karen Doddson. He waited for a response from the woman inside the house.

"I don't know who you're talking about. Now get off my property or I'll call the police," The voice said.

"I think you do, Karen. Please talk to me." He hoped using her real name would put some pressure on her to listen to him.

Again a pause, then, "Karen's dead. Go away."

John smiled because he then knew he was at the right place. Now he was more determined than ever to get her to talk to him.

"I know about the cube. Please talk to me."

"I have nothing to say. Go away right now." The voice exclaimed.

"I want to show you something. I'm not from the government. I'm a teacher at Stanford University. I'll be right back. Please wait just a minute?" He backed away from the door and hurriedly walked to the car where Carol waited. Reaching the car, he opened the passenger door.

Carol immediately made her feelings known to John. "Hurry up and get in so we can get off the mountain." Carol's tone indicated she was not happy with their present situation.

"Are you crazy?" replied John.

"No, the woman inside is crazy and so are you if you don't get in the car." Why he wanted to talk to some crazy woman was beyond her understanding.

"Wait, I'm not leaving. Give me the copy of the picture of the structure."

"What? Why do you want it?" Carol asked, now sure he was missing some screws.

"Give me the copy, now," John said as forcefully as he could. He was tired of trying to appease her.

Seeing a determined look in his eyes she had not encountered before, Carol reached in her bag and retrieved the picture for him.

"Are you coming? You don't want to be left out, I assure you."

Not knowing how she felt about John, she wavered, mumbling to herself about how she wound up in this predicament and becoming more involved. Getting out of the car, she said, "This better be good, buckaroo!"

Walking back to the house next to John, she stayed on the side of him away from the fence.

"Trust me. You won't be disappointed," John assured her. He suspected she was having second thoughts about him as well as the lady in the house. Turning the corner and in front of the door, John knocked and waited.

"What have you got to show me?" The voice said.

John noticed a different tone in her voice-more calm and less agitated. He felt more confident now the woman would concede to talk to them about her past.

"To demonstrate my good will and to prove I'm not here to hurt you or make fun of you, I want you to look at a picture. After you see it, you'll know why I'm here."

"What are you talking about?" Carol asked. "Whose in there?" John put his finger to his mouth and shook his head as signs to be quiet.

"Slide it through the crack in the door," The voice said as the door opened just a bit.

Doing as instructed, he pushed the picture of the broken orange and black igloo shaped object through the door and waited. Carol started to say something, but John gave her a quiet sign again. He didn't want to do any-thing to jeopardize the chance to talk to someone who knew about the cube.

Nothing happened for what seemed like an eternity. The sun was bear-ing down on Carol and John as they both started to perspire from the intense rays and heat from the afternoon sun.

Finally, the door slowly swung open. Carol and John took a step back. There stood an elderly woman barefoot, in jeans, and a ragged long sleeve shirt. Her white hair fell well below her shoulders. It looked like it hadn't been brushed or combed in ages. What caused them to back up though, was what was sitting on each side of her. She stood between the two animals that earlier had nearly torn the fence down trying to get at them.

CHAPTER 18

The rose appears to us a lovely flower and we cherish its sweet beauty unless we graze over the stem feeling its thorny bite. We shy away from beggars in the street fearing the harm they may do us, when only a few years ago these same people may have been the pillars of their communities. First impressions don't always reflect the true nature of someone. Happy Valsen's demeanor was not enticing to either Carol or John and when she invited them in, they both pointed to the animals and refused to move.

"Yard!" She barked and the two animals left the room.

Carol, caught off guard, nearly jumped out of her shoes when the lady yelled in her screechy voice.

"I don't have guests so they are unaccustomed to seeing other people in my house. You may come in now. It is safe. They won't harm you," She assured them.

All the assurances in the world wouldn't be enough for Carol so John took her arm and told her to stand behind him. She did, and they edged their way into the house squinting their eyes attempting to scan the interior for the animals. The curtains were closed and the light from the outside had been so bright their eyes were taking a long time to adjust to the darker interior. After entering, Carol slowly shut the door, keeping her hand on the doorknob, alert for the return of the animals.

John said in as polite a way as he could muster, "Miss Valsen or Karen Doddson. Which would you prefer?"

She eyed John and Carol as if it was a contest to see how much she could remember about their persons. "My name is Happy Valsen," She replied standing in front of Carol and John.

"I'm John-John Kirkwood and this is my friend, Carol Jacobs," John informed her as he looked over the room. Returning his gaze to Miss Valsen, he said, "It is our pleasure to meet you."

180

"If you will follow me into the kitchen," She instructed them. "We can sit and talk."

As their eyes adjusted to the dimmer light, they could see the room was filled with stacks of books, magazines, newspapers, and leaflets. John assumed from what he saw Karen must be an avid reader. One chair with a lamp beside it was the only piece of furniture not covered by some type of reading material. A narrow path led through all the books and magazines into the kitchen, which also contained a myriad of publications. She had to remove some to provide them a place to sit.

Eventually, the table was clean and three seats were available. Happy Valsen stood with her back to the cooking area and John and Carol sat across from her. After sitting down, John looked out the sliding glass doors to a view similar to the one he had witnessed outside. The kitchen area was one room with the table area surrounded by bookcases filled with books. At the other end of the room were the stove, sink and refrigerator. "You have a lovely view here on the hillside," John told her.

She made no response. Standing by the table facing John and Carol and staring at them through her glasses, she pulled on her hair and pressed it to the sides of her head in an attempt to keep it from falling over her face. Finally, she spoke. "Would you like to tell me why you're here."

Carol was still nervous not knowing where the animals were located. "First could you tell us where the big dogs are?"

A slight frown crossed her forehead as she looked at Carol and replied, "They're not dogs and you're safe as long as I am here with you. They have never harmed anyone as of yet."

Not happy with Miss Valsen's assurances, Carol asked, "If they are not dogs, what are they?"

"They're wolves."

Her statement did not make Carol or John feel the least bit safer. "Wolves! Where did you get wolves?" Carol asked.

"I raised them from the time they were puppies. A man I know trained them for me. I've had them eleven years. You still haven't answered my question. Why are you here?"

John eyed the lady, taking in the messy gray hair and the wrinkled face. He guessed her age to be around eighty or more. She most certainly read a lot and did not have very good grooming habits. The frizzy hair hung down around her head, not having been brushed or combed. Her fingernails were dirty and she had a slight odor, which probably meant she had not bathed recently. "I'm a professor at Stanford University and Carol is an engineer for the Jet Propulsion Laboratory in Pasadena. I think you know from the picture I gave you why we are here to see you."

Miss Valsen started to say something, then held back. She looked at the two of them with searching eyes determining in her own mind if what John and Carol had said could hold water.

She pulled the picture from under her shirt and placed it on the table in front of them.

First looking at Happy, Carol then turned toward John with a questioning stare, saying to herself, tell us John, why are we here?

"Where was the picture taken?" She asked as she gingerly picked it up with her bony fingers and eyed it with close scrutiny.

"The Asteroid Belt. It was taken by a space probe called NEAR," Carol answered.

"NEAR landed on Eros didn't it?"

Carol was taken aback by Happy Valsen familiarity with the probe cooped up here in her house.

"Miss Valsen, Carol has no idea why we came to see you either, and the picture belongs to her. He was beginning to understand that the lady called Crazy Happy is extremely intelligent. If she is who he thinks she is and she knows what he thinks she knows, she could be a gold mine of information.

She brushed the hair back from her face again, then pointedly asked Carol, "I haven't seen this picture in the news, any journal, or on the Internet. Where did you get it?"

Carol was surprised by the abrupt direct question. She shifted in her chair, uneasy with the question. "Let's just say I have it and leave it at that." Carol wasn't keen about revealing to a strange woman her personal problems.

John could tell Happy was not satisfied with her answer.

"I'll ask again. Why are you here?"

John collected himself, then responded, "I know you came to New Mexico in the early fifties and worked with Dr. Senval Happard on a program under the cover of a secret plan called Project Mogul. How am I doing so far?" The look in her eyes told John he had surprised her with the information he just imparted.

"I'm still listening." She responded hesitantly, sitting down for the first time.

John could almost detect Happy Valsen's ears perking up under the matted hair.

"So am I," Carol said giving John a questioning look he knew meant 'what are you talking about?'.

"You worked with Dr. Happard investigating an alien artifact in the shape of a cube. You retrieved information from the object, using it in some way. Am I still on target."

"I haven't stopped you have I."

"I'm here to find out all I can about the artifact," John said putting his desires on the line. He had been leaning with his elbows on the table and now he moved back in his chair waiting for her to respond.

"From what you have said, I think you may have mistaken me for someone else. Your story of an alien artifact is interesting."

She may think she is going to slip out of this, but John was not about to give up. "You may have fooled others since you changed your name, but I know who you are and I know anyone else besides Karen Doddson would not have let us enter."

You could feel the tension in the air as Happy responded. "If I was Karen Doddson and I did know something, what makes you think I would tell you anything?"

John was ready for her question. He had been tossing it around in his mind for a long time. "Because I think something happened in the fifties changing the way the artifact was being used, and I think you want to tell someone, in fact I think you have been dying to tell somebody." John spoke to her in a direct straightforward manner.

Happy stood and walked to the glass doors. Carol punched John with wide eyes and whispered, "Why didn't you tell me?"

"I'm telling you now, so listen," He said with a little smirk. He had the impression Carol didn't think much of his ability to ferret out what they were looking for, so now she can listen and learn.

Happy stared through the glass toward the white sands in the distance, then returned to the table and sat facing them, saying, "Let's assume for the moment, I am who you believe me to be. How did you find me?" She fingered the picture on the table then looked up from the picture at John.

"I talked to Joyce Carter last week. She mentioned your name," John said matter of factly.

"Who is Joyce Carter?"

"Joyce Happard, Dr. Happard's daughter. She told me you worked with her father." John and Carol could sense Happy was remembering her past as her eyes glazed over.

After a moment, she replied, "My, I haven't seen her since she was a little girl. Did she tell you where to find me?" Happy asked, inadvertently confessing to be Karen Doddson.

"So you are Karen Doddson!" John said.

"No one has called me by that name in over fifty years."

"Would you prefer we call you Karen instead of Happy?"

She stared through both John and Carol showing her mind was in another place. "Please do, it has been so long. Now how did you find me?" Karen Doddson asked.

"I have a friend who found you. You were last known to have lived in Albuquerque."

"If you found me, then they can find me and I am safe no longer," Karen said in a dejected way. She was obviously distraught about being found. "I'll have to make some new arrangements."

"Who are they and why are they looking for you?" John asked.

"If I am who you think, then we will talk about who 'they' are later and now, what do you intend to do with any information I may give you regarding the artifact?"

"I want to expose the cube so it will be used for the benefit of all mankind. I am not investigating the cube for personal gain," John said hoping his statement would increase her trust in him.

Karen cleared her throat. "Carol, why are you here?" Karen asked noticing Carol had few words to say.

Carol, unprepared for the question glanced at John then responded. "I knew nothing of the cube till now. I'm here to find the answer to why the picture you have in your hand was deleted from JPL's records and not shown to the analysts or anyone else."

"I'm not sure who to trust. I don't trust the government." Karen again fingered the picture as she spoke.

"I have an arrest warrant out for me for taking the picture from JPL so I'm definitely not in good favor with the government." Carol also wanted to help John ease Karen's fear.

"Will you vouch for John?" Karen asked, giving them the first sign of a friendlier look.

Carol hesitated, looked at John and smiled. "I guess we can trust him, besides he's kind-a-cute."

John looked at Carol and winked.

Karen observed them both and said, "How well do you know each other?"

"We just met yesterday."

"I find that hard to believe," Karen said seeing facial signs between the two showing more intimacy than she would expect in one day.

"Why do you not trust the government?" John asked.

"One moment." Karen stood and walked over to the stove and sink area and returned shortly with a tray containing three glasses of ice tea. She set the tray on the table.

Karen's gray hair seemed frizzier now than when Carol first saw her with the wolves. If Carol lived by herself for a long time and had few visitors, would she let herself go like Karen seems to have done?

"Thank you for the tea," Carol said.

Karen picked up one of the glasses, took a drink, then said, "You asked why I don't trust the government. It is a long story. I'll give you the short version. I disappeared in 1962 because I feared for my life. I had my suspicions that they killed Senval in 1959 and that I might be next."

Now John was confused, "Who do you think killed Dr. Happard?"

"The people in control of the cube. You have no idea how much power and money is involved. It is mind-boggling. When I skipped out, it was a combination of the intelligence community and the Defense Department, but not necessarily the people we would normally think of as being in charge such as the CIA Director and the Secretary of Defense. It was others in less well-known agencies and departments who are in control. Senval helped set it up in that fashion to try to prevent politics and greed from becoming the main factors in using information from the artifact," Karen explained to them.

"Someone threatened to kill you?" Carol asked.

"No, the people in charge after Senval died let it be known that no one leaves the project unless they say so," Karen returned, her voice getting screechier.

"What happened to Dr. Happard?" John asked.

The topic was a very difficult for Karen to discuss without bringing back some pain. It was one of the saddest times of her life, though she did begin to answer John's question partially. "Originally, Senval was connected to the State Department, I think he told me it was through Sumner Welles, but he was fired or left and others slowly began to take over.

Eventually in the late fifties, Senval, the scientists and the rest of the people in control of the cube began to be pressured by the intelligence and military people. Senval threatened to go public with the knowledge of the cube. He hinted he had evidence, which would leave no doubt in anyone's mind the alien artifact existed. It wasn't long after he threatened them he was found dead of a heart attack, yet he had no history of heart problems." Her voice was beginning to break up so she paused and collected herself before continuing.

"I wanted an autopsy, but somehow his body was embalmed before it could be performed. Within a few months, a different group of people were overruling the ones associated with Senval and slowly taking charge of the cube and sadly, there was nothing I or my friends could do to stop them," Karen said.

In all of John's concerns about the search for the artifact, he never considered the possibility of someone wishing him dead. The investigation into the where-a-bouts of the cube just put on a completely different and more dangerous face.

CHAPTER 19

Cherished by all is the American dream, which imparts the opportunity to every citizen to create something which others may desire and each citizen in turn, the right to reap a profit from the same. The possibility that creations have been manipulated by a group of people flies in the face of fairness the American dream propounds. John was anxious to hear Karen's explanation of how the cube was used and for whose benefit.

Staring at John as the three sat around the table, Carol saw a different person than she had perceived during the previous night and during the morning. One who she took to be a user of people to get his way was turning into an extremely intelligent, competent, and caring man. She realized he had to be intelligent to be a professor at Stanford, yet he could also have been a snob or a nerd. He definitely was neither. She was impressed with the amount of data he had gathered about this mysterious cube and the concern he illustrated toward Karen.

"You want to know about the cube, do you," Karen said in her squeaky voice and with squinty eyes behind the glasses she wore.

"All you can tell us," John said again leaning over the table toward Karen. He couldn't miss the chance to get important information after searching for the past week and realizing almost everyone was dead who had knowledge of its initial use.

"Have you got all day?" Karen said with a slight twist of her lips.

He didn't know whether it was a smile or just a tic. "First, if you will, tell us how you became involved with the project?" John asked.

Karen put her hands on her forehead as if she were squeezing the information out of her brain, then laid them back on the table before beginning. "Yes, so many years ago. I was right out of college and a young girl ready to take her place in history, but in 1945 women were not supposed to be career oriented. Happy, I mean Dr. Happard recruited me anyway."

"Since you were, what, only twenty-one. Why would he recruit you at such a young age?" John said puzzled by her statement.

"Because of my field, my degree, and my intelligence. He offered me less money than the industries and pharmaceuticals that were courting me had put on the table. I was tempted to go for the money, but Senval had a way of convincing people to go for the greater good and so I took the job in part because I found Happy to be a wonderful person." Karen stopped and stared off into space. It was clear there was some connection between the two in addition to their work.

"What was your field. It must have had some relevance to what he was trying to find?" John asked.

"Let me explain to you why I was added to the staff. First Dr. Happard wanted young minds with cool heads, which hopefully had not been corrupted by greed. The cube was brought to Wright Field in Ohio and Happy was concerned, as were some others that the cube would wind up under the control of the Army or Navy. Afraid they might use it for war purposes, Happy made a deal with President Roosevelt. Let him and a few others control the use of the cube, keep it secret, and they would make sure it was used for the good of all people, not just Americans. In return for agreeing to those conditions, the President told them their first priority had to be finding a way to cure or prevent polio. As I'm sure you know, the President had polio and was partially crippled by the disease. I became a part of the group involved in this effort because I had a degree in chemistry and biology, and graduated top of my class from Columbia. I was a prime target as you might say for recruitment by Dr. Happard."

The last bit of information cleared up several questions for John going back to his conversation with Joyce Carter. Carol was still in awe of what was being discussed around Karen's kitchen table. These two people were speaking of cubes, airfields and curing diseases. She jumped in with a question for Karen. "I thought Jonas Salk found a vaccine for polio?"

"Your right, he did in the early fifties. It was one of the major breakthroughs of the twentieth century."

"But I thought you just said you-", Carol attempted to ask as Karen interrupted.

"Carol, John, listen. Here is what we did. We would try to get the information from the cube, which was not easy. Once we had something, and after testing it, we would seed the field so to speak, much like you seed the clouds, hoping to make rain. In the case of polio, we buried a report about weakened viruses in a study at John Hopkins University. People at John Hopkins found the research paper we had planted and used it to stimulate anti-body production. Salk in turn used their work to help him find the solution for a vaccine," Karen explained.

John got it. By slipping the information in, no one would ever suspect secret information was creating these advances and discoveries in the various fields. His premise about the German scientists he had given to his friends was closer to the truth than he realized.

He leaned his chair back away from the table. "You must have discovered lots of things from the cube. What else did you seed?" John inquired.

"I was not privy to all the seeding. I know the maser and laser were seeded. As I said, it wasn't easy to get information from the cube." Karen took a drink from her glass of tea.

"Why did you leave the project since you were doing things to help all people? To me it would have been the most fantastic job in the world," John said.

"I told you the agreement Dr. Happy had with FDR. It started going downhill during the Eisenhower Presidency. During the 1950's, the Department of Defense was constantly pushing for more military information," Karen said.

"Did you give it to them?" Carol asked.

"Dr. Happard tried to keep his promise to President Roosevelt and it no doubt led to his death. I'm not proud of what we did, but remember, we were Americans and it was during the beginning of the Cold War. I'll give you one example. The military needed a new spy plane. They had a plane called the U-2, but feared it was too slow, especially with the development of missiles able to shoot planes out of the sky. The military wanted a plane so fast it couldn't be shot down.

A U-2 spy plane was shot down over Russia during the last years of the Eisenhower term and was a huge embarrassment for the United States. President Eisenhower felt he was close to a world agreement on nuclear weapons and banning tests of these devices when the plane was shot down, which ended his chance to get a signed agreement. Even before these events, the military was pushing for a super fast plane."

"Do we have a plane like the one the military wanted? I mean one that can fly so fast it can't be shot down?" Carol asked with an inquiring frown.

"Are either of you familiar with the A-12 Oxcart?" Karen asked.

They both looked at each other, then back at Karen shaking their heads no.

"It was a jet plane that could travel over 2,100 miles per hour. A group at Lockheed called the "skunk-works" built the plane. The plane would fly so fast that the frame would swell in size from four to eleven inches during its flight. When it landed, no maintenance people could touch it because its skin temperature would be over 600 degrees. Now how do you suppose the United States came up with the knowledge to build a plane like the A-12 in the 1950's?" Karen relayed to John and Carol.

"What happened to the plane?" Asked John.

"The Defense Department used its design to build the SR-71 Blackbird, which was retired in 1990. Only twenty eight were built and when production was over, Secretary of Defense MacNamara specifically ordered the destruction of the tooling so the SR-71 variants would not compete with the planes being developed such as the F-15 Eagle and other combat aircraft. The Blackbird to this day still holds the speed record for a jet airplane at almost 2200 miles per hour which it did in 1976."

"So you did provide information to the Defense Department," John stated.

Karen hung her head down like a child who had committed a wrong and gotten caught. "That was the beginning of the end. Once we let them in the door, they couldn't get enough. Remember when Eisenhower's term was about up he gave a speech in which he coined the term, military-industrial complex. He told how dangerous the Defense Department and their contractors were to the civilian control of the military. I believe the words he used were something like 'the potential for disaster lies in the rise of misplaced power in the hands of this machinery and public policy could itself become a captive'. If only he knew what we did, it would have scared him to death," Karen said.

Karen's knowledge and ability to recall details impressed Carol and John. "You mean President Eisenhower didn't know about the cube? He was the President," Carol said in an exasperated way.

"FDR is the only President to my knowledge that knew about our Project? It had been kept secret from all the other presidents."

"How is it possible something like an alien artifact in the hands of the United States Government is kept secret from the President?" John asked.

"You'll have to ask someone else. I don't know," Karen said.

To Carol and John, the story being told was mind-boggling, almost more so than the artifact itself. Another question John wanted to get in. "How do you get information from the cube?"

Karen, pulling on her long frizzy hair, stood and excused herself.

Carol took the chance to needle John by saying, "You rat, all this time you knew a lot more than I did and you never gave me a clue until this afternoon. Even then I thought you were making it up."

John looked at Carol, smiled, and said, "Your pretty when you get riled."

She could say nothing. She stuck her tongue out at him like a teenage girl might, turned her head away and then swinging back returned his smile.

Karen returned with her hair in a more presentable fashion. She sat down at the table-stared at the two people before her and said, "Now, how did we get information? Any kind of information was extremely difficult to obtain. One thing helping us was each face of the cube contained different topics. For example, as best we could tell, one face had to do with biology, medicine, health, and chemistry. I dealt with this face most of the time. Another contained physics and mathematics, another dealt with language and so on. So the first thing you had to decide was which face might have the information you wanted," Karen explained.

"Then how did you retrieve it, just ask," Carol asked, unaware of the description given John by Dr. Cable.

"Oh, if it had been so easy. It would have been unbelievable, the things we could have learned and the discoveries we could have made for humankind. To answer your question, a plate was pressed against the face and wires connected the plate to a helmet like device we wore. It was found to be the most efficient way to retrieve the information; in effect our brains were wired to the object. While I was there, we never were able to interrupt their language so when we were hooked to the cube, we garnered whatever information came into our heads.

Some of the scientists believed everything was in code to prevent others from doing exactly what we were attempting. Others thought certain information was locked in like how they were able to move from one star system to another.

After we broke contact, we had to write down all the symbols we saw and the sounds we heard if possible. The group would do the same thing for weeks, eventually a symbol or a diagram would come through the system we could understand enough to test it. If it worked, we gave it to the council who decided whether to seed it or not. There was a lot of trial and error involved," Karen said.

"I don't understand. You mean you wouldn't pass on all the information or discoveries. Why wouldn't you seed something?" Carol asked.

"You can't. Sometimes the world is not able to handle a new invention. An example would be a method to make diamonds," Karen said offhandedly.

Carol and John reacted to her last statement by raising their heads and looking at Karen with wider eyes. They were beginning to connect a lot of the data they had accumulated recently. "Why couldn't you seed a way to make diamonds?" Carol asked.

"Because they used the interior of a small star as a pressure furnace to make these large diamonds. We don't have the ability to use a star for anything like a furnace and won't in all likely hood for thousands of years. The cube was originally made using the same process. I'm sure it was much more complicated than we could ever imagine. You must understand; they were so far ahead of us our minds have difficulty comprehending their abilities. Even after studying the cube, we still didn't understand how it worked. Somehow the data was stored inside the diamond."

"I read recently where diamonds are being studied as a replacement for the silicon chip because diamonds can withstand higher temperatures. Could the idea have been planted by those who are in control of the artifact?" Carol asked.

"Very possibly. I read a similar article, maybe the same one you saw, and it crossed my mind that it might have been seeded by them," Karen replied.

"In our discussion you keep referring to they or them. Who is "them"?" John asked.

"We don't know. We called them the Alpha-Omegans. Not knowing their language or their speech, we are blind most of the time," Karen said.

"Why that name?" Carol asked.

"Alpha to omega from the Greek alphabet. The phrase encompasses everything like our A to Z. We assumed they knew everything there was to know. Of course if they did know everything, why would they come visit our system?"

John was intrigued by her discussion of the Alpha-Omegans and he had to ask, "Karen, what did they look like?"

She laughed at the question. "I'm not making fun of your question. It was a common item discussed among the people who worked with the artifact. From all the information we had, they were taller, thinner, and had more hair. Their general appearance was a bipedal hominoid of some sort we think."

Carol and John were trying to imagine how they looked from her description, and then Carol switched to another area. "Then can you tell us the connection between the picture in the Asteroid Belt and the cube?"

"All I know is they look to be made of similar materials. I don't know how one is here and the other is in space millions of miles away. There were some suggestions other artifacts were scattered throughout the solar system."

"What happened to the Alpha-Omegans? Are they still around," John inquired.

"You're probably not going to understand what I say," Karen said as she stood and moved to look out the sliding glass doors again.

John sensed Karen's connection to and knowledge of the artifact had dramatically changed her outlook on the world and on life.

As she looked out the glass doors, she said, "It's all so relative. Who are you? Where are you? But more important in the Universe is—When are you?" She turned and faced John and Carol. "The Alpha-Omegans left the cube here, as best we can determine, approximately two hundred million years ago." She waited to let her statement sink in. "We believe they were here to study the dinosaurs, not us. Something must have happened, because as far as we can determine, they left and never came back leaving some of their stuff behind."

Sometimes there is just so much information and disclosures an intelligent person can handle at one time. John and Carol's minds were trying to correlate all the data Karen was describing and at the same time relate the information to their own life and surroundings. It was not an easy chore, given the amount of material Karen was dishing out. The two hundred million years was an example.

Comprehending that length of time is difficult for any human given we live less than a hundred years, and what happened to the Alpha-Omegans over the last two hundred million years. Where did they go? Where did they come from? Why did they come to our Solar System? The questions were endless.

As John pondered these thoughts Carol asked, "Have you lived here ever since you left?"

"No, I resided in Las Cruces and Truth or Consequences for many years. I have lived here for the last twenty years," Karen said to them as she returned to her chair and sat down.

"Why did you stay in New Mexico?" John asked.

"I like it here and it was as safe as any place."

The lady had been in hiding for over forty years. How had she supported herself and purchased her home. John was curious so he asked, "How have you made a living, if I might ask since you have been in hiding for so long, where do you get money to live?"

"I'm not proud of what I did, but I bought stock in the Hamilton Watch Company in the early fifties. We seeded them in the late forties or early fifties with information on how to create an electric watch. They did in 1957 and their stock shot out of sight making me wealthy. I never told Senval, and I'm glad he never found out," Karen said, again hanging her head down as if repenting.

As she finished her confession, John's cell phone rang. He answered the call. It was from Peter and all he said was check Duke immediately and hung up.

John was confused. Why hadn't Peter just told him over the phone what he wanted? He looked at Karen and asked, "Would it be too much to ask if you have an Internet connection and could I use it to check my e-mail."

Carol looked at John with a funny stare wondering why he would ask that while they were getting so much information from Karen.

"Yes, you may use it if you need to," Karen said. She got up and led John into the room they passed through when they entered the house, then into a smaller room where her computer was located. This room was full of books and material like the others. She clicked the screen to the search engine page so he could get to his email, then left him alone.

Karen returned to the kitchen table where Carol waited.

"Why did you come out west from Ohio?" Carol asked.

"The cube was transferred to the air force base here because of too much scrutiny at Wright. After the war, Wright was too active, too many people, so Project Mogul was assigned serendipitously to the "Air Material Command". It was a special weapon-testing group involved in part with the CIA, which wound up assigned to Kirtland Air Force Base outside Albuquerque. This allowed the movement and existence of the artifact to he hidden in covert activity and also gave it a new home out west under the cover of the Command."

"The location for the cube was called site Able and construction began in 1947 in the foothills of the Manzano Mountains. With completion, we moved to site Able in 1952 changing the name to Manzano Base which was supposedly operated by the Air Force and of course 'top secret'."

"Is the cube there now?"

"Some people were talking of moving and the last I knew it was moved, but I really have no idea where."

In the other room, John called up the email account set up by Peter. The new message appeared:

PEOPLE AT APACHE LODGE LOOKING FOR YOU AND MS JACOBS DO NOT RETURN TO LODGE MY RENTAL CAR WILL BE AT THE SANTA FE TRAIL PARKING LOT FOR YOU TO USE THEY MAY KNOW YOUR RENTAL CAR KEYS UNDER REAR FLOOR MAT SUGGEST ALBEQUERQUE AS DESTINATION PC

John got up and walked into the kitchen and said, "Carol, would you go look at the email I received." Carol got up and walked into the room with the computer and read what was on the screen, then she read it again. She turned and walked back into the kitchen where John was waiting with Karen.

"Who sent the message," Carol asked.

"A friend of mine who is watching our back."

Karen was listening in and asked, "Is there a problem?"

"We are going to have to leave soon. It's getting late anyway and your information has been invaluable in our quest to learn the truth. One more thing you might help us with-is there anyone that we could contact who might have more recent information about the cube?" John said.

Karen didn't respond immediately, John assuming it meant she was in thought. Dropping her forehead into her hands, John worried they might be over-taxing her strength. Eventually she raised her head and said, "The only person I can think of who might be of some help is a young girl who started working just before I ran away. Her name is, oh what was her name?, Amanda, that's it, Amanda-Amanda Bowers, yes, Amanda Bowers. She had a degree in an engineering field. I can't remember which one. I do know she didn't seen overjoyed with the way things were done with the cube so she might be more willing to talk to you," Karen said.

"Thank you for your time. We probably need to get going," John said looking at Carol giving her a nod as well.

"Why don't you stay for dinner. I don't cook much. I could find something for all of us," Karen said. Her attitude had changed immensely after conversing with John and Carol. John was sure she was starved for conversation and the two of them had whetted her appetite.

"No thank you. We've already put you out too much," Carol said moving closer to John.

"Is something amiss. Your tenor has changed since you used the computer?" Karen asked with a frown on her face.

She was a perceptive lady. Should he tell her someone was after them? "Miss Doddson, you deserve to know the reason after all you have given to us. People are searching for us at our hotel, so we need to get out of town, so to speak," John said beginning to worry for Karen's safety.

"My, do you want to stay here?" She offered.

"No!" Carol blurted out. In no way was she going to stay here with two wolves running around. "I mean you've done too much the way it is," She said in a calmer tone.

"Will you be safe here? I hope we have not blown your cover so to speak." John added.

"Don't worry about me. I've been in hiding for fifty years, so they will never find me because I don't exist," Karen said with a smile.

John and Carol thanked her again and told her they would be back in contact with her in the future, which she agreed to by giving them her e-mail address and phone number.

Now the difficult part. Where to go?

CHAPTER 20

Reading books with characters like Sherlock Holmes and James Bond might help in Carol and John's present situation. Neither of them were avid readers of these types of books. Now they were thrown into, using Dale Belfer's terminology, a cloak and dagger escapade in which the two were not proficient in performing the kinds of acts usually associated with these stories. Both had done a surprisingly good job thus far in avoiding being caught or watched.

As they walked down Karen's short drive to the rental car, the sun was slowly disappearing behind the San Andres Mountains to the West. After getting into the car, Carol stared at John with a scowl and said, "Since you've left me in the dark on everything, are you going to tell me who or what is watching our backs."

As he watched her give him a mild tongue-lashing, he saw her nostrils flare the least little bit and her lower lip tighten up after the words were spewed out. Seeing her this way, with those blue eyes glaring at him actually was intriguing because there was an inner beauty coming out at him he hadn't noticed. Carol was a person who didn't back down from anything, except maybe wolves.

"I told you before, I couldn't tell anyone, but now you know almost as much as I do. The person who is covering our asses is Peter Cozid, a private detective I hired. Now can we decide what we are going to do about our situation."

Carol's anger began to fade as a gentler hue came over her face. In part she was mad at herself for being such a bad judge of character. John was obviously very competent and diligent in his effort to find the artifact and she marveled at his ability.

"If someone is searching for us, we better get out of town as soon as possible."

Peter had suggested exchanging cars. John wasn't sure switching cars would be the best move. "What's your opinion on exchanging cars with Peter?" He asked.

"It's a good idea. Did you write down your license number when you registered?" Carol asked, sure that he did or the hotel security might have checked.

"You're right, let's get to the Santa Fe Trail and take his car. Wait, I have to go back. I didn't ask her the most important question; where is the cube?"

"She doesn't know."

"What!"

"While you were on the computer, I asked her. She doesn't know where it is now, but it was near Kirtland Air Force Base close to Albuquerque."

"Then it could still be there and the people we are looking for should be in the area: Robert White and Amanda Bowers."

"I suppose, though Karen thought differently."

Carol started the engine and they sped away down the mountain. Because the mountains blocked the sun as it descended in the west, the air was much cooler and it was darker in the valley. Arriving at the restaurant and finding Peter's rental, John parked and they were preparing to get out when two cars and a van pulled into the parking lot and surrounded John and Carol. The headlights of all three vehicles were directed at their car creating a glaring brightness in the late evening shadows.

Two men flashing badges and wielding guns approached the car yelling for them to get out and put their hands on top of the car. Looking over his shoulder and squinting his eyes, John tried to discern who the men were with no success.

He turned, looked at Carol, raised his shoulders and said, "Maybe it wasn't such a good idea. Don't do anything foolish."

"Me! It's been one surprise after another since I met you. Are you going to get out or just sit here?"

The men outside their car were still yelling for them to get out so John and Carol opened their doors and exited the vehicle, putting their hands on top of the car as the men directed.

The two men came nearer, frisking each for weapons, John supposed. As they were handcuffed, one of the two men told them they were under arrest and led them to the van.

As they walked toward the vehicle, John asked, "What's this all about?" "We've done nothing wrong or illegal. This is tantamount to false arrest."

"Save your speeches for someone who cares," one of the men said in reply to John's outburst. "The charge is treason."

"Treason!" John exclaimed. "You are crazy. Do you know what they are talking about?" He directed the question to Carol, expecting some response. She said nothing so John stared at her with a frown and said, "What gives, Carol?"

Carol, again gave him no response.

Nearing the van, the doors opened and a man and woman stepped out, helping them into the van. Carol and John sat in the middle seat, the woman who got out of the van sat in the back seat directly behind them, and two people were in the front seats. As they drove away from the restaurant, Carol could see the crowd of people that had congregated being directed back into the building by two police officers. The people were the last thing she saw as the agent behind them said she was going to blindfold them, which she did under great protest from Carol and John. The blindfolds were black ski masks turned backwards making them completely blind.

"PC must have given us away," John said in a whisper to Carol who was on his left.

The person in the front seat turned, looking at John over his shoulder and yelled, "Keep your mouth shut!"

Driving for what John estimated to be ten to fifteen minutes, then stopping, John and Carol heard a window open and words exchanged between the driver and someone who must be on the outside. Carol could not understand the words except the last statement from the outside voice was "Yes Sir".

The van moved again, only for a minute, then it stopped and they were ordered out of the van. After being helped to the ground, they were led to what Carol assumed was a building. As she entered Carol could tell they were walking on wooden floors. She could also sense that John was not with her and yelled out in a muffled cry, "John, John, where are you?"

Carol heard nothing in reply, as she was pushed through what she sensed to be a door because her shoulder brushed the door jam. From the echo of the footsteps, she knew it must be a small room.

She was guided to a chair and told to sit down. Carol's blindfold was removed and before her was a nemesis she couldn't seem to shake. "What are you doing here? I might have known," She exclaimed in the same snarly tone she had used with the Agents Feathers and Johnson in her office days ago. Her ire was up because sitting across the table was Colonel Gil Pratt in full uniform.

"You are not very nice to an old friend," Colonel Pratt said as he leered at Carol. "You have lost some hair since we last met."

"Your no friend of mine. I wouldn't want you as a friend if we were the last two people on earth," She spouted defiantly. The room she found herself in had no windows, a wooden floor, a table, two chairs and one door. It looked and felt old, with a musty smell you might find in a room that had not been used in a long time.

He stood, walked around the table, standing behind Carol, and then continued circling the table, like an animal cornering its' prey. "I see you haven't changed a bit since I booted you out of JPL. The next question is what to do with you and your lover?" He had the smallest of smirks on his face that caused Carol's eyes to water and nose to flare out.

"You can arrest me and try me. If you do, the tale of the pictures will come out at my trial and the world will know, so go ahead, and he's not my lover, I'm sorry to say," Carol said adding the last words in defiance!

Glaring at her with that holier than thou look, he said, "How naive you are Mrs. Jacobs. Let me explain something to you. You have no proof of any picture because we found the discs in the bag you were carrying as well as the photos. Dale Belfer gladly gave up all of his copies."

"What did you do to Dale? Is he okay?" Pangs of grief went through her body with thoughts of Dale.

"Mr. Belfer has seen the light. He is back at JPL, doing his work as he should have done till you coerced him," He replied as he sat back down across the table from her.

Carol started to come back at him again, then closed her mouth. Thinking over what he had said she responded, "You may have the evidence. I still have my voice and I can tell the world how evil you are."

"From Guantanamo Bay, Cuba. I doubt it. You will waste away." Colonel Pratt sat more erect in his chair like he was trying to stick his chest of medals and ribbons into her face.

"I'm a civilian. You can't send me to Cuba," She said without really knowing if he had the authority to carry out the threat.

"My dear, I can and I will if you continue your crusade. Haven't you heard of the Patriot Act? You will be sent as a suspected terrorist, never to be heard from again." He leaned back in his chair and seemed to be enjoying the banter, which caused more anger to swell up in her gut.

Sadly, the scenario outlined by the Colonel was likely true, yet she did not want to give him the satisfaction of knowing she agreed with him.

"Maybe we can come to some arrangement," He suggested.

"What kind of arrangement are you talking about?" She probably wouldn't like the answer to her question since her feelings toward the Colonel were very much out in the open.

The Colonel put his hand to his chin, then said, "We can work something out where you might return to your job, and no retributions will be inflicted."

She couldn't back down; not after all of the trouble her efforts had created. "Where is John—Dr. Kirkwood?"

"He is being taken care of and none of your concern since you say he is not an intimate friend. You better worry more about Carol Jacobs." He again gave that smirk irritating her to no end.

Concentrating, she attempted not to show any outward appearance indicating she was concerned. Having sparred with these people before, she worried John might not be prepared to deal with the agents. She more than anything wanted to talk to him.

Shortly after John entered the building, he was turned to his right into a room. He knew Carol was not with him. He thought it strange that in only a couple of days, he had this innate sense letting him know when she was near.

Being seated, the mask was removed, and before him stood two men. John's first words were, "I protest the blatant intrusion into my life and the usurpation of my rights as an American Citizen. Who gave you the authority to arrest me and on what charge. I demand to see an attorney. I want one here before I answer any questions, and by the way, where are we?" John exclaimed in his most demanding voice almost out of breath from the litany.

Neither of the two men seemed affected one way or another. They stood across a table from John in a room containing the one table, two chairs, a mirror, and one door. Finally one of the men sat down in front of John at the table, looked him straight in the eye and said, "Dr. Kirkwood, if I were you, I would be worrying more about staying out of prison than your rights being violated. Here is the situation. You are a collaborator to a suspected terrorist who might be plotting to attack the United States."

John couldn't keep quiet. He eyed the agent sitting across the table, knowing he had to rebuff the man. "One, I am an accomplice to no one and two: I know of no terrorist plot of any kind, so what you just said makes no sense."

The man sitting looked at the one standing, who was now leaning against the wall clipping his fingernails. John hated it when someone used one around him.

"Dr. Kirkwood, Let's review the events. One, you have been transporting and abetting a Carol Jacobs and two: She has been arrested for stealing government property for the purpose of conveying it to an organization bent on destroying the United States."

"You've got to be joking. Carol-Ms. Jacobs is no more a terrorist than you or me," John replied, "and where is she anyway?"

"How long have you known the woman?" He gave John a surly grin.

"Long enough to know she is no terrorist." Unless he had completely misjudged Carol, the entire line of questioning must be a fabrication.

"I'm sure you have-yes, I'm sure you have," He said with a wide grin as he looked over at the other man and winked.

"I don't know what you are implying. My relationship with Ms Jacobs is purely professional. Now where is she?" John fired back at him as he stood up, upset with himself for his emotional outburst.

"Sit down Dr. Kirkwood.-Sit down," He repeated. "She is in good hands."

"I want to know who you are and what authority gives you the power to detain me?" John sat back in the chair taking some time to evaluate his predicament as the two men took their time in answering.

"We are agents of the Government-the United States Government. I'm agent Johnson and he is agent Feathers. Now I'm going to lay it on the line. With the passage of the Patriot Act, we can send you to Guantanamo Bay

Cuba, as a terrorist where you have no rights or you can cooperate with us and possibly be released," Agent Johnson said.

"You can't send me there. I have rights," John said still upset.

"You had rights. Now are you going to help us?" Agent Feathers chimed in as he stuck the fingernail clippers in his pocket.

John was confused and disoriented. He always had control of his classes, his relationships, and his life. He found the control slipping away from him in this little room as his emotions began to take over his actions. Concentrating on keeping intelligent command of his behavior had to be his top proirity if he intended to keep on top of things.

"I know little you could possibly use in your investigation or what ever you are investigating," He returned.

"Oh, I wouldn't be so hasty. Have you seen the pictures Ms Jacobs had in her possession?"

Now John was at a crossroads. Telling these men about the pictures could only help put pressure on Carol. No way was she a terrorist. She couldn't be, so this had to be an effort to keep the pictures and the cube a secret.

"I have no idea what you are talking about," John said defiantly. "I want a lawyer."

"You're digging your own grave, Dr. Kirkwood," Agent Johnson said as he stood up and moved toward Agent Feathers.

The agents continued to grill him for what must have been five to six hours. Finally, they led him from the room, down a hall and into another room that looked like a cell. The room had no windows and the door had a bar across the side next to the hall. The building was definitely old and appeared to be rarely used from the creaks and groans the structure emitted.

A cot was in the room and an open doorway led into a restroom. Told he could rest for a short time, he used the restroom then lay on the cot trying to figure out the events leading him to this place. Who were these people and what connection did they have to the cube? Worried about Carol, he got up, walked to the door, tried to open it and found it barred from the outside. He guessed it to be early Tuesday, maybe three or four o'clock in the morning. His legs were weak from the many hours without rest. Returning to the cot exhausted, he lay down again and shortly fell asleep.

In another room similar to John's, Carol was so weak and tired from the interrogation, she couldn't keep her eyes open. She tried to evaluate her situation when sleep overcame her the same as it had John.

CHAPTER 21

Rain was such a rarity in Alamogordo, when it did occur, everything was brought to a stop and people viewed the falling water with adulation. The force of the raindrops striking the parched ground spewed the earth into the air creating small dust clouds. These were quickly dissipated by the continuing onslaught of the rain, which if it persisted, could produce flash flooding.

John was awoken first by the thunder and then by the relentless pounding of rain on the metal roof of the building where he was imprisoned. He was lying on his side with his back to the door when he sensed movement by the door. Glancing over his shoulder, he saw the door to his room open and someone enter, closing the door behind them. A soft drink logo was on the back of their shirt, and when the person at the door turned around, John got a huge surprise, which had lately been a common occurrence in his life.

Peter Cozid stood in front of John, your local beverage man, completely soaked and dripping water off of his face.

"You order some sodas," Peter said with a large grin on his face.

"What-Where did—," John mumbled as Peter cut him off whispering to him, "Be quiet and listen. We don't have much time. We have to find your female companion and get out of here within the next ten minutes or we are all done for. Got it?" He wiped his head and face with the blanket on the cot where John was sleeping.

"Yes," John said in a low voice, "Where are we?"

Peter returned, "Holloman Air Force Base. Now come on. First let me check." Throwing the blanket down and looking out the crack in the door, he saw no one around. He motioned John to follow as he replaced the bar across the door. The wooden floors creaked with every footstep, but the rain hitting the roof over-shadowed the sound of the footsteps. Near the end of the hall was a door that had a bar across the jam. Quickly they removed the bar, opened the door, and entered. Carol sat up from the bed, observing the two men with a dazed look on her face.

Realizing one of the men was John, she blurted out, "John, what's happening?"

He put his finger over his mouth signaling her to be quiet. Sliding his arm around her waist, he whispered to her that they were getting out. Peter cracked the door checking the hallway again as the rain continued to roar as it hit the metal roof.

"Come on, let's go," Peter motioned to them to go out the door as he moved in a stealthy way by crouching and walking on tiptoes. Reaching a door, he opened it and the three of them crowded in a very small room containing cleaning supplies. Peter was busy opening a small window that was chest high to him.

He motioned John to move to his side. "The doors to the building are all guarded so we must go out here. Slide through the window like you are diving into a pool. I'll hold your feet till you hit the ground. Hurry, time is running out," Peter said to them with a great deal of urgency.

The rain was pouring down as he put his head through the opening and slid over the edge. Holding his feet, Peter eased him down until John's hands touched the wet ground. As Peter let go, John did a forward roll in the mud. He quickly got up to help Carol.

Reaching up and grabbing her under the arms after she had stuck her head out the window, John pulled her through the opening as she held on to his shoulders and neck. She felt light in his arms as he let her feet touch the ground and get some footing.

He didn't immediately let go. He liked the feeling of her body against his and the softness of her short hair against his cheek.

Carol whispered in his ear, thanks and didn't let go right away either.

Sticking his head out the window, Peter broke the moment saying, "How about me?" They turned and together pulled him out.

Leading them away from the building to cars parked thirty feet away, Peter herded them behind a large SUV as the rain relentlessly pounded their bodies and faces. The rain was so heavy they had trouble seeing more that a few feet away.

"We're going to have to run from here to the truck I came in. It is parked about a quarter mile away and we have less than five minutes. Are you ready?"

Nodding their heads, they followed Peter as he ran along a gravel road. John's jogging was a godsend and Carol was staying close by his side.

The rain slowed their pace, as did the pools of water they sloshed through. The rain increased in intensity and pounded against their heads, faces, and bodies. Even with these hardships, they reached the truck in less than three minutes.

Both Carol and John started to get in the cab. Peter blocked their way and directed them to the back where he helped them climb up to the top of the truck.

They laid flat down on the top of the vehicle, the rain beating against their backs. Peter got in the truck, started the engine and drove toward the main gate.

"Your friend, Peter, is quiet resourceful."

"Yes, he has turned out to be a remarkable detective and seems to have many other talents in his repertoire."

"How did you find him?"

"Believe it or not, over the Internet."

John must be a very lucky guy or the tealeaves looked kindly on him when he got on the Internet.

As the truck rounded corners, their position became more precarious. The rain slapped at their bodies and ran down their faces causing each of them to squint their eyes so they could partially see. They braced themselves by laying face down and pressing their hands and feet against the ridges in the roof of the truck. Carol wrapped one of her arms around John's waist, feeling safer clinging to him with the sides of their bodies pressed together.

Nearing an entry gate, the truck slowed as the guards signaled it to stop. One guard chided Peter for leaving during the rainstorm and causing them to get wet. Peter was asked by the other guard to open one of the compartments so he exited the truck walking back to the first compartment, where he opened the door. One guard shined his light into it, his eyes following the beam. Peter knew the guard was getting wet since he could see the water running over the brim of his cap down onto his face. The guard wiped his face, looked at Peter and started to ask him to open another compartment, but instead told him he could go ahead.

Pulling the truck through the gate, Peter drove gingerly down the road for a half-mile until he was out of site of the gate. Carol and John needed no cue to get down and into the truck, both completely soaked and water logged.

Continuing down the road, John asked, "How did you find us?"

Not taking his eyes from the road, he explained. "I saw them arrest you at the restaurant and followed you to the base. I then had to come up with a way to enter and free you. I asked at a gas station near here and they told me the Soft Drink Truck delivered early every morning. I gave the driver some money to use his truck before he started the rest of his route for the day."

Finally the weather was a godsend that just happened to come along. Once in, I drove around till I saw one of the vehicles that took you away. I then drove the truck to where the real driver told me it normally parked and ran to your building where I was able to get in through the same window we went out.

"Now, having escaped, where are we going?" John asked as the rain slowed its torrential down pour into a light steady drizzle.

"My rental car has been moved to an old factory not far from here. I want you to drive to Albuquerque today, find a place to stay and call me tomorrow morning." Peter said.

"I have nothing to use to pay for rooms or anything else we might need. They took all my credit cards and credentials," John said. Carol added that she had no money.

"Here is a credit card to use. You'll need clothes. Don't stop for them in Alamogordo. Get on the road first and away from the city. I'll work on fake ID's," Peter explained as they drove into the lot of the abandon factory. The rain had completely stopped and the clouds were beginning to break letting the sun peek through the morning haze.

Getting the keys to the rental car, Carol and John exited the truck, thanking Peter. John got behind the wheel and after both were in, he headed the car north toward Albuquerque. He turned the heater on high hoping to warm up his and Carol's cold wet bodies and dry out their clothes. The morning was cool due to the rain, so rolling down the windows was not an option they could use to dry out.

Since lying on top of the truck, Carol and John had exchanged few words with one another, but now in the car together, they began a lengthy conversation.

"I need to get out of these wet clothes."

"I'll stop at the next town big enough to have a clothing store of some kind."

Carol unbuttoned the denim shirt she had been wearing and took it off leaving herself in a bra. John looked over at her and said, "I'll stop. I promise."

"Am I embarrassing you," She said, looking over at him with a questioning stare.

"Not at all," He replied as he looked at Carol out of the corner of his eye.

"Then how about watching the road instead of me before you kill us both."

John focused his eyes on the road ahead, yet his mind was on Carol. She was becoming in such a casual way, a part of his life and he didn't mind the least little bit.

After about two hours of driving, they arrived at Socorro, New Mexico, which contained a small strip mall with a department store. Carol had put her shirt back on and the two fugitives proceeded to get out of the car and enter the store. The sales clerk, a young girl of around twenty, eyed them with circumspection as they each gathered up a couple of sets of clothes, jeans, underwear, socks, towels and such and piled them on the counter. The sales clerk asked, "What happened to your clothes?"

Carol looked at her as serious as she could and said, "We are building an ark and we decided to test it with a "wet run"."

John gave a little laugh as the clerk rolled her eyes and said, "Sure."

204

The clerk rang up the clothes and John paid with the credit card Peter had given him earlier. Leaving the clothing store, they entered a shoe store three doors down the mall walkway, each purchasing a pair of athletic shoes and slip-ons.

Their wardrobe complete now, they needed a place to change out of their sticky wet clothes. Returning to the clothing store, Carol asked the girl if they could use the changing room to put their new clothes on. John thought the clerk was afraid to say no.

"I could still use a hot shower." Carol said as they walked over to the dressing rooms.

In due time, they were in dry clothes and on their way to Albuquerque.

"I think I have purchased new clothes two or three times and left a trail of items along my path to here. Someone could follow me by following the trail of clothes," She joked. The nursery rhyme came to mind where bread-crumbs were left along the trail and the birds ate the markers foiling the clues. What was its name? Ah, yes-Hansel and Gretel.

"You come across as having been one step ahead of these people? How about telling me who is chasing you and why they think you committed treason."

"I'm not sure who they represent. I'm positive they're connected to the military in some way. I don't know if the CIA is involved or if any other governmental agency is playing a part, but they want to make sure the copy of the picture no longer exits."

Carol then took the time to relate to John her entire ordeal at JPL, including copying the pictures and the theft of the computers at her house. It gave him a better understanding of her and reinforced the opinion he had already formed about her personality. She was a highly intelligent and very determined woman when she set a goal.

"Carol, why have you put yourself in such a dangerous position? You could have simply given the copy back and received only a reprimand I would imagine."

"If I had, I wouldn't have met you," Carol said wishing she hadn't expressed it quite that way. She had put her self out on a limb. John looked over at her and she recovered by saying, "Of course, I was just teasing. The real reason is I knew in my heart something was important in these pictures and I wanted to determine why others wanted to hide them, no matter where it led me."

Her last words reminded John of his remarks to Dr. Cable when he decided to go on the search for the artifact.

Another hour or so put them in Albuquerque. Stopping at a drug store, they purchased personal items and a cell phone. The atmosphere between them became more cheerful as the threat of being caught began to recede and they continued to feel more comfortable with each other's company.

The conversation during the trip from Alamogordo ran the gamut from experiences held in common to special times unique to each.

After the drive to Albuquerque, John suggested they find a place to eat. Carol said she wanted a hot bath and then eat. John acquiesced. Since he had purchased a hat and sunglasses back in Socorro, he used them to help disguise himself as he rented adjoining rooms at the Holiday Inn while Carol waited in the car.

Each went to their respective rooms, carrying their clothes in the shopping bags from the stores back in Socorro. After reaching his room, John was glad he let Carol have her way. He knew a shower would put some new life into his tired abused body. The warm water flowing from head to toe washed away the cold dampness from the earlier rain.

John put on a pair of shorts and a T-shirt from the clothing he had purchased and waited for Carol. Knowing if she took a bath it would take longer; the desire for food grew greater as time passed. Deciding he could wait not longer, he knocked on the adjoining door to see if Carol was ready.

The door opened and Carol stood before him wrapped in a towel drying her hair with another towel. "Are you getting hungry?" Her blue eyes sparkled as she eyed him from underneath the towel on her head.

Making no response, he only looked at her face with eyes that weren't blinking. The craving for food dissipated as he gazed at Carol.

Carol quit toweling off her hair and smiled, realizing the effect she was having on John. There was electricity igniting the air in the space between them and it acted like a magnet attempting to draw them together. All it would take was the slightest movement by either one.

John started to raise his hand toward Carol at the same time she was moving hers in his direction. They melted into each other's arms, the touch of their bodies igniting the passion, which had been building in each the past few days. Their lips met in a sensual kiss as their bodies molded to each other. Dropping the towel used to dry her head, Carol wrapped her arms around John's neck letting her body flow against his as their tongues met in an erotic dance.

Moving his hands to her waist, then with one around her thighs, lifted her and carried her to the bed. He fell on the bed with her as they rolled around together for a moment, then John whispered, "Should we do this, you're a married woman."

Carol's only response was, "Don't talk."

The towel slipped away from her body as she pulled at his shirt and shorts and when their naked bodies made contact, each knew there was nothing that could stop their love-making.

The sensations in each were so great that little foreplay occurred and their union seemed over almost before it began. They lay together afterwards; their bodies still encased like two anacondas.

Under his heavy breathing, John asked, "Can I talk now?"

Carol cooed, "Yes."

His only word was "Wow."

John and Carol lay in each other's arms for a long time, waiting for their bodies to come down from the high and the tingling to subside. After a time of snuggling together, the earlier passion slowly and quietly came over them again and they began making love once more, this time much slower exploring more of one another's bodies. John reveled in the soft curves of her body and Carol delightful in the hardness of his. Looking into each other's eyes, they knew there was a special connection between their two souls, but their thoughts were soon overtaken by the ecstasy consuming their minds and the passion possessing their bodies as they reached their peaks together for a second time.

CHAPTER 22

Connections between people occur often throughout life and in some rare cases those bonds can assimilate into unique relationships. Seldom is known the long-term outcome initially, yet again in those rare cases, a sensation that an affinity for another person is special can happen. Neither Carol or John knew exactly how the other felt, but there was a hypnotic efflorescence in the air signifying their union was not an "overnight fling". More passed between them last night than either could grasp at the moment.

After their lovemaking, they ordered food from hotel room service. Being sated from the sex and food, they crawled into bed and embracing each other fell asleep, both exhausted from the past two day's events.

Awakening Wednesday morning, stretching and touching one another to make sure the previous night was not just a dream, they caressed and kissed, wrapped in each other's arms. Neither spoke, both unsure what to say, then Carol arose, slipped John's T-shirt on and went into the bathroom. After she closed the door, John called Peter.

Peter answered, "You won't believe it. You're on the news. Escaped terrorists wanted by the FBI."

John, still with cobwebs in his head, didn't react immediately.

"Did you here what I said," Peter said frantically, "Your pictures are on TV and in the paper. You are lucky they didn't display them yesterday while you were driving to Albuquerque."

"You are joking-aren't you?" John said rubbing his eyes, trying to clear his head and focus on Peter's words.

"I am not joking. I have some good news and some bad news. Which do you want first?"

John's mind was still whirling from the terrorist statement, and now on top of everything Peter wanted to play games. He answered as he reached for the remote control to the television. "I thought being on TV was the bad news. Give me the good news. I definitely need some." He clicked on the TV to CNN.

"Okay, the name you gave me-an Amanda, eh, yes, Bowers-I've found her location. She is married and her new name is Amanda Patton. She and her husband live in the Cincinnati-Dayton, Ohio Area."

Dayton, Ohio-John repeated to himself. It comes up again. He had a strong feeling the artifact was back in Ohio, because when Amanda Bowers was hired in the early sixties as Karen said, it would have been in New Mexico. The coincidence of her winding up back in the Dayton area after applying for a job in New Mexico was too great. The cube had to have been moved. He still wanted to be sure. He asked Peter to find out what he could about Manzano Base at Kirtland Air Force Base.

"I will see what I can come up with."

"Very good. Now if you must, tell me the bad."

"I won't have your fake ID's until late today. We will also have disguises for your fake ID's."

John was wide-awake now, sitting up in bed leaning against the headboard. Turning up the volume on the TV, he saw Carol and his pictures plastered across the screen. The commentary was something to do with a terrorist plot. "Your right. We will have to do something with our looks. Our faces would be recognizable. I'm seeing them on TV right now. We will wait it out here at the Holiday Inn in Albuquerque. Where are you?"

"I'm still in Alamogordo tying up some loose ends. I will be at your hotel tomorrow morning at eight o'clock. We'll get you and the lady set up for travel. By the way, where do you want to go?"

He was wondering what loose ends he had to tie up as he clicked off the TV when Carol came out of the bathroom yawning, stretching her arms over her head. "Who are you talking to?"

Admiring her tall slender body, John didn't react to the question for a moment, then said, "Peter. He will have fake ID's here tomorrow morning. Do you want to go to Cincinnati with me?"

She cocked her head slightly, opened her eyes in a questioning look and said, "Yow, I do!"

Happy with her response, he told Peter Cincinnati was their destination unless he came up with information on Manzano Base. He was sure the artifact was moved from there to some other location and since Amanda Bowers-Patton was in the Dayton area, it seemed the best place to go.

"Peter, how difficult would it be for you to get an ID showing that Carol and I are agents for the FBI?"

"Why do you want those?"

"Call it intuition. Can you get them."

"Yes, but not by tomorrow morning. I can have them waiting for you in Cincy."

"That will work."

"Okay. Keep a low profile until I contact you again. I'll take care of all the arrangements. See you tomorrow." He said as he ended the call.

After John put down the cell phone, Carol asked, "Why are we going to Cincinnati? I thought you wanted to check out Kirtland."

He gave her his logic on why he felt the cube was back in Ohio. John told her about Peter finding Amanda Bowers back in the Dayton area and reminded her of Karen's belief it had been moved. Then he said, "Peter will be here tomorrow morning. Until then we are to keep a low profile."

Crowding back into bed next to John's naked body, she said coyly, "How low?"

She folded into his arms as their lovemaking started slowly building into a crescendo that took them to the same peaks they had ascended the night before. Carol's T-shirt disappeared, as their bodies seemed to mold together again, both conscious of tingling sensations wherever their skin touched.

Afterwards, Carol was lying on top of John, the perspiration of sex gluing their bodies together. Both were taking a long time to come down from the mountain they had just soared over as their heavy breathing slowly subsided.

It was as peaceful as John and Carol, each in their own way, had felt for a very long time. Neither spoke, letting the time flow without words.

Finally, he related to her the terrorist news stories with their pictures on the tube. Carol started to say something, then changed her mind, nestling against John's body, not wanting the moment to be ruined by the news.

After showering and dressing, they spent the day together shopping for clothes, luggage, and other items they needed. The first purchases they made were for a hat and sunglasses for Carol. They were constantly leery of making themselves noticeable and were always on the lookout for police or someone recognizing them. The mall they were shopping in also had a movie theater, so they opted to go to an afternoon matinee.

Leaving the theater after the movie and forgetting to put their sunglasses back on, they walked out the door and started down the mall corridor when John noticed a man and woman across the way pointing in their direction. He was not sure if they were pointing at Carol and him till the woman ran to a security person and pointed their way again as she conversed with the guard. During this time, Carol was talking to John about the movie assuming he was listening to all she was saying.

John interrupted her saying, "Carol, don't say anything, just move faster and when we get around the corner of the corridor, start running."

She responded by nodding and as they turned the corner, both took off in a dead run, jockeying their way through the people. As they neared the exit door to the mall, another security person outside the door was getting out of a vehicle with flashing yellow lights. He walked toward the exit door so John grabbed Carol's hand and pulled her into a large department store.

They hurried through trying to draw as little attention as possible. Reaching an escalator, they ran up the steps to a second floor of the store. Trying to keep from breathing heavily, John asked a sales person where the nearest exit was located. She directed them to a door leading into a passageway with windows overlooking the parking lot. The passageway led to a two story-parking garage, which they quickly ran through to the ramp leading up from ground level.

As they ran down the ramp, John could see the entire parking lot on this side of the mall. He located their rental car far in the distance. It would be a long run for both of them to reach their car before being spotted. In the distance, sirens resounded louder as they ran down the ramp.

Reaching the bottom, they zigzagged their way through the parked cars, bending over to make themselves less visible. Another security car drove down a lane near to them and to avoid detection, they ducked in behind a large van and waited until it passed. Looking at each other and saying nothing, they held hands and ran the last few yards to their rental car.

Carol got behind the wheel as John entered the passenger side and she eased the car out of the parking space and down the lane. The sirens could be heard from all directions as they neared the exit to the street. Carol maneuvered onto the avenue just prior to a police car pulling up to block the drive. She continued to drive along the street, glancing over at John knowing they had narrowly escaped capture.

Returning to the room, they both let out a sigh of relief. Carol turned on the TV and the local channel was showing a news bulletin about John and Carol being spotted at the mall. The pictures shown on TV of Carol and John were obviously taken at Holloman Air Force Base when they were in custody, because Carol's hair was short. Staring at the TV without saying a word, both knew they were fugitives on the run.

Carol broke the silence. "We are in big trouble."

John nodded in agreement and said, "I need to call someone." He had not told Carol about Dr. Cable and he decided she should know.

Carol, sitting in one of the chairs in the room, said, "Who do you have to call?"

Not sure how to explain Dr. Cable, John considered carefully his next words. "I met a man who induced me to get involved in the search for the cube. You might say he is my benefactor, since he is paying my salary, Peter's bills and all my expenses."

Carol looked up from her chair, starring at him with her icy blue eyes and said, "And who might he be?"

How much to tell her? John didn't mind her knowing yet was unsure what effect the story might have on her life. He was getting paid for his efforts and she, on the other hand, was out in the cold, on her own as far as finances were concerned.

"His name is Dr. Henry Cable. He is ninety years old or more and was an archeologist of some renown in his heyday. He approached me about the cube."

Carol, moving from the chair to lay on the bed diagonally, with John sitting up against some pillows and the headboard, said, "I want to know it all. Tell me."

He began with the meeting in his office and spent the next hour telling Carol all the events occurring to him in the past two weeks. She listened patiently throwing in questions now and then.

Afterward, John used the cell phone to call Dr. Cable.

Hearing him answer, he said, "Yes sir, this is John. I'm sorry I haven't checked in sooner."

"No need to apologize. I see from the news you've been very busy. Who is the mysterious woman you're connected too?"

John relayed to Dr. Cable Carol's history and how they had come together as well as how important she had become to his investigation. He exhibited through the inflection in his voice a keen interest in the pictures she had and wanted John to fax copies to him.

"The agents took them and the computer disc so we have no proof the pictures even exist." No immediate response came from Dr. Cable. John was sure he was disappointed. "Dr. Cable, are you there?"

"Yes, I'm here. Where is your destination now?" Dr. Cable asked in a very weak voice. John could barely hear his question.

"Cincinnati. Are you feeling okay?" The concern in John's voice was apparent to Carol.

"Call me when you get there," He said as he ended the call.

John was not surprised by Dr. Cable's brevity. He seldom wanted many details. John was concerned because sometimes during their conversation Dr. Cable's voice sounded weaker than the last call and a couple of times he spoke slow like he was sleepy or on drugs. Maybe when you get to be ninety, you sometimes talk that way.

"What did he say?"

"Not much. Usually I just report what I've been doing and he asks some questions or gives some suggestions. This time he seemed far away. He was very interested in the pictures we don't have anymore."

"I have an idea about the pictures. I'll let you know later what I find out regarding them." Carol interjected a tidbit of information for John.

Knowing they didn't dare take another chance on being recognized, they ordered room service and spent the evening in their rooms. They lay on the bed relating to each other more of their individual life histories, along with stories of their accomplishments and disappointments. Talking until two o'clock in the morning, they reached a point where they both fell asleep.

The next morning, John answered a knock at the room door. He had rolled out of bed early, showered, shaved, dressed and then woke Carol. She was in the shower when Peter entered their room.

He came carrying a large attaché case, which he set on the table under a lamp. He started to say something and John interrupted. "I don't want to hear it."

"Oh, your no fun. I had a couple of good lines to use on you and the lady," Peter said disappointedly.

"I'll bet you did. Another time maybe. Were you able to dig up anything on Manzano Base?"

"Of course," Peter said in his usual self-praising way. "The base was combined with Kirtland in 1971. Prior to 1971 it was very hush-hush. It was controlled under a special weapons group that was disbanded a few years later. Does any of this help?"

"Yes, thanks. You've answered the main question for me. Now, can you get us to Cincinnati without the FBI or some other agency putting us under arrest?"

"Have I ever failed you? Let's sit down," Peter said as he sat at the small desk while John went to the bathroom door, knocked, and said, "Carol, Peter is here."

"I'll be right out."

John sat in another chair as Peter opened the case showing him an Ohio driver's license for Carol and saying, "I could get you fake Passports, but you don't need those unless your going out of the country."

"How are we going to do the picture?"

"I have the disguises for you before I take your pictures."

Carol entered the room in jeans and a shirt, eyeing the two men sitting at the table. She greeted Peter. "John said you looked out for him. It's nice to see you again."

"So he said that, did he!" He looked at John with a grin on his face. Addressing Carol. "I'm happy to see you looking refreshed."

She smiled knowing what a mess she was at the base when Peter helped them escape.

Peter showed them their tickets for Cincinnati with a stopover in St. Louis. He had a make-up kit, with wigs for Carol and a mustache for John. The three worked on the disguises for almost two hours until they had something all of them agreed would pass as reasonably authentic and would make it difficult for others to recognize their faces from the pictures in the paper and on TV. The long hair together with some dark glasses gave Carol an entirely different look.

John kept the mustache and his hair was dyed light blond. At last Peter took his digital camera and made pictures of both John and Carol in their disguises. He gathered up the camera, ID's, and departed. He would develop them to use on their fake driver's licenses he had obtained from a supplier he knew in Cincinnati.

After having brunch downstairs in the hotel, John and Carol returned to their room. No one seemed to pay any attention to their new looks, so they felt confident they would pass.

"What are our plans John? Let's talk about where we are going and what we can do," Carol said as she was taking the wig off for the time being.

Thinking about their future for a moment, he replied, "Yes, we do need to develop a plan. I can see two things, one would be to talk to Amanda Bowers, and another would be looking for some way of proving the cube and the object in space exist and have been kept secret from the American People as well as the rest of the world."

Nodding her head, she agreed with everything John had said with one addition. "If you remember, Karen said Dr. Happard had something that would prove the cube existed, but she never knew what it was. If we could determine how Dr. Happard could prove the artifact's existence, then we might have some leverage in accomplishing our goal."

"Yes, we should talk to Karen again and ask her if she remembers any more about this so called proof." John stared far into the distance. His mind was deep in thought.

Seeing John with that odd look on his face she had noticed several times in the past, as if he were in a daze, Carol surmised he was devising some other scheme and said nothing.

His eyes finally focused on the immediate surroundings. "Carol, if we are to prove the artifact exists and let it be known, I see a need for a public figure to champion our cause. Finding someone, let alone persuading them will not be easy. The best bet would be the President."

Carol had a questioning stare. She asked, "'The president of what?"

"The United States," came the reply from John.

Carol was stunned. How could they persuade the President an alien artifact was in the United States, much less getting information to the President? "Well, just tell me the answer to this question; how can we get to know or see the President of the United States?"

"Make it impossible for him not to want to talk to us," John replied.

"And just how do we go about making this happen?"

"I don't have the foggiest idea—yet!"

CHAPTER 23

The political battlefield is a gaming arena in which the experienced have the upper hand. Besides considerable connections, influence, and money, most politicians have a talented staff to run point for them and guide their decisions. Attempting to persuade the President of the United States of a mystic cube, much less getting an audience with him seemed like trying to climb Mount Everest walking backwards.

When Peter knocked at the door an hour after he left, Carol let him in, surprised at how quick he completed the ID's. He presented two Ohio driver licenses displaying their pictures in the new disguises. He also gave them two credit cards in each of their new identities along with two thousand dollars in cash.

"These credit cards are for identification purposes only, so don't use them to charge any items. Also, a woman will meet you at the Cincinnati airport with the FBI identifications and keys to a car. She will have a red coat with a blue scarf around her neck and black hair. When you see her, walk up to her and say 'I'm a friend of Dr. No'."

Their flight would depart Albuquerque in less than two hours, so they began packing and preparing to leave. Neither of them was happy with the names Peter chose for their fake ID's, but had little choice since they were his creations.

"What are you going to do?" John asked of Peter since they were leaving for Cincinnati.

"You're always worrying about me. Carol, does he nag at you like he does me? Never mind! Don't answer that question. Here is the address of Amanda Bowers, now Patton. It's just North of Cincinnati. Give me the keys to the rental car and I'll take care of its return. You can take a cab to the airport. I will be back in Cincy this afternoon, actually before you two arrive."

Starting to inquire how it was possible for him to beat them, John began his question, then stopped. No-as often as Peter amazed John, he decided to just accept Amanda Patton's address and go on.

Peter walked to the door. "I will see you in Ohio, soon I'm sure," He conveyed to them as he exited the hotel room.

The guy is strange, Carol thought to herself. He pops up everywhere, and according to John, finds people who disappeared tens of years ago, and he seems to have the answer to every question. "He is quite a maverick," She said to John across the room as she finished packing her bag.

"Yes. He never ceases to surprise me. I was lucky to have obtained his services."

After packing and checking out, they took a cab to the airport, picking up their boarding passes with no problems. Their new disguises and identities were working perfectly. No one seemed to give them a second look so they became very confident in their appearances.

Losing time as they flew east, the trip in regional time took two and one half-hours, only stopping in St. Louis for a few minutes, but it was late afternoon in Ohio when they arrived at the Cincinnati area airport. They walked along the corridor passing security and finally saw a woman standing along the side of the walkway wearing a red coat. She had black hair and an average body size for a woman of five feet. The high heels gave her a taller appearance as John approached her saying, "I'm a friend of Dr. No." Her eyes lit up as she reached in her purse and moving close to John slipped him an envelope. She turned and walked away without saying a word.

John turned to Carol and said; "Now that was right out of James Bond."

Inside the envelope were the forged FBI papers and a set of keys with directions to the parking lot where the car was located.

Finding the car, they took a chance on Amanda Bowers being home and drove to her house using the directions supplied by Peter.

Heading north on Interstate71, they exited at mile marker 32 and drove toward Lebanon, Ohio. Eventually, winding through the country, they proceeded along a gravel road to a home in the woods near the Little Miami River. The lane passed through tall oak and hickory trees and was lined by a split rail fence on one side. At the end of the lane sat an English Tudor home in brown and white surrounded by a garden of flowers.

The sun was beginning to fade in the west as Carol and John parked in front of the house and walked to the front door. John clanked the door-knocker making an unusually loud noise startling Carol as she adjusted her wig. Almost instantly, the door opened causing her to jerk her hand away from the wig.

The man who stood looking at the two of them appeared to be in his late fifties, overweight with a large belly and wore shorts and a T-shirt with the Cincinnati Bengels logo on the front.

John began. "Good day. I'm Curt Wood and my friend is Jane Cobb." He used the fake names given to them by Peter. "We wish to know if an Amanda Patton is present. We would very much like to talk to her."

The man looked at them suspiciously. "What might this be in reference to," He asked in a very noble tone defying his lack-a-dazical appearance.

Carol availed herself. "We are acquainted with a friend of hers who directed us to your locale. We have some inquiries which she might help us answer."

His reaction was stolid, then he yelled, in a much less regal tone than before, "Amanda, you have visitors. Come in if you want. Let me take you to the rear of the house." They walked through a hallway into a kitchen, and then out French doors onto a deck. The view from the deck was spectacular. The hills in the distance were covered with trees and in the valley below ran the Little Miami River.

As they took in the view, a voice behind them said, "Can I help you?"

Turning, Carol's eyes met a very large woman with dark black hair. Carol replied, "Why yes, are you Amanda Patton?"

Her reply was quick, "Yes." Her eyes gave the impression she was checking out John and Carol in her mind as she scanned them from head to toe.

"We know a woman who worked along side of you many years ago," John explained. "She sent us to talk to you."

Looking at them with suspicion, she asked, "To whom are you referring?"

John replied, "Karen Doddson is her name."

As she stood thinking, a different complexion came over Amanda face as she stepped back. Carol knew she must have suddenly remembered the name because her attitude instantly changed.

"I must ask you to leave. I've never worked with anyone by that name in my life. I always worked alone, so you are mistaken or have been mislead," She said as she turned to lead them back through the house to their car.

John was quick to respond. "We are not mistaken Mrs. Patton. We know you dealt with the cube."

She hesitated in her movement, then moved again toward the door. When she reached the French doors leading into the house, she turned saying, "Again, I must ask you to leave."

Carol moved toward the woman. She said in a soft voice, "We know everything Amanda. Now won't you talk to us and answer a couple of our questions."

Just as Carol finished, the breeze picked up around the house blowing the seeds from the trees onto the three people gathered on the deck. When John was growing up in the Midwest, they would refer to these floating pods as helicopters, due to their spinning motion as they cascaded slowly to the ground. Time seemed to freeze as the three people gazed at the decent of the small acrobatical flyers.

As the wind eased, the eyes of the three people on the deck returned to each other with Amanda saying, "If you know everything, why do you need to ask me questions?"

Seeing she was beginning to soften her attitude, John continued, "We just have to clean up some points before we return to Washington, D.C."

"Who do you work for?"

"We are not at liberty to disclose what agency we represent. Rest assured, we work for the highest levels of an investigative arm of the government."

"It's about time someone looked into this matter. If I talk to you, I could lose my pension and they could have me arrested and put in jail." She spoke with a worried look that gave Carol the impression her words were under-lined with a great deal of fear.

Seeing this hint of fear in Amanda's eyes as she made the last statement, Carol added, "Amanda, we are sworn to secrecy and are not permitted to divulge where we receive the information we obtain. Our agency works for the good of all the people of the United States. No one will ever know we were even here to see you." She continued the charade John had started.

Amanda looked at the two strangers standing on her patio. Not moving, she turned to look out at the valley below, then turned back to Carol and John. "I am sorry, but I can't risk the loss of my pension and possibly going to jail. You will have to leave."

John reached in his coat pocket and pulled out his fake FBI badge and ID. "If you must know, we are FBI agents and you will answer our questions here or in custody. It is your choice."

The breeze stopped its whistling in the trees completely and the deck and valley below, in an instant, were devoid of any sounds. The air was full of tension created by John's decree.

Looking at the two, Amanda's eyes moved back and forth from Carol, who had pulled out her fake FBI badge, to John, who remained statuesque before her. Speaking in a calmer voice, she said, "Please have a seat." She pointed toward a wooden table with wooden chairs near the railing of the deck.

Taking a seat, Carol felt extremely confident in her masquerade. "We are interviewing people connected to Project Mogul. You are just one of many," Carol explained, attempting to put her at ease.

As they sat down, Amanda said, "You realize they do not recognize the FBI's or anyone else's authority except their own security department."

"What kind of security department does not have to listen to the FBI?" Carol asked.

"The one supposititiously connected to the Defense Intelligence Agency, which is part of the Pentagon. The security was at one time part of the CIA, but someone long ago discovered they could be a section of the DIA and have less scrutiny by Congress."

From Amanda's description, John believed a shadowy intelligence group must have been established to protect the cube, and they were the ones spying on them.

"Why have you come to me. Many other people are more knowledgeable and better qualified to answer your questions."

"Exactly who are you referring to?" John asked.

"The people at Wright, as well as the Defense Department come to mind. I was just one of the engineers who worked on the project."

"Are you speaking of Albuquerque?" Carol asked.

"No, of course not. We moved back to Dayton a long time ago. Don't you know where I worked?" She said with quizzical eyes.

John jumped in to explain. "Of course. We prefer you to answer the questions so we can complete our file. We knew you worked at Manzano Base. Exactly where did you work at Wright?"

"After we moved back to Wright, I worked there until I retired eleven years ago. Are you sure the information I give you won't affect my pension?"

"We are sure, and for the record, how much is your pension and who provides it to you?" John asked.

"Presently it is $95,000 and it goes up each year. As to where it comes from, all I know is I get a check the first of each month from the Harriston Bank of Cleveland, Ohio."

John and Carol turned, looking at one another and Carol raised her eyebrows as if to say 'wow'. She could tell John was having the same reaction.

John said, "Your pension is quite large." To him the amount seemed exorbitant and must be an example of the money involved in the use of the artifact.

"So now you know why I don't want to do anything to jeopardize my pension and my husband wouldn't like it either."

"Did you work in or near to building A-19?" John asked.

"Of course, except as you know it was in the underground complex below A-19."

John shook his head in acknowledgement of what she said as if he already knew. "Were you connected to the cube, and if so for how long?"

Amanda stretched her large arms across her huge waist as she replied, "The first five years I was, then I moved to an administrative position, and finally to the Council of Determination."

"How many people were involved in the effort to extract information?" Carol inquired.

"Hundreds, maybe thousands. I'm not sure. I must tell you that very few of the people involved were aware of the cube. Only a select few knew of its existence. I did not know everything. Each person was denied some knowledge. I always had suspicions part of the organization was outside Wright Field."

"How did they keep it from all the other people?" John asked.

"The story given to others was that we were working on very important secret research dealing with the national security of the United States. Most people had no idea where all the new ideas and data were coming from except that it was being developed by a team of scientists."

"Tell us about the administrator's position you had and the council," John asked.

Staring away from the two visitors, she looked off into the distant hills and the fading sunset. "I am leery about telling you or anyone about the inner workings of the project. The security around the project is purported to be among the tightest in the entire U. S. Government. One of the security people told me once their motto was 'take no prisoners'. I'm sure that is just a saying, but it gives you the idea of how dedicated they are in keeping the knowledge of the cube under wraps. Of course, most security people knew little about an alien artifact; they were defending our National Security."

"We know of the efforts to keep it under control and are willing to accept the dangers we may encounter. Please go on." After his last words, John looked over at Carol hoping she agreed. His look received a conferring nod.

"After five years on the cube, most scientists and engineers are burned out and given another job. Mine was external denial. I was part of a group that analyzed material and data from the world media that might lead someone to suspect something was amiss. My particular section dealt with preventing various military departments stumbling on to something related to the cube."

"If you could explain what you mean because, Karen Doddson said, 'even the President of the United States doesn't know about the project'. How did you keep it from the President? We both thought the President knew everything," Carol stated.

"You both are a little naive. Many things have been kept secret even from the President. Project Shamrock is a good example," She said.

John had a quizzical look on his face. "What is Project Shamrock?"

"During World War II, President Roosevelt authorized the Defense Intelligence Agency which later became the NSA or National Security Agency to wire tap anyone they felt was a security risk for the U. S. After the war, President Truman agreed to continue the practice because of the cold war and the nuclear scare. He was the last President to know that the NSA was tapping the phones of any citizen in the U. S. suspected of doing anything against the government. If the FBI was interested in someone, their name was passed through the Intelligence Community until NSA got it and they put a tap on the person's phone."

"The wire tapping went on until the 1970's when the Weatherman, a supposedly subversive group opposed to the U. S. Government, were put on trial for their activities against the Government. Their attorneys asked the Justice Department for all records and information on how they collected the evidence to prosecute these people. Well, much of the information came from wiretaps from the NSA. The NSA didn't want it revealed that they were tapping everyone's phones so to keep from divulging that little item, the case against the Weathermen was dropped. Later, President Ford found out about the executive order and rescinded it, but for thirty years no President knew anything about the illegal wire tapping of normal citizens."

"Now you ask me how the cube is kept from the President. It is really not hard to do."

"Then how did you keep the funding for it a secret?"

"The Project Mogul was buried in the budget of the CIA under covert ops never to see the light of day. You see, their budget is not public record. Other money was obtained through the Defense Intelligence Agency. A select few had knowledge of its existence, and where the money came from to support it. These people were non-political appointees, so as the Administrations changed, the personnel with the cube remained the same. Today they probably make so much money from the ideas derived from it, they need little government funding," She said.

Both John and Carol were absorbed in all the information Amanda was telling them. The conversation became quiet as they attempted to analyze all the revelations.

Eventually John inquired of Amanda, "Who were the higher ups who knew?"

Carol took out a pen and a notepad to write the names.

Amanda started with a Senator from Texas, two Representatives, one from Alabama and another from South Carolina and a former Assistant Director of the CIA along with others John did not know. When she finished, John stared at her amazed at the caliber of the people who had knowledge of the cube. Amanda admitted there might be many more people who she was not aware, with knowledge.

He asked, "All of these people knew that the U. S. had an alien artifact providing them with information?"

Her response was, "Oh no. They were told the information was stolen from the Russians and everything was in an unusual code. The people I named knew we had secret information. As I said before, only a small group were aware of the artifact."

"What is the entire story?" Carol wanted to know.

"I'm afraid you'll have to ask someone else. All I know was that we possessed an alien artifact. I always presumed it was obtained in the Roswell incident in 1947 where they said an alien space craft crashed."

Something distracted Amanda's attention as she stood and excused herself.

Looking over his shoulder, John saw her husband standing on the other side of the French doors. Shortly, he and Amanda were in a discussion and it appeared to be quite heated. Seeing John staring at the house, Carol also could see the two in an argument and started to comment to John when Amanda came out of the house with a dire look on her face.

"You will have to leave. You have to leave right now!" She said with all the urgency she could inflect into her voice.

"What's wrong?" responded John.

"My husband thought you were bringing trouble into our lives and called the people. You don't have much time. You must leave and calling your friends at the FBI won't work because they can't get here before the other people."

"What other people?" Carol asked.

"The ones from the Project. You must go. If they catch you, well, you don't want to know." Amanda was becoming frantic to the point of trying to push them toward steps leading off the deck. She was directing them to use the path at the bottom of the steps.

John grabbed Carol by the arm. "Let's go Carol." They went down the set of steps to the pathway leading from the deck around to the front of the house. As they were turning the corner of the house, John pushed Carol back after seeing two cars approach the house sliding in the loose gravel along the drive.

Turning, they ran to the back of the house meeting Amanda. She pointed to another trail and said, "Follow the path down the hill. It takes you to the river. Our canoe is beside the small building. Take it quickly."

"Thanks Amanda for all your help and information," Carol said as she and John took off in a lope down the hill.

It was a steep incline with the path winding through the woods. It was difficult to traverse with the sun light almost completely gone. They ran the best they could, moving quickly to the bottom. Upon reaching the end of the trail, there was, as Amanda said, a small building and dock, with a canoe leaning against the side of the building.

John slid the canoe off the dock into the water while Carol looked for paddles. She opened the door to the shed and found them hanging along the wall.

Within a few seconds, they were paddling downstream close to the shore along the side directly below the house. Placing the paddles quietly in the water so as to make the least amount of noise, each stroke sent them farther down the river and away from the people after them. Having used canoes on some of his expeditions, John knew sound traveled a long way in a river valley.

They were nearing the turn in the river where they would be out of view of the dock when two loud bangs echoed along the river valley. As the noise occurred, John heard two pings and small splashes in the water near the canoe.

Carol looked over her shoulder at John. "What was that?"

"Keep paddling with all you might and don't look back. I think they are shooting at us."

An adrenaline rush went through John's body as the fear of being shot entered his mind. He seemed to have super-human strength as he propelled the canoe with new vigor. Shortly they were out of sight of the house above and the dock upstream.

"I can't believe they were shooting at us." Carol spoke frightfully and full of fear.

Having a sense of security and thinking they had evaded capture, they both relaxed, catching their breath from the hastened escape. Carol's ears perked up as she heard a noise above the trees. Looking over her shoulder and raising her hand to point skyward, she directed John to look where she was signaling. He could see a helicopter far in the distance.

Their feeling of safety quickly slipped from their minds as they again paddled with a new sense of urgency.

"We must find a place to hide," John conveyed to Carol. "We can't out run the helicopter."

As he spoke to Carol, they passed through some overhanging trees and Carol's wig became entangled in the limbs. As the canoe continued to slide downstream the wig was jerked from her head and dangled on the end of the limb.

John reached for it, but couldn't grasp it. Not having time to turn back, they left the wig hanging from the tree limb. "I'm sorry Carol, I couldn't reach it."

Nothing could be done about the wig so Carol, riding in the front of the canoe, searched the dark areas along the river bank and pointed, "There, just ahead. It looks like an opening in the trees." She directed the canoe toward the opening on the right. They found a small stream entering the river located where Carol had seen the opening, probably supplied by a spring somewhere in the hill above them.

The stream was not deep enough for the canoe to navigate so they stepped out into the water. Carol felt a cold sensation as the water surrounded her feet and she scrunched her toes as the water filled the small spaces around her digits.

Pulling the canoe into the ditch the small stream had carved out over hundreds of years, their view from overhead and from the sides was adequately blocked by walls of dirt, leaves and tree limbs. John pulled up some small bushes growing in the wet mud and put them near the entrance to the ditch to block the view from the river.

The helicopter flew overhead following the river and as it passed their hiding spot, seemed to hover before continuing downstream. Soon it would be completely dark and they would attempt to extricate themselves from yet another predicament.

CHAPTER 24

The ripples in the water on the Little Miami River reflected the moonlight reminding Carol of the mirrored balls hanging over the dance floors at many wedding receptions and parties she had attended. A cool breeze carried the dying winter chill through the bushes on this beautiful clear spring night and the stars twinkled throughout the night sky.

As they waited for darkness to completely descend, Carol had tried to use her cell phone to call Peter, but in the river valley, the signal was too weak. John's cell phone was in the rental car back at Amanda's house. Staring at the first stars beginning to brighten the night sky, she told John, "You know they will be searching along the river for us. They know we are in the boat or on foot." Her voice quivered from the cool air and damp feet encased in the wet shoes.

"Yes, we need to get to a position where we can call Peter and see if he can help us escape. I think it is dark enough now for us to continue down the river."

Quietly as possible, John and Carol pushed the canoe back to the main channel and after slipping in they began to paddle downstream. Steering the canoe just inside the shadow of the trees, they were able to remain in the dark yet use the moonlight to navigate down the stream. Without some illumination, it would have been impossible to venture out on the water.

Very few words were spoken between them since the slightest sound might give their location away. The canoe glided silently through the water as they neared a turn in the river. The hope of lights from a town or city was in their minds as the canoe edged around the bend in the stream.

"I see a light," Carol whispered from the front of the boat.

"I see it too!" Just as John finished responding to Carol, he began to hear a noise similar to a hum. As they proceeded the hum began to increase in intensity. "Steer to the bank quickly," John urged Carol.

Carol turned her efforts in the direction John had instructed and guided the canoe toward a fallen tree along the water's edge.

"Let the boat float in behind the tree," John said in a hushed tone.

The sound of a motorboat was very plain now as the canoe slid in behind the trunk of the large tree floating next to the riverbank. John held on to a limb to keep the canoe in place as he and Carol lay down in the canoe hovering below the side.

As the motorboat approached, a beam of light was shone back and forth along each side the river. When the light passed over the log and bank where they lay, it hesitated. For a moment, Carol was sure they had been spotted until the light moved farther upstream and the boat continued without slowing or stopping. The tree had done its job of blocking the view of the canoe.

After they were out of sight, she and John returned to their upright positions and continued downstream.

"That was a close call," Carol whispered to no one in particular even though she and John were the only two people around.

What seemed like hours was less than thirty minutes when they both noticed a glimmer of light coming from beyond the next bend. Both paddles were stroked with caution as they moved toward the light. As they neared the glow they began to hear the sounds of traffic, a great deal of traffic. The noise from what must be tractor-trailer trucks began to drown out any sounds from the paddles, which were stroked with more urgency.

Carol riding in the front turned, looking back over her shoulder and informed John, "We're crossing under a highway."

"I see. It may be an interstate with the sound of the traffic."

"Let's get out and follow the highway to an exit. I'll try the cell phone again," She suggested.

After these words, they ditched the canoe under the two bridges carrying the traffic and made the trek up the steep embankment to the highway over the river. As difficult as the climb was, they both safely reached the end of the bridge and gathered their bearings.

Finding themselves next to the southbound lane, John determined the highway to be Interstate 71, the same road they had traveled from Cincinnati. Seeing no mile marker, they were undecided on which direction to choose.

"I think I see a sign on the north bound side," Carol informed John.

"Let's go, but we will have to stay off the road and out of sight as much as possible. We don't want some driver calling 911 when they see people walking along the road." Thankfully a large swath of grass lay next to the southbound lane where they were walking and the side of the road sloped down toward the woods giving them more cover. They moved north and again the trek was rough going. Having to stay in or close to the weeds and bushes, Carol was becoming fatigued.

It turned out Carol had been right about the sign across the Interstate on the northbound side. Walking along the southbound lane against the traffic to the entrance ramp, they were happy to see gas stations and other businesses located at the exit.

Walking in behind a culvert where they were out of visual range of any car coming down the ramp, Carol tried her cell phone again. Here she had service and as Peter's number began to ring, she handed the phone to John. "Here, he's your employee."

Taking the phone from Carol, he waited until Peter came on the line.

"I've been hoping you would call. A massive manhunt is underway in the Lebanon area and it is for you two terrorists."

"We know. We're at an exit on I-71. I believe its exit 36. Listen, can you get us out of this mess?"

"Haven't I always. It's becoming a full time job."

Not replying to his comment, John said, "I believe an abandoned gas station is located on the South side of the crossing highway. We will hide behind it till you get here, but hurry."

"Will do. I'll flash my lights on and off twice so you will know it's me. See you soon."

After ending the call they waited until no traffic was coming down the ramp then ran over and climbed the fence running along the Interstate. They followed the fence until they were almost to the crossing highway with the abandoned gas station on their left. Then staying in the shadows, they scurried over to the paved area around the empty gas station. In behind the building were some old barrels and two trash bins running over with garbage. John did not mention anything to Carol, but was sure he saw rats in the vicinity.

"Let's get to a place where we can quickly slip off into the dark if a police car happens upon our location."

Carol answered, "It looks like the two barrels on the other side of the building are close to a ditch. It will be ideal for our needs."

"Great, lead the way." The Mini Mart across the road and the little bit of moonlight provided just enough light for them to see their way without running into anything.

Carol took off at a fast pace in behind the building then out to the side and in back where the two barrels were located. Just behind the barrels was a drop-off down an embankment and into a wooded area with lots of underbrush.

Each picked a barrel and sat down leaning against it and facing away from the highway and towards the ditch.

Her wet shoes and socks were causing her feet to itch, but she knew if she took them off, she may not be able to get them back on as sticky as the shoes seemed to be.

John caught his breath, then looked over at Carol. She had not faltered an iota on their most recent escapade and it gave him some pride in having her as a companion. She had made the search for the artifact more interesting and exciting in a way he never expected. He knew a decision needed to be made quickly to expose the cube because if their pattern continued, eventually they would be apprehended and not even Peter would be able to save their skins.

As he sat mulling over ideas, he began to nod off. He said to himself, this is no time to sleep. He needed to be alert because hopefully Peter would soon be pulling into the abandoned station. John was tired since he and Carol had stayed up talking most of last night.

Jerking his head back to an erect position and glancing over at the barrel next to him, a shiver of fear ran through his body. Carol was not leaning against her barrel. Rolling over on his stomach, he looked around the edge of his barrel scanning the area near the vacant building.

Seeing no sign of her, he tried to think of reasons why she would have left without telling him. He could see the Mini Mart across the road with all the bright lights and several cars filling up with gas, but no indication she was in the vicinity and her cell phone was still lying beside the barrel. Maybe she had to use the bathroom and went down into the ditch or across the street into the mini mart. Surely she wouldn't be taking a chance like that knowing there was a manhunt out for them and without the wig, she would be more likely to be recognized.

Becoming anxious waiting for her to return, he considered leaving his hiding place and searching the area when a car pulled in front of the vacant building and flashed its lights two times. Realizing Peter might leave if no one came, he knew he had to get to the car. Finally he picked up Carol's cell phone and eased around the barrel, dashed to the front of the vacant building and slipped into the front seat, happy to see Peter's smiling face.

The smiles quickly disappeared as Peter asked, "Where's Carol?"

Slightly embarrassed to admit, John said, "I don't know. I dozed off for a second and she was gone."

"The longer we hang around here the greater the chance of being spotted and questioned," Peter said. Just as Peter finished, several police cars, lights flashing, but no sirens were exiting the interstate on the highway and pulling into the Mini Mart across the street.

"We need to leave. It's too dangerous sitting here," Peter said as he put the car in gear and began to pull onto the highway.

As John said, "I won't leave Carol," his worst fears came true. Across the street, she was being led out of the Mini Mart in handcuffs and put into one of the patrol cars. He reached over grabbing Peter's arm.

"Yes, I see her too! We can't do anything for her now. I'm sorry John."

Shaken by his inability to help Carol, his anger was building to a high boil. He watched the patrol car drive away with her as he and Peter passed the Mini Mart and proceeded along the highway. Leaning back in his seat and feeling helpless, his mind started working on some decisive action to bring about a resolution to the mystery of the alien artifact and free Carol in the process.

On the way back to Dayton, John used Carol's cell phone to call Karen Doddson in Alamogordo where it was two hours earlier.

"Karen, this is John Kirkwood."

"Yes-hello Mr. Kirkwood, is everything okay. I've seen your picture and Carol's too on the TV."

Karen's voice gave John the feeling she truly cared about their plight. "Yes, I'm sorry to say Carol was picked up tonight and she is in custody. I need your help on a matter we discussed at your home."

"Of course. What can I do?"

"In our discussion, you mentioned Dr. Happard once told someone he could prove the artifact existed and would if they tried to remove him from the control group overseeing the cube. Can you enlighten me in what he might have been referring to in his statement."

A short silence was followed by Karen's answer. "It happened so long ago. I had the impression Happy had an object or device or something to prove to the world the cube existed."

"Did he have it hidden someplace?"

"No. I don't believe he did. I felt someone else was involved, that is-another person had the proof or possessed something. I can't be absolutely sure. I think that was the feeling I had at the time."

"Do you have any idea who the person might be? Was it someone he worked with?"

Again a pause. "I'm not sure. I believe it might have been someone involved from the beginning. I don't know if that means anything to you. John-John, are you there?"

John's mind was reeling. Things were beginning to connect in a shocking way. Could what he was thinking be true? Peter glanced over at John and asked if he was okay. He shook his head and answered, "Karen, yes I'm here. Anything else?"

"No, I can't remember any more concerning any proof. If I think of anything else I'll call you."

"Better if you contact me through the email address I gave you. Thanks for all your help." He ended the call.

Turning to Peter, "When we get back to Dayton, I want you to find out everything you can about a Dr. Henry Cable."

Peter acted disturbed by the question and an expression came over his face that John had not seen previously. He responded with a hint of anger in his voice. "Why do you want to know about him?"

"Just do it!" John snapped at Peter with anger and impatience of his own.

"Alright, but remember I didn't steal your girlfriend from you." Peter said, still with anger in his tone.

John did not respond. He stared out the window lost in his own thoughts. Could the recent revelations and his interpretations of these events be correct? His mental techniques used to analyze archeological sites were operating in high gear as he tried to connect all the dots.

Not wanting to chance taking John to his place, Peter checked him into a motel near his office. "Take a shower. I'll be back shortly with clean clothes and I'll check into what they did with Carol."

Not having much choice, John did as Peter suggested. As soon as he cleaned up, he would take a new path. Now he had two missions-to free Carol and dispel all questions regarding the alien artifact.

CHAPTER 25

Long ago it was once believed to be a fact our Earth was the center of the Universe and everything in the heavens circled around our little world. The notion was not easily dispelled and convincing people their home sphere was just a lonely little planet, part of a star system no more special in its location than any of the other millions of bodies in the night sky, took many decades to accomplish. John was heading to a point in his world where things might not be as they appeared and conveying these ideas to others may be just as difficult.

After cleaning up, he sat on his bed wrapped in a towel. He used Carol's cell phone to call Dr. Cable and receiving no answer, he recorded a message saying he would get in touch tomorrow.

A knock at the door caused him to pull the curtain back slightly to see Peter standing with a sack at the motel room door. Opening the door Peter entered handing him the sack, which contained clothes for John. "I hope these fit and last until you can get some of your own. You go through clothes faster than a fashion model."

"I'm sure they will be fine. Anything is better than the damp, wet and muddy ones I had been wearing and I'm glad you brought some shoes. Mine are all wet."

"I know-I could tell by the way they squeaked when you walked. I checked into where they took Carol and I can find no record of her being in custody. The Lebanon Police say they do not have her in their jail."

As John donned the clothes from the bag, he replied, "Why not? We both saw the Lebanon police pick her up at the Mini Mart." As they talked, John put on the clothes from the bag.

"I know, but the Lebanon Police say they did not arrest anyone tonight."

"I bet the agency pursuing us has taken her from the local police and told them to say nothing about her being captured."

"Your probably right. I'll keep checking. On a different subject, I have received a package today from Seattle, Washington. There is no return address and inside are four pictures of something. Could they be connected to your inquiry?"

John grabbed the envelope and quickly opened it. Inside were the pictures from NEAR and Talaria. Who could have sent them to Peter? Who knew Peter?

As he sat thinking, Peter said, "Are these meant for you?"

"Yes-but I can't think-wait a minute. Carol said she had an idea about copies of the pictures, but she never confided in me how she planned to get them. The guy in Seattle must have kept copies and Carol has contacted him and—-.?" John was not really talking to Peter, just to himself, but out loud.

Peter took all of it in still baffled by what the pictures represented. "What are these pictures?"

"I'll tell you another time."

Peter shook his head not enjoying the position of odd man out. "I also looked up Dr. Henry Cable. I just found the man to be a retired archeologist and very old."

"That's all?" John exclaimed as he looked at Peter with suspicious eyes.

Sitting in the one chair in the room, Peter turned his head to face John. "The truth is John, technically you do not pay me."

"Of course I do. I gave you a credit card number to charge your-it was Cable's credit card. Wait a minute. Do you mean to tell me you have been working for Dr. Cable?"

Peter eyes had a saddened expression as he responded. "In a way yes. Everything I've done I have reported to him just like I reported to you."

Now John knew why Dr. Cable asked him very few questions when they talked because he already knew most of his activities through Peter. "That crusty old man. He has been playing games with me since the first day we talked."

"Not so fast John. Don't curse the man out yet. He was paying me to make sure you didn't get into trouble and if you did, to get you out."

"Did you know him before I hired you?"

"No, he contacted me after you hired me. We worked out an agreement where by your trust with me would not be compromised by his pact with me."

John saw indecision in Peter's face for the first time since he had met him and his confidence in Peter had taken a nose-dive. Trust in this man would be suspect from now on. He continued to stare at Peter disappointed in the talented young man.

"You're not telling me something. I'm still your employer. I pay you, now let's have it. What else do you know about Dr. Cable?"

Peter was looking away from John's stare. He was definitely hiding something. "Out with it Peter or you are done, here and now."

"I really don't—."

"I really don't care," John exclaimed, cutting him off in a loud voice, his frustration beginning to show. "Tell me what you know or walk out the door and consider our contract ended."

Peter sat contemplating his response to John. He knew he had made a mistake accepting Dr. Cable's deal and now he had to make another decision. "You must know John, I had no choice."

"No choice for what? One question Peter. Who do you work for now?"

"Technically-"

"Not technically anything. Is it me or Dr. Cable?"

Peter hung his head staring at the floor. Looking up he answered the question. "You then."

"Okay, tell me what do you know about Dr. Cable?"

"He is as I said before with one addition. He is one of the wealthiest men in the United States and maybe the world."

"You mean wealthy wealthy. How did he get his money?"

"The record shows in the past, he made some of the most lucrative stock purchases bringing in millions of dollars. It seems he had a crystal ball telling him what stocks to purchase."

John's brain was telling him the information confirmed some of his previous suspicions. There was only one way to satisfy his suppositions. "Where is he now?"

"At the Mayo Clinic in Minnesota. His health had taken a turn for the worst."

"That's in Rochester, isn't it?" Not waiting for an answer, he continued, "Get me on a plane tomorrow. I'm going to see him." John said emphatically.

Peter nodded in agreement.

John's thoughts turned to Carol. He felt impotent not being able to free her from her captors.

Thirsty and hungry, wet and cold, Carol sat behind the barrel eyeing the Mini Mart across the road. Sitting here doing nothing was making her colder by the minute as the nighttime temperature continued to drop.

She decided she was going to get something to eat and drink. She turned to John to ask him if he wanted anything, but he sat with his chin on his chest asleep. Her plan would be to run quickly to the Mini Mart, grab a couple of snacks and drinks and be back before John knew she was gone. Checking to see that she had money in her jacket pocket, she followed the shadows to the road. She watched for a clear path, then ran across the highway to the Mini Mart, entered quickly, grabbing two packages of snacks and a couple of sodas, walked to the check out counter which had a line of people paying for food and gas.

Now becoming jittery, she had not planned to stand in line for any length of time and the lady behind the counter was taking so long to check people through. One man's credit card wouldn't work so the clerk had to run it again.

Carol looked over the store and noticed a young man near the rear corner of the building looking at her. Fear began to spread through her body as the thought of someone recognizing her became a distinct possibility. Without her wig, the chances someone might were much greater. She was at the counter now and began to feel safer as the lady rang up her snacks and drinks.

Just as she was giving the lady the money, police cars began pulling up in front of the store. Carol dropped the snacks and looked for a way out the back. Seeing an exit sign near the rear of the store, she hurried to it but it would not open. Turning, she faced three police officers with their guns drawn and knew it was hopeless.

Putting her hands against the wall, she spread her legs as directed while one of the officers frisked her for weapons. She noticed the young man again smiling at her dangling a key in his hand; no doubt the key was to the door she had attempted to open. Damn, she was so foolish and John was not going to like her sneaking off and getting caught.

Leading her out of the Mini Mart handcuffed, the officers put her in a patrol car and drove away. She looked to see if John was at the vacant building as they passed, but it was too dark to determine if he was still hiding behind the barrel. She was mad at herself for being so foolish, but glad John was still free.

Reaching a point about three miles from the Mini Mart, they ran into a roadblock. The two officers in the car with her got out and were approached by two men in regular clothes. After a discussion, which appeared to be heated at times, the two plain-clothes men came to the car and opened the door telling her to get out of the car.

She was taken to one of the cars in the roadblock and in quick time, was off again with these two men. Even though they had not shown her their badges, she was sure they were agents from the same group associated with Colonel Pratt. No doubt he would be entering the picture shortly and he would make sure John or Peter did not rescue her again.

Driving her along a highway until they reached Interstate 75, they headed north toward Dayton. She suspected Wright-Patterson might be their destination. The agents in the front seat said very little as they pulled up to a gate manned by security people.

After showing credentials, they were allowed through the gate into a place called "Cubical Industries". Winding between buildings, then driving down a ramp into an underground parking garage, they stopped at an elevator sign. The two men got out and pulled her from the car into a lobby area containing three elevators, two on one side and another directly across the lobby.

They pushed her into one of the two elevators and hit the button for floor four. Expecting the elevator to go up, she was caught off guard when it started moving downward. One of the agents grabbed her by the arm to keep her from falling. She looked at the buttons on the panel in the elevator. They went from one to six, but must all be below ground except the first floor. They must have entered on floor two.

The elevator dropped quickly two floors and opened into a hallway manned by three security people. Two of the officers took Carol with them and the agents exited back into the elevators.

Carol was led to a room entirely different from the one at Hollomen Air Force Base in Alamogordo. The room was carpeted with wood paneling and a large conference table with twelve nice padded leather chairs spaced around the table. She was directed to sit in one of the chairs and wait. Left with handcuffs on, she waited twiddling her thumbs and still upset at herself for getting caught.

After fifteen minutes, the door opened and she had never been so shocked in her life, because standing before her was the director of the Jet Propulsion Laboratory, Ben Hagen.

CHAPTER 26

'Nothing appears to be what it appears to be'-John wasn't sure if the saying was from some philosopher like the Frenchman, Jacques Derrida, or something he just thought up on his own. He knew it represented a great deal of truth to him at the present time.

Leaning over and looking out the window, he could see the ground slowly passing below him even though the plane was traveling over three hundred miles per hour. The Rochester Minnesota Airport should be appearing soon after his flight from Cincinnati to Chicago where he changed planes. Thinking ahead, it may be difficult for him to confront an ill Dr. Cable if he can not respond and John didn't want to brow beat the man, only to get at the truth.

After landing and taking a cab to the Mayo Clinic, he approached the information desk and asked to see Henry Cable. He was told to return tomorrow, as Dr. Cable was not allowed visitors today. When asked for his name, he gave the receptionist the fake name, Curt Wood that Peter had put on the I.D.

Leaving the clinic, he hailed a cab to take him to a nearby hotel; he could not resist the Best Western Apache. He would have to bide his time for nearly twenty-four hours.

Confronted by Ben Hagen, Carol made no reply, just sat quietly staring at the huge man. Ben Hagen was six feet five inches tall and large, but not overweight, just big. His appearance made him a formable adversary simply because of his size and yet after what Carol had been through, his size had little effect on her resistance and defiance.

He walked over to where she was sitting and stood above her like a towering giant as he spoke. "You have caused us a great deal of agony Miss

Jacobs. I venture to say you will not be a problem for us again now that we have you at our facility."

Carol straightened herself in the chair replying, "Who is us and what facility is ours?" The handcuffs were uncomfortable as she twisted her hands around in her lap in an attempt to relieve some of the pressure.

Walking around the table to the side opposite Carol, he again stood facing her. "All in good time-first things first. Are there more copies of the Talaria or NEAR pictures?"

Replying immediately, she said, "Of course, I had many copies. I sent them to Universities all over the country."

He laughed at her remark and walked to the end of the table, pulled the chair out and sat down. "Don't give me a lot of lies. If you do, I have no choice other than to let them take you to Cuba. Would you prefer to go there?"

Carol began twiddling her thumbs again, knowing her responses needed to be carefully thought out before answering any questions. "I have no desire to go to Cuba or anywhere else against my will. If you have anything to do with the artifact, then your time is coming."

"Artifact! What artifact are you referring too?"

"You know, the one in the picture and the one here in Dayton. You're not an ignorant man, are you? Did you think I didn't know about the cube? What hole have you been hiding in the last few weeks?" The awareness of the nerve she hit became apparent when he recklessly pushed his chair back from the table. Obviously he was surprised by her knowledge and anger began to fill his eyes.

"Maybe I have under-estimated you, Miss. Jacobs. You seem to have more knowledge than is good for you. Do you know the value of what you think we have in our possession?" The glint of anger in his eyes gave an austere cast to his face.

Whether to let him know how much she knew or to play dumb was the question going around in her brain. She decided to let him have it all.

"Of course I know its value. You've been garnering information from it for over sixty years making yourselves and everyone else connected with it rich. You have to be the most selfish bunch of crazies in the world." Carol was not sure about the money, but she thought it was a good bet they were making a lot of money from the cube or how else could they pay Amanda the large retirement amount.

The anger continued to well up inside Ben Hagen and his face started to turn red. "What we are doing is for the betterment of the people of the United States and the compensation awarded us is well deserved for our efforts in protecting our great country."

After his statement, he stood and walked out of the room.

Carol wondered what kind of pickle she had put herself into with her last comments. He had left the room seething because of her remarks. She remained in the room for over an hour until the door opened and Ben Hagen entered with one of the officers. The officer walked over to Carol and removed her handcuffs.

"Miss Jacobs, you will be taken to a room where you can clean up. A change of clothes will be provided and tomorrow, we will talk more about your suspicions," Ben Hagen said, most of the anger gone from his face and voice.

Carol was led away through a hallway making several turns and ending at a room similar to a motel room. It had a bed, desk and chair, dresser and bathroom. Resting on top of the bed was her suitcase from the car she and John had driven to Amanda Pattons.

She looked over the room and bath checking for hidden cameras and microphones. Sure they were here, yet not able to find any, she took a shower anyway, too cold and wet to care whether someone would be watching. As she dressed, her mind was thinking about the future and whether she would ever see John or the light of day again.

During the evening, John called Harry in California as he had promised. He gave him the entire story blowing Harry's mind away. Harry's life long desire was coming to fruition and he was excited to the point that John could not answer his questions fast enough. They talked for almost two hours, Harry craving every detail John could recall.

"I'm going to sit down and analyze everything you have told me and I will come to some conclusions and speculations, so when you call again, I'll have some ideas for you. Also if you need any help, call me. I would love to get in on the action."

"Thanks Harry. I have appreciated all your help and am sorry for having to keep you in the dark for so long. If I need you, I'll let you know." With that John ended the call feeling better after bringing Harry into the loop.

The next morning, riding in the taxi back to the Mayo Clinic, John thought about Carol and the ordeal she must be enduring. If he had not dozed off, she would be here by his side, safe and helping him to decide what steps to take.

Reaching the clinic, he was informed it would be another hour before Dr. Cable could see him in his room. While sitting on a large couch, he took note of the importance of the Mayo Clinic and its influence in various health decisions made by the Department of Health and our own National Government.

After an hour and some minutes, a lady approached John and said, "Curt Wood?"

Having rarely used his fake name, he did not react right away to her calling it out. Looking up from his couch, he finally replied, "Yes, I'm Curt Wood." He stood and faced the woman.

"Mr. Wood, I'm Shirley Knight. I'm a patient facilitator here at the clinic." She offered her hand to John, which he took and shook, then invited him to sit down as she sat on the couch next to where he had been sitting.

She turned the clipboard toward John. "I need some information from you before you will be able to visit Dr. Cable."

Nodding yes, she inquired about his background and lastly requested some form of identification. John made up information about his being a book editor and fed it to her as she asked the questions.

She eyed the Driver's License from Ohio, then asked for another form of ID. John offered her the fake credit card and she copied the number along with the Driver's License number.

"Now, Mr. Wood, why do you want to see Dr. Cable?"

John replied, "I am visiting friends in Rochester and I knew from another associate that Dr. Cable was here at the clinic. Dr. Cable was an author who I worked with and a well-known archeologist. I had a great deal of respect for him and wanted to say hello before I left town." He was proud of himself on how cool he was answering the questions posed by Ms Knight.

"You are very kind. I did ask Dr. Cable if he knew you and he said yes, but I thought he referred to you as John."

John did not reply.

"If you will follow me, Mr. Wood, I will take you to Dr. Cable's room."

Miss Knight stood and John followed her to the elevator. She vouched for John with security, then directed him into an elevator which went to the third floor. Exiting they proceeded through the hall to a room where she knocked and a nurse opened the door. Entering, Miss Knight approached Dr. Cable's bed and said, "Mr. Wood is here to see you."

Dr. Cable turned his head slightly, then nodded searching the room for John, finally making eye contact. Miss Knight backed away from the bed and turning to John, "You may have twenty minutes."

"Could we have some privacy?" John asked.

"I suppose."

"Thank you." John said as Miss Knight and the nurse excused themselves from the room.

John scanned the bed and Dr. Cable, seeing first hand the man was very ill. Walking around the bed, he looked at the IVs attached to his body. One was a morphine drip connected to a button in his hand whereby he could give himself the drug when he was in pain. John surmised he had some type of cancer, which he must have known about when he visited John in his office. John remembered the phrase he spoke saying something like, 'my time is limited here on earth'.

"Dr. Cable, do you know who I am?" He spoke in a rather loud voice wanting to make sure he heard his question.

John leaned over his bed and Dr. Cable opened his eyes and looked directly into John's. In a weak voice he said, "Yes."

"I need answers and your help. You didn't tell we the whole truth about you and Dr. Happard. I want it now. Carol has been taken into custody and I don't have much time."

Seeing Dr. Cable push the morphine button, John reached over and clamped the line on the drug. He wanted him awake so he could get the information he needed. "Talk to me Dr. Cable." He seemed to have his attention. "How did you make your money?"

Slowly he began to respond. "Dr. Happard —- me bits of ————- on what —— were finding." His voice was weak and his tongue acted like it was in spasms as he talked. It was difficult to understand his words and John was missing every second or third one.

"You had proof the cube existed and black-mailed him into giving you the information for your promise of silence. What was the proof?"

John shook his arm trying to keep him awake. "What's the proof, Dr. Cable?"

He looked up at John with sad eyes and asked, "You be —- my -tory?"

"Yes, I believe the cube exists. What's the proof? Please!"

He smiled the grin that John remembered from the hallway at his office- the one that spread across his face, then his eyes turned sad as he looked at John. Reaching out for John and pulling him close, he whispered, "Brian Dover, an att —- in —-ago. Tell him I sent —-." John knew he was in agony as Dr. Cable said, "Give him the -ord 'ahnee' with a—." Grimising in pain, his head fell back and his eyes closed.

"What was the word and with a what?" John did not understand. "Was the word cahnee?" He tried to awaken him, but to no avail. He could see him pushing the button. Saddened, John reached over and released the clamp on the pain drip. Shortly he saw relief ease across Dr. Cable's face. Leaning over, he grasped Dr. Cable's hand with his own and whispered, "Don't worry, I will let the world know." Raising up from the bed, John solemnly stared at the white haired man who had changed his life and knew he would never see Dr. Henry Cable again.

John opened the door and the nurse entered as he exited and slowly walked down the hall with his head hung down. When he looked up, he saw Miss Knight coming toward him with a security guard. He stopped, reversed his step and looked for a set of stairs.

Mrs. Knight yelled at him to stop as he passed through two swinging doors into another hallway just like the one where Dr. Cable's room was located. He ran through the hall turning right at the first corner, and pro-ceeded down this hall until he saw an exit light at the end of the corridor. Picking up his pace, he reached the door to the stairs, opened it and ran down the four flights of steps. At the bottom he found an emergency door, which he pushed through setting off an alarm.

Seeing a street to his right, he raced to the corner of the block and crossed to the other side. Catching sight of a cab, he flagged it down, hopped in and directed the Driver to the Apache. On the way, he called the airlines to get a flight to Chicago. If he hurried and was lucky, he could just make it to the airport in time to get on the plane. Rushing to his room, gathering his things and checking out, he grabbed a cab to the airport.

Reaching the airport with time to spare, he was relieved when the plane took off for the short flight to Chicago. As he sat in his seat, he wrote on a pad the word 'ahnee' and 'cahnee' asking himself the question 'with a what?' If he didn't come up with the answer, the attorney might not give him the information from Dr. Cable. He wrote the word in various ways, with more letters and with fewer letters. He continued for most of the trip using print and cursive, when at last the answer came to him-'acne'.

CHAPTER 27

The size and complexity of a large corporation like General Motors or Wal-Mart can overwhelm the average person. What seems to be a simple store in which to purchase items actually involves thousands of people behind the scenes building, organizing, creating, shipping and hauling to provide you with the opportunity to buy a product.

When Ben Hagen came for Carol Saturday morning and took her through the underground maze at Cubical Industries, she was in awe. Rooms filled with people performing various tasks attempting to interpret the information gleaned from the artifact astounded her in the size, scope and diversification of the operation.

As Ben Hagen walked her through the various steps set in place, he demonstrated a great deal of pride in what he had helped develop. The artifact had in effect created a complex organization whose main function was to garner anything of value, analyze it and release it to the general business public if deemed feasible. Carol feared making money might be the most important thing to people like Ben Hagen rather than items good for all the people.

Opening another door for Carol, he explained, "In this area we attempt to decipher the language of the 'almegs'. It is so complex, even after all these years we can not interpret any of words or phrases. We have been able to classify words in regards to their general subject area, but not their specific meanings."

"How do you get any information?" Carol inquired.

"It is difficult. We have hundreds of people review all the data given to us by the recorders. The recorders are the people who are connected to the cube and take down everything they see and hear in their brain after their listening time or session as we call it. Once you are attached, the recorder has no control to write anything down. Everything must be from memory after their connection to the cube is broken. Most of the information is in the form of diagrams or symbols the recorders remember seeing. The basic design of a hydrogen atom should be the same throughout the entire Universe"

"How much data do you get?"

"Follow me." They left the language area and entered a hallway, and then up some stairs into a large room. It was filled with rows of people in cubicles sitting in front of a computer.

"Here we review and catalog all the data we have received over the past fifty years. All the information from the cube is gone over many times looking for bits and pieces missed in previous examinations. We are constantly trying to connect those bits and pieces anyway we can much like you would attempt to find pieces in a jigsaw puzzle. When these people think they have found something, it is routed to one of the specialized areas dealing with that topic. There they try to develop the data into useful information."

The size and complexity of the organization overwhelmed Carol. "How can you possibly keep it a secret?"

"Very easily. By never letting one hand know what the other is doing. If you were to ask any of the hundreds of people in our plant what the cube is, they wouldn't have the slightest idea what you were talking about. Only a handful of people know the artifact exists and now you are one of the few."

"And who are the other few?"

"That is none of your concern." He ushered Carol out into another hallway and into an elevator. The elevator descended many floors, stopped, but the doors did not open.

"What's wrong?"

"We are being scanned?"

"Scanned for what reason?"

"Firearms, explosives, and our pictures are being run through a data bank."

A red light came on, then a voice said, "Mr. Ben Hagen, you are cleared, but Mrs. Carol Jacobs is a terrorist and is denied access."

Carol started to protest, but Ben raised his hand. "Allow her entry on my authority, code orange-1A3B-yellow."

After a long pause the voice said, "Clearance allowed on your code."

The elevator started again, but this time it moved sideways, traveling at a high rate of speed causing Carol to grab the handrail to keep from falling.

After the elevator stopped, Carol steadied herself as the doors opened. Ben led her through a hall into a room the size of a typical school classroom containing a dozen or so people.

"In here we try to discover ways the data can be used in the everyday world. This room is dedicated to medical research. If we come up with a new drug, then we test it and put it out in the public."

"How do you put it out in the public?"

"In the past we would seed it someplace and let it develop on its own. Now one of our agents will contact a pharmaceutical company and offer it to them."

"Yes, and I suppose you get a fee for the drug, as well as a percentage of the take."

"I wouldn't put it that way, but we do have expenses to cover."

"I bet you do." Carol was becoming sick, thinking about these people getting wealthy on something which should be shared by everyone on the planet.

"Let me ask you a question Miss Jacobs. How do you think we were able to squelch the pictures at JPL from the Asteroid Belt?"

Carol knew now why Colonel Pratt was at JPL when pictures were returned from space. "One question for you Mr. Hagen. What told you there was something in the Asteroid Belt causing you to begin a program of concealment?"

She could tell he first was going to avoid answering her question, then stopping, he turned and said, "From the face of the artifact dealing with astronomy, a diagram of our solar system was seen by one of the recorders. Beacons in the display were judged to be the location of monitors placed here by the Almegs. The largest of these beacons was in the Asteroid Belt except in the drawing there was not as many pieces floating around in the orbit. From this we surmised there could be something in the Asteroid Belt connected with the cube so we monitored everything associated with it."

Carol was stunned. So much knowledge was simply put away, kept secret, and she was only getting a smidgen. Somehow she had to bring an end to this conspiracy.

"I still don't understand how you have been able to keep all of this a secret for so many years. You have tax reports to file and other government agencies coming to your plant examining and checking various aspects of your operation. Sometime, somebody has to stumble onto knowledge of the cube," Carol said.

"It is actually very simple," He said with a sly grin. "There is only one way you can keep a secret in a democracy."

"What pray tell could you be talking about," Carol said in a condescending way.

"The government investigates everything except one item and when they look into it, they only do it from behind closed doors, and since there is no press to give the congressman air time on TV, they only give the inquiry cursory effort. The answer is National Security."

"I don't believe you can keep it a secret by just saying it involves National Security."

"Oh you don't. Have you been burying your head in the sand? History is full of people hiding things under the guises of National Security.

Eisenhower flew spy planes over Russia. Nixon in the Watergate Affair set up his own Gestapo called the 'Plumbers' in the name of National Security. National Security was used in the Iran-Contra deal to justify selling guns to our sworn enemies who are now terrorizing us. The difference between these events and our operation is they got caught. How many other secrets are hidden in the Government under the classification of National Security that you don't know about?"

"In our Government, what you have to worry about is snooping reporters, headline grabbing Congressmen, and do-gooder watch dog groups. The only way you can shut these people out is under the auspices of National Security. Even the courts don't want to get involved."

"You have to give the courts the information. You can't hide it from them." Carol spoke in a fiery tone.

"My innocent Ms Jacobs. In 1953 your Government, before the Supreme Court of the United States refused to give the court information about the crash of a B-29 because they said it involved National Security. We now know it was a lie. It had nothing to do with National Security. The plane simply malfunctioned, but the Government didn't want that known. They won the case by claiming National Security and the court believed them."

"It sounds so Un-American." It was the only comment Carol could foster.

"It's the American way. Why the only reason 'Cubical Industries' stays connected to the Military is for the sole purpose of using this shield, otherwise we would break away and become an independent corporation."

The short flight from Rochester put John in Chicago at 2:30 in the afternoon. He called from the airport for a room and also checked directory assistance for the number of Brian Dover. Having no listing for him, he remembered Dr. Cable's law firm that sent him his agreement was located here in Chicago. In the cab on the way to his hotel, he tried to remember the name and getting no where called Peter.

"Peter, what is the name of Dr. Cable's law firm?"

"Gentry, Ames and Ames, I believe."

"Thanks. Any news concerning Carol?"

"She was transferred to the Feds by the police who arrested her and more than likely they have taken her to Wright-Patterson. I have nothing else regarding her capture. How are you getting along?"

"Fine. I'm in Chicago and will be here for a day or two. Keep checking into Carol's disappearance and call me the moment you have any news." John then ended the call.

Calling the firm of Gentry, Ames and Ames, he asked the receptionist to put him through to Brian Dover."

"He is gone for the day. Can I take a message or transfer you to one of our other attorneys."

"No, will he be in tomorrow?"

"Yes, until noon."

"Thank you." John knew he had found the man he was looking for.

Arriving at the hotel, checking in, and going to his room, John relaxed for the rest of the evening ordering from room service. The evening wore on as he worried about Carol and wondered what situation she now had to combat. He called Harry inquiring about his ideas on the story he gave him the day before.

"John, I have been going over the information from yesterday and I have formed some conclusions. First, I would suggest to you that the Almegs as you call them were visiting our Solar System because there was life here. Granted, the dinosaurs ruled the earth and may be a unique species to the Universe, but they were not sapient as far as we know. I would propose to you that life might be very rare in the vastness of space and that is the reason they came to our system. Remember there is still a possibility life of some kind existed on Mars as well if your date of two hundred million years ago is correct."

"If your analysis is close to the truth, do you have any idea why they never returned?"

"How do you know they never returned?"

John took a moment. An interesting idea of Harry's. Once Karen had told him it was millions of years ago, he never considered anytime recently. "How recent do you think they may have come back?"

"Remember, John, we are not talking about decades or even centuries and maybe not even thousands of years so if they returned-let's suppose it was every one hundred thousand years. At this rate over a period of ten million years they could have come back here one hundred times and still it would not have been close to two hundred million years."

"It is hard to imagine a million years. What happened to the Almegs?"

"Ah, yes, what happened indeed. When discussing this amount of time, the possibilities are endless. Maybe their civilization died or was conquered by another. It would be hard to imagine intelligent beings so advanced disintegrating. They may have decided it wasn't worth returning. The main problem is the items they left here. They suggest something else, but I have no conclusions in this area yet."

"It is definitely a mystery. Thanks for your input. I'll get back to you soon."

The rising sun tried to take the chill off the morning air in downtown Chicago as John stepped out of his cab and entered the Thompson Building. The information board on the wall in the lobby told him the law firm he was here to see was on the ninth floor.

Stepping off the elevator into the reception area, he asked for Mr. Brian Dover. Gentry, Ames, and Ames must be a large firm because they have use of the entire ninth floor of the building.

The receptionist sitting behind the counter was dressed very prim and proper, an older lady who no doubt had worked here many years. She replied, "May I ask who is calling?"

John started to give his fake name, then thought better recalling the incident at the Mayo Clinic. "I was sent by a Dr. Henry Cable to see Mr. Brian Dover."

"What is your name?"

"Please, just tell Mr. Dover what I said."

The receptionist was not pleased with John's refusal to provide his name. Asking him to have a seat, she pushed the intercom and John sensed there was more than the usual relay of information taking place. Soon a man in his late fifties or early sixties walked up to John. He was very distinguished looking with a large swath of wavy gray hair.

"I'm Brian Dover. Are you the gentleman sent by Dr. Cable?"

"Yes, I am." John stood and offered his hand to Mr. Dover. Reluctantly he gave his hand in return, which put John on his toes and he became alert to all that was transpiring.

"What is your name?" He spoke very direct with the hint of a demand.

"I'd rather leave that for a little later." John was pushing the envelope with Mr. Dover. He had to be exceedingly careful since he had a feeling his time was running out.

Just like the receptionist, he too was not happy with John's refusal to give his name. "Would you please follow me to my office."

John did as instructed and when in the room was offered a seat in front of a large desk. Mr. Dover walked around his desk and sat in the equally large chair behind the desk. The office was spacious with wooden floors and wood paneling. Area rugs were dispersed around the room and oil paintings adorned the walls.

He fumbled with some papers, then looked at John. "When did Dr. Cable send you to me?"

"Yesterday," John replied thinking the question seemed unusual.

"I find that hard to believe, because Dr. Cable passed away yesterday."

John's eyes dropped in sadness. "I didn't know, but I did talk to him yesterday morning. Also, I would like to hire you as my attorney." John's brain was working fast because if this man considered calling the authorities after John told him his name, it would be more difficult for him to do so if he represented John.

A little surprised by John's request, he asked, "Before I can agree to that, I need your name."

"I will tell you my name as soon as you agree to represent me."

"Why should I represent you Mr. Whoever?"

He eyed Mr. Dover. Dr. Cable had chosen well because John was of the opinion this man had ice water in his veins-very cool, collected and calculating-a man who would rarely find himself on the short end of the stick.

"I'm a friend of Dr. Cable and I am to give you the word 'acne'.

Now Mr. Dover looked closely at John with a frown and his eyes emitted a coldness from inside the deep sockets as he stared at him. He looked at John for an extended period to the point of causing John to feel a little uneasy. Pushing a pen and pad of paper across the desk, he asked John to write the word down.

John had the sense of mistrust on the part of Brian Dover. Taking the pen and paper, John wrote the word acne except he spelt it with an 'i': acni and slid the pad back toward Mr. Dover.

He looked at the word, then said, "Yes, Inca backwards. I will represent you, now what's your name?"

"Dr. John Kirkwood."

Now it was Mr. Dover's turn to be a little uneasy. A concerned look came over him as he said, "The terrorist?" John had slipped one over on him and he was not happy.

"One and the same." Replied John.

Over the next half-hour, Mr. Dover questioned John on why he needed representation. John related most of the story including the part about the alien artifact. He also requested he represent Mrs. Carol Jacobs who was now in custody with some agency of the Federal Government.

Brian Dover's uneasiness disappeared as the discussion continued. John knew his identity was safe now, but he did recommend John turn himself in to the authorities.

Knowing that was not going to happen, John asked, "By my having given you the word acni with the letter i, aren't you supposed to tell me something?"

Mr. Dover slid his chair back and stood, walked over to a picture on the wall. The picture had hinges on the side and he swung it out from the wall. He then turned a combination dial on a wall safe located behind the picture, and reached in retrieving an envelope. Closing the safe, he returned to his seat.

"Even though I have this envelope, I know nothing about its contents, but I was to destroy it on the death of Dr. Cable. If I took his instructions literally, I would not hand it over, but your story seems so preposterous that the package must be a part of the tale."

He pushed the envelope across the desk to John. John picked it up and put it in his pocket. Standing, he thanked Mr. Dover and asked him again to look into Carol's captivity, then walked out of his office.

The envelope was not opened until he was in a cab on his way back to the hotel. Taking his finger and running it along the fold, he tore it open and took out the contents. It contained no note, only a piece of cardboard with a key taped to one side. The cardboard was an advertisement for the First Town National Bank.

CHAPTER 28

A treasure hunt can be an exciting adventure if at the end of the search the treasure does exist and the reward is real. For the past weeks, John wasn't positive the alien artifact did exist. He only had the word of people he had just met-strangers who may have their own agendas to proclaim. They all had interesting stories, and so did Dr. Cable, but was there any truth in them?

When telling the cab driver to take him to the First Town National Bank, the reply he received was not one he wanted to hear.

"I've never heard of a First Town Bank," The driver replied.

He looked at the card again and read the address off on the advertisement: At Madison and Clark.

"I can take you there if you want," the cabby said.

Pulling up to the intersection, he saw a sign for the Sailors Premium Bank. John paid the driver and entered the bank. From the character of the structure, he knew it was built many years ago. The building's interior was massive and the effect was like stepping into the recent past.

The floor was a tile of very small squares. Massive pillars reached up to the fifteen-foot high ceiling and the teller's windows were glass framed in a mahogany looking wood. The film industry could have used the bank as a movie set for old time bank robberies of the Bonnie and Clyde era.

Approaching the first teller, John asked, "Who do I see about getting into my safety deposit box?"

The young girl smiled, then pointed to a stairway as she replied, "Please see the person at the bottom of the stairs behind you or take the elevator in the rear."

Descending the stairway to the bottom, he was greeted by a man stationed behind a desk. He was an older gentleman, which fit the antiquated décor of the room. Looking up at John, he said, "How can I help you sir?"

"I'd like to view my safety deposit box. Here is my key."

The man took the key and examined it. He rolled it over in his fingers. "My-my, this is one of the old ones." He gave John a paper to sign and told him anyone with the key could have access, which was unusual. Signing his name as Curt Wood and showing him his ID, he was led to the vault. John waited by the door while the man entered the vault, which also had the appearance of age. He inserted John's key and another key from the bank, turned the keys, opened the door and withdrew the box. He led John to a cubicle the size of a closet, put the box on a shelf in front of a chair and closed the door, which left John and the box alone in the small room.

The lock-box was approximately the size of a very large shoebox similar to the boxes the new gym shoes are encased in today. A shiver ran through his body as he speculated in his mind what might be waiting inside the box. He was anxious and the palms of his hands were sweating; a trait he displayed when investigating a new find at an archeological site.

Setting down at the table, he looked over his shoulder as if someone might be spying on him. His suspiciousness reminded him of Dr. Cable's posture when he was in John's office telling him about the cube and worried that someone may have been listening. John turned back to the container, reached out with shaking hands and opened the box.

A large piece of folded paper lay just under the lid. He took it out and spread it on the table next to the box. The paper was the size of a dining place mat and contained a map with no legend or description. Because of what Dr. Cable had told him in his office weeks ago, John recognized it to be a drawing of the chamber where they found the cube. If it hadn't been for his previous knowledge, he would have had no idea what the map represented. Everything seemed to be as Dr. Cable had described except behind the altar-there were markings showing a recess in the stone wall. He did not recall Dr. Cable mentioning any such detail.

Pushing the paper aside, he looked in the box and in the back was a small cardboard box the size of a softball. He lifted the container out of the lock box and set it on the table in front of him. Opening the lid to this box, he discovered dark blue plastic sheets crumbled up on the inside. He lifted the sheets out of the box and realized they surrounded a hard solid object. He began peeling away the plastic sheets like they were petals and he was revealing the flower inside. When he had removed enough of the plastic to see what was inside, he was stupefied.

The box contained a perfect crystal cube slightly smaller than a baseball-more like the size of a billiard ball. It was glowing in a bluish white hue and it sparkled as it reflected some of the light from the overhead lamp. He gazed at it in wonderment and was sure he had never seen anything as beautiful in his life. He sat eyeing the crystal for many minutes appraising all the ramifications this large diamond represented. The vision of a woman having it on her finger crossed his mind causing him to smile and emit a little chuckle.

250

Slowly he reached toward the cube and delicately touched a face with his finger. At first it was like a static shock as he jerked his finger back, then he reached to touch it once more. Again a shock of less intensity ran through his arm and spread over his body. He closed his eyes and began to see flashes of stars. Clusters of stars, giant suns, solar systems, and gas clouds flashed before him, then as it settled down, he could concentrate on one object and realized what he was seeing. Laser like red rays shot from a central point spreading out over the starry black night.

In his opinion, he was looking at star maps and routes from one point to another, a three dimensional roadmap of the heavens. Focusing on one of the laser lights, he was quickly swept into the line and he moved along the light so fast that the stars around him began to blur. As he slowed, he was coming into a solar system like our own, but not ours, one similar with a star sun in the center and several planets orbiting around it.

His mind's eye was taken to a tiny moon orbiting a mars-like planet about halfway between the outer planets and the star. On the moon was an object that looked like an igloo, black in color and as he neared it a portal opened. Inside were reddish orange colored crystals. His mind was about to enter when someone called out his name. He tried to concentrate on the igloo when his name was called again shaking him back to reality.

"Mr. Wood! Mr. Wood, are you all right. You've been in the cubicle almost an hour. Are you okay?"

John pulled his hand back breaking contact with the small cube and began to get his wits back. "Yes, I'm fine. Thank you. I'll be out in just a moment."

He stared at the cube and smiled. Everything Dr. Cable had told him must be true and here before him was proof. It was a mystical event giving him great pleasure and satisfaction. Now he could relate to the experience Dr. Happard and Dr. Cable had in the chamber in Peru and a better understanding of how they felt. One thing that puzzled him was how they kept it a secret for all these years? John wanted to announce it to the entire world.

Carol entered his mind and he wanted to share his discovery with her. As he thought of her, reality began to creep back into his consciousness.

He folded the leafs back around the cube, now knowing it was wrapped in plastic to prevent being put in a trance when handling it. He slid the small cube in the side pocket of his jacket, placed the paper and the small box back inside the lock box and shut it, then stood and walked out of the cubicle. The attendant came over, picked up the lock box and returned it to the vault. After getting his key back, John left the bank hailing a cab and told the driver to take him to the law offices of Gentry, Ames, and Ames.

Returning to Brian Dover's office, he pressed the receptionist to let Mr. Dover know he had returned and needed to see him immediately. Finally relenting, she contacted him and he agreed to allow John five minutes after he finished with his present client.

When John was let in, he walked over and stood by Mr. Dover's desk. "Are you familiar with what Dr. Cable had in the lock box at the bank?"

By his slow movements, he made John aware of his reluctance at having him in his office again. "I would guess it is some kind of artifact from his expeditions, and now it is yours. Is there a problem?"

Not sure if he knew its worth, John continued, "Do you know the value of the artifact or what it does?"

Leaning back in his chair, he smiled saying, "No, but any artifact is valuable and I have no idea what it does. Is it some kind of tool?"

"Let me show you. You are my lawyer-right?"

"Yes, anything you show me is privileged as long as it is not illegal to have in your possession."

John reached in his jacket pocket, pulled out the cube wrapped in the blue plastic and put the artifact on Mr. Dover's desk. John slowly peeled away the dark blue sheets. He wanted to create an effect on Mr. Dover so the last few sheets were slowly pulled back disclosing the cube to him. He could see his eyes grow large and his mouth hung open, then he quickly returned to his steely lawyer face.

"Is this what I think it is?" His eyes in part and his voice betrayed the stolid character he was trying to present as he stared at the crystal.

"Yes, the largest diamond you have ever seen," John said.

"Is this an example of what you referred to earlier as an alien artifact?"

Not answering his question, John said, "I want you to touch it with your finger. You will need to relax your mind and don't worry because it will not harm you in any way. You might feel a slight shock like static electricity. Will you do that for me, please?"

He looked at John with a frown, nodded and slowly reached out with his hand and pulled back before touching it. "Is this some kind of joke?" Not waiting for John to answer, he touched the cube, quickly jerking his hand away. "Is it radioactive?"

Again John assured him it was safe by touching it with his own hand then pulling away. Brian held his finger against the face of the crystal and John watched the expression on his face. He looked like he had gone into a trance. John gave him several minutes before breaking contact by pulling his arm away."

Settling back in his chair, he looked at John saying, "Why did you pull me away?"

"You were touching it for several minutes."

"Really, okay, what do you have here?"

"Mr. Dover, listen carefully. The object contains a map of part of the galaxy and as you must realize, it is an alien object, not from our solar system. It validates everything I recounted to you earlier."

After a pause he replied, "If it is, it is the most important discovery in the history of human kind. Why did Dr. Cable keep it locked up all these years?"

He could see skepticism on Mr. Dover's face. John let the silence continue for a moment. "That is a long story. Right now I need your help. I want an audience with the President of the United States and I need it soon."

"You are asking for quite a lot. I do have contacts in the government which I might be able to use." He put his right hand on his chin tapping his index finger against his jaw.

"Use them or I'm afraid Carol Jacobs may never be heard from again."

"Are the people after you the ones in control of the other artifact?"

"Yes, and they are very powerful."

Moving his hand from his chin to his desk, Brian Dover sat drumming his fingers on top of his desk looking at the artifact then raised his head eyeing John with a questioning stare trying to decide what to do. "Have a seat. Let me see what I can do."

Carol was escorted back to the room where she had showered and changed before and was told to rest and relax. A TV was in the corner of the room and the guard told her she might be here for a long time, like maybe days so the TV could help to kill the time.

After over two days locked in the room, Carol was at the end of her rope when a knock at the door was followed by the door opening and Ben Hagen standing with his aide and a guard.

"My aide will accompany you to a waiting area. Please follow his directions or you will not like the consequences. Agreed."

Reluctantly, Carol nodded agreement. "Where are you taking me now?"

"You'll find out soon enough." Ben walked away leaving Carol with his aide and the guard. The aide was a thin handsome dark haired young man in his mid twenties.

She thought she would try something. "Do you know where we are at the present time?"

Giving her a funny look, he answered, "Of course-Cubical Industries, where do you think we are?"

"What is the room we are in now?"

"The security area for Cubical Industries. Are you feeling all right? You're asking strange questions."

"Do you know about the alien artifact?"

"Now, I have no idea what you are talking about. Maybe I should take you to the clinic first and have you checked out."

"No, I'm fine. You've answered my question."

Maybe Ben Hagen was right when he said most people were not aware of the artifact. He led her through the underground maze to a large waiting area divided by glass partitions. Two other people were here, one in handcuffs with attendants and guards accompanying them. She was directed to have a seat in one of the partitioned areas

Late in the evening she was led by two men through a hallway into a large conference room. The conference tabletop was shaped like a "V" with her sitting in a chair in the open part of the "V" facing the people sitting on the opposite side of the "V" shaped tabletop. Ben Hagen was sitting in the center left seat.

Eyeing the people, some looked familiar, but she could not place any names except Ben Hagen. In the room were six people in total four men and two women plus her. Three sat on one wing of the "V" shaped tabletop and three on the other. On Ben Hagen's right were a woman and then a man. On the other wing nearest Ben was a man with a device in his ear, next to him the other woman and finally the eldest looking man to her left.

Ben Hagen spoke giving a short synapse of who Carol was and how she came to be here before the Council of Six.

"The woman on his right spoke after Ben was finished. "Miss Jacobs, did Mr. Hagen explain to you why you are before us?"

"Not really."

"We are going to determine the rest of your life for you. With your cooperation, it can be pleasant and probably exciting or it can be basically a jail sentence for your remaining days."

"Who are you anyway? And what gives you the right to make a decision regarding my life?" She stared at the woman making the statement, then glared at the remaining five ending back with the woman who spoke.

A man on her right blurted out loudly; "We've taken the right on behalf of all Americans to protect our way of life and to improve it for the betterment of everyone. You have no idea of the responsibilities we have on our shoulders."

The self-serving statement ate at Carol's insides. "You said you took the responsibility on behalf of Americans, yet you stole it from the Peruvians, so don't give me the holier than thou bullshit. Tell your lies to someone else." Carol was surprised by the anger built up in her these past days locked up in the room. It was coming out and all of it was directed at these six people.

The other lady of the group spoke with a high pitched and a sharp edged voice also stirring Carol up. "So you know a great deal about our artifact, but you have no idea how important it is to protect the people from those who would use its power unscrupulously."

"I noticed you said 'our' artifact. What gives you the right of ownership? Can't you just let the whole world in on the information?"

Ben Hagen replied, "Miss Jacobs, you don't understand. All we learn from the cube can't just be handed out to the public. For example twenty-two years ago we developed a device increasing the energy of gasoline so cars would get four times the mileage. So if your car presently was getting twenty mile per gallon, with the device, it would get eighty mpg."

"I've never heard of a device improving gas mileage to the extent you say."

"Of course not, the two men who we seeded eventually came up with the device then sold it to the Oil Companies, never to hear of it again. All we did was make two men filthy rich. Then there was the cold fusion fiasco more recently. Sometimes people are not ready for advanced knowledge."

"Who replaces you when you die or quit?"

"We pick our own replacement. Curious you ask because it is one of the choices we may consider concerning your future," the woman with the high pitched voice added.

Carol thought her suggestion was simply a bribe to shut her up. "I can assure you I would never agree to be a part of your elitist group of self-glorified demi gods. You are a pathetic bunch of—."

"One moment Ms. Jacobs." Ben Hagen said cutting her off.

The man on his left was listening to a cell earphone type device and had raised his hand to signal the others to be quiet. Finally he lowered the device and signaled to the guards who came through the door and escorted Carol from the room. As she was leaving, she heard the man with the ear phone say in a lowered voice, "We have a problem in Chicago."

CHAPTER 29

The tradition of the Government of the United States is to take ten times as long to accomplish a goal as it would a private individual or a group to perform the same function. Brian Dover's efforts would have to move mountains quickly if John was to see any fruit from his labors.

Returning to Mr. Dover's office from the canteen in the basement of the building, John was stressed out do to the lack of activity. His trip to Rochester and back had been full of dead time and it was beginning to wear on him. Sitting and waiting were not characteristics of his persona, especially when someone special to him is in trouble. He entered Brian's office and sat in the chair facing his desk as Mr. Dover was finishing a phone call.

As he replaced the receiver on the phone, Brian looked at John and said, "I have contacted many people in the past two hours and am waiting for a return call."

John replied, "I will wait with you. If you don't mind, would you keep this key for me?" Brian shook his head yes and picked up the lock box key and inserted it in an envelope writing John's name on the outside.

Neither spoke for quite some time as each eyed the cube resting on Brian's desk and imagined the consequences it presented by existing. The ring of his phone broke the silence and after a conversation with the caller, he faced John. "A representative of the President's Science Advisor, a Dr. Conway Stefford will be here in my office in an hour. We or you can present your evidence to him."

"Are you acquainted with Dr. Stefford?"

"No, but he is a close friend and colleague of the President's Science Advisor, Dr. Richard Banks, and can relate the information you provide through him to the President."

John was leery of the arrangement, yet he had little choice in the matter at this time.

Dr. Stefford arrived at Mr. Dover's office in less than an hour. He was a short pudgy individual with greasy hair and a large nose.

After the introductions, John related a synapses of his story, getting frowns and questioning looks from Dr. Stefford the entire way. Dr. Stefford was not going to be an easy one to convince.

After ten minutes, John and Brian presented him with the small cube. Still looking skeptical, he watched as John pulled away the covering and the bluish white glow lit up the top of Mr. Dover's desk.

"Are you sure the object is a diamond."

Dr. Conway Stefford's attitude was upsetting John. He had not been impressed with the man the instant he entered the office and the snide way he reacted to the story increased John's indignation toward him. John stood, grabbed up the cube in its covering, walked to a mirror behind Dr. Stefford and raked one edge of the cube along the mirror creating a distinctive scratch in the glass. "Satisfied." He turned to Brian. "I'll get you a new mirror."

"No need, I will leave it on the wall-a great conversation piece now, wouldn't you say."

Dr. Stefford's attitude and expression changed after the demonstration. John had him go through the procedure of touching the cube. He was quite shaken. Standing, he walked to a corner of the room and using his cell phone, placed a call. After several minutes, he moved back to where John and Brian were sitting. "I have contacted Dr. Banks and he is informing the President."

John stood, gathered up the cube in his hands saying, " If I don't talk to the President soon, I'm leaving with everything and you might not see it again."

An expression of fear came over Dr. Steffords face. "Wait Dr. Kirkwood. Let's not get hasty. I'll make another call."

John was worried about Dr. Stefford being on the up and up and did not want to let the cube out of his possession. Right now it was the only leverage he had to free Carol. "Yes, I think you better." The tone of his voice was full of anger.

Again, after more calls by Dr. Stefford, John was connected to Dr. Banks. "I understand your concern Dr. Kirkwood, but the President is a busy man-."

Interrupting, John said, "And so am I. If he is not connected to me in five minutes, I'm gone and so is the artifact. I wonder if another country might be interested in possessing this small crystal."

"Now Dr. Kirkwood, No need to do that. Let me see what I can do."

Dr. Stefford was stunned by John's words to the President's science advisor, but Brian Dover only smiled, amused and amazed by John's actions which could easily have been his own if he were in John's shoes.

Shortly, Brian's phone rang again and after answering; he handed the receiver to John. "It's the President-the President of the United States."

President Mitchell Fielding was in his first term and had enjoyed a stable economy and relative peace during his first couple of years. A small man, making up for his short stature with a booming voice and a keen intellect that overshadowed any physical shortcomings.

"Dr. Kirkwood, this is President Fielding. I understand you have acquired an interesting object."

"Thank you Mr. President for talking to me. I don't know what information you have so please listen carefully. The object I have is proof that earth was visited by an alien culture many years ago. There is another alien artifact much larger than the one I have in use by the United States Government at Wright Patterson Air Force Base and has been in U. S. control for over sixty years. The people in possession of the device also have my friend in custody, a Carol Jacobs, and I very much want to obtain her release."

"Dr. Kirkwood, if what you say is true, the government would have been keeping the artifact as you call it a secret for all these years. That in itself is hard to believe and besides, aren't you being referred to as a terrorist by the law enforcement officials?"

"Mr. President, I'm not—Mr. President—." The connection was broken. John looked at Brian, then at Dr. Stefford who had a slight grin.

"What's happening?" John demanded. Now it was John's turn to show an expression of fear.

"You'll find out shortly." Dr. Stefford said now smiling. "The government has a plan if at any time there is some sign showing aliens might be involved."

Slowly edging his way over to Brian, John whispered, "Is there another way out of the building? I have a feeling we are going to have visitors."

Brian responded, "Yes and I agree. We will have guests." He nodded toward another door in his office. "A private elevator is located through that door, down the hall and on your left. No one uses it except the lawyers and some technical people."

"Thanks, I'll be in contact."

John moved over to the desk and picked up the cube. He started to leave, but Dr. Stefford reached out and grabbed hold of the cube also. They began to struggle with the cube and as they did it squirted out of the plastic wrapping and went flying across the room toward the main door of the office.

As the cube rolled on the floor, the door burst open and men dressed in black, armed with weapons began entering the room. John assumed they were Special Forces sent by the Government. As Dr. Stefford rushed toward the men, the cube still sliding across the floor, he yelled, "Protect the cube-protect the cube."

John backed toward the door Brian had pointed out and as the intruders looked at Dr. Stefford and the sparkling object rolling across the floor, John was through the door and running down the hallway. Punching the button on the elevator, he waited for the doors to open. Just as they did, the office door opened and one of the armed men came through running toward John shouting at him to stop.

Having stepped into the elevator just as the man raised his weapon and fired, John kept trying to get the doors to close faster by pushing on them. It seemed like an eternity for them to shut and they did so an instant prior to the man with the gun reaching the elevator. John did not relish getting shot at again nor did he intend to let it become a regular event in his life. His whole body began to shake all over from the incident.

As the elevator descended, he could not be sure if the President had any knowledge of the cube. The question would be if he didn't would he do anything to investigate what John had conveyed to him over the phone or would he think it was just the ranting of a terrorist. Reaching the first floor, the elevator doors opened and to his left was a door appearing to be an exit. He opened the door slowly seeing a sidewalk and looking left and right, no armed men were present, so he exited and walked hurriedly along the street flagging down a cab.

He told the taxi driver to take him to Elmwood Park, a suburb of Chicago. The address was Roger Fry's, his college buddy.

While on route to Roger's home, he called Peter on his cell phone.

"What's up John, are you in more deep shit?'

"Yes. Would I be in anything else! Have you anything more on Carol?"

"A short distance outside Wright Patterson's property line is an industry. I think it may have some connection to your investigation."

"What about Carol?"

"I'm getting to her. Just wait a minute. By the way, where are you?"

"Chicago, now what info do you have?"

"The name of the plant bordering Wright Airfield is Cubical Industries." Now Peter had John's attention. "John, you want me to continue?"

"Yes, go on." John recalled Amanda Patton mentioning in her conversation a feeling that parts of the group were outside the Airfield.

"It seems Cubical Industries has many connections with Wright Patterson and the Defense Department."

With the name Cubical and its proximity to Wright, John was sure there was a connection having to do with the artifact. "Can you obtain a pass to get me into the Company?" John noticed the cab driver staring at him in his rear view mirror. John made eye contact through the mirror and smiled hoping his disguise continued to be effective.

"How did you know you need a pass?"

"I've needed one to get almost everywhere I've been lately, besides, if it is connected with the Government, I'm sure they keep it secret. I have an idea Carol is being held either at Wright or at the Cubical Industries you just mentioned."

"I have to agree with you in regards to the location of Carol. I'll work on the passes to get into Cubical. I'll have a better chance there than at Wright to get us in. How did things work out in Rochester?"

"I saw Dr. Cable, but it went downhill from there. I had something that probably would get Carol released, and then lost it. That's why I need to get inside Wright or the plant. I plan on being in Dayton sometime early in the morning. I'll call you when I am close. Plan on around one or two in the morning."

"See you soon."

Next, John called Roger's home and received no reply, so he called his office. The person who answered told him Roger had just left and gave him his cell phone number. Calling the number, Roger answered with a "Hello".

"Roger, John here."

"John?-John? Oh yes John, you have become famous since we last talked. Are you on the run?"

"Yes, and I need a favor."

"If I help a terrorist, the world will come down hard on me." After which he laughed long and loud.

"Roger, you know I'm not one. Let's just say I have discovered some things the government has been doing in secrecy and they are not too happy about my knowing so they put out the fake story."

"Does it have anything to do with the German scientists you mentioned the last time we talked?"

"In a way. Now will you help me?'

"Yes, what do you want?"

John was relieved by Roger's offer. "I need a car. Either let me borrow yours or rent me one, and I need it now-I mean right now." John knew he needed to get out of Chicago quickly and tried to convey the urgency in his tone of voice.

"Let me do this for you. My wife and I have two cars. I'll let you take mine and I'll rent one tonight to use till you return mine."

"Great, Roger, I really appreciate what you are doing. When everything is over, I'll fill you in on the whole story."

"Where are you now?"

John gave Roger the location of the cab and he made arrangements to meet at a gas station at Cicero and Division. There he would give John the car then Roger could hail another cab to take him to a rental agency. He didn't want the cab driver to be able to connect him to Roger's car.

After making the connection and exchanging vehicles, John was on his way to Dayton. He pushed the Lexus at first, then decided to obey all the speed limits. Getting caught speeding would be the end of his attempts to find Carol or the cube. Thoughts of Carol and the excitement she had put into his life flowed through his body like an elixir and he knew then, it was more important to him personally to find her than it was to locate the artifact. Hopefully, he could do both.

CHAPTER 30

The glare from the rain on the windshield and roadway reflecting the lights from the other cars can numb a person's senses. John had recently stopped twice to avoid falling asleep at the wheel. The monotonous hum of the wipers was like a lullaby slowly enticing him toward a peaceful rest. He hoped the nasty weather would soon improve as he drove toward Dayton.

John had gone over many times in his mind his failure in Chicago to keep the small cube in his possession. He had been such a fool to trust Dr. Stefford. The next time, if there were a next time, he would go by his instincts, which had told him Stefford was a shifty individual. Now he couldn't complain about Carol's mistake of going to the Mini Mart since he had fouled up as well.

He had called Peter and made arrangements to meet him at five-thirty in the morning at the Lampton Inn, which was located near the entrance to Cubical Industries. He let Peter know things had not worked out as planned in Chicago. John would get a room there as soon as he arrived in Dayton and sleep for a few hours. He wanted to find and free Carol any way possible.

The alarm rang at five am waking John from a sleep that felt like no sleep to his tired body. He had checked into the Inn at two thirty this morning, which had not given him much time to sleep. Dazed after the long drive, he headed for the shower and hoped it would help him wake-up and improve his alertness.

After the shower, he brushed his teeth and shaved using items he had purchased at gas stations and food marts along the way. Reviewing in his mind the plan he and Peter had engineered on the phone while he traveled to Dayton, he tried to forecast possible problems in their attempt to get inside Cubical Industries. His cell phone rang and it was Peter wanting to know his room number. Shortly a knock at the door told him the time had come.

Opening the door and letting Peter in, they sat on the bed rehearsing their plan. As they talked, John dressed in the work clothes provided by Peter. Peter had come up with maintenance uniforms from Cubical Industries for both John and him along with ID tags with their pictures.

Even though John had protested adamantly, Peter would not be denied the opportunity to accompany him in his attempt to find and free Carol.

Again reviewing the procedures at Cubical, which Peter had learned from his investigations, they left the motel and drove to the maintenance entrance at the plant. As they approached the gate, John filled Peter in concerning the alien artifact and gave him a general description of what he and Carol were trying to find. He related Dr. Cable's role in the effort and how the people Peter had found for him fit into the story. Much of what he said Peter had previously guessed or had been told by Dr. Cable, but the artifact drew a stare from him as John expected it too. Anytime he mentioned something alien to anyone; he would get a questioning look or response.

They fell into a long line of cars at the entrance gate. A large number of people must work at the plant and John hoped they changed regularly so his and Peter's new faces would not be a big deal to the guards or other workers. John's mustache and blond hair continued to help him avoid recognition.

When their car reached the gate, they flashed their fake picture ID's and the security guard waved them through. The ID cards were on cords which John and Peter had hanging around their necks. Following the cars ahead of them, they parked and followed the other people toward an unmarked door. As soon as they were through the door, Peter and John's eyes scanned the area looking for exits and places they could use to get into other sections of the plant.

John motioned Peter to follow him into a room filled with lockers probably provided for some members of the staff. The lockers created a maze, which they navigated through in between the benches and the few people sitting or standing at their lockers. In a group of lockers devoid of any workers, they found tool belts and immediately strapped them around their waists. They returned to the hallway and melted in with the other employees coming into the building.

At the end of the hallway was another security station where people swiped their cards through an instrument much like you would run your credit card through at a store check out. He looked at Peter with a frown and Peter returned a grin giving John the impression everything would the okay.

They passed through with flying colors and now were inside the main part of the building. The room was large and reminded John of a small flea market under one roof with stands containing various items to buy. Instead of selling items here, the compartments were workstations with one or two people at each handing out assignments to the maintenance and cleaning staff. Peter shook his head at John telling him not to go to any of the stations.

John and Peter walked to their left and Peter, seeing a large stepladder leaning against one wall, picked it up and told John to carry the other end. In this fashion, they worked their way to the other side of the room and for all appearances, they were workmen heading to a job.

Upon reaching the opposite side of the room from which they entered, they now were presented with a dilemma. The wall they faced contained a double door with a space of fifteen feet then another double door and so on for a total of four double doors.

They walked along the wall, looking for some sign to lead them to choose the correct door. Above each door was a letter, but no explanation of where the entrance led. Finally John put down his end of the ladder and walked over to one of the work stations and asked a young woman, "Miss, I'm a little confused and embarrassed. We were to repair a light in the security area and I have misplaced my work order so I don't know which door I'm to enter." He smiled at the woman with as much charm as he could convey and when she returned the smile, he knew he had a chance.

"We're not supposed to tell anyone unless they have an order, but I understand. Why don't you return to your station and get a copy?"

"I would, but I'm new and I don't want to start out on a bad foot." He smiled at her with every bit of enchantment he could muster.

She finally said, "Okay, but don't tell anyone. You want door C."

John provided her with another smile, thanked her and returned to Peter standing with the ladder. He signaled Peter to follow and they carried the ladder to door C.

"Act like we own the place," Peter said.

Entering the door marked C and toting the ladder, John, in the front led them through a hallway to another set of double doors. After entering these, they stopped to take stock of their situation. Again, they found themselves in a hallway, except at the end of this one was an elevator.

"Looks like we have to decide which floor this time." Peter relayed to John as they picked up their ladder and carried it toward the doors. To this point they had been extremely lucky to get through without being stopped, but Peter was sure their luck would not hold.

"Let's see what options we have after we get in," Replied John.

The elevator was large, no doubt for service personnel only and the ladder fit inside with little room to spare. When they looked at the floor panel, there were buttons only for three floors below them.

It appears we are going down," Peter said.

"Pick a floor, John."

He eyed the panel and hit the button B-3, thinking security is usually on the bottom floor. The elevator shook as it began its decent and when it stopped and the doors opened, a much larger hallway approaching thirty feet wide appeared before them with people, many in security uniforms moving through it. Across from the elevator was a counter with a woman standing behind it talking to four people.

John looked over his shoulder at Peter. "Pick a side."

"Left" responded Peter and off they went with the ladder over their shoulders.

As they moved to their left and down the large corridor, John noticed a board on the wall behind the woman at the counter with names and room numbers. He motioned Peter to circle around and pass in front of the counter so they could get a better view.Walking past the people and counter both he and Peter looked at the board, then moving down the hall they stopped to compare what each had seen.

After discussing the information, they decided that if Carol were here, she would be in the section labeled "Rooms B 309H through M-Security Cells." The next step was to determine where these rooms were located. As they continued along the corridor, they came to a hallway leading off to the right with a sign above labeled, 302-A to I.

They both picked up the pace moving along the hall, which seemed to go on forever. Ahead were two maintenance people working on an air vent in the ceiling of the hallway.

"John, move over so we pass by the workers ahead and slow your pace."

He did as instructed and nearing the two men who were on stepladders, Peter swung over close to the work cart containing tools and materials, passing along side of it.

John saw him take something from the cart and they proceeded down the hall eventually reaching B309H-M and turning left into the hall, which had another security station a short distance from the entrance to the hall.

Both instinctively slowed their pace viewing the two men at the guard desk, one sitting at a desk and one standing near by. "What now," John whispered over his shoulder to Peter.

"Trust me."

John had heard him say those words so many times he actually did trust him. As they approached the desk, the guard sitting stated, "Let me see your work order."

John pointed to Peter behind him and Peter set his end of the ladder down and walked toward the desk eyeing the two men, both in their late fifties and probably doing this easy job to finish out their careers before retiring.

"I'm new on the job so I hope I have the right place and tools. They changed our orders just before we left. I don't think anyone knows what is going on in this here place. If I had a nickel for every light fixture I had fixed in this damn place, I could of retired a long time ago."

Peter went on and on in a down home dialect as he handed a paper with orders on it that he had picked off the other workers cart when they passed by it in the hallway. He had smudged the area where the location was marked so the guard couldn't tell what the number was supposed to be.

During Peter's continuing jabbering, the guard with the order showed it to the other guard who shook his head indicating he couldn't read it either. The one with the paper eyed John and Peter in their work uniforms, and giving a scowl at Peter, said to John, "Sign here. How do you stand this guy all day?"

As John signed, he said, "I've only been with him for an hour. I'm not sure I will make it all day."

Again they had to swipe their ID tags and then pass through the corridor and turning left approached a group of doors one after another labeled "Security H to M".

Propping the ladder against the wall, John tried the knob to H. The knob had a keypad above it, which he assumed was opened by combination. The knob turned and the door opened despite the keypad. Reaching in, he flicked the light switch and the room lit up. It looked like a motel room, clean and deserted. As Peter fooled with the ladder, John continued along the hall trying other doors and finding the same situation in each as he had in room H.

When he came to K, the doorknob wouldn't turn. He motioned to Peter and he moved the ladder in front of the door where John stood. They both stared at the door John could not open then their heads slowly turned to look at each other.

CHAPTER 31

The phrase 'trapped like a caged animal' has significant meaning to one who is so confined. After a day in a room only seeing a guard three times bringing meals, she was near the end of her sanity. She paced back and forth, watched television, and attempted to sleep finding it would not come easy or for any period of time.

When she heard a noise at the door the next morning, she expected a guard with her morning breakfast. When no one entered, she laid back down on the bed. She had spent the last day and a half in sweat pants and a sweatshirt seeing no reason to dress.

Again the noise at the door, yet no one entered. She walked over to the door and listened. Hearing no sounds, she started talking to herself asking if she could be hearing things. Shaking her head she turned on the TV.

Neither Peter nor John could think of a way to get the door open except with brute force. They were about to attempt knocking it down when John caught site of two guards walking their way. One carried a tray of food and the other walked along side. Neither seemed to be armed except for an object resembling a nightstick swinging from each of their waists. The two guards approached the door John and Peter had been looking at and the one without the tray nodded at them, then started pushing in numbers as the other guard stood by his side.

Just as the door opened, Peter grabbed the ladder at one end and wheeling it similar to a baseball bat, awkwardly swung it with all his might and the ladder came around just missing John's head, but striking both guards squarely on the back of their heads and necks.

The guard with the tray crumpled to the floor like a wet blanket, but the other guard staggered, reached out for support from the wall, and stayed on his feet. John took a wrench from his tool belt and hit the still standing guard in the side of the face sending him to the floor with the other guard.

"Nice shot John for a college professor," Peter said with a grin on his face.

"It would be nice if you would let me know ahead of time what you planned. You nearly knocked me in the head with the ladder." John did not have a grin on his face as he spoke these words.

Carol rushed through the door jumping into John's arms.

"Come on you two, we have to get these guards inside the room."

Carol began to let go, as did John, all the time staring into each other's eyes with looks few people would have trouble understanding.

"Are you all right?" John asked.

Carol responded, "I am now. I'm sorry for leaving. It was stupid of me."

"I've done some stupid things too-now we are together. Let's not look back."

Peter yelled at the two again as he attempted to drag the guard John had conked in the face into the room. Carol and John quickly helped and once inside, removed their uniforms and tied the two up using the electric cord from the lamps and TV. One of the guards moaned and was trying to speak so they gagged them both using strips of cloth from the sheets on the bed.

"I know you two are valiant heroes, but the halls are monitored with cameras. Other security people will be here soon," Carol informed them after the guards were bound. She then went into the bathroom to change out of her sweats.

"We have to leave right away. Carol, do you have any ideas since you've been here?" asked Peter as Carol came back into the room.

"The security is tight everywhere. I think I know of one place we can go for awhile till we come up with something better."

Trying to button the guard's pants, Peter exclaimed, "This uniform is too tight. Damn John, why didn't you take this one?"

John made no reply and after Peter was ready, they exited the room and followed Carol, continuing opposite to the direction from which John and Peter had entered the hallway. Moving quickly, they turned a corner and began running along another hallway. As they did, Peter took out a tiny spray can that looked like a can of mace, and sprayed black paint over the camera lens above the hallway door.

Running down this hall, Carol said to take the stairs midway along the hall.

Peter said, "No, keep running down the hall. They did as directed going through another set of double doors and here Peter sprayed paint on the camera. Now he instructed John and Carol to back track to the stairs Carol had mentioned earlier.

As they ran back, Peter added, "Hopefully they will think we continued down the hallway and most places don't have cameras in the stairwells."

"Good thinking Peter, but I don't know where we are going," John said.

"Up one flight of stairs," added Carol. She had a place in mind for them to hide.

Reaching the door to the stairwell, they entered just as two guards came around the corner behind them. Luckily, they did not see any of the three going through the stairwell door.

Proceeding up one flight, they stopped in front of the exit door.

Carol opened the door a little and peeped through the crack. "Across the hall is a research room that has never been occupied by anyone, at least the two times I have passed by it has been empty, and the door is always open. We can hide in it until we come up with a plan to escape." Looking across the hall, she said, "The door is not open now."

Peter said, "I'll go across and see if I can open the door."

All three could hear noise in the stairwell. "Hurry Peter, we don't have much time," John warned.

Peter casually walked across the hall as if he was a guard checking doors. The door was locked, but this one had a key lock and Peter had it open in a matter of seconds.

Peter entered and checking the hall signaled the other two to cross over into the room. If they had any luck, who ever was watching the cameras would miss John and Carol darting across.

Closing the door and feeling safe for the moment, they turned on the lights revealing a room about the size of a school classroom. To John and Carol's amazement the walls were lined with blow-ups of the pictures from NEAR and Talaria. John and Carol stood in awe as they swung around the room 360 degrees taking in all the poster size pictures of which most were new to them. The room also contained computers, cabinets, lockers and worktables. Making a full turn Carol said, "These must have been taken by another space probe. A secret military satellite or something".

Peter added, "These posters are similar to the pictures I received in the mail."

Neither John or Carol responded, too much engrossed in what they were seeing. At one end of the room was a large table covered with plastic parts like you might find in a child's set of building blocks or an erector set. They were being used to construct a model of what they believed to be the object in the picture on the wall. An igloo shaped building or container of some kind similar to the one in Carol's picture from NEAR.

It was made of orange and black pieces. John could see they were trying to speculate on what the rest of the structure would look like before it was damaged. "Carol, it appears others have been as curious as you in attempting to determine what the object in space represents."

Carol examined carefully each part of the model. She then read some of the papers lying on the table along side the model. After looking at some of the material, she responded, "I think I know what the structure represents."

John gave her an inquiring frown then commented, "How can you come to a conclusion so quickly after only seeing the model for a few minutes?"

Smiling at John, she replied, "Because I'm good."

Peter and John looked at each other, then back at Carol. John said, "Okay, tell us oh great one."

"The object in space is a control station. The Almegs put devices throughout the solar system to monitor developments on each of the planets. The Asteroid Belt would be the ideal place because it is close to halfway between the inner most planet, Mercury and the outer most planet, Pluto."

"I understand, but where does the cube fit into your analysis?" John queried.

"I don't have an answer for your question, but John, I'm sure the cube is here in the complex," Carol said.

He returned a normal response to such a revelation. "Have you seen it?"

"No, but from what Ben Hagen said, I'm sure it is close at hand. He led me to believe it was in the complex."

The thought of finding the cube filled John's mind; even the possibility of taking it with them was a consideration. He picked up some of the pieces on the table and tried to attach them to the unfinished model of the object in space.

"We better be more concerned on how to get out of here," added Peter. Just as Peter finished his remark, the door from the hallway opened and a man in a lab coat entered, at first not noticing the three people then abruptly stopping when he did see them.

"What are you doing here?" He asked in an authoritative tone. He was average height and build with black rimmed glasses and a pocket full of pens and markers reminding John of a character in the movie, 'Nerds'.

John took the lead. "We have a prisoner who escaped and we just found her here in your lab."

"You should have her in handcuffs." The Man said not believing wholeheartedly John's explanation.

"We will, but we became interested in your work and were admiring your efforts," added Peter.

This seemed to ease the Man's mind as he acted proud to have someone praise his work. He probably received very little adulation buried here in this room. "Why, thank you. Not many people care much about the object in space."

"What is it?" asked John, hoping to get some new information and ideas.

Walking over to John and shaking his hand, "I'm Louis Todian. I am a structural engineer as well as an astronomy buff, so I landed a job trying to find out how the Russians got this into space and what it is supposed to be and how it is used. I work here when I have time. A few of my colleagues help once in awhile."

All three, John, Carol, and Peter looked at one another with half-hearted grins and frowns wondering where he came up with such a story.

Carol said, "They keep it a secret by giving mis-information and keeping the people who work here in the dark. See, he doesn't know parts of it are made of diamonds."

"Yes, and they must do it very well, because Louis here knows little yet he works on the piece in space and has blow ups of the pictures," John said.

Louis was taking their conversation in, but understanding little. "What do you mean I know nothing and why do you talk to your prisoner like you do?"

Carol looked at John and said, "Shall we?"

He responded, "Why not. Be my guest. Louis, our prisoner knows a lot about your work. Listen to what she has to say."

He backed away while Carol approached Louis. "Louis, I'm going to answer questions you have been trying to solve since you've been here, so sit down and keep your ears open."

Carol spent the next twenty minutes reviewing and answering questions from Louis. At various stages you could see his face light up because Carol was giving him solutions to problems he had been working on for years.

When he finished, Louis sat lost in thought absorbed by what he had learned. Carol left him and walked over to Peter and John who were playing with the model discussing how they were going to escape without getting caught.

"The man might be able to help us get out," Peter said.

"He also might take us to the cube." John was still enthralled about seeing the artifact.

Carol's eyes lit up too as the possibility of seeing the cube raced through her mind. "Let's ask. It can't hurt."

Carol swung around and said to Louis, "Louis, come over here. I want to introduce you." He stood and walked over to where John and Peter were sitting and Carol standing next to them.

"Louis, I would like you to meet Peter Cozid, a private investigator here in the city of Dayton and sitting next to him is John Kirkwood, History Professor from Stanford University, and I'm Carol Jacobs, a scientist for the Jet Propulsion Laboratory in Pasadena, California."

After hearing the story and being introduced to the people, Louis was at a loss for words and in a numb state. His world had come crashing down on him in one fell swoop. All his problems he had been working on for the past four years were answered simply and in a few minutes.

He stared around the room at the pictures, then directed his eyes to the three people before him. "I have thought about all you have told me, and normally I wouldn't believe you except it all fits. Even though your story of aliens seems preposterous, it works. If I could see the cube, I would believe."

"We believe the cube is somewhere here in the complex. Do you have any idea where it might be?" Carol asked.

Louis sat down, thinking for a moment, turned to one of the computers in the room and used it to look at some schematics. "Yes. I believe I have an idea where it might be. It will be difficult to get to it. From the diagram, security around this area is extremely tight. What ever is located here is important." His printer started up and was making a copy of the diagram on the screen.

"They are looking for us. How can we escape capture?" asked Peter.

"For one thing the camera in this room has not worked for months." They all turned and looked for signs of a camera. Louis informed them that it was behind boxes stacked on top of cabinets. "At first, others would come to check on my progress, but the last couple of years, seldom does anyone show any interest in what I am doing. I'm only here when I'm not scheduled with my normal group.

"What's your normal group?" asked John.

"I'm working with other engineers. We evaluate secrets from the Russians-we were told they were from them."

"You have helped me, now let me help you." Louis replied.

He walked over to a cabinet in the corner of the room where several lockers were located. He opened the lockers taking out white lab coats and surgical hats used by him and his colleagues. Quickly the three donned the jackets and hats, John and Peter not crazy about wearing the hats as they joked at each others looks.

"Hurry, we need to get going. We have a long way to go."

"Where are we going?" Carol asked.

"Wright-Patterson," Louis replied.

"Is that where the cube is located?" She asked.

"If I guess right, the cube you described might be there," He answered.

"Wright Airfield is a long way from here. Are you going to magically get us there?" Peter asked.

Ignoring Peter's question, he handed Carol and John a clipboard each and gave Peter a large Poster size map rolled up to carry. He told Peter and John to hang their ID cards on the outside of the lab coat. He went to a locker and retrieved one for Carol. "Here is an old one for you. It's not your picture so keep the picture side turned against your coat."

At Louis's direction, they left the room and walked down the hallway to a group of elevators. Louis used his card to open the elevator doors and the four entered.

The elevator descended several floors until it stopped. Here lights began to flash as a red light came on. "Allow all entry on my code, yellow-8A8B-orange. Delete passage record on Security Code red-1A1A-red," Louis said to no one in particular.

A voice responded, "Clearance and deletion allowed on your code Mr. Louis Todian and SEC Code."

Suddenly the elevator moved sideways causing Peter and John to reach for the handrails. Both Louis and Carol were prepared and smiled at John and Peter. "You must have been here before," Louis directed the statement to Carol.

"Yes, once and the voice identified me."

"You learn some things after working here for four years. I've made some friends who have provided me some extra clearance codes, which help when I take visitors or big shots from the Pentagon around the complex. The elevator is taking us to Wright Airfield." Louis informed them.

John understood the connection between Cubical and Wright. A quasi-governmental business industry located partly underneath a military base. Something he remembered Karen Doddson mentioning President Eisenhower was worried about.

Traveling almost a mile underground, the elevator came to a halt and the doors opened. Louis had warned them to act like they belonged and follow his lead. Exiting, the people they met paid little attention to them.

Walking along a hallway similar to those John and Peter had orchestrated to get to Carol; they entered another elevator and dropped several more floors to a section marked service level. As they descended, Louis reviewed the print out. The drawing turned out to be part of the blue prints of the complex.

Exiting the elevator, Louis guided them through some hallways and down some steps into a room full of large equipment. The noise was deafening as air conditioners, heaters, generators and dehumidifiers all contributed to the roar. John felt like they were going deep into the bowels of some mechanical giant.

"If what you have told me is correct, the room housing the cube is somewhere near here. There has to be a service entrance or tunnel close," Louis said.

"They each spread throughout the room looking for exits. Carol yelled for the others to come to her side. She was standing in front of an opening the size of double doors containing conduits, air and water pipes, heating and cooling tubes and a walkway along the side leaving just enough room for a person to ease by.

"Does anyone have a flashlight?" asked John.

Peter pulled out a little pocket light and said, "Don't I always have what is necessary." Peter went first as they edged their way into the dark tunnel and moved along side of all the pipes. The temperature began to rise and all four were sweating by the time they reached the end.

What they came to was a metal gate with a chain and padlock blocking further progress. Peter easily picked the lock with the tool he used on the door back at Louis' room.

Telling everyone to be quiet, Louis continued through the tunnel, having more room now since some of the pipes had disappeared, obviously going to their intended destination.

Finally the passageway ended with a ladder ascending upward for what looked to be two stories. "Let me go first in case I have to pick another lock," Peter said. "Be careful and don't look down."

He climbed up the ladder, and at the top was a very heavy man hole cover. Peter tried to get in a position where he could put some pressure to lift it and try as he might, he couldn't budge it. John was below him and he wedged his way up next to Peter to help and the two together were able to lift it enough to slide it sideways until the opening was large enough for Peter to climb through.

Peter helped the others through the hole and into a small room the size of an average bedroom. It contained pipes and monitoring devices with a door which Louis opened a crack. He looked through the opening and could see a little because there was some background lighting.

Again using his small pocket flashlight, Peter worked his way around Louis and aimed it into the darkness. Before him was another walkway like tunnel that you might see at sports stadiums, where they have ramps leading down into the stands where the fans sit. He could tell it opened up at the end approximately thirty feet ahead.

Peter shut off his light and informed the others that there is enough light to see once their eyes became adjusted. He suggested they exit the small room very quietly. Louis took the lead followed by John and Carol with Peter bringing up the rear.

As they neared the end of the hallway, all four could see that they were entering a very large room. As Louis reached the end of the corridor and looked to his left, he suddenly stopped and made no movement.

"What's wrong?" John asked.

Louis made no reply. He slowly raised his hand and pointed to something above and to the left of him.

John moved around Louis and looked to his left, and it was Carol's turn to ask, "John, what's the matter?" She and Peter pressed ahead next to John and Louis and they halted as well.

Before their eyes was a crystal cube the size of a small TV, floating in mid-air emitting the hazy reddish orange glow Dr. Cable had described to John weeks ago.

CHAPTER 32

Being confronted with the proof of a new idea, especially one we had considered impossible can cause our minds to have trouble adjusting our thinking to the multitude of changes our knowing dictates. Even though John and Carol had strong suspicions the artifact was real, they were still not prepared for the experience of coming face to face with it. It shimmered in an orange and reddish light that spread throughout the whole room giving the effect of a haunted house on Halloween. This contributed to the mystic nature it conveyed to the beholder.

It was a glass-like cube, a glistening diamond the size of a small TV and all four people stood gazing at the artifact mesmerized by its beauty and luster. It had a trance like quality and as Carol's eyes continued to absorb its radiance, she started to weave on her feet until she grabbed John by the arm.

It was a perfect diamond crystal resting on a wire thin almost invisible pedestal creating the illusion it was floating in air. The pedestal rested on a platform, much like a stage. No doubt the person who designed the room intended to increase the enchanting effect it had on the viewer.

No one moved as all four viewed the artifact and reveled in the significance its existence meant. It was, to say the least, a mind-altering event.

John reacted to Carol's touch by turning to look in her eyes and she responded by returning his stare and they simply communicated through their thoughts. Neither needed to speak any words, each sensing the others intoxication.

Louis started to move toward the stage like area on which the pedestal was sitting and stumbled in the process reaching out to brace himself on Peter's shoulder.

Peter held Louis back as he broke the eerie silence. "I don't believe what I'm seeing. John, I thought your explanation of what you and Dr. Cable were looking for was crazy and now looking at the thing here in front of me, it is still hard to accept. I'm sure no one on this Earth made something like this."

"It is the most beautiful thing I have ever seen in my life. Those who made this are remarkable beings," Carol said.

Louis was awe struck with amazement and upset too, since most of his years of work could have been answered in the flash of an eye. "I wasted so much time trying to determine how the object in space got there and people here knew all along." He slipped from Peter's grasp and started to climb up on the raised platform to get a better look.

Peter yelled, "Don't Louis, stay here." but it was too late. As his hand moved over the platform, alarms sounded and two heavy metal fences dropped from the ceiling. Peter pulled Louis back just before the fence struck the stage. It came with such force Louis would have lost an arm if not for Peter's quick reaction.

Scrambling to find a way out, neither Peter nor John could see anyway to counteract what happened. As they were surveying the area the cube began to descend into an opening in the platform and was soon out of sight.

The four-trapped people stood looking at one another each hoping someone would come up with a method of escape. John knew they were caught and nothing he or Peter could do would get them out.

Security people began to enter armed with guns and one pushed a lever and a section of the fence began to rise. They were told to stand still and raise their hands above their heads. When the fence was above them, the six guards surrounded them with two of the guards putting handcuffs on the four intruders.

They were led up a ramp and out of the room into a large elevator, which moved sideways very fast. Eventually the guards took them to the room Carol had waited in before her audience with the Council.

Addressing Peter, John said, "Got a rabbit to pull out of your hat now?"

"I think we may have reached the end of the line." Peter answered shaking his head.

"I was brought to this exact room a couple of days ago and I was put before the Council of Six."

"Who are the Council of Six?" asked Peter.

"They are the ones who are in control of the artifact."

"What did they want?" asked Louis.

"They gave me three choices. I could become a part of their organization. I could be sent to Cuba, or I could disappear," Carol said emphasizing the last.

Peter added some information. "John, I hadn't told you, but it may be pertinent now. I found Robert White. I'm not sure you will want to know what I found."

"Where is he?" John inquired.

"The same place David Hanson and Frank Wisner-resting peacefully. He committed suicide."

John stared off into space. The odds these three people all committed suicide were highly unlikely. It may be what Carol referred to as disappearing. Two of the guards entered and escorted Louis out of the room.

"Any suggestions now," Carol asked of Peter.

"I think we will have to deal with the events as they occur. I see no way to escape at the moment."

John looked at Carol remembering the time they spent together, and enjoying the warm feeling spreading through his body as the memories played out. He reached over and held her hands, handcuffed as they were. He started to convey these thoughts to Carol, but was interrupted as the guards entered again and told the three to move out of the room.

They were led to the same Council Room Carol had been in before, except this time all three were left standing in the open part of the "V" and their hands cuffed in front of their bodies

The six council members entered and took their seats as they had with Carol. John recognized Ben Hagen from his appearances on TV and Carol had told him he was one of the members of the committee. He scanned the others and two faces were familiar, one could be a member or former member of the CIA he had seen on CSPAN in front of a Congressional Committee. The other he could not recall where he had seen her.

A lady to the right began. "Miss Jacobs, would you do us the pleasure of introducing your partners."

Carol did as she was told.

The Lady continued. "You three have caused us a great many problems. It has been the worst two days I have spent on the Council and I've been a part of it for over twenty-one years. I for one am not giving you any choices this time Miss Jacobs."

John replied to the Lady's comment saying, "We don't require any choices, Miss Whoever you are. It is you who will need the choices. You have convinced yourselves of your importance only in your minds. You six people are no more than self-anointed gods who have the gall to think you are so enlightened you can determine the future for all human kind. How pathetic you look." John finished his speech looking each of the council directly in the eyes as he moved around the table with his stare.

Ben Hagen reacted to John's statement. "I will not sit here and listen to you speak without any knowledge of what we do."

"Well listen to my words. I know the artifact belongs to the people of Peru if it belongs to anyone specifically. You stole it from them. I know you eliminated people who are a threat to your almighty power such as Robert White and David Hanson. You will do anything to protect your kingdom," John replied.

Ben Hagen answered John's charges. "You have no idea. We think we may be able to contact the Almegs soon."

Carol replied, "And just who are you going to say is calling, a few power hungry people or are you going to lie and say the people of earth are calling?" She gave the people a stare similar to the one John had given the six.

"Easy Ben. Don't let these traitors get to you." The man to his right said.

"Even if we aren't able to expose you and the Government ignores your secrets, there is a group who will eventually ask for your atonement." John drew all six member's attention with his statement.

Ben Hagen responded to his remark. "And just who might you be referring to my terrorist friend."

"First, I'm no terrorist and certainly not a friend of yours. I am speaking of someone who you have no control over. The Alpha Omegans."

Everyone looked at the other members of the Council inquiring with their eyes what could he possibly be talking about. Carol and Peter also eyed John with questioning stares, as they too were speechless.

The woman across from Ben Hagen gave a reply this time. "Dr. Kirkwood, you are losing your mind. The Almegs were here over two hundred million years ago." The woman grinned at John thinking she had surprised him with information new to him.

John gave the lady a big grin of his own. "I know they were here two hundred million years ago. Did you think you were telling me something I didn't know? What I propose to you is that they never left." Now it was the Council's turn to sit back and think about his words.

Ben Hagen asked rhetorically, "And how could they survive millions of years?" Some of the other Council members chuckled.

John came back with, "And how could they use a star as an oven to create diamond cubes in such a large size, and how can they travel among the stars, and how can they develop a language, which you in over sixty years have not been able to translate."

All members remained quiet, thinking over John's ideas. John reached inside his shirt with his handcuffed hands and pulled out an envelope. He tossed the package with his two hands on top of the council table in front of Ben Hagen. "While you are thinking about the Almegs, you might want to also consider how you will explain these."

Ben Hagen grabbed the envelope and opened it, pulling the pictures out. They were the pictures Peter had given John earlier. He passed them around the table. "Where did you get these?"

"It doesn't matter where, they are around and will become common knowledge eventually no matter what you do to us." John could see the concern in the Council's faces as he added, "I'm sure you thought all copies of these were in your possession. They are not and there are many more where these came from."

The man with the earphone was noticeably disturbed as he said, "Let us decide and get this over. It's time for a vote."

"What kind of vote are you talking about?" Carol asked.

"Don't concern yourself. You will know in due time," The man with the phone said.

All six seemed to be looking down and pushing buttons on the table in front of them, then looking at an object sitting at the top of the table protruding up about four inches. John assumed it was giving the results of the vote.

The Lady with the screechy voice spoke. "Our agents will escort you out. I'm sorry to have to do this."

Peter started to protest as Agents Johnson and Feathers entered with three other security guards. "Take these three to the jail cells, not the rooms. They are to be dealt with," The man with the earphone said, "and we will have no further trouble from these three."

Just as the agents started to lead them out of the room, everyone heard a loud boom. From the looks on the faces of the council, it was not a normal occurrence. The five members looked to the man with the phone and you could tell he was listening.

"We have to evacuate," he said and they all started to file out of the room when another boom occurred, this one very near. When one of the council members opened the door, a cloud of smoke entered the room and shortly an armed soldier entered followed by three more. They looked to be Special Forces of some kind dressed like the ones who entered Brian Dover's office in Chicago.

"Everyone put your hands behind your head and turn and face the wall. Johnson and Feathers started to pull out their guns, but the firepower of the Special Forces looked too overpowering, so they put their hands behind their head. Everyone did except John, Peter, and Carol who were handcuffed and they simply put their hands up showing the handcuffs.

One of the soldiers spoke into his mouthpiece. "General, Captain Monroe. I have three people in handcuffs and a bunch of others who could be first at the trough." After a delay, his only other words were, "Yes sir."

CHAPTER 33

The morning was bright with sunshine, an unusually warm day. The cherry blossoms of spring were gone and Washington was abuzz with the news the President of the United States had asked to speak before the United Nations in New York this evening. All the news stations had speculated on what would be so important to change the United Nations schedule so the President could address the General Assembly.

In their room at the Freedom Hotel, John and Carol knew the topic of the speech, but had little knowledge of what part they were to play. The last two days had been a whirl wind ordeal of interviews, questioning, and travel to the capitol. After the first day, secret service agents were assigned to them for their protection and to guide them around. John was sure it was more for their comfort than to counteract any threat to them.

After the Navy Seals and Army Rangers took over "Cubical Industries" and part of Wright Patterson Air Base, Carol, John and Peter were taken to the intelligent section of Wright Field where they were interrogated by agents from the Federal Bureau of Investigation. All three had to recount everything that had occurred for the last few weeks. A representative from the White House sat in on all the interviews with John and he found out later they also witnessed some of the testimony of Carol and Peter.

When the President's science advisor had presented the President with the small cube from the lock box, he knew John's story could be true, and after some effort to break down the barriers set up for over fifty years, the President's staff were able to determine the artifact had to be at or close to Wright Patterson Air Base.

Not trusting any individual or group to investigate, he sent in the Rangers and Seals to secure both Cubical Industries and the part of Wright-Patterson that was involved. The FBI was then brought in to do the investigations since no one was sure who was connected to the use of the cube.

After twenty-four hours, the President was given a preliminary report informing him of the general information relating to the internal operations of the Council of Six and their ability to keep the artifact a secret.

After receiving the report he ordered John, Carol and Peter flown to Washington, D. C. and used as sources in the continuing investigations. After some interviews, Peter had nothing further to add so he opted to fly back to Dayton and get back to his business.

John and Carol met him in the lobby as he was checking out. They accompanied him to the top of the steps leading down from the front of the hotel to the waiting car.

"Peter, I don't know how we can ever thank you enough for your help and advice," John said as he shook Peter's hand.

"You are a very special person, Peter and I will miss having you around to save John and me when we get into trouble." Carol gave Peter a hug and kiss as she said these words.

"I was just doing what you handsomely paid me to do. I will miss you both. I'm sure my life will be much more peaceful." All three laughed at his remark. "Remember, you have my number if you get in anymore scrapes and why, for some reason, do I think I've not seen the last of the you two." Peter grinned and gave Carol and John a wink as he went down the steps to the car with the Secret Service Agents.

"I'm going to miss having him around," John said to Carol as they watched Peter get into the car with the agents.

Carol's only reply was, "I know."

They hadn't been back in the room more than ten minutes when John answered a knock at the door. A Secret Service Agent told them they had fifteen minutes to get ready to leave for the White House. They quickly changed into dressier clothes knowing little about the purpose for their trip.

Riding in the back seat with two agents in the front, they made a quick trip to the White House. After going through security and entering they were taken to a small room and told to wait. John and Carol had shared with one another their conjectures on what was happening. Basically both were in the dark on why they were at the White House and neither could come up with a logical reason for their presence.

In twenty minutes, a woman came and guided them to the Oval Office and President Mitchell Fielding. He greeted them with a big politician's smile and introduced them to the others present, then asked them to sit on the couch.

Even though they knew President Fielding was small in stature, they were still surprised by his size in person, but his demeanor and commanding voice over shadowed any lack of height. The President sat on another couch facing them. Coffee and tea with pastries were on a coffee table between the two couches and they were told to help themselves.

As would be expected, both Carol and John were nervous in this setting, so neither opted for the drinks or snacks. As John scanned the room
he felt impotent in these surroundings and was sure Carol was having a similar feeling. If it had this effect on two people like John and Carol who were
very forceful and audacious in expressing their opinions, it would be more
consequential on those who were less adamant in their beliefs. The aura of
the Office of the President of the United States, without a doubt the most
powerful place in the world, might reduce some people to babbling sheep.

In the room with the President were Carl Huffman, his chief of staff,
and Richard Banks, his science advisor that John had talked to on the phone.
General Gaff who was in charge of the artifacts was also present.

The President began, speaking first to Carol and John. "I want to thank
you for your efforts in exposing this deceit of not only the American people,
but the citizens of Earth. You both acted with a great amount of courage
and I want to offer my apologies for the way some of people in the Military
and Government treated you in this matter."

Carol responded to the praise. "Thank you Mr. President. We were honored to help bring about the re-discovery of the artifact for the benefit of all
people."

John added, "My thanks as well. May I ask why we are here?"

The President looked at his chief of staff, who responded to John's
question. "Now that we have the artifact, there are going to be many decisions to make regarding its use and location just to name a couple. Someone
or some group is going to have to take on the responsibility of this immense
task." He nodded to the President who continued.

"We would like to know if you and Miss Jacobs would be interested in
playing a part in this process?"

John and Carol turned to each other with excitement in their eyes and
a flush look on their faces. From their expressions the President knew their
answer.

John spoke first saying, "I would be honored." He turned to Carol
waiting for her response.

"I also would be honored to participate," Carol said.

"Mr. President, What will be our responsibilities," John asked.

"I'll let Carl add some information."

"You will be a part of a committee of five people who will make final
decisions regarding the artifact. The only person who can over rule you in
these early stages would be the President. The other members will be Dr.
Banks, Amar Assaden, former Secretary General of the United Nations, and
Dr. Hi Bin Liu from China, recent winner of the Nobel Peace Prize.

We are going to ask you, Dr. Kirkwood to chair this committee."

John noticed a glaring look from Dr. Banks, no doubt because he
expected to be the one to head the committee.

Carl continued, "The artifact will be kept at Wright for the foreseeable future until your committee has gone over the intricacies of the organization that controlled it. You will have an adequate staff to perform the day to day operation and provide you with the data needed to make the necessary decisions regarding its use."

The President finished the meeting with some words for Carol and John. "I'm happy both of you have agreed to serve. I am putting a great deal of trust in both of you. I hope you do not let me down. Carl has assigned aides for each of you to help get you settled in and set up in offices. You will start in a few days. For now enjoy the Capitol."

Leaving the White House and returning to their hotel room, John and Carol both felt like they were walking on air. They spent the afternoon making love and discussing their lives. So much had changed for both in the past few weeks.

Lying in bed, they turned the TV on to listen to the President's speech. Later they would dress and go out to dinner.

President Mitchell Fielding stood on the podium in front of the representatives of most of the countries of the world.

"Ladies and Gentlemen, citizens of the world, it is with both pride and sadness I come before you today. I am here to give all the people of Earth great news and also an apology on behalf of the citizens of the United States.

First the news we all have dreamed about yet never expected to hear. I have recently been informed by my science advisors and many experts throughout the country of a discovery of immense magnitude. We have undeniable proof demonstrating the Earth, our planet has been visited in the past by an intelligent species from somewhere else in the galaxy."

The buzz from the representatives carried to the podium causing the President to pause.

"I know it will be difficult to accept only my word so the United States is in the process of making available the evidence of my statement to all scientists of the world. The two artifacts left by an alien people have convinced every scientist who has examined them that they are in fact not of earth or our Solar System. I will present more on our efforts to provide access to the artifacts through my staff.

I now want to express to all countries of the world my most humble apologies because even though I was just informed of the existence of these items, some people in our country have known and possessed them since 1938."

Another buzz went through the hall.

"I was as shocked as you to find some of my misguided countryman decided on their own to keep it a secret not only from the people of the United States, but from the highest levels of government.

I assure you this will not happen again.

Now to some more important news concerning the artifacts. We have found in the study of the objects that information can be obtained from them to further the advancement of the human race. I am here before you today to offer this knowledge to all the people of our special planet, Earth."

"It is my belief and my countries hope that with this new knowledge we can all work toward a better and more peaceful world society.People of Earth, we are not alone."

John and Carol slipped on robes and went out on the balcony of their room overlooking the city. As they stood gazing at the thousands of lights beginning to illuminate the Capitol, John broke the silence. "I have a revelation to share with you."

"Is it about the Alpha-Omegans having never left?"

"No, but I believe they might be like Robinson Crusoe who was stranded on an Island. What if they came here on an impulse without any of their companions knowing where they were going and something happened and they couldn't get back? They had no means to communicate their plight to their home system and were left stranded. Remember our solar system is on the outskirts of the Milky Way Galaxy."

"Or it could be like the movie Castaway," Carol said, "Maybe they decided to set sail so they left hoping someone would find them as happened in the movie. Can you imagine stuck here with the dinosaurs? What happened to them if they didn't leave?"

"I have no idea. It could be interesting. This is not the revelation I wanted to tell you."

She snuggled up next to him and asked, "What is the revelation oh soothsayer?"

"I might know where more cubes are located. Dr. Cable left a map in the lock box."

"Is it in Peru?"

"Yes." Neither spoke for a time. John looked up at two stars beginning to shine in the fading sunlight and Carol thought about exploring in the Andes. After a moment, John turned to face her. "I have never been happier at anytime in my life than I am now. I would like for you to stay with me and together we can explore the Universe? I don't want to do it without you."

Carol grasped his hands in hers. "I too cannot remember ever feeling better than I do right now. I always wanted to investigate space and now thanks to the Almegs, I will be able to go, using the cubes, to places in the Universe I never imagined and on top of everything, I get to do it with you."

They folded into each other's arms as the sun, setting in the West, emitted through the evening clouds a reddish-orange hue.

Epilogue

hrough Brian Dover, it was discovered Dr. Cable had no living relatives and his entire estate of almost two billion dollars was left for the purpose of constructing an institute for the purpose of preserving and investigating the artifact with one condition. The center must be located in Peru.

Karen Doddson came out of hiding and still remains in her home overlooking the white sands.

Ron Williams kept trying to contact John, but John never returned his calls. Ron was appointed History Department Chairman after Dr. Calway retired.

Joyce Carter sought help to overcome her issues with her Father.

Harold Anker had made several copies of the pictures and after the President's speech, he made them available to all on the Internet.

Colonel Garland Martin died three months after John visited him in the home in Maimisburg. Charlie is still watching the birds.

John discovered Don Webster's only relative was his deceased younger Sister's two daughters who had recently come into a large sum of money. He surmised it came from Dr. Cable.

The gold plate described by Dr. Cable in the chamber has never been found.

Cheryl Roberts replaced John at Stanford University permanently.

The movie Carol had on her mind when she had her haircut was 'Steel Magnolias'.

Amanda Patton had to take a reduction in her retirement, but it remains a very nice income.

A month after the meeting with the President, Carol and John flew to Cincinnati and spent an evening with Peter, then drove Roger's Lexus to Chicago. They spent a weekend with Roger and his wife before flying back to Washington. They gave Roger and his family a week's cruise in the Caribbean.

Harry returned Robin's Camry to her and Carol gave Robin her Jeep in appreciation for her help.

Dr. and Mrs. Hillvale continue to teach and live in Stanford, California.

Ben Hagen and the rest of the Council of Six were found guilty in Federal Court of multiple charges and are serving sentences along with Agents Johnson and Feathers. Ben Hagen's comment about making contact with the Almegs was a lie.

Colonel Gil Pratt was discharged from the military and much of the wealth he had accumulated was confiscated.

A project is in the works to send a manned mission to the Asteroid Belt to investigate the object, which has taken on the name of "the igloo".

The committee straightened out the mess at Cubical Industries and Wright Airfield. John and Carol were appointed co-chairs of an organization assigned the duty of establishing an institute in Peru for the purpose of studying the Almegs. They proposed it be named the Cable Institute and Research Center, Andean or "CIRCA". They are now overseeing the development and construction of the buildings and campus using the money from Dr. Cable's estate. Carol purchased a Jeep upon arriving in Lima.

John and Carol hired Harry Calvert to work with the artifact, which will be moved to "CIRCA" when the construction is completed. He still has a yard full of flowers.

Louis Todian was hired as a part of the staff of the committee and plans to move to Peru to work at "CIRCA" after the artifact is moved there.

Peter Cozid expanded the Kinkle Detective Agency with branches in both Cincinnati and Columbus, Ohio. He is still single and lives in the apartment above his office. A crew is presently refurbishing the outside of his building.

Dale Belfer took over Carol's job at the Jet Propulsion Laboratory and is considering moving to Peru to work at "CIRCA".

Carol was quickly divorced from Bob and she and John live together with plans to marry at the dedication of the Institute. Together they explored Machu Picchu and discovered another small cube at the ruins using the map from the lock box. They announced to the world their find at the groundbreaking ceremony for the institute in Lima. They have a home outside Lima in the highlands on the side of a hill looking out over the Pacific Ocean and the setting sun. They are still searching for the Alpha-Omegans.